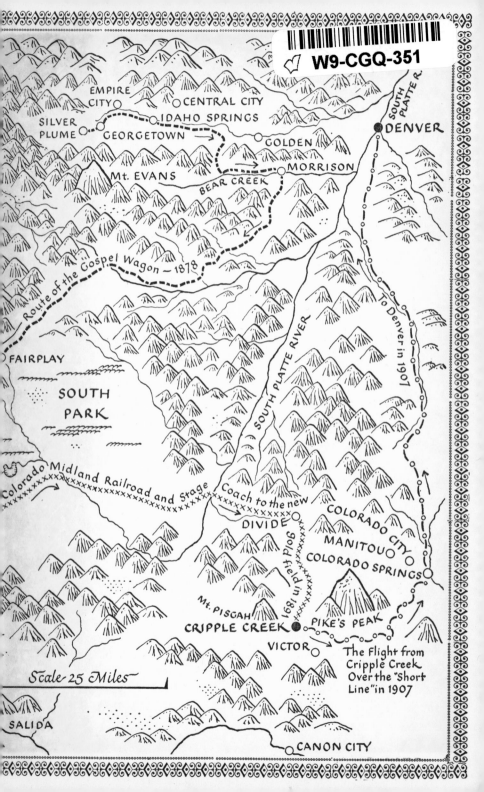

EMPIRE CITY

CENTRAL CITY

SILVER PLUME

IDAHO SPRINGS

GEORGETOWN

SOUTH PLATTE R.

DENVER

GOLDEN

Mt. EVANS

MORRISON

BEAR CREEK

Route of the Gospel Wagon ~ 1878

To Denver in 1901

FAIRPLAY

SOUTH PARK

SOUTH PLATTE RIVER

Colorado Midland Railroad and Stage Coach to the new

DIVIDE

COLORADO CITY

MANITOU

COLORADO SPRINGS

Gold field in 1891

Mt. PISGAH

CRIPPLE CREEK

PIKE'S PEAK

VICTOR

The Flight from Cripple Creek Over the "Short Line" in 1907

Scale 25 Miles

SALIDA

CANON CITY

THE GOLDEN FURY

THE GOLDEN FURY

BY MARIAN CASTLE

WM. MORROW & CO.

NEW YORK, 1949

THE GOLDEN FURY

CHAPTER 1

THE COLUMN OF DUST-FURRED VEHICLES JOLTED TO A HALT. SINCE early morning the wagon train had moved westward across the vast mountain-rimmed lake of grass called South Park. Now it was forced to pause here at the base of the Mosquito range so that the drivers could help each other over Weston Pass.

As the creaking and rumbling of heavy wagons ceased, lesser sounds stood out in the chill autumn brilliance. The delicate, metallic chatter of bit rings and tug chains; the relaxed snuffles of horses stamping and shaking themselves; the routine cursing of freighters as they unhitched their teams.

To most of the passengers, the Pass was the final perverse obstacle between themselves and quick riches. On the other side of that austere range lay Leadville. So near, as the squawking crested blue-jay would fly; so far, as the tired horses must plod and strain. With poor grace, the travelers settled back to wait during the tedious process of double-hitching the teams, of hauling some of the vehicles to the top of the 12,000-foot Pass, and then of coming back for the rest. For, almost without exception, they were young and greedy and in a rush. A Colorado mining boom in the fall of 1878 was no place for the old or the calm or the resigned.

Only two in the whole line welcomed the delay, and they were to be found in the last wagon, whose tattered cover bore the legend, "Gospel Wagon," on one side, and on the other, "Brother, Are You Saved?"

Perched on the high front seat of the wagon was Carolina Lawler, a taut, watchful little girl of six, with bronzed, bristling braids and a leashed eagerness. She welcomed the delay because it would take her father up ahead and permit her to carry out a certain forbidden project of her own. Tossing wearily on a pile of quilts in the back of the wagon was her mother, Hester Lawler, who thanked God for the respite from the interminable jolting,

1

but who feared it, too, knowing that her pains might not hold off until they reached Leadville.

Carolina, with the wariness of an intelligent little mongrel who has learned to dodge kicks and cuffs, sat immobile while her father, with vicious jerks of buckles and straps, unhitched his scrawny team. Jude Lawler fought inanimate things as hard as he fought sin.

She held her breath so that he should not sense her pounding heart and straining curiosity. So often had he snatched what she desired right out of her fingers at the very last moment. But inwardly she was crying out, Oh, hurry up, Pa—do hurry up—I want to visit the pretty ladies.

The others in the stalled cavalcade killed time as best they could. Those freighters who were left behind tightened ropes and tarpaulins over bulging loads—at ten cents a pound—of blankets and hand steels and faro tables and flour and bacon and barrels of whiskey. Dudes, in light buggies, anxiously snapped the covers of plump gold watches and squinted at the sun climbing the thin blueness. The four women in the next to the last vehicle tried to smarten their plumes and touch up lips already cracking under layers of dust and rouge.

At last the little girl saw her father lead his horses up ahead, with her nine-year-old brother Elick strutting behind. Now was her chance!

Ever since the Gospel wagon, on its journey from Clear Creek Canyon to Leadville, had attached itself three days earlier to the loosely formed caravan going up from Denver, Carolina had been in a fever to get acquainted with the ladies in the carriage just ahead. Thus far, her father had prevented her. Yet, no matter how hard he tried, he could not break away from their contaminating presence. For the Gospel wagon was always breaking down or the harness giving way, leaving it in the rear. And Leander, the ladies' colored driver, spent so much time with his head thrown back in rich African laughter, displaying a gold tooth as shiny as his horseshoe stickpin, that his team always dawdled along in next to the last place in line. The Gospel wagon and the ladies' carriage seemed destined to bring up the tail of the procession together.

The thin birdlike child slid down over the high wheel until her foot found the hub. Carolina did not bother with even a backward flick of her light, brown-gold eyes—queer eyes, people called them, the color of ale—toward the wagon where her mother lay, her body making a gross bulge under the quilts; or at twelve-year-old Letty who was tending her mother; or at Mat, the present baby, unconcernedly playing beside the bulge.

Carolina thought simply of getting away. She tossed her raveled, rust-brown braids back from her face; braids that were drab with dust now but which, when they were clean, shone in the sun with the unearthly prismatic glints of a peacock's train. She wanted to get away, not only because she longed for a closer view of the ladies whose lovely laces and petticoats foamed out over the edges of their carriage, but because she was bored with the scene behind her. Had she known what that bulge portended, nothing could have pried her out of the wagon.

But Carolina did not know. Perhaps some Victorian reticence on the part of her parents had kept them from telling her. More likely it was because birth was such an old story to Jude and Hester Lawler. Already, four home-made headstones in lonely places along the trail marked the graves of those four babies who had not been tough enough to survive the rigors of the jolting wagon and the bitter cold of the high country winters and the fact that Hester's milk always dried up too soon. Four headstones and four living children and one on the way—no wonder birth was a commonplace in the Lawler family.

Whenever she questioned her mother about her own birthplace, Hester was vague.

"Let's see, it was either Georgetown or Silver Plume or Empire City, dear. I guess it was Empire. No, that's where little Mat was born. I'm not sure——" So often had they trekked up and down Clear Creek Canyon from Idaho Springs to Silver Plume, and over to Central City and Black Hawk and Caribou, and then back. Hester Lawler had had so many babies. When her time came, all gulches looked alike to her. And Jude was forever setting off to a new one where the creeks ran gray with mill tailings, and times were good, and men were bad.

Carolina landed with a thump and a puff of dust, picked up her long plaid skirts and ran ahead to the carriage, stalled because its driver was waiting for someone to help him to the top of the Pass. In the meantime he was up ahead exchanging pleasantries with the freighters.

Already the child had discovered that three of the ladies were

3

young and pretty, while the fourth spent her time trying to order them around. At the moment, they were eating their lunch. Carolina, who was always hungry, swung herself up, with one scuffed shoe resting on the step which hung downward like a small iron hoe. The women were grabbing at the contents of the basket and talking with their mouths full. Carolina, likewise devoid of manners, in spite of her mother's constant weak pecking at her, stood and stared, her eyes covetously following each lifted morsel. Except for her eyes, she was gray with dust, the exact gray of the camp robber, the cheeky thin-legged bird that haunted the route of the caravan.

As her slight weight tilted the carriage, the quartette turned to stare, their sandwiches halted before open mouths, a quick, inimical greed in their eyes . . . They hadn't any too much food along; it was still a long way to Leadville; who knew when they might get anything more to eat in this Godforsaken country?

The youngest and prettiest broke first under that fascinated scrutiny. She choked on her dry bread. Then she thrust something toward the child's dirty little talons.

"Here, take my jelly tart. You're worse'n a little dog, following every move when a body raises her hand to her mouth."

Carolina clutched the tart with one hand while she clung to the door frame with the other. She swallowed it in two gulps. Then she licked off the crumbs with a questing tongue and sniffed.

"My, but you Sodomwhores smell nice," she said.

The youngest and prettiest found herself unwillingly moving over to make room for the dirty child.

"Us what?" demanded the bossy older one called Hattie, whose face seemed never to be creased by frowns or smiles.

"Pa keeps saying, don't look at your wagon, it's full of Sodomwhores."

The three younger ones giggled vapidly. The Madam pondered. Whores she could figure out. But Sodomwhores? Something uncomplimentary, of course.

"He says the fires of hell will roast you till your vile souls frizzle and fry like grease," explained Carolina conversationally. Her father's predictions were too old and too frequent to matter much; besides, none of them ever seemed to come true.

"This sure feels nice," she said presently, caressing the silk dress beside her. "Softer than anything, ain't it? Softer even than our baby Mat's cheek, I'll bet."

4

The women looked mollified. They, who could scarcely have been called bulwarks of family life, invariably melted at the mention of a baby.

Carolina, however, had not finished with her observations.

"You got funny hair," she remarked to the Madam, staring at the purplish-black hair that fell away from pallid roots at the part. "She *has* got funny hair, ain't she?" she inquired reasonably of the other three.

The three giggled again, but a little less certainly this time. The Madam stared straight ahead as if she had not heard. But she *had* heard.

Hattie Merkle, who prided herself on her stony expression, hated the nastily observing brat. She hated the girls, too, for being young. She had known all along that she should have had her hair touched up before she left Denver . . . This parching mountain wind and sun—that dawdling, witless driver—and a whole week on the way, tossing around like corn in a popper. They should have taken the stage. The stage did not have to stop to double up to get to the top of a pass; it ran straight through like a tireless machine.

But she had been tempted into buying this broken-down hack because, with a coat of shiny paint and the top thrown back, it would be just the thing for her girls to take their afternoon rides in around Leadville. That was always a good trick. And the driver would be useful about the place, once she had located a house.

This was her last chance, and she knew it. No one would ever back her again. As they had told her down in Denver, if she couldn't succeed with a sporting house in Leadville now, she wouldn't be able to sell a mint julep in hell.

Carolina settled back with unaccustomed sensual delight. The nice smells, the jelly tart, the swish of silks, the soft cushiony thighs she was wedged between, and the up-and-down giggles of the girls . . .

Thus did she make her acquaintance with one of the strongest influences of her early life: the prostitutes of the mining camps. Always her father would fight them, and always the young Carolina would feel drawn to them. To him, Leadville's State Street would be synonymous with Hell. To her it would be alluring because in State Street they laughed. What matter whether the laughs were drunken or amorous or despairing or merely empty? She was famished for the sound of human gaiety.

5

The Madam glanced up the road. Her lips stretched into a near smile.

"Here comes the old fool back. Guess he didn't have any luck finding somebody else to double up with—guess he'll have to team up with the sporting women's carriage after all. Better get along to your wagon, youngun."

"I ain't going to. It stinks," stated Carolina, burrowing deeper among the flounces and overdrapes and bustles. "I aim to stay here and ride to the top with you."

Hattie's mouth tightened. Then it relaxed.

"Be a good joke to play on the old skate. Well, scrooch down then and keep your mouth shut."

Carolina scrooched. The girls on either side spread their ruffles over her like mother hens. It was a game, and they liked playing games. They laughed with the empty, artless malice of children.

And so the bawdy house Negro, Leander, and the itinerant preacher hitched their two teams together, and both men climbed up on to the high front seat of the carriage. At his father's command, Elick reluctantly returned to stay with the Gospel wagon. Jude kept his eyes fixed sternly straight ahead, as if, like his horses, he also wore blinders.

The carriage set off for the long climb. First one driver and then the other tried his hand at guiding the four-horse team. In either case the progress was erratic, for the Negro was too slack, and the preacher was too harsh. The carriage swayed and rocked.

There were moments on that ascent when the hard-faced older woman, who had looked down the bore of a gun and witnessed beatings, rape, and murder in her time, blanched and shut her eyes. Such moments as when the outer wheel crossed an open notch in the edge of the road, beneath which the cliff dropped sheer and pitiless. Or when the front wheels of the carriage rose straight up over great boulders, letting the carriage pitch forward almost on to the backs of the horses in the descent beyond.

It was not a road. It was only a recent trail over which countless mules and horses had already clawed their way to the top of the Pass, a trail which had to be gouged out and shored up afresh on every trip by tired drivers. Here and there, far below, could be seen the remains of luckless wagons and animals that had gone over the brink in a shambles of broken harness and splintering wagon tongues and the frenzied screaming of men and mules.

6

None of the occupants of the carriage had the faintest interest in the swiftly changing pageant of vegetation. It was fall, and the frost had singed the high country. The carriage soon left behind the familiar region of lodgepole pines and aspens, which last still managed to hold on to a quivering patch of gold here and there. It left behind, too, the rich dark belt of spruce spires whose branches were sometimes tipped with blue, reminding Carolina of candles on the Sunday School Christmas tree.

Now the trail wound up among the last gallant outposts, the ragged bristlecone pines, deformed by the wind into scarred old dwarfs. Great cracks spiraled around the trunks, which always twisted in the same direction, giving mute evidence of the ceaseless assault of the winds. Finally even these stubborn warriors were left behind, flaunting their tattered flags of branches. All that remained were the bushy mats of fir and the low leafless thickets of Alpine willow that crawled up the last bitter slopes together.

Timber line! The carriage entered a high, barren, breathless region of boulders and of rills trickling down from under the edges of snow patches. The husks of foot-high mountain sunflowers which had bloomed in August rattled in the wind. A thick moss studded with minute dried flowers hugged the ground like fur.

Carolina's ears popped and felt thick. She peered out and drew in a breath that was like the blade of winter piercing her skinny chest. She cowered back quickly again in the warmth of the plump bodies beside her.

When it seemed that the four horses could not strain another foot, the grade leveled off, and they drew up on the flat, rock-strewn crest of the ridge. Back of them to the east lay the vast, shimmering, opalescent basin of South Park. Ahead of them to the west lay the sharper, narrower valley of the Arkansas river, backed by the jagged majesty of the Sawatch range.

The Madam stared ahead at the cruelly massive peaks, eighteen miles away, that formed the spine of the continent. Somewhere below in the valley that separated this craggy ridge on which they stood and those cruel peaks lay Leadville. She shuddered. God! They'd earn their money in a country like this. She longed to be back in Denver, with its cozy grate fires and cheerful gaslights. She spoke sharply to the girls telling them to get out and stretch their legs.

Carolina remained crouched inside the carriage until her father and the Negro had unhitched their teams and were preparing to

7

head back down the trail together to bring up the Gospel wagon.

The Pass was a stopping place where the first wagons had assembled for a noon meal and to wait until the last ones could be dragged to the top. Campfires built from brush picked up along the climb crackled in the thin air. Coffee, which bubbled quickly at this high altitude, sent out its sharp invitation; and saltside sizzled in skillets. Bearded freighters stood around and wolfed down food. The dandies shivered and wondered if it was such a jolly adventure after all. A gambler tentatively riffled a pack of cards.

But they all brightened, as one man, when the shabby carriage disgorged its load of women in their plumed hats and narrow-waisted jackets and pear-shaped, draped skirts that belled out over exaggerated bustles and narrowed in seductively at the knees.

The women bridled and took mincing steps and acted their time-less roles. The men gallantly spread coats on rocks for them and offered them coffee and a nip of something to warm their insides. There were jokes and laughter.

Carolina forgot her father. She gravitated to the fringe of men about the women. A freighter who had obviously had more than a nip had hold of the youngest and prettiest girl by the arm. He was urging her toward his covered wagon. The girl demurred.

At that moment Carolina's father returned. Perhaps he had heard her shrill treble. Perhaps he had forgotten something. Perhaps he merely wanted another look at his adversaries, those painted damned creatures who were the devil's first assistants.

When he recognized his own child, jumping up and down on the edge of the unholy fringe about the women, he stared unbelievingly. His reddish mustache bristled like an angry collie's ruff. Fires leaped in his queer tawny eyes.

"Carolina! What are you doing amongst these whores straight from Sodom and Gomorrah? Come along with me."

Carolina cringed back among the women. For a moment she had been happy.

Even in his rage, Jude Lawler was reluctant to approach too closely. But everyone was watching. He had no choice but to stride in among the flounces and pleats.

"Give me my child!"

The Madam was revenged. A sardonic dent ran down from one corner of her mouth.

Jude made a grab for Carolina and caught her by a skinny shoulder. She tried to wriggle away.

Coarse remarks popped all around . . . "She's choosin' kind of young, ain't she, parson?"

The fires in his eyes blazed higher. He shook his child. She wrenched away, but he caught her again. She struggled and clawed. He cuffed her, and she bit back like a snarling lion cub. He held her off at arm's length this time. Only then did she cry, the tears streaking down through the dirt and jelly; but they were tears of ignominy and helpless fury, not of pain. She was beyond pain; she was a seething bundle of rage.

Carrying her like a thrashing little animal, he climbed up on the back of one of his horses. Black Leander started to accompany him, since it was his turn to help the parson bring his wagon to the top. But that was more than Jude Lawler could stomach now. It was bad enough to have had to help haul the fallen women's carriage to the top. But to have been tricked, so that he had carted his own child up amongst them——

"I don't want your help!" he thundered down at Leander. "Stay with your Sodomwhores, and go ye hellward together." He looked truculently around at the others. "Surely there's one of you will let me have the use of his team to get my wagon up?"

He dared them to refuse, and they took his dare. After all, it was the colored driver's turn, and he was plainly willing to go. Had Jude Lawler been in real need, several might have gone to great lengths to help him. But he was not in real need. He was refusing the Negro for moral reasons only. This was no country for the squeamish or the overscrupulous.

Jude read their answer. He dug his heels into his horse and headed his team down the east face of the Pass. A wind that seemed to blow from the outer spaces of eternity swept his hat off; it sailed far out into the canyon. He did not glance after it.

Down and down the horses plodded, guided by a bare-headed Jeremiah who held a gasping child caged in his left arm. Far below waited a solitary gray wagon where a woman tossed and moaned.

Carolina sniffled and fought spasmodically against that relentless grasp. She could not know that what her father had been trying to beat out of her were his own frailties, his own weaknesses of the flesh, his own burning temptations. Every time he looked at this strange child, who had his own eyes and his own stubborn furies,

9

he saw himself in her, and he was both shamed and fearful. But she was young. He still had a chance to save her. She must never have to fight the devils he had battled—the driving lusts of the flesh—the craving for soft living that the world called beauty—the hunger for approbation that the world called fellowship. The love of God must be enough . . . forsaking all others. Yes, he would beat it out of her.

What he did not know was that you cannot beat a child's paternity out of it.

CHAPTER 2

WHILE HE WAITED BESIDE THE GOSPEL WAGON FOR SOMEONE TO come along, Jude's wrath had time to cool. For once, he was forced to share in the panic all women know, facing the inexorability of childbirth. Always before, he had escaped it. Now he was terrified, alone here in this high basin, with no one but God to call upon. For the only answer he received to his tormented prayers was the sigh of winds pouring down through the draws from the peaks, and the petulant scolding of chickaree squirrels in the timber alongside the road, and the frightened whimpers of his own children within the wagon. Almost accusingly he explained to God that He would have to come to his help. For he could not bring himself to admit that it might have been better if he had accepted even the tainted assistance of Leander in order to reach Leadville in time.

He paced up and down the road, shading his eyes with his hand and peering across the vast floor of the valley for signs of an approaching wagon. The beauty of the place was lost upon him. He did not notice the rippling meadows, laced with glinting creeks, that stretched away toward dim azure peaks; nor the pressing hands of the winds that made moving wavelets across the brownish autumn grasses. But he did feel, all too plainly, the cool astringency in the air that lifted the hairs on the back of his neck and reminded him that winter was coming. He noted the steady progress of the sun across the limpid sky that warned him that night was coming too. And he heard the moans from within the wagon that told him that his wife's hour was drawing near.

When he saw the creeping speck of a wagon in the distance, followed by its rolling ball of dust, he ran to meet it. The freighter would have to help him out. God could not turn a deaf ear to him now.

The wagon rumbled to a stop. The freighter, a leathery little man with a face as wrinkled as a last year's walnut and almost as dark, from wind and sun, looked down at him in concern.

"What's wrong, man?"

"It's my wife—her birth pains are starting, even though she always takes a lengthy time to it. I've got to reach Leadville, and my team can't pull my wagon to the top of the Pass. Will you double up with me?"

Jude paused, looking up at the freighter in angry despair. He half-expected a refusal; he was braced for it in fact.

But when the freighter's face softened, and he said, "Sure, sure. Jump up on the seat here, quick," the bristle seemed to go out of Jude's bushy eyebrows and the iron out of his backbone. So God *had* heard.

When they reached the stalled Gospel wagon, the stranger leaped down and began to unhitch his own rugged four-horse team to add to the parson's spiritless beasts. He kept his eyes politely averted from the canvas-covered interior from which issued premonitory groans. But, looking at the gaunt Gospel team, he could let loose some of the pity that welled up within him, but which was not fitting for one man to show toward another's wife.

"Poor, ga'nted creatures. It's galled you are, and why not? With no collar pads to speak of, and your harness a-chafin' and your check reins jacked up too tight. Wait till I rub a little of my good wool fat on you." He rubbed lanolin on crusted sores and loosened a buckle here and tightened one there. "No wonder they say this country is fine for men and dogs but hell on horses and women ——" He stopped with a contrite look as a moan from within the wagon attested to the truth of the last part of his statement.

Red to the ears, he unhitched the Gospel team first and tied it to the endgate of the wagon. His own four-horse team could pull the load to the top easy, he assured Jude Lawler, and rest these poor scrawny beasts a mite.

11

Jude was silent during the unhitching and hitching, although he awkwardly tried to help. For, after all, the little man was an answer to prayer. When they were ready, the freighter swung Elick and Carolina up on to the wagon seat between himself and their father, and the wagon set off smartly up the slope.

Leo Cobb, the man said his name was. "Horse doctor by trade, but freighter by necessity. More money in freighting. And it gives me a chance to buy up poor, mistreated, beat-out horses. Look at those fine beasts." He pointed. "You never saw a sorrowfuller string than when I bought them from a freight outfit that figured they was worn out. But I cosseted them, till today they'd bring a thousand dollars easy. Take care of your critters, and they'll take care of you," he reproved.

Jude listened with unwonted meekness. He was not used to being reproved; but even less was he used to kindness, and the man had been kind.

"You should see my Nellie's colt," Leo went on boastfully. The two children brightened. "The mother was the worst done-up nag that ever laid down by the side of a road to die. But I found her in time and helped bring her foal into the world, and then I put the old girl out to pasture like she deserved. Her colt's going to be a great little race horse, come two years or more——"

Jude tried to frown. "Where there's racing, men make wagers. That's gambling."

"Sure, and do you think you'll stop it?" chuckled the freighter. "I know folks, parson, that would rather have a full house in their hand than mansions in the sky." He clucked to his horses.

Jude did not offer to help with the driving. Leo Cobb had a way with horses.

He had a way with children too. Once, he stopped the wagon to dart over to break off a chunk of resin from an old spruce tree. It stuck to the children's teeth at first, but presently they chewed it down to a bricky red gum that had a pungent, comforting taste. They chewed until they fell asleep hours later.

Another time, he slowed the team to let a dumpy, furry animal with a black face cross the road. It gave a short sharp whistling sound that ended in a rounded call.

"That's a whistle pig," he said. "Though some would call it a ground hog and maybe others a woodchuck."

Carolina clapped her hands, and the marmot broke into a run

12

that became an undulating gallop as it finally ducked under the rocks at the far side of the road.

"It looks like a muff on legs!" she squealed.

Leo's eyes squinted into slits of pleasure.

On an easy stretch, while he let Elick "drive" with the lines that dangled below his own skilled fingers, Leo managed to twist a bandanna handkerchief into a doll baby which, when he held it in the crook of his arm, magically sat up with a jerk and said, "Go along with you now!" or else lay back in his arms and sighed, "Lack-aday, but I'm sleepy!"

True, the doll, after he gave it to Carolina, did not exactly talk out loud, but it did snuggle back in her arms in a satisfying way. She cradled it against her chest and loved it. She had never had a doll before. She looked up at the man with worship in her eyes.

All the way to the top the freighter talked cheerfully. And the moaning from within subsided, as if there were communicated to Hester something of his sympathy and his cheer.

"Planning to stay long in Leadville, parson?"

"As long as there are gamblers fleecing young men and tippling houses making sots of them and brothels leading them to hell."

"I guess you're planning on quite a stay," replied the freighter innocently. "They say there's a couple of hundred men arriving every day in Leadville, and over thirty thousand in the gulch already. The post office does the biggest business of anywheres between Kansas City and San Francisco. The line waiting for mail is so long, a fellow at the head can sell his place for five dollars and start over. I hear Tabor has thirteen mail clerks working for him— he's the one made the big killing last spring out of a grubstake he gave a couple of fellows that located the Little Pittsburgh mine. He gets a third of everything."

But Jude was not interested in any except the rich veins of sin. Yet once, when Leo Cobb executed a particularly perilous turn, with the road caving in just behind them, he was disconcerted to have the little man remark blithely, "I always say on this stretch, 'If I'm lucky I reach Leadville; if I ain't, I see the Holy City.'"

Jude's ginger-colored brows drew together. He ought to be the one to warn of the imminence of the hereafter, not this twinkling-eyed heathen. But he found himself strangely tongue-tied.

It was twilight when they reached the top of the Pass. The wind, straight off the continental divide, knifed through the men's rough

13

jackets and the children's thin cloaks; it pierced the canvas sides of the wagon and the tattered quilts covering the woman.

Leo assured Jude Lawler, while he unhitched his own team and put the Gospel horses in their place, that he would not need any help himself to make the climb.

"You'd best be getting on to Leadville, sir," he urged.

Jude could not argue. He thanked the freighter gruffly. He did not know how to tender thanks gracefully, either to man or God. For man had done him few favors, and God had meted out more afflictions than benisons, thus far. He lifted a hand in farewell.

Leo Cobb seemed to understand.

"Remember, parson, to chain a log to your hind axle when the grade gets steep so you don't have a runaway," he called back.

Jude nodded and headed down the west face of the Pass, leaving Leo to retrace his course down the east slope.

The Gospel wagon creaked and jolted downward over the same twisting, headlong route that thousands had followed this past year. A few had struck it rich; countless others had lost everything, even their lives. Men died of pneumonia from sleeping on sawdust saloon floors, of "cholera morbus" from eating tainted food, of simple starvation, and of "lead poisoning."

There were few complaints. The populace gave a not unsympathetic shrug and buried the dead—now and then striking a rich ore pocket in the digging—reckoning merely that another poor devil had lost his gamble. There was always the chance of winning, and every prospector was a gambler.

They did not stop to figure that the odds were against them, that nature had rigged a gigantic game where "the house" took an unfair percentage of their health and hopes and youth. All of them were young and strong of body and will. Careful plodders seldom left home in the first place, and the weaklings who started either turned back or died along the trail.

Some worked hard, like Leo, and acquired only calluses. Others, like Jude, received wounds to the spirit that became festering sores.

The solitary wagon reached the meager shelter of the pines, whose branches tossed in the wind like hearse plums. Their sound was like the hollow moan inside a giant seashell, or like a rehearsal for a storm that was coming.

The short, thin, sober twilight swiftly gave way to night as the

14

sun dropped behind great Mt. Massive in the range across the valley. Jude lighted a lantern and hung it under the wagon. He fastened a log to the rear axle as Leo had advised. But he dared not stop. He gave the horses their head and hoped they would not all go crashing over the mountain side.

When at last the long descent was completed, the trail turned north again, winding along the base of the range among scrub-covered hills until it neared the Arkansas river, which was only a small stream near its source here.

It was long past midnight when they turned east up a wide draw called California Gulch, which made a shallow gash on the western slope of the Mosquito range. Three or four miles ahead lay Leadville, at the foot of the low rounded carbonate hills that jutted out like steps at the foot of the range.

This was Leadville's second boom in eighteen years, and it would not be its last. In 1860 several Gilpin County gold hunters had found surface gold here and, in a burst of hope, had named it California Gulch. Soon the whole length of the skimpy six-mile-long creek was preempted, and men stood all day in freezing water while they washed gold in pans or rockers or sluices. The storekeepers of the settlement of Oro weighed the gold dust and accepted it as it came from the sluices at eighteen dollars an ounce, in return for whiskey and flour.

But the boom was soon spent, and California Gulch finally became as dead as a three-day-old corpse which, in miners' jargon, was considered "too dead to skin."

During the years, a peculiarly heavy sand had made washing the gold in sluices difficult, and inordinately heavy boulders in the stream bed had had to be tugged out of the way. Suddenly, in the middle Seventies, men discovered that those heavy sands and boulders were made of carbonate of lead, carrying silver.

Silver! The word spread. Prospectors poured in to "gopher" the hills with diggings. In '77 a sampling works to test ore went up; a smelter for roasting and refining it followed. Charlie Mater came up from Granite and built the first store. Horace Tabor, whose hard-working wife had baked for the miners and nursed them and kept their dust safe for them, moved his stock of goods down from Oro and opened the second store.

Leadville was named in January of 1878 for those magically heavy lead boulders, and the rush was on. New discoveries were made every day, until prospect holes on Fryer Hill were thick as pits on a strawberry. People no longer said, "How are you?" They said, "How deep are you?"

The highways were choked with lines of freight and immigrant wagons, with stage coaches, and with people on foot. The population rose quickly from 300 to 30,000. There were twenty times as many saloons as churches.

II

IT WAS INTO LEADVILLE THIS NIGHT IN THE FALL OF 1878 THAT JUDE Lawler brought his brood.

Carolina suddenly awakened. She and Elick had been sleeping limply against their father. She sat up and sniffed. There was something in the air. Not just that it was thin and heady, two miles above the ocean. But it was filled with a queer, acrid, nose-tickling smell—sulphurous and Satanic. In time, this stench from the smelters would become so familiar to her that all other air would seem flat and savorless. In time, it would seem only natural to live in a town where the smelter fumes killed the trees and blighted the wild flowers and made tiny holes in the washings hung on the lines. But now the smell was strange and exciting.

The starry night was punctuated by blasts of flame from the smelter furnaces. And here and there, near the sides of the gulch, showers of crimson sparks shot skyward, as great spurts of molten slag were poured from slag pots down over the edges of the fast growing smelter dumps.

Past straggling huts and tents they jolted. The night was made hideous by the screech and whine and rasp of a dozen sawmills laboring to satisfy the mines and the shivering population, three-fourths of which were still housed in tents. The better tents had board floors and a square of tin sewed around the protruding stovepipe. The raw new pine cabins were mostly one-room boxes. Those with plain gable ends were dwellings; those with a flimsy false front slapped across the gable were stores and saloons and assay offices.

Suddenly Leadville lay before them, ablaze with kerosene flares and torches and lamps backed by reflectors. Night in Leadville was far livelier than day. The wagon wound its way up the chief thoroughfare called Chestnut Street, laid out a little crooked like the street scene on a theater curtain, and bordered with high, uneven wooden sidewalks. A dozen bands blared through open doorways. Great muslin banners across the fronts of the buildings announced the very attractions Jude Lawler had come to abolish.

Carolina's head turned as on a pivot. From the high seat she looked down on a milling confusion: freight wagons standing every which way with their bare ribs arching over them, saddled horses drooping hipshot beside the hitching racks, strings of burros with dainty hoofs and huge packs picking their way around the stumps that still protruded from the streets. Piles of lumber were dumped at random, as well as stacks of stove wood and bundles of shingles. Great tents bore the painted announcement, "Lodgings from 50¢ to $1.50."

Jude halted his team before the handsome three-story frame Grand Hotel. Ordinarily he shunned such costly places; but tonight, in his extremity, he would try anything. But when he saw the long queue of men waiting to register, he shook his head helplessly and drove on.

Men, men, men, everywhere, thought Carolina. But where were the ladies and the little children? When they turned a corner she saw the ladies, leaning out of windows right on a level with the street, their arms bare and flowers in their hair and smiles on their faces. She smiled back at them, but she was afraid they did not see her. The laughing all about her grew louder.

Carolina was intoxicated. Her dusty bronze braids stood straight out. The bruise she had received in her scuffle with her father on the Pass was already blackening around one eye. She sniffed the air and heard the shouts, the shrieks, the brassy tom-tom music, and everywhere the ribald laughter.

Jude called down to a man in a thick frieze jacket and a round felt hat to ask if he knew where one could find a doctor or a midwife.

The man shook his head. "I been here two days and I ain't found a bed to sleep in myself."

Jude drove on to the end of the street and up the slope which was dotted with tent houses and dugouts, with here and there a flickering campfire. He drew up under one of the few remaining pine trees and cramped his wagon to hold it on the side of the hill.

He went around to the back of the wagon to leave the lantern while he was gone. As he looked inside he saw that he must indeed hurry. Letty was crouching beside her mother, whimpering

17

with fright. Elick, wide-eyed, peered in under his father's elbow. Little Mat was asleep. Only Carolina, still perched on the front seat, was oblivious. Her eyes were fastened on those beckoning lights below.

"I'm going to find ye a doctor or a midwife or at least a woman, if I can, Hester," he said, laying his hand on her awkwardly. Then he turned and strode down the hill.

Carolina, on the wagon seat, became aware presently of the suffering behind her. She was suddenly engulfed in love and terror for her mother. She tumbled off the seat and down into the wagon bed.

"Does it hurt, Ma? Don't cry, Ma!"

For once Hester could pay her no heed. Letty, who was twelve and a "regular little woman," was scornful of such ignorance, although a moment before she had been weak with fright herself.

"She'll be worse before she's better, silly!" she announced sagely, as she had heard grown-up ladies say. "You and Elick better run down and find Pa." Her voice broke; she was only a little girl again. "You know how Pa forgets."

They knew. Carolina, still clutching her bandanna doll, scrambled out of the wagon and took hold of Elick's hand. Together the two children stumbled down the hillside, away from the moaning hump that was their mother and toward the town's luring lights, already beginning to fade against the paling sky.

They were too scared and too intent to heed the first rosy coloring on the crest of the massive Sawatch range, as the sun, hidden as yet from their view deep in the valley, reached across and painted the tips of the peaks to the west.

They headed straight for the main streets, still brightly lighted and busy with the interminable buying and selling of claims and mining shares and building lots. Where there were lights, there they would find Pa, preaching against "the playing cards that the devil uses to fan the hellfires with," and "whiskey, the first downward step on the greased stairway to hell."

But they could not find their father. They stopped in relief when a four-horse team drew up beside them. Leo whom they loved grinned anxiously down at them.

"What you two fryin'-size chicks doing out alone?"

"It's Ma," explained Carolina. "She hurts. Pa came down to

find somebody, but Letty says maybe he forgot. Ma hurts bad. She's crying. Letty's crying too," she finished solemnly.

Leo muttered under his breath and turned and stared hopelessly up and down the street.

"Where's your wagon?"

"Under yonder pine," Elick pointed.

"You younguns keep on till you find your father. Bring him back if you have to drag him. I'll see what I can do."

He drove straight toward the hill to which Elick had pointed. The children walked on uncertainly.

As soon as Leo Cobb had located the Gospel wagon, with the lantern light shining through the gray canvas sides, he left his team and hurried toward it. When he spoke to the suffering woman inside, his voice was as gentle as it had been the time he found old Nellie at the roadside where she had lain down to die.

"Easy now, old girl," he encouraged the tormented woman, using the only words he knew, horse talk. Hester relaxed at once. That was what she had needed, reassurance and comfort. "Steady now—everything's all right. Don't be in a hurry. Easy does it. That's the girl——"

Hester sighed and went on with her eternal task of bringing Jude Lawler's children into the world. A moment before, she had thought she was dying. She had wanted to die. Now she rallied her forces to do as this kind voice told her.

Hester Davidson had grown up in a small Ohio town, trying to obey her mother's injunction to be a lady, which proved the worst possible preparation for life with Jude Lawler. She had turned into a pretty, pallid, mouse-drab girl whose only emotional release was obtained at revival meetings.

The traveling revivalists represented romance to every starved young female in a town that had lost most of its virile young males to the California gold rush in '48, or to the Colorado gold rush in '59, or to the War in the '60's. So when this tall, vehement young preacher, attracted by Hester's shy breeding and pale charm, bent his fiery head toward her and turned his fiery glance upon her, she was his for the taking. Quite literally she was carried away by him—not on a prancing charger, but in a rented livery rig to the next town on the revival circuit.

Her mother was first taken aback and then elated. Hadn't every girl in the congregation openly set her cap for him? Later, after

19

Jude's split with the recognized church in which he had been ordained, she was not so complacent. But by then Hester had several babies and had moved westward with her hothead.

The marriage was ill-fated from the start. During the first years before Jude left the aegis of the church, he was forever quarreling with the clerical hierarchy, shaking a sinewy fist and scowling with his lion's brows. He was unable to compromise or to listen. When Hester was about to have her third baby, Jude had his final dramatic schism with the church and they moved out west. He ought to have traveled alone. Instead he was check-reined and hobbled by a wife and an ever growing family of children.

He was not a good provider of anything but seed for his progeny. And Hester's only vigor was at conceiving. She lacked the ruggedness to stand up to him or his children or to life. Everything was too much for her. So when he felt the Call to come out to this country of sheer peaks and barren gulches and drunken brawls and casual death, Hester had simply stopped struggling.

It was a country few women could cope with anyhow. For it was a man's world, without law and order, without gentleness, without ease. It was savage and dramatic and thrilling—but not to Hester Lawler.

She hated a ribald land where the town's noisiest brothel elbowed a church until the church was forced to move. Where men played poker until they were naked, and then let one of their number wander tipsily outside to freeze to death, a grisly joke on himself.

She hated the hurried violence of a country that had neither rocking chairs nor old people, those signs of a leisured kindly land; where a dry gulch one day became a raging flash flood the next, only to revert to a dry gulch again on the third day; and where babies died of colic or croup or summer complaint—or just died. She wanted security and ordered calmness; Jude Lawler gave her want and savage crusading.

Yet from some queer tenacious loyalty she always defended him to her children.

"You don't understand your father. He *has* to act the way he does. He *takes* life harder than most—he fights himself harder——"

Elick, who could read, was slowly pronouncing the names of the saloons and variety theaters and gambling houses to Carolina, who as yet could only spell. But they could not find their father before any of them. Not outside the fashionable Tontine restaurant, or Pap Wyman's, or the Zoo, or even St. Anne's Rest, which was the noisiest spot on the street. They were ready to give up when they saw a knot of men in front of the farthest lighted doorway, from which issued stale music and staler odors: the sour, yet sweetish fumes of beer and whiskey.

High above the tired music and the shouts and the laughter sounded the thundering invective of a man arguing with God and the devil and his own soul. They saw a demanding fist above the clustering heads. Pa, all right.

They wormed their way in between the unsteadily balanced legs of the drunkenly repentant or the drunkenly derisive bystanders. When they reached their father, Elick plucked at one sleeve while Carolina tugged at the other. Leo had said to bring their father back if they had to drag him.

Rapt, carried away by his own pleas, Jude Lawler shook them off.

A half-hour before, he had been a worried father and husband as he strode in among the fleshpots to inquire about a doctor or a midwife, or even a warm room to which he could take his wife. But in all this greedy, sensation-craving crowd, he could find not one who would listen. It was inevitable that, goaded by this fact, he should launch forth on a peroration about No Room at The Inn.

Presently his eyes were flashing and his tongue had loosened, while his mane tossed and his voice thundered. Against their will, men stopped to listen. They had to listen to this torrent of pleading and hate. And it was more hate than pleading. For to Jude Lawler the flames of hell were hot and close, and the mercy of God was a cool abstraction it was best not to bank too much on in a sinning world.

Carolina reached up and stubbornly tugged again. And while she tugged, up on the hillside, a gnarled little man was saying, "There, there, old girl—it's a fine little foal—girl-child you got——" as he delivered the baby that was to be called Rosalie.

Exasperated by the repeated tugging and pulling, Jude Lawler finally shook himself free. He did not even notice that it was his own child he sent sprawling in the sawdust and gravel. A knotted red bandanna was jolted out of her grasp. Before she could regain it, heavy boots had trodden on it. She darted in to snatch it up, but she was too late. It had come untied. She stared down at the bedraggled thing in her hands, shock and unbelief in her eyes. The magic was gone. It was only a limp and trampled bandanna.

Slowly she backed away from the cluster of men surrounding her father, her face white under its dirt. Her brown-gold eyes with their wide black pupils were blazing. Her pinched face had grown suddenly wolfish.

Standing there with the tears scoring runnels down her cheeks, she looked down at the lifeless, dirty piece of cloth in her hands. Then she hurled it to the ground, turned toward that booming voice and lifted a grubby fist, shaking it high above her head in a gesture so like her father's that it was both absurd and sinister.

C H A P T E R 3

CAROLINA BANGED DOWN HER IRON WITH DISGUST AND REACHED FOR another damp roll in the clothes basket. At sixteen, she could already hold her own with her sister Letty when it came to ironing. But today she had far outstripped Letty. Carolina had never known her sister to dawdle so; stopping at intervals at her board on the other side of the dark little kitchen to sing hymns or to tuck up a tan wisp of hair or even to hold off a chemise to admire it. As if time were not terribly short and growing shorter. And unless they got the ironing delivered to Hattie Merkle's place on West Fifth Street in time for Floss to pay for it before supper, she would never be able to buy the dress in the window of the Palace of Fashion. And if she did not have the dress, she could not go to the Assembly Ball in the Armory tonight with Bert Damon; and if she did not go to the ball, her life was ruined.

"You are under condemnation, careless sinner,
And the judgment day is surely drawing near——"

Letty's nasal alto, loud from years of trying to drown out tipsy laughter and brassy bands on street corners, droned on.

Carolina thumped her iron down again and then lifted it hastily. Floss was nice and easy-going and full of fun, but she would not take kindly to a scorch on the front of her petticoat with the ten rows of hand-whipped lace and the lace edging on the dust ruffle. My, the girls in the parlor houses had stylish clothes!

> "Depart from my presence, the Judge will proclaim;
> Depart from my presence in everlasting flame!"

Letty's just like Pa, thought Carolina. She really enjoys thinking about all the sinners sizzling and basting in the great oven of hell. Carolina herself liked pretty songs, not hymns. "The Blue Alsatian Mountains," and "Waiting," and "Never Take the Horseshoe from the Door." But Letty was as bad as Ma about singing hymns to please Pa.

At the thought of her mother she scowled and rammed the point of her iron into the gathers of the dust ruffle.

Already, at sixteen, she sensed her mother's overwhelming defeat at the hands of life and Jude Lawler. When Hester had died last year giving birth to a stillborn child—her tenth—Carolina had been torn with pity for her mother and with fresh hatred for her father. She had been too prejudiced to face the fact that nothing but death could have dragged her mother away from Jude Lawler; that it was more than duty and convention and the word of God that had bound her to him. At fifteen, there is always something embarrassing, even repugnant, about the bond between one's parents. Added to this was Carolina's own sense of grieved protectiveness toward her mother.

She had been forced all this past year to contain her resentment toward her father, while she continued to attend school and help Letty at home with the washings which her mother had formerly done. They washed openly for the respectable ladies of the town and on the sly for the parlor house girls. The latter paid the best, of course, but Letty and Carolina had to be careful not to let their father find out. For although he never stayed at one job long enough to maintain his family in any kind of comfort, and was always making sacrifices which, Carolina muttered darkly, took more out of the family than they did out of himself (food and warmth and nice clothes had long since ceased to mean anything to him), still he would have raised a righteous hurricane if he had known that his daughters were washing for the light women of the town.

Once, this past year, he had struck her when she remarked pertly, "I don't see why you have to pick on the fancy women all the time, Pa. They and us both follow the strikes. Miners seem to be easy marks for either religion or sin." . . . In his sermon that evening, her father had warned a sodden crowd (and his own daughter): "For a whore is a deep ditch—her feet go down to death and her steps take hold on hell——"

So while she was waiting to be old—say, sixteen—Carolina had helped Letty and darted around the edges of life picking up whatever came her way. There was still much of the eager, inquisitive, terrier quality about the adolescent Carolina. At home she had unwittingly soaked the Bible into the marrow of her mind. She had read her father's volume of Spurgeon's Sermons and a book on Exegesis and Homiletics, and her mother's copy of "Barriers Burned Away." At school she was good in "mental arithmetic" and poor in "composition," and she quickly but stealthily learned the waltz and the polka during her lunch time.

Leo Cobb, whose own reading ended with the labels on bottles of horse liniment, brought her books all the way from Denver. Leo also taught her how to tie a diamond hitch and to stay on a horse. When she rode, she wore an old skirt of her mother's and hooked her right knee over the pommel of a man's saddle (no lady could ride astride like a clothespin) and went clattering off alone up Iowa Gulch to some promontory where she could survey the splendor of the great Sawatch range. In spite of the bleakness of her home surroundings, she was not a stranger to beauty. She knew a winged soaring of the spirit during those moments when she sat gazing up at brooding Mt. Elbert or Mt. Massive.

From the women for whom her mother, and then Letty, washed she learned many things. From the doctor's wife she learned that you scalded out the pot before you made tea. From the wife of the man who ran the sampling works she learned that you bathed every chance you got, not just on Saturday nights. From a visiting Miss Lovelace who taught elocution she learned to keep her voice low; only in temper did she forget Miss Lovelace's injunctions.

From the sporting women she learned that she was turning into a beauty. The respectable women would never have told her, for fear of turning her head. But actually it gave her a needed confidence. Floss Kittredge, who was twenty-one and a comparatively new girl at Hattie Merkle's place, had told her so with emphasis and relish, and had promptly become Carolina's best friend. They did not see each other often, but when they did, they giggled together at respectable Leadville and somehow healed the wounds inflicted on Carolina by that same Leadville. And Carolina was starved for somebody to giggle with.

Not that the nice girls of the town did not giggle. They were downright silly, Carolina thought enviously—only not with her. True, she had few chances to meet them, with their walled-in lives of private school and dancing school and hand-picked parties; fewer chances even than she had to meet Floss of West Fifth Street. For whenever she approached these well-brought-up young ladies of the town, they joined ranks against her like a party of emigrant wagons forming a tight circle against a band of marauding Utes.

She had no way of knowing that this cabal was not altogether due to their snobbishness. Rather, it was because they were afraid of both her and her ranting father. He was wild-eyed and queer. And she threatened them—their supremacy, their dominion over their young men. But Carolina knew only that they had fun and she did not. And even while Floss was calling them prissy, whey-faced sluts, she was passionately longing to know what they laughed at with their gasping little lady-giggles.

Tonight would narrow the gap between them, she told herself. Tonight they would accept her, for wouldn't she be escorted by the most eligible boy in town, the son of the superintendent of the third largest smelter? She could see all the girls envying her new dress and crowding up to share those delicious little jokes with her. She could see the boys crowding up, too, to ask for the pleasure of the next waltz—or the schottische—or the polka——

Her brown-gold eyes burned bright. She tossed her head, and a curl of rusty brown, the same rusty brown of a scrub oak leaf in late fall, sprang loose from the knot at the back of her neck. It had a vigor all its own, coarse and strong and warmly colored like Carolina herself. She had no way of knowing that it was her hair that had bewitched poor Bertie Damon that day in the hardware store. It had looked so alive he had wanted to touch it; he could not keep his eyes off it all the time he was talking to her.

He had not intended to invite her to the Assembly Ball. Even as his halting words issued from his lips, another part of him was regretting them. What would his folks say? He could hear his mother protesting, "Bertie! That wild untidy young thing. Why couldn't you invite some nice girl in your own set on Capitol Hill?"

. . . And his father, "Hm. The Lawler gal. Isn't her old man that fist-waving preacher from down in Stringtown that smashes bar mirrors and stirs up the miners? If I recall, they ran him out of town once and wouldn't let him show his face around here again for a couple of years afterwards."

But now Bertie had her on his hands and he did not know what to do about it. Life for him had held few problems until a mane of glowing hair and a lower lip that pushed out entrancingly had snared him just as he was buying a new coffee mill for his mother. He did not want to take her to the dance, and yet every time he thought of her, he was filled with the strangest, maddest feelings.

Carolina folded the last beautiful cambric chemise, tucked a piece of old clean sheeting over the basket and looked around for eleven-year-old Mat to carry it over to Hattie Merkle's. Such a boy! Never there when you wanted him. If only Elick had not run away soon after Ma died. He had had some sort of a quarrel with his father and had disappeared between sundown and sunrise. A penciled postcard from the Nevada gold fields saying he was cleaning up twenty dollars a shovel was all they had heard from him since.

She peered up at the walnut clock that had come all the way from Ohio. In winter, until the lamps were lighted, one had to peer; for the ugly little rented shack was one of the earliest in the gulch, built when window panes were carted from Denver. In winter, the house was as dreary, she sometimes said, as a dugout roofed with "dirt shingles." The ceiling, which was made of the original stretched muslin covered with paper, sagged so sharply in the middle that Carolina, who was tall, always ducked instinctively when she crossed the kitchen.

In summer, with the doors open, she could forget how she hated the dark little house. Besides, until this past year when she was suddenly grown up, she had spent all of her summers out of doors anyhow. There were so many things a girl could do outside while she was still only a rangy tomboy; but she had to stop doing them when she was sixteen and had "filled out." Things like wading with the other Stringtown girls in the ice-cold water in the wooden flumes, holding up her skirts and screaming; or scrambling up the hillsides for wildflowers to bring home and cram into a cracked tumbler—furry pasqueflowers in the spring, lupines and larkspur and Indian paintbrush in the summer, and in the fall the

26

scarlet-berried kinnikinic that always made Carolina's mother sigh
and talk of holly wreaths.

Sometimes Carolina brought home stalks of reddish, rank-grow-
ing fireweed that covered recently burned-over areas with masses
of pinkish bloom in summer and in the fall with foliage that
shaded from pale buckskin to glowing browns and claret. She
was not sure she liked it, but Leo always championed it.

"Fireweed's a pioneer, Carolina. First into a region after a forest
fire, even before the aspens can seed and the slow pines get started.
Sure, it's pushing and rank and high-colored and full of get-up-and-
git. Wouldn't survive if it wasn't. And it's prettiest after the frost
has nipped it. Like all pioneers, it's at its best in hard times." He
had smiled at her, his squinty eyes full of wisdom.

II

SHE FUMBLED FOR HER SHAWL IN THE DARKNESS BEHIND THE KITCHEN
door.

"Oh, you can't carry the washing yourself. To a bawdy house—
in daylight! It wouldn't be right," protested the shocked Letty.
She was always protesting. At twenty-two Letty was an old maid,
timid and disapproving and barren of laughter.

"Well, if I don't take it, how can I get the money to buy the
dress?" Carolina asked impatiently. As if Letty did not know! "I
plan to stop at the store on the way over and ask them to hold
the dress till I can get back with the money."

Five dollars, the placard in the window, pinned to the cream-
colored surah with the cherry velvet bow, had said. With what
Floss would pay her today, she would have enough. She had not
dreamed that a boughten dress—any dress—could be so beautiful.
For up until this last year she had not thought about clothes,
with her skirt hems always torn from skating, and one mitten missing, and a tear in her cloak. Most of her dresses were only drab
hand-downs from Letty anyhow. But now she would have something all her own, something perfect.

She hoisted her basket up on to one hip, opened the door and
started across the snowy back yard. It was spring by the calendar,
but winter held on long and jealously here. The black frozen
weeds clutched at her skirts. The snow squeaked under her heels.
She drew in sword-sharp breaths. But she did not mind cold
weather, so long as she could be out in it battling it; not the deep

27

relentless snows that piled up in four-foot walls on either side of the street, or the pitilessly cold and starry nights, or the fact that winter lasted so long here that the miners claimed that the Leadville climate was "eleven months winter and one month late fall."

Oh, if only she could manage Pa tonight. What good a new dress and a handsome beau and an invitation to the ball, if Pa kicked up trouble? She had washed and ironed to that refrain all day . . . She had to manage Pa.

No one in Stringtown paid any heed to her or her basket. Stringtown was merely a long untidy settlement bordering a street that ran like a soiled ribbon from the business district of Leadville down past the smelters toward Malta. Here, women were always starting off with a basket; they carried burdens naturally.

But when Carolina reached the business district of Leadville, she began to attract attention. Men turned to stare at this tall girl with the basket on her hip and the shawl slipping off her glowing hair. She pretended not to hear their admiring murmurs.

"Whew! I bet that one would assay mighty high." Or the more impassioned: "Man, oh, man! I'm on the down-grade and can't reach the brake lock."

A girl who had lived all her life on the tattered hem of a redlight district grew used to flattering or tentative or even persuasive remarks.

She flirted her skirts and admired Harrison Avenue, which had taken the place of Chestnut Street as the main thoroughfare.

Elegant sleighs streaked along frozen ruts, the horses breathing out vapor plumes. Ladies, pink-cheeked against fur tippets, held their muffs coquettishly up before their faces. Gentlemen, with frost-rippled whiskers, sawed masterfully on the reins.

How much more citified it was, she thought, than when she had arrived as a little girl. All these fine new brick buildings had gone up since. Her glance flicked up and down the street, briefly touching Mr. Tabor's theater and his new hotel (although the Clarendon was still nice even if it was old—ten years old at least), and finally the courthouse, which had a statue of Justice on the top with one of the scales missing.

She had heard much masculine talk about these improvements. She liked to hear men talk; she always gravitated to a bass rumble. Already she had begun to sort out the opinions you could expect from different kinds of men. She found that they thought differently on Capitol Hill (optimistically named for the future state capitol buildings that were to be located there) from the way they thought in Stringtown.

On Capitol Hill you heard no sarcastic comments on that scale missing from the hand of Justice. You heard only comfortable assurances that Leadville would certainly become the railroad center and capital of the state in time; that silver was as limitless as was the demand for it; that anyone was a traitor who hinted that Leadville's best days were over. What if the population had dwindled? That was only because more labor-saving devices were used in the mines. What if the ore was becoming lower grade all the time, and harder to smelt, and water was coming into the mine workings? Next year they'd strike a new and richer stratum.

That was not the way the men of Stringtown talked, the miners and smelter workers. They laughed cynically at the missing scale and said sure, why not? Did you ever try to buck one of the mine operators in a lawsuit? They said Leadville was on the toboggan already, and they were easing out next week to try their luck in Aspen, or Rosita, or Silver Cliff.

III

AT THE STORE SHE SET HER BASKET DOWN ABSENTLY AND WENT TO ask about the dress in the window. Her eyes were on it. It was so beautiful, compared with that ugly old mustardy thing of Letty's that she had first thought she must wear.

The clerk came toward her. He was a youngish man with a weedy, broom-colored mustache and a pensive expression. He, too, had come west to make his fortune, but the fortune still eluded him. Something told him that the only difference between himself and the men who had struck it rich was simply that they had dug in the right place and he had not. He was resentfully aware that while they were buying matched teams and garnet bracelets, he was losing his own savings and those of his parents, until finally he had been forced to take this job in a dry-goods store where his boss assured him he had a real forte for trimming windows.

He lived in a boarding house and on Saturday nights went to one of the gambling places, dubbed "silver exchanges," that lined Harrison Avenue and State Street. He liked Hyman's Club Rooms because the keno games were electrically operated and hence squarer. Sometimes he tried his luck at faro; or again at roulette or poker or slough. Next week he would make a killing and buy some mining stock. That was the way the big ones got started. Look at Leiter and Guggenheim and Tabor . . .

Carolina pointed toward the window containing the cream-colored surah on the wire form, with the draped polonaise and the cherry velvet bow and the lace bertha.

"Please, will you hold that dress for me until I can get back with the five dollars? I'll have it in a few minutes. You won't sell it to anyone else, will you?" She stammered in her excitement.

The clerk's eyes filled with a superior kind of pity. For answer, he went up to the wire figure in the window, turned it around, and drew out the few pins that held the length of stiff, creamy surah, just as he had unwound it from the bolt.

The blood rushed to Carolina's cheeks. Why it wasn't a dress at all! It was merely a piece of goods, draped around an iron shell, with a bow and a bertha pinned on. But it had looked like a dress. Anybody would think it was a dress.

"We don't carry boughten dresses, Miss," he explained loftily to this ignorant young thing who did not seem to know that no lady would ever dream of buying a ready-made dress. "That is, except for the very cheapest wrappers. And this material is five dollars a yard. If you were to take, say, fourteen yards—then there'd be the findings—and you'd have to hire a dressmaker——" He began to compute superciliously under his breath.

"Too bad you don't hire out yourself!" snapped the girl as she turned away hurriedly to hide her shamed tears. "You'd make a lovely dressmaker."

Then she was gone with her basket, leaving a youngish man looking angry and pinched and deflated, for she had made fun of his only talent. Suddenly he knew that he would never strike it rich, but that he would grow old draping lengths of cloth around adjustable forms in store windows. And he hated her.

Carolina hurried along the street setting her heels down hard and breathing fast. She turned on to West Fifth Street, where gentlemen kept their mistresses and where the parlor houses were located. It was not a rowdy street like State Street, whose saloons and variety theaters and cribs were patronized by the miners and smelter workers. West Fifth Street was "select."

Again she was impervious to the sly glances and remarks of passersby whose curiosity was stirred by so much flaming color accompanied by a glint of tears.

Her religion-blinded parents never dreamed how early Carolina acquired an armor against male advances. For while they thought they were protecting her by leaving her without a single unguarded evening, what really protected her was the lesson of Stringtown. All about her she saw sordid or diseased or work-warped women who had been betrayed by the fact of their sex. Carolina would have none of it.

She had awakened late; her body was only beginning to assert its demands. Thus far, all she wanted from life was fun—laughter and friendliness and gaiety. Once she found out how to achieve them in this unlaughing, funless world, she would lose no time in going after them. But as yet she was not sure.

She had watched the women of the underworld fascinatedly ever since she could remember. She was without a conscious moral code. She watched them critically and weighingly and hopefully, to find out if they had what she wanted from life.

Sometimes she was almost sure that they had, when Floss told her amusing things about the anonymous customers who frequented Hattie Merkle's place, making the life there sound impudent and gay. Occasionally she even wondered about the noisy girls in the variety theaters, dancing the can-can, going through their sentimental and bawdy stage acts, and plying the men in the curtained boxes with champagne between acts (for a commission). Although she had never been inside one of these variety theaters, certainly the laughter that issued from them was loud and continuous. The crib women she disregarded because they were not really gay, and it was gaiety she wanted. She watched all these women consideringly. She would have to be very sure first . . . or very angry.

CHAPTER 4

It was nearly supper time when Carolina arrived at Hattie Merkle's house with her basket. The shades were tightly drawn, as they always were during the day. Business did not get under way until nine in the evening.

She rapped, and Leander opened the door. The same amiable, childlike Leander who had driven the carriage to the top of Weston Pass ten years before; only a little older and blacker and showing more gold teeth now. She liked Leander, as she liked Leo Cobb, because both were easy-smiling men. She was sorry that Leo's business brought him less and less to Leadville, since the advent of the railroad, and that Leander was the factotum of a sporting house, so that she saw him only when she stealthily delivered washings.

Leander, who had respect for the proprieties, barred her entrance now to the front hall. But Carolina could see beyond him into the parlor at the left, with its flowered carpet and square piano and rich draperies that were stiff enough to stand alone. No wonder the better establishments prided themselves on being called "parlor houses" as distinguished from the boxlike cribs on State Street.

At that moment Carolina saw Floss coming down the stairs. She pushed Leander out of her path.

"Floss, oh, Floss!" she cried out.

"Why, you poor thing, you've been bawling," commiserated Floss as she dug deep into a pocket in her flounces for the money to pay for the washing. "What's happened, honey?"

Carolina, who had never known the exquisite solace of a confidante before, told her. About the uppity clerk and her terrible mistake and the Assembly Ball tonight and her not having anything to wear now except that hideous old merino of Letty's.

"It's the same nasty color as a dose of sulphur, Floss!" she wailed.

Floss tapped her teeth thoughtfully with her forefinger. Then she turned and ran up the Brussels-covered stairs.

"Wait a minute. We'll see if this won't do," she called over her shoulder.

Presently she was back, carrying a billow of pale-green silk over her arm.

"See," she said with generous eagerness, "the neck's edged with little moss rosebuds, and the basque is lovely and tight, and the rosebuds kind of peek in and out of the drapery. None of those prissy, wheyfaced Capitol Hill sluts will be able to hold a candle to you."

Carolina's eyes widened, at first incredulously, and then greedily. It put that hoax of a dress in the store window clear in the shade. She held the frock up to herself.

32

"Do you suppose it's maybe a tiny bit low?" she asked anxiously, willing to be overpersuaded.

"Low!" scoffed Floss satisfactorily. "You ought to see what some of the girls around here wear." And neither of them saw anything unsound in such an argument. "You can have it for keeps. I've worn it as much as I dare, here. We always march down at nine in our best evening dresses and parade around," she explained gravely. "You got to keep in style in this business."

Carolina knew that this was true. Everyone admitted that Hattie Merkle ran a high-toned establishment.

Twice on the way home she had to lift the sheeting to touch the green billows in the clothesbasket. Maybe Letty would allow her to use the curling iron tonight on her front frizzes. Usually Letty said that it would spoil her natural curl. She would twist the rest of her hair up into a great silken coil on the back of her head. She was glad she had washed it only yesterday in the water from the tank at the mine; it felt slippery-clean. She would wear that practically new bustle Miss Lovelace had given her before she went away. A dress like this would need a bustle. She had never owned one before; a bustle signified that you were a woman grown.

How kind Floss was! Holding Floss's dress in her arms, she stood on the back stoop of their Stringtown house and looked up and down the darkening street for her father. He always curdled everything the minute he came home. Perhaps he would be late tonight, she thought hopefully. Sometimes he stopped to preach or pray or "do a good deed" on his way.

Her lip curled with the contempt of youth for what it considers the hypocrisies of its elders. Praying—preaching—good deeds! She was sick of all of them. Her mind turned back to her father's rescue of the hurt miner. It was following their two-year banishment from town due to Pa's smashing the saloon mirror with a hammer. The family had been forced to trek from town to town in the Gospel wagon—from Ruby to Gothic to Gunnison. Only after her father had made that heroic rescue, carrying the injured miner on his back, on snowshoes, all the way down Old Woman Gulch to a doctor, did the city authorities permit him to return with his brood.

Carolina had always grimly discounted his deed. After all, her father was strong as a mule; he hadn't expected to get his feet

33

frozen, she told herself. She was puzzled by both the miner's excessive gratitude and by the town's sudden half-ashamed respect toward her father. With determined hardness she always turned her face away from him now on winter nights when she saw him slip off his boots to rub his aching feet—those feet that would burn and hurt in cold weather for the rest of his life.

The town's esteem had lasted a year or two before it began to wear thin and the old impatience to show through again; the impatience of the solvent and the well-fed for the ragged zealot . . . Ranting on street corners about God and hellfire and souls, when there were rich lodes to uncover—and champagne corks to pop—and roulette wheels to spin——

But most of all, Carolina was sick of the preaching and praying. Her face set bitterly as she remembered the time Letty had sent her to look for her father when he was late. She had found him on a hillside near the smelter, praying aloud in a lonely, terrible voice, his gaunt body flung across a boulder, his face turned toward the sky.

"How long wilt thou forget me, O Lord, for ever? . . . How long wilt thou hide thy face from me?" he groaned.

She had looked away quickly, ashamed. The praying was too loud and too close to the path where the men hurried home from work. She had only distrust for praying that was so carefully timed and so picturesquely posed. She had turned and run from him and all he stood for. Nor would she let herself remember afterwards how one passerby had jeered at him curiously, while another, less gentle, had tossed a small rock that grazed his cheek; and that her father had not flinched or slackened in his supplications.

II

SHE STEADIED HER BASKET ON HER HIP AND OPENED THE DOOR OF THE kitchen upon the hot smoky interior. Letty was frying saltside as usual. Salt pork and potatoes and biscuits and milk in cans; that was their fare. She remembered Leo Cobb sighing over the puny little Rosalie.

"It's greens she needs. Plague on a soil that'll grow silver but no vegetables!"

She looked over at Mat now, whittling beside the wood box, and at Rosalie, who was ten, dressing a china-headed doll Leo

34

had brought her on his last trip. Carolina hurried on through the kitchen to the bedroom she shared with her sisters and pushed the basket out of sight under the curtain in one corner.

As she heard the outer door open, her heart sank. Pa was home! All day she had tried to figure a way to outwit him tonight. To Jude Lawler balls were Godless carousals. He never called them anything else.

She saw him washing the smelter smudge off his face at the tin basin by the door. She supposed this job would not last long either, and then they would all go on shorter rations until he found something else. He was always shifting to a new job—carrying mail on snowshoes in winter, prospecting in a high gulch, or cutting timbers for the mines. And preaching, preaching, preaching, whenever anyone would listen.

She longed for a job of her own. Why weren't there things a girl could do besides washing or giving music lessons or working out?

"Supper's on," called Letty.

Carolina went out into the kitchen.

The atmosphere had changed, as it always did, the minute her father came in. Rosalie had tucked her doll out of sight. Mat had stopped whittling. They all waited in strained silence to see how Pa was going to act tonight.

He bowed his head and began his usual lengthy blessing. But thank goodness, Carolina thought, he was not praying for her tonight. There were so many Bible injunctions about honoring your parents and so few about parents being nice to their children. And her father had all the ones about obedience at his tongue's tip. She squirmed whenever he prayed for her in front of the other children. For Letty always looked so smug, with her eyes downcast and her mouth pursed. Letty never seemed to need Pa's praying.

But tonight he was praying only for mankind in general. The prayer went on and on. As he grew older, he subsisted more and more on prayers and less and less on food, until he was as thin and taut as a rawhide thong. But prayers made poor victuals for growing children, Carolina thought. From one corner of her eye she saw Mat reach stealthily for a piece of bread. Oh, God, don't let anyone make Pa mad tonight, she prayed, glaring at Mat and shaking her head. Mat jerked his hand back and squeezed his eyes shut. This one night they must keep Pa peaceful and get him out of the house for his street preaching.

After supper Jude Lawler sat and thumbed through the Old Testament for a text for tonight's sermon. Job was his favorite.

"Man that is born of woman," he read to himself, "is of few days and full of trouble." True, true, he thought sadly. "Man dieth, and wasteth away: yea, man giveth up the ghost, and where is he?" Ah, Job understood. "My days are swifter than a weaver's shuttle, and are spent without hope——" Ten years, he thought in despair. Ten years in this wicked town, and what had he to show for them? Oh, yes, the "regular" churches had prospered well enough, with their tittle-tattle ladies' meetings and their choir squabbles and their quilting bees. But did they drag the man out of the saloon and the woman from the crib? Sin—sin, everywhere. He had failed! And the time was so short, and life itself was so short—and hell lasted so long . . .

Jude watched his daughter, the way she walked and moved her hips and held her head. Something about her disturbed him to-night. He looked across at Letty, spare and washed-out and safe. Like her mother, Letty was. But Carolina, now—ah, Carolina was not safe. He did not finish the thought that Carolina's soul was in danger because she was not like her mother, but was like himself instead. He knew only that she was a brand to be rescued from the burning, and that he must rescue her.

"Come, girls," he warned. "Be quick with your tasks. I shall want you both tonight. It is cold out; we'll need some stirring tunes to warm folks up and make them gather around."

"Yes, Pa," said Letty meekly. "As soon as I hang up my dishrag."

Carolina's heart did a somersault.

"I can't go tonight, Pa. I've got a headache."

"Since when have you had a headache?" her father asked with a frown.

"It's been coming on all day. I told you, Letty, didn't I, how I could feel it coming on?" she answered, talking fast and saying too much. "First I had an ache low down at the back of my neck and then a pounding all over my head like little hammers." In her flurry Carolina was parroting her dead mother. How often had they heard Hester complain about that headache starting at the back of her neck and then pounding all over like little hammers.

Her father cleared his throat. "I see," he said.

And she should have seen, too; but she did not. Instead she relaxed with relief. How easy it had been. Now to get him out of the house so she could dress in peace and leisure. The beautiful dress . . . handsome Bertie Damon . . . the wonderful ball . . . exquisite life.

Letty was nervous. While their father was shrugging on his greenish-black coat with the verdigris of age upon it, she managed to whisper to Carolina.

"I wish you hadn't lied. You oughtn't to lie. Don't you think you better wear your cloak even if it is old? That broché shawl of Ma's won't be warm enough, although it is prettier. Tell him not to drive up in front of the house when you come home—Pa'll hear——"

"Everything will be all right," Carolina whispered back.

At last they were gone. Carolina got Mat and Rosalie off to bed after haggling and bribes. She had the warm, steamy little kitchen to herself. She drew the curtains and bathed in the tin basin set on the open oven door; bathed all over in warmth and privacy and luxury. It was seldom that one could do that in the Lawler household.

The shack contained no mirror larger than her head, so she had never seen her own reflection below her breastbone. But she liked soaping her firm, curving young body with its length of limb and its high triumphant breasts.

Carolina knew quite well that it was a lovely body, not from having seen it in a mirror, but because Letty always sighed and drew her mouth down and said, "I don't think you ought to wear your basque so tight, Carolina. It shows too much—I mean, you're too——" And because Floss had said, "With a shape like that, it's a damn' shame to waste it singing hymns!" Then she had laughed, and after a moment's faint confusion, Carolina had laughed too. After that, when she walked, she switched her skirts and held her breasts high and delighted in this recently discovered body of hers.

All the past year she had been sure she was just waiting for something wonderful to happen. Tonight must be it.

She wished Floss had given her some underwear to go with the dress, for she had nothing decent of her own. But she managed, by wearing Letty's best petticoat and by leaving off her high-necked corset cover and letting her chemise drop off her sloping

37

rounded shoulders. She laced her cracked old corsets tighter than usual to make her waist small and push her breasts higher. Then she combed her hair and slipped into the dress. Smoothing its sea-green billows with her hands, she looked down in proud modesty at her uncovered shoulders and bosom. She had seen pictures like this in Godey's, but she had never dreamed—— A thudding triumph beat through her veins. She was beautiful and she knew it.

A step sounded on the stoop. She had been so absorbed in her finery that she had not heard any wheels. She grabbed up her mother's rich broché shawl, flung wide the door in an exuberance of youth and anticipation and faced—her father.

He stood there in his old coat, his head bare, his hair standing straight up. And suddenly the always smouldering embers in his eyes burst into flame. His searing glance flicked over her bouffant skirt, the tightly laced waist, and above it—like some rare and waxen double-petaled flower bursting out of a lacy holder—the ivory bosom.

Carolina took a step backwards, instinctively shielding her skirts with her hands. Step by step, she moved away from those marauding eyes, from those slowly clenching hands.

He followed her across the doorstep and into the room until he had backed her against the farthest wall.

Carolina never took her eyes from him. She did not even see the white, self-accusing face of Letty behind him. Letty who, because she was eaten with jealousy and the pain of being young and not wanted, had let it slip, in answer to her father's probings, that perhaps Carolina did have other plans for tonight. Like tossing a tiny pebble that starts an avalanche, she had said those words. And now, when she would regain the pebble—unsay the words—it was too late.

"Wanton!" A huge sinewy hand that had pounded a hand steel and wheeled a slag pot reached out to tear the dress from her, to wrench off the moss rosebuds, to strangle the billows of sea-green that pushed up between him and his daughter.

And then he stayed his hand. He backed away, looking down at her and panting.

Carolina was frightened. Far more frightened than if he had torn the dress from her. His eyes were queer.

"I'll take it off, Pa—I'll take it off!"

"No, you'll leave it on. You'll leave on your vain tinsel that you

38

wore to arouse the lusts of men—exposing your body—glorying in it. You'll leave it on, I say——"

She stared at him uncomprehendingly. She had never met his controlled venom before. She understood his rages better.

"Come along. It's time for the preaching. Pick up your shawl."

"Not on the street corner——" she whispered, shrinking back. "Not—like this."

"On the street corner—like that!"

Dazedly she picked up her shawl. She was too stupefied to wonder what would happen when Bertie Damon knocked on the door and got no answer.

In silence, the two sisters, one in her lead-colored bonnet and lank skirts, the other in her autumn-toned shawl and her seafoam ruffles, followed their father along the street of straggling huts that led up to the town. The darkness was merciful to them all, as it was merciful to those huts which, only a short decade ago, had been of pale new yellow pine smelling freshly of the forests, and that now were warped and gray and smelled of wet woolens and unaired beds.

Slowly Carolina began to feel again. As they neared the lights she cringed. Her light dress looked startling against the winter's dourness. On the corner nearest the "Concert and Novelty Hall with 15 Attractive Lady Waiters," Jude Lawler took his stand. She made her feet follow Letty's. She made herself take her place in the circle.

Men shouldering by, heads bent against the wind, slowed down to stare at her.

Carolina stood like one frozen. She was frozen. But not by the wind which lashed down off the slopes of Mt. Massive.

Dimly, from far off, she knew that her father's words were pouring forth, but she heard not one of them. She saw Letty, who could not meet her eyes, leading a hymn. But she heard none of the threatening old warnings.

As her father preached on, the usual drunks gathered around. A crib woman began to snivel because she was old and the wind was cruel and customers were few since the railroads had come in and put all those freighters out of business. This was no night to be out of doors listening to words about the flames of hell.

Carolina stood there tall and still. But inside, she was no longer frozen. Sixteen years of resentment and humiliation were building up to the explosion point. A flake of snow wandered down. She did not even feel it touch her hot cheek and turn to a tear and slide down. She was a charge of dynamite waiting for someone to light the fuse.

And then someone lighted it.

Perhaps the ball was not one of the best this year; perhaps the cotillion favors had been a little silly; perhaps the chaperones had merely become lax. Anyhow, a crowd of young people had left the hall to go exploring, as had become the fashion, dressed in one's fine clothes and straggling down the middle of State Street. The young men with their collars turned high, laughing and nudging each other self-consciously. The girls in their fur mantles and warm carriage boots to keep out the snow, squealing a little in a ladylike way . . . Oh, look, there's that queer old character ranting on the corner again . . . Ooh, see the girl, will you—and in that dress! What on earth——? . . . Peggy, Sally, Fanny, look, isn't she the one——?

Carolina's nails dug into her palms under the shawl. She held her head up, eyes straight ahead, her cheeks shamed scarlet flags.

The preaching voice went on and on, rising and falling with a peculiar penetrating timbre that was both moving and ridiculous. No one was paying any attention to it—and suddenly everyone was paying attention to it.

"Forgive this erring daughter before us who so shamefully bedizened herself to attend a Godless carousal," prayed the voice. "Oh, God, keep her from tasting the bread of wickedness, thou who rainest snares and fire and brimstone——" Up went the clenched fist in the old familiar gesture—savage, demanding, chastising.

He was talking about her! He was pointing her out to everybody, exposing her nakedly.

Carolina heard a snicker. She saw the young people drawing back, half in alarm, half in derision. Why, there was Bertie Damon. Once, long ago, she had dressed in a sea-green dress to go to the ball with Bertie Damon . . . A roaring thrummed in her ears.

The young people faded away uneasily into the darkness.

The plea of a righteous man, of a violent man, came to an end: "And so, oh, Lord, we beseech thee to take back this straying daughter ere her feet go down to death and her steps take hold on hell—— Amen."

He looked up sadly. For a moment he was cleansed of all fury and strife. There was the same weaving circle of bums, the same sin-etched old drab wondering if a dose of laudanum might not be the best way out, and his daughter Letty.

But Carolina was gone.

CHAPTER 5

AS CAROLINA RACED ALONG THE HIGH, ICE-COATED WOODEN SIDEWALKS away from the vibrating twang of her father's praying voice, she had no idea where she was going. She could not go home; she would never go home again. There were no respectable ladies to whom she dared turn; which was just as well, as they were the first to whom Jude Lawler rushed when it penetrated his startled brain that his daughter had actually defied him and run away in the cold of a winter night. He pried their names out of Letty. But through some instinct of self-preservation or belated loyalty to Carolina, Letty did not divulge the names of the prostitutes for whom they washed.

Carolina was running wildly but aimlessly along Harrison Avenue when suddenly she knew where she was going. She was going to the only person who had always acted as if she cared what happened to her—to Floss at the parlor house.

She slowed to a walk. Her side ached from running in the cold in her too-tight stays. In front of Hattie Merkle's house she paused.

She had never seen it at midnight before, with the gas lights streaming out through the front hall transom and making splinters of light around every drawn shade. She heard a piano being brassily played inside by one of Hattie's girls. Floss perhaps. Floss had a rollicking repertoire, she knew. The house had a completely different personality now; not secretive and withdrawn, as in the daytime, but bold and inviting like the music. She climbed the three steps falteringly and went around to the side door.

Leander took a long time to answer her knock. Customers seldom came to the side door and seldom knocked so timidly. He opened it and peered out.

41

"Miss Cahlina!" he gasped. "You can't come here this time a night." Bad enough, he meant, for her to come in the afternoon with the washings.

He started to shut the door in shocked disapproval, but she would not let him. She held on tenaciously to the knob.

"I've got to see Floss, Leander. I've simply got to."

He frowned. He ought not to let the girl in, but it was bitter cold outside, and her face looked queer and set.

"Side in quick then into the Madam's office and don't let nobody see you," he scolded. "You shouldn't a come. You likely have to wait; Miss Floss busy now."

He reluctantly unlatched a door at the left of the narrow hall, which opened into Hattie Merkle's tiny office, with its tall secretary desk and haircloth chairs. Here the Madam kept her accounts and paid the help and checked over her wine bills and collected her take from the girls. He closed the door firmly after her.

Carolina sat well forward on a straight slippery chair with a cluster of hard walnut grapes at her back. The sounds of discreet revelry filtered in, but she did not hear them. With anguished egotism she was concerned only with her own plight and her own hatred and her own revenge.

When at last the door opened, it let in a louder blast of music along with two women, Floss and Hattie Merkle.

The Madam looked more than ever like something carved out of streaked and weathered gray limestone. She was dressed in a prim, high-necked—almost prudishly high-necked—black silk dress, garnished with heavy gold jewelry. She looked ageless, as if her heart had long ago calcified to match her face.

Floss wore a lavishly low-cut gown of pink chiné, a little askew on one shoulder. Her smile was wide and loose and faintly askew too. Her eyes could not quite meet Carolina's, and her gait had a roll to it. But Carolina did not notice. All she saw was that the loose mouth was kind and that the vague eyes were full of pitying alarm.

"Now what?" inquired Floss with good-natured haste. It was a nice time for the girl to show up! With business a regular stampede and Hattie making money off the drinks faster than you could clean up a rich ore pocket. "You better get on home, child."

"I'm not a child, and I can't go home. I've run away from my father."

"Well, you can just run back to him," stated the Madam flatly. "This here is a parlor house."

"I know. But Floss is the only friend I've got," the girl said thinly. "There's no place else to go——"

Hattie Merkle looked her over with narrowed eyes. She hated the old bastard that was the girl's father; he had almost ruined her business one week by taking up a preaching stand out in front. She had never cottoned to Carolina either from the time she was a brat. But business was business, and the child had grown into a striking wench. If it weren't for that wild, stubborn look in her eyes, she might be turned into one of the house's biggest attractions. But she wasn't sure about those eyes. The girl was plenty old enough, sixteen or so, and that was older than Floss when she started . . . If she could just knock the idea out of Floss's head of starting up a house of her own. That was the trouble with a good girl—as soon as you got her trained in, she started planning competition for you. She guessed she'd have to start taking steps . . .

"What do you think, Floss?" Hattie asked dubiously. "We really ought to drop her like a hot potato, with that crazy father of hers due to come raving around any minute looking for her—he might even sick the church folks on us and padlock the place. But she's a looker, and healthy——" She was staring at Carolina as if the latter were a piece of goods displayed on a counter.

Floss was troubled. Her vague eyes were clearing; her confused brain was clearing too. Yet the image before her was still cloudy. Perhaps for an instant she was seeing another girl, younger than Carolina and with ash-brown hair and a too ripe body and a too amiable smile—who had had no one to care what became of her.

She started to speak, but Leander opened the door to summon the Madam. The demand for champagne in the front parlors could no longer be staved off. Hattie left the two girls alone in the little office.

"You know I'm your friend, honey," Floss began gently. "But like Hattie says, this is a sporting house. You couldn't stay here. You don't know what you'd be getting into."

"I don't care!" Carolina's voice was taut with hysteria. "I know what I'd be getting out of."

"Your old man would locate you right off. Because you'd have to be licensed first thing."

"Licensed?" Carolina looked at her.

43

"Every one of us girls—and there's several hundred in this town —has to pay five dollars a month to the city treasury. All the public places have to pay—the gambling houses and variety theaters and saloons and dance halls. He'd find out about you then."

Carolina, who would have to be either very sure or very angry before she could take the final step, was very angry now.

"That suits me fine, just fine. Jude Lawler's daughter in a parlor house!" She mouthed the words vengefully.

Floss shook her head.

"You're only thinking of getting back at your old man; you aren't thinking of what you'd be doing to yourself."

"I don't care. I'm sick of his talk of saving souls from hell, while he drives his own children there. He's mean; he's bad. Look at my mother—he killed her. Look at Elick—he drove him out. Look at me!"

Floss did look at her—thoughtfully. Maybe this would be as good a time as any to break away from Hattie, she reflected. Hattie had been acting queer lately. She's scared I'll start up a place of my own, Floss decided shrewdly. She knows I'll take half her customers with me, the old vinegar face. And in spite of all her taffy about me being the most reliable girl she's got, she wouldn't stop at a knife in my back to stop me. I ought to be pulling up stakes, and the sooner the better——

Her expression gave no hint of her thoughts. She stood up with an air of decision.

"You wait here. I've got an idea. I want to talk to the Madam about it." She went out, closing the door carefully after her.

Carolina sat there, lacing and unlacing her fingers. She lost all track of time, although she sensed that the house was quieting down, that doors were closing, that the piano was stilled at last along with the popping of corks and the bass rumble of men's voices and the raucous giggles of the girls. It was nearly dawn when Floss and Hattie returned. They had been arguing.

"It's just like I was afraid, Floss. Leander says he's on the warpath hunting for her. Raging around town like a Comanche full of firewater. I don't want him burning down this house like he smashes up saloons. I say, turn her out before trouble starts."

"I hate to, Hattie. We'll be gone before he gets wind. I'll take all the risk. All you have to do is give me a letter to Stelle Bogart at Aspen. Come on, Hattie; you won't regret it."

Hattie considered the idea. After all, it would put an end to the worry about Floss starting up another place here.

Floss read Hattie's answer even before the latter gave it grudgingly. She beckoned to the immobile girl.

"We got to hurry," she admonished Carolina.

Carolina followed Floss stiffly out into the dark hall, with its stale, imprisoned odors of liquor and tobacco and scent and sweat, and up the thickly carpeted stairs to the big front bedroom that was Floss's. It was the preferred room in the house, like the star's dressing room in the theater, and awarded for the same reason. No wonder Hattie hated to lose her and yet was afraid to keep her.

A maid was making up the bed in a room that was very grand, Carolina thought, with its black walnut furniture and heavy draperies. She looked longingly toward the bed; she was worn out with the day's and night's events. But Floss was firm.

"No, you don't. I'm a heap tireder than you are. But we got to catch that early train. Here, put these on." She stood in the closet doorway and pitched clean clothes out to Carolina. "We'll burn those rags you call underwear," she added briskly. "Better shuck clear to the skin."

Carolina obeyed. She had washed and ironed some of these lovely garments that Floss tossed to her, but she had never dreamed of wearing them. Handmade petticoats and chemise and corset cover. Floss even gave her a stiff new corset, with a high rounding bosom, that hooked down the front and ended just at her hip bones, squeezing her waist in very small and letting her bosom and stomach bulge fashionably above and below. There were striped lisle stockings and buttoned shoes with scalloped tops and spool heels and pointed toes, that had come straight from The Famous Shoe Store.

Carolina was young enough and feminine enough to feel a reviving flicker of interest at sight of a new dress. Floss had not worn it even for an afternoon carriage ride. The moss-green velvet basque was fastened down the front with green silk frogs; the copper-colored cheviot overskirt was draped crosswise over her stomach, with the bulk of the material carried around to the rear where it fell in a handsome waterfall over her bustle. Two lifelike copper birds were poised on top of a green scuttle of a hat, as if momentarily resting on their flight northward.

Floss tied a dotted green veil over Carolina's face, which only

45

emphasized her tawny hair and her several freckles and her queer light eyes. Through it all, Carolina stood as rigid and lifeless as the iron form in the window of a drygoods store.

"There!" said Floss with satisfaction. "You're decked out like the prize lunch basket at a box social. If you don't run the bids up good and high, I've sure wasted some elegant dress goods on you."

While Floss dressed and shouted orders and waved her hairbrush and screwed in ear bobs, the maid threw things into valises and telescopes. Still in a state of suspended animation, Carolina looked on.

Leander was waiting with the closed carriage. They did not go toward the depot, but headed instead for the Junction, which was the next stop after Leadville. As they clopped past a certain weathered four-room shack in Stringtown, Floss gave a swift sidewise look at the girl. Carolina was staring straight ahead, her throat working as she tried to swallow past a knot.

"You wouldn't like to change your mind—tell your old man you're sorry?" Floss suggested kindly.

Carolina turned and stared at her in horror.

"I never want to see him again. All that makes me feel bad is running off and leaving the young ones. But I've got to." There was no softening of her resolute features.

At the depot she said an absent good-by to Leander and waited stolidly while Floss bought their tickets. It was Floss who paced up and down the platform, craning to look back up the road over which they had just come; it was Floss who nervously shooed Carolina up the steps of the puffing D. and R. G. train and into the hot, plushy coach with the crackling little stove in the far end.

Carolina had never been on a train before. But she was unheeding of her surroundings. So anaesthetized was she by her resentment that she was unaware of the irrevocable quality of the moment. That at sixteen she was saying good-by to Leadville and to her father and her home, as she ran away to join the inmates of "the Row" in Aspen. Aspen, that newest bonanza across the divide to beckon with silver fingers to the reckless, the ambitious, the desperate, and the venal.

The engine grunted and puffed, readying itself for the stiff climb ahead. Floss dared relax.

"God! I sure expected your old man right up to the last," she admitted.

"What made you go to so much trouble for me, Floss?" Carolina asked wonderingly.

Floss looked embarrassed.

"Tush. I was ready for a change anyhow. I've got to be thinking of my own future now, and I'd overstayed my time at Hattie's; she was sharpening her hatchet for me. They say this Stelle Bogart is a pleasant-spoken woman and easy on her girls. It was a good time to get out."

Carolina wondered if Floss was lying, but she was too wrapped up in her own troubles to probe further. She sat stiffly, looking unseeingly out the window.

In spite of her barbaric love of color, she did not even notice that the willow shrubs in the creek bottoms were putting on their early spring show. Without a leaf as yet, their thickly massed twigs offered the only color in a landscape that was otherwise all white and black and rusty green. There were rich golden-bronze patches of willows, the color of Carolina's eyes; there were silvery-purple patches shading to wine, subdued yet glowing, like her mother's broché shawl.

Ordinarily she would have been as excited as a child as they crossed the continental divide and she realized that from here on, a raindrop sought the Pacific instead of the Atlantic Ocean. Even when the train went through a tunnel and the coach was filled with acrid fumes, and the passengers knew the pleasantly suspended sensation of belonging to no world at all, Carolina only sat and stared at the place where the window had been.

She paid no attention to the other passengers. She neither knew nor cared that she and her companion were eyed with avid interest by every male on the coach; furtively by the married men, openly by the young blades. She did not notice that the conductor collected their tickets so hastily that he all but tore them out of Floss's fingers.

"The scared old Cheap-John!" Floss muttered scathingly, her professional pride injured. "I reckon he never patronized any but cribs except that once. Scuttling by us like we had cholera. Don't the poor fool know that no high-toned sporting house girl ever recognizes a man—any man at all—when she meets him in public?"

But Carolina was not interested in the code of the courtesan. She had not noticed the conductor, any more than she noticed the handsome, slightly dandified young man wearing the very latest in cravats and massive watch chains and round-domed hats and silken sideburns who made an extraordinary number of trips up and down the aisle. On each trip he looked significantly at Floss, trying to indicate that he would like to meet the cataleptic beauty at her side.

But Floss was granite. One simply did not recognize former customers in public, even pleasant, unattached ones like Roger Walling Jardine III of Denver, whom the Madam treated, if not with outright approval, at least with measured respect. Naturally the respect was intended for the senior Jardine, who had made the fortune, but it included the son as well. And it was generally agreed among the solid male citizenry of Leadville that a meager smile from Hattie Merkle was the equivalant of a top rating with either Dun's or Bradstreet's.

On his tenth trip down the aisle, Floss managed by some legerdemain to convey to him that perhaps in due time his wish might be granted . . . Just perhaps, her manner said.

The young man had to be satisfied. He returned to his seat and settled once more to a weak pretense of reading a treatise on mining law.

Floss's calm, handsome face was preoccupied. It was a long chance, she thought, but after all, she had no other cards to play.

The young man never turned a page. And every time the copper birds on the hat ahead so much as described a quarter circle, a little cord tightened down the side of his freshly shaven jaw, and a hot eagerness brought a flush to his fair skin and an unwonted light to his amiable blue eyes.

The dry words of the law journal, bearing on the case he had come to help try as a fledgling lawyer, made no impression whatever on him . . . He let the treatise fall to the plush seat and gave himself up to a fixed and rapturous contemplation of the copper birds.

C H A P T E R 6

RESENTMENT IS A POWERFUL DRUG. DURING THE LONG TRIP TO ASPEN Carolina was both dulled and supported by it.

On the ride through the streets of the new town, another boom town with the smell of quick riches in the air and the taste of quick riches on every tongue, she only dimly heard Floss's chatter. She sensed that it was an attempt to pry her out of her brooding.

They were going to like it here, Floss assured her. It was so much lower than Leadville; why, she'd heard they could actually grow vegetables in Aspen. Wouldn't Carolina dearly love to chomp her teeth on a nice raw carrot or a crisp radish? Though after the kind of cold and naked feeling you had in Leadville, as if you were sitting on top of the world, she wondered if a body might not feel cooped up, deep in this cozy valley ringed with steep hills.

Carolina made no answer. Obediently, but unseeingly, she turned her head this way and that at the behest of the hack driver, who proudly pointed out with his whip all the fine new brick and stone buildings.

"That's the Jerome hotel; it'll be done this summer. Yonder's the brand-new Wheeler Opera House; it's just opened. That saloon they call 'The Brick.' " Then, as if he had strung the wires himself, he commanded proudly: "Cast your eyes, ladies, on the first electric street lights in the state."

Like one pointing to a Supreme Being, he gave a reverent upward flick of his whip toward the source of all this good: to the mines on the slopes. To the Molly Gibson and the Smuggler and the Aspen and the rest, with their freshly trammed-out dumps.

"This is one mining town that's being built substantial," he boasted. "Aspen ain't no poor man's camp; only the big fellows with capital are operating here."

Carolina was still drugged by her own emotions when they reached Stelle Bogart's house in the Row, that line of parlor houses and cribs, a few blocks south of the business district, that backed up against the foot of Aspen Mountain as if it had retreated there for a last stand.

But a faint ripple of curiosity roiled the sluggish surface of her mind as she and Floss entered the front door. It was her first unobstructed view of a parlor house. Leander had always barred her way at Hattie Merkle's in the daytime; and last night, Floss's carefulness and her own distraught state had combined to keep her from observing anything of Hattie's establishment during business hours.

She glanced about her with a certain interest now. The whole first floor was as still and waiting, at this hour, as an empty stage

set. She thought with surprise, that held an element of disappointment, that this might be any of the respectable homes for which
her mother had washed. The same thick Brussels carpets and gilt
picture frames and mantel figurines and gilded cattails and doily-
spotted chair backs. She had half-expected things to be different:
for the very chairs and tables to wear a profane and carnal look.

Of course there was no mistaking Stelle herself and Trixie and
Mimi and Doll and the others for respectable women, with their
painted faces and unnecessarily fine figures and too fashionable
clothes. Floss introduced her laconically to them at the table.

"Her mother died and her father married again, but her stepmother was mean, and the old man beat her——"

The girls nodded. Those were the orthodox reasons you always
gave for leaving home. People were forever nagging at you to tell
them "how you happened to fall into this kind of a life." The stock
explanation, which Floss had just given, served as well as any and
forestalled a lot of time-wasting talk.

However, if you were a Madam, it was different. Then you made
an asset of your past. You were deliberately mysterious, without
making an outright statement, of course. You just let it seep out
that you came from a fine old Southern family (or New England
or Philadelphia) and had gone to a convent (or an Eastern finishing school) and had a brother who was an Admiral or a Senator.

Floss went on to tell them that Carolina's name was Cara. She
hesitated at that point, her burst of originality expended, and
added lamely, "Smith." So Cara Smith she became.

The girls warmed to her, and she to them. They gave her a sense
of solidarity against the world that comforted her and strength-
ened her. She desperately needed such strengthening.

That first night Carolina and Floss slept twelve hours. Carolina
heard none of the traffic up and down the stairs to the second
floor because Stelle Bogart, at Floss's insistence, had given her a
tiny room on the third floor with the maids. Nor did she know
about the altercation that took place between Floss and Stelle soon
after she had gone up to her room.

The two sat in Stelle's office, a rococo cubbyhole lavishly
decorated with tasseled "throws" and luxuriant fringe and thick
red plush. Stelle was convinced that the male nature was peculiarly responsive to stuffy warmth and cluttered red-and-gilt opu-
lence.

She sat before her desk, breathing heavily, either from umbrage, or high blood pressure, or tight lacing. Her immense bosom was thrust out and up by her armorlike corsets. Her hair was an elaborate, frowzy pile of yellow straw that was almost the badge of the light woman of her day. Her florid, good-natured face was bloated by years of rich living. Only on second glance did one notice that her eyes were not really good-natured. They were cautious agate marbles set deep in folds of flesh. Stelle Bogart looked much the way Floss might look in twenty years, if Floss achieved her ambition to become a Madam of consequence.

"Nobody puts on airs in my house and don't work!" Stelle puffed. "What do you think this is—a young ladies' seminary?" She went on to state in succinct terms the curriculum offered by a parlor house.

Floss was unmoved. She repeated what she had been saying to Stelle ever since she had arrived that afternoon with the tall, silent, almost stupid-acting beauty at her side.

"You'll do a lot better, Stelle, if you follow Hattie's advice. What you want to do is make her out as something rare and special— keeping her out of circulation, though parading her in public— till everybody knows she's a prize that goes to the highest bidder. It'll give the house a reputation for getting hold of extra fine girls. It'll add tone. I'm just thinking of your own good, Stelle. You know how Hattie's place is thought of in all the camps?" Floss paused adroitly.

Stelle meditated, her lids narrowed. There might be something to what this Floss Kittredge said. Certainly Hattie, in her letter, had spoken highly of Floss's good sense, as well as of her ability to bring in business. She could use an experienced and reliable girl right now, regardless of how the younger one panned out.

Floss was quick to follow up her advantage.

"Like those slick New Yorkers that come out here to make a to-do over some particular mining stock in order to send the quotations up and then cash in on it themselves. Not——" Floss added hastily, "that this girl isn't worth all I say. I knew her folks. She was never out of her mother's sight—and then the mother died, and her old man started being mean to her—but I got hold of her in time."

Stelle gave a bored wave of the hand that said, "You needn't waste that stuff on me."

Floss shrugged. Funny how the truth could sound like the biggest lie sometimes.

"Well, all right," Stelle gave in at last. "But only for a day or so. I'll start showing her off tomorrow—maybe take her riding with the other girls. And I'll let her mingle with the nine o'clock crowd downstairs at night. Then we'll see how big a bank roll looks her way."

"Not too fast, not too fast," objected Floss. "It might take more than one day to send the quotations up on her. Suppose you let me handle this, Stelle? She's fractious, you know. But I'll guarantee she'll catch the eye of some big mogul before the week's out. You let me handle her——"

Stelle agreed grudgingly. She was not sure she liked this shilly-shallying. But if Hattie Merkle advised it . . .

The girls in the house were less amiable on the second day when they discovered that Carolina was not to join them yet. That instead, she was to be put through a course of baths and hair-washings and perfumings, as well as lessons in the deportment of the enchantress. They sensed the potential danger in Carolina and they united against her, as had the nice little girls of Leadville, because they, too, felt that she was a threat.

Still lethargic toward them all, Carolina lent herself to Floss's plans. There was little to be done; chiefly to see that her copper-bronze hair was so clean that it shone in the light like the glinting wings of a dragonfly, and to heed Floss's instructions to "walk tall and stately, like you was rolling on casters, see?" Beyond that she was merely to look remote and beautiful. Which would not be hard; for she was beautiful, and her remoteness was unfeigned. She scarcely existed in this world in which she found herself.

So she was not deeply affected when the girls made scathing remarks about her antecedents, or childishly elbowed her out of the way at the table, or even baited her in an attempt to start an open fight. But she was puzzled. Where was all the pagan joyousness, the happy freedom from the conviction of sin, and the openhearted kindness she had expected to find?

She tried to put her perplexity into words to Floss as the latter brushed her hair that afternoon. She had been here exactly a day, and already her ideas about the denizens of a parlor house had undergone upsetting changes.

"What did you expect?" Floss shrugged. "They're a mean bunch, when nobody's looking, as well as liars, one and all. Reason you thought they were kind is they're always kind when they can team up against respectable folks. They make a big show of being generous then. Behind the scenes—well, that's different."

She tried a curl of Carolina's hair over her finger, tipping her head back to survey the effect in the glass.

"As for the girls standing by each other—Stelle says last year Mimi got jealous of another girl and threw acid in her face, and the other girl about died. Disfigured for life, she is. A sweet bunch you've joined up with," Floss finished coolly.

She hoped she hadn't laid it on too thick. Though, God knows, it was the truth. She had to jar the girl loose from her hate of her old man long enough to start her thinking about herself. She guessed she'd made a dent, for Carolina was staring back at her in the glass like one hypnotized.

"But I thought—fancy girls had fun, Floss. They always seemed to laugh a lot. You did yourself. You were the only girl I ever knew that laughed a lot. Remember?" How could Carolina explain the importance of that laughter?

"Well, sure, you got to grin like a Chessy-cat in this business. And why would I tell you the truth? Nobody runs down their job to an outsider. But now you aren't an outsider, you're one of us —or you soon will be, if Stelle has her way. And it'll be just the turn of a roulette wheel how you'll end up yourself . . . drugs—disease—an alley suicide."

If she could just get Carolina to help instead of to hinder, she might be able to figure out something. As yet, she had only the vaguest idea. She must have more time. And every influence—Stelle's greed, the other girls' resentment, and Carolina's own lethargy—was rushing the girl toward that short, steep path that was so easy to take and so hard to return from. Of them all, only Floss herself was trying to hold Carolina back.

Carolina broke in on her musings with a frightened whisper.

"Then what about you, Floss, if you stay here? How will you end up?" She was gripping the marble top of the bureau.

The question was the last thing Floss had expected. Wasn't it just like the crazy girl? Here she was, worrying about Carolina, while Carolina was scared to death over what was to become of her.

"Me?" Her face looked suddenly pinched. "Oh, I'll get along. I'm different from you. You're the thunder and lightning kind that often ends in a smash. While I've got a real head for business. The life of a girl in a house is short. I know that only too well. So I'll be giving it up soon. Either I'll start up a place of my own or get married. That's not such a wild idea. We girls make good wives—never look at another man—know how to keep a husband satisfied——"

II

FLOSS'S WORDS HAD FINALLY ACCOMPLISHED THEIR PURPOSE; THEY jolted Carolina out of her intense preoccupation with herself. That night at supper she watched the girls with newly sharpened perceptions as they snatched at the food or quarreled among themselves or complained to the Madam about not getting their share of business. She looked at their loose, painted mouths, at their feral eyes, at their burned-out faces. Why, they were nothing but evil children, she thought—with women's bodies and women's lusts. Somewhere far back in her mind echoed the somber words: "For a whore is a deep ditch . . . Her feet go down to death; her steps take hold on hell." She had the swift, frightened knowledge that she had been tricked. These girls were no more carefree than Letty; and they were without Letty's stern dependability.

The enormity of the step she had taken rushed over her. She tried to think of a way out, but there was none. She was one of them, Floss had said. Floss had tried to discourage her before they left for Aspen. Even Hattie Merkle had tried to turn her back. But she would not listen. If she had been tricked, she had tricked herself. She had stubbornly insisted upon throwing her life away, and now it was too late to ask for it back.

On that second evening on the top floor of Stelle Bogart's house, she sat rigid and desolate, waiting for the summons to go downstairs. She knew that the evening's traffic got under way with a stately showing of the girls in their handsomest frocks at nine o'clock. It was as stilted and formal as the routines of a geisha house; and it was doubly provocative because its prim overlay only thinly concealed the license underneath.

Tonight she wore an amber lansdown dress of Floss's which dropped low off her shoulders and surrounded her full high bosom like the chalice of a flower. She twisted a fragile fan in her fingers. It was past nine o'clock now. Why didn't the maid come for her as Floss had said? She listened with morbid concentration to every

54

creak of the stairs, to every footstep outside. Each time the steps passed her door, she sank back in relief; then she made herself sit up straight again. She had got herself into this . . .

She did not know that while she waited, Floss and a young man talked in the back parlor, with the folding doors closed against the rising hum of conviviality in the front rooms. He had been besieging Floss for the last half-hour. In fact he had been trying in vain to communicate with her ever since she had arrived the day before.

"Look here, Floss," he said imperiously, "I want to know, who is she?"

Roger Walling Jardine III and Floss were old acquaintances. He had known her first in Denver; he always asked for her when his father's law business took him to Leadville. They had built up a mocking but respectful regard for each other.

Floss did not pretend to misunderstand. She grinned back at him.

"No good asking, Roger."

"Come on, old girl, it isn't like you to be niggardly. Or jealous either. I've got to know. I haven't been worth a chunk of fool's gold since I saw her on the train with you. I came over here last night, supposing of course she'd be on parade. But Stelle Bogart said you were both done up and were sleeping the clock around. I tried to send you a message this morning, and no one was up. As soon as the house opened tonight, I was at the door asking for her. But Stelle acted most mysterious. Said she couldn't tell me a thing. The new girl was completely in your hands."

"That's right, Roger."

"What's this game anyhow? I'm taken with the girl, Floss. I can't keep my mind on my work." He sounded aggrieved.

"I don't wonder."

"One of Hattie Merkle's imports from Chicago or Denver, I suppose?"

"Well, I brought her from Hattie's, as you saw. But she's never worked before. Hattie sent me along to break her in. Wants her to get a good start; there were reasons for not keeping her in Leadville."

"Reasons?"

She ignored his query blandly.

"Hattie has big fish in mind for her—she's pretty bait, you'll have to admit—and you know how much it means to some old parties to

55

be first?" She was matter-of-fact; a woman discussing a business transaction with a friend.

He jerked about to stare at her incredulously.

"Oh, come now! You're not trying to pretend——?"

"Yes." With maddening leisureliness she sipped the champagne he had ordered. "Stelle doesn't carry quite as good liquor as Hattie, do you think?"

Roger Jardine was not here to compare vintages.

"What's that you said about her?" he prodded.

"That she's green as grass."

He continued to search her face and was misled by her hint of a smile. He threw back his head in relief and let out a shout of cynical laughter.

"Floss, you tease! You almost had me believing you! That's almost as good as the one you tell about how your own mother died and your father married again and your cruel stepmother drove you out and a mean old neighbor took advantage of you—so that's how you got here."

Floss's smile gave way to an affronted scowl. Her smooth cheeks reddened under their paint. For she had almost made herself believe that stock tale of every prostitute. When she had told Carolina that all sporting women were liars, perhaps she had halfway included herself. Few indeed there were who could bear to recall the naked truth, and Floss was not among them.

She continued to look incensed at the young man's mirth.

"All right—all right——" he gasped at last. "I'll swallow your own story, cruel stepmother and all, but I won't be hooked by this one about the new girl. She's here at Stelle Bogart's, isn't she?" And then, his jaw squaring, "And I want her, Floss, I want her." He reached for a very clean handkerchief and wiped his glistening forehead.

Floss continued to sit there enigmatically.

He was not used to being balked.

"I'll give six months' salary—I'm going straight out to talk to Stelle this minute. Maybe she'll listen to reason, if you won't."

Not to reason, but to money, thought Floss in quick alarm. She put out a hand to restrain him. Stelle would give in at once.

"There's no use your asking her, Roger. As Stelle told you, the girl's in my charge. Hattie put her there——" And thankful enough to get rid of her, she thought. "She's completely out of season for you, young man. She's big game, and only a millionaire can afford a hunting license." She looked at him with pretended regret. And then an inspiration came to her. "Last thing Hattie said was, 'Either find her a rich protector or a good husband, Floss.'" If Hattie ever found that out!

"Well, I'm not either of those, I'm afraid. But I'm bound I'll have her. Stelle said I was to ask you——"

The small rootlet idea was growing. Floss looked at him speculatively. She knew a good deal about the Roger Jardines of the world. Nothing fanned the flame of their desire like some teasing bait held out and then snatched away. Nothing drove these educated young gentlemen so wild as not getting their own way at once. Many a mother with a marriageable daughter had played on the same weakness, she knew; and many a high-toned match had been founded on the maxim that only a wedding ring buys what you want, young man.

"If I send for her, you can talk to her for just half an hour. *Talk*, I said. That's all. And remember, I'll be sitting across the room all the while. I'm only giving in for old times' sake, Roger. Nothing can come of it."

"Miser," he grumbled. But he was plainly elated. "I never thought to see you in the role of Latin duenna, Floss, but even to look at her will be better than nothing."

Floss sent the maid to summon Carolina. While they waited, she watched him. Roger Jardine was as fidgety as a cat on a hot griddle. She smiled to herself. These young blades that thought they were so worldly wise! Why, they were actually only spoiled and stubborn children. Deprive them of a lollypop, and it suddenly became the most desirable sweet on earth. If she could just manage to hold off Stelle long enough; and if she could get the least bit of cooperation from Carolina . . . So far, everything was going as smooth as a crooked dealer's shuffle.

Admiringly she watched Carolina enter the room and pause with her back to the door. The girl was an actress. She could run rings around Miss Fannie Louise Buckingham in "Mazeppa." Look at her now, with her great big tragedy-queen eyes—bedroom eyes, if she ever saw any—combined with that uppity, don't-touch-me look.

Actually, Carolina had to stop and lean against the back of the door because her knees had turned to jelly. When the maid had knocked and said discreetly, "Miss Cara—the back parlor——" she had thought: "Here it is. And I can't go through with it. I'll kill myself first." Yet, step by jolting step, she had descended the long stairs. Two steep flights. Then the narrow hall. Now the back parlor.

Fear had glazed her eyes until she could not focus them upon the occupants of the room, but could only stand there, arms outstretched against the back of the door. Fear had sharpened the planes of her face and made each freckle stand out against the dead whiteness of her skin.

Then a tall, slightly built, carefully tailored young man stood up from the damask-covered settee beside Floss, and all thought of self-destruction left Carolina. For his expression was merely one of rueful admiration.

"Here's a young gentleman that's been begging for the pleasure of meeting you, Cara," Floss said drily. "His name is Roger Walling Jardine, the Third, of Denver. Roger, this is Cara Smith." Pointedly she refrained from saying where Cara came from.

"Cara," he repeated with rapt stupidity. "Cara. That means dear!"

"Dear!" laughed Floss rudely. "Much too dear for you, Roger. To the highest bidder, like I told you." Her round white shoulders shook. But, like any Victorian chaperone, she subsided into a chair across the room. All I need now, she thought, is a roll of knitting.

Carolina was just emerging from her nightmare. For while her first glimpse of the gentleman had been reassuring, perhaps she had hoped too soon. Perhaps this was only a preliminary move. She lifted anguished eyes.

Roger Jardine did not know what her look portended, but it turned him giddy with emotion. Automatically he begged her to be seated; he darted to bring a cushion for her back; he picked up her lace-edged handkerchief when she nervously dropped it. He had been a polite little boy who always went to dancing school and never gave his mother a moment's trouble.

He had become a polite young man, thoroughly conventional even to the sowing of his wild oats. Young men of his time and class considered that a tour of the dance halls and variety theaters and sporting houses of a mining town was an orthodox part of their educations. It was almost incumbent upon them to be on first-name terms with at least one of the famous Madams of the day, so that they could casually refer to a Roxy Riordan or a Sadie Purple in their smoking-room conversations. But they would have been profoundly shocked at the idea of falling in love with a "soiled dove."

Roger himself would have been shocked at the idea. He had not the faintest intention of falling in love with such a girl. Making love—ah, that was different. He told himself that he was merely infatuated with the most desirable little piece he had ever seen, and that he had only the usual pursuit and capture and conquest in mind. He admitted that he was mad about her (which was quite orthodox, so long as one's intentions remained strictly dishonorable), but he did not admit to what extravagant lengths he might be willing to go, to get her.

Life had not equipped him to fight against his own desires. Until he had seen Carolina, he had never wanted anything that was not his for the asking. And now he wanted her, and Floss prevented him from having her, and so she took on a fabulous value in his eyes.

"You were on the train. I couldn't keep my eyes off you," he confessed boyishly.

Her heart slowed a little in its hard thumping. This did not sound alarming. This might have been Bertie Damon inviting her to the Assembly Ball. She smiled up at him uncertainly.

"But I had a deuce of a time tracking you down," he complained. "Floss certainly keeps a short rein on you."

"Floss has been wonderful—simply wonderful to me."

"Have you known her long?" He had known Floss for some time himself, but he had never heard her mention a girl named Cara Smith.

"Yes, a long time."

"Then your home is in Leadville?"

She retreated quickly.

"I've—I've lived in several places."

He frowned a little. Reluctantly, because he did not want to believe Floss, he forced himself to ask a question.

"Look, Cara, does—does your family know where you are? The kind of a place you're in?"

Alarm leaped to her eyes. This would never do, she thought.

"I haven't any family. I'm alone in the world." God knows, she was. And she could not have him telling her father where she was.

He settled back in relief. He let his shoulder touch hers tentatively. But she jerked away as if the brief contact had scorched her; the look in her eyes was one of such terror that he was instantly contrite. If she wasn't a novice, as Floss claimed, she certainly gave a remarkable imitation of one. None of his sister's prissy friends in Denver could have acted more shocked. Well, he could play the game too.

"Do you care for the theater, Miss Cara?" he asked politely.

She looked blank; then her face lighted.

"Oh, I think I would. I've never been, you see."

He looked incredulous. That was carrying things pretty far.

"I've tickets for 'The Black Crook' at the Wheeler Opera House tomorrow night. A box, in fact. I wonder if I may have the pleasure—the honor—of escorting you two ladies to the performance?"

Floss gave him a quizzical look. Carolina only stared blankly. This was the last thing either of them had expected.

"A box!" ejaculated Floss. "Can't say I ever sat in a box before. They don't sell 'em to the profession if they can help it. Sure, we'll go. Stelle will be delighted for us to. But I warn you, Roger, you're just wasting your money. It's only a stop-over for her." She nodded toward Carolina. "Her ticket still reads the same. And now your half-hour is almost up."

Carolina looked uncomprehendingly from one to the other. There was some secret interchange going on here. Roger Jardine flushed. Floss sat back and resumed her study of the wallpaper.

"Did you ever notice how time races when you're happy?" he asked Carolina with a lover's startled discovery. "Whereas all day tomorrow I'll just be pushing the clock's hands ahead."

"So will I." She smiled shyly at him.

He bent nearer and spoke in a tone too low for Floss to hear.

"And I'll be remembering you exactly as you are this minute, Cara."

Which was not to be wondered at. For Carolina's eyes were luminous . . . He had invited her to the theater. He wasn't treating her like a tart; he was treating her like a lady. Nobody had ever treated her like a lady before.

"And I'll remember—you——" she answered softly, and then her words died away. He had to bend close to hear—close enough to be bewitched by the perfume of her hair and the nearness of

60

her mouth. That red, red mouth whose underlip thrust out like a lovely child's.

She heard him catch his breath and mutter something—imprecation, supplication—and then Floss's crisp voice interrupted.

"Time's up, Roger. Cara has to get her beauty sleep. A girl's only capital, you know——"

Reluctantly he stood up, bending over Carolina's hand for longer than was strictly necessary. After a look of reproach mingled with gratitude for Floss, he said the last of several good-bys and was off.

Roger Jardine walked back to the hotel that night, shouldering the clouds. Could Floss have told the truth after all? Every gesture of the girl confirmed it. Yet how did she happen to be here? It was queer. Yet he could not think of a girl in Denver who could even approach her . . . That last look, the way her underlip trembled, the sweep of her lashes on her young cheek. Her throat —her bosom—— If she was all that Floss said, and if she might be his—— He was pleasantly beside himself by the time he reached his room.

Carolina was in a similar delightful turmoil. Why, he was a gentleman. The way he bowed over her hand—and brought a cushion for her—and picked up her handkerchief. He was the first real gentleman she had ever known. And all day tomorrow he would be pushing the clock ahead . . .

She climbed to her room on the top floor too bemused to heed the revelry going on all about her. As in Leadville, she passed through it without its touching her, strangely knowing, yet strangely innocent too. Her dreams that night were as sweetly romantic as if she slept safe in a maiden's bower, guarded by doting parents and wafted off to sleep by the sound of sleepy birdsongs.

The only one of the three who was not in a pleasurable turmoil was Floss. As she finished letting Roger out the door she turned to face Stelle's scowl . . . Where was Floss's business sense she'd heard so much about? Stelle wanted to know. Letting a young man leave—almost pushing him out the door, in fact— after he'd bought a single bottle of champagne. She'd been a fool to listen to Floss about the new girl, too.

"So you sent the young gentleman along home and the girl up to bed? My, my, ain't that just too sweet!" Stelle repeated, with lumbering sarcasm. "I told you this was no young ladies' seminary.

I got several customers in there this minute, and not enough girls to take care of them. I'm tired of all this geeing and hawing. I'm sending up for her this minute."

Floss's heart gave a bound of fright. But she managed to speak with composure.

"Young Jardine has invited us to go to the theater tomorrow night and sit in a box. It will be a fine chance to show the girl off. We'll hook a rich one yet."

Stelle looked dubious.

"Sure, you're much too smart to spoil a fine haul like that," Floss cajoled. "If you insist on starting her in now like she was any cheap little chippy, we'll both have to pull out. There's plenty of places would like to have me—— What say, Stelle?" She waited in apparent unconcern.

Stelle considered. "All right, all right," she said at last; then turned toward the front parlor sullenly.

CHAPTER 7

LUCKILY CAROLINA WAS TOO WRAPPED UP IN A SENSE OF PROFOUND and happy fatalism to be more than vaguely conscious of the growing animosity of the other girls the following day . . . They had never seen the likes—all this washing and perfuming and curling and preening of Cara—and then no business transacted after all.

They glowered as the two drove off that night with Roger Jardine in a rented carriage to attend the theater. Right in working hours too!

Rapturously Carolina settled back in her corner of the carriage, that smelled of leather and horse blanket and livery stable, while she listened to the *slup—slup* of hoofs in the spring slush. This was far nicer than any of those novels Leo had brought her to read. For Roger Jardine was a glorified Bertie Damon, only richer and older and more agreeable. She no longer had a thundercloud of a father to ruin everything. Her clothes had come straight from the Palace of Fashion. And Roger—well, Roger acted as if he thought she was wonderful. She regarded with naive wonder the fact that not until she had come to live at a sporting house had she been treated with either deference or gentleness.

The brilliant lights of the Opera House, the gilded boxes at either side with their draped-back velvet curtains, the swimming sea of faces below, and the heady thrumming of the orchestra all combined to intoxicate her. She chose a chair a little in the shadow of the curtains, while Floss sat well forward in the box so she could see. Roger sat between them.

Floss, who looked handsome and not very fast, gave calm attention to both the audience and the performance. She did not think much of either, she told them. The people "gawped" at their box, and the acting was poor. She was certainly shocked that Stalacta appeared wearing tights. What was the world coming to, she wanted to know, when women on the legitimate stage made an indecent spectacle of themselves?

Roger and Carolina neither knew nor cared what the world was coming to. Their world, this night, consisted of themselves. If Carolina had had any doubts that she looked enchanting in Floss's frock, which was the waxy-white of a yucca blossom, Roger soon dispelled those doubts. Each time he looked at her, he swayed toward her, as little able to control that swaying as an iron filing can withstand a magnet. Each time he picked up her fan, which she was continually dropping from nervousness, he handed it back with a look which said, "Here is my heart."

Occasionally he was forced to drag his attention away from her to answer Floss's irreverent questions about the audience. It was as if Floss interrupted on purpose . . . Who was the tart in the second row with the feathers in her hair? Roger answered reprovingly that she was the young wife of the president of one of the largest mining syndicates. But Floss remained unimpressed; she knew a tart when she saw one. And the old ewe with the spy glasses—did she have eye trouble? . . . Roger grinned. No, opera glasses were merely the style. Her husband was a banker, and they lived in a big house in "Bullion Row," the nickname for the fashionable new residence district. Floss grunted disparagingly. Hm— wrinkled and warty as an old squash, wasn't she? And what about the dapper little man beside her that looked like a chipmunk? Was he the banker husband? . . . Roger explained: he was Henry Gilson, one of Roger's—well, Roger's father's—clients in the present law suit. He was a sort of a widower; at least his wife was reputed to have left him in spite of the fact that he had interests in several mines, with thousands rolling in weekly. Roger stopped hastily as if he had said too much.

"Thanks, Roger." Floss's grin was pure malice. "I wouldn't wonder if you'd put me on the track of something."

He slumped, as if her words carried a sinister meaning.

"He's sure kept his eyes glued on this box ever since we came in, Roger; and they haven't been glued on you or me."

"Forty, if he's a day!" he snapped, with all the scorn of twenty-five for complete senescence.

"That's what I said. It's the rich old ones. They've got the——" She made the age-old mercenary gesture of rubbing her thumb against her bunched-up fingertips.

For some reason unknown to Carolina this remark plunged Roger into the blackest gloom. But it did not diminish his admiration for her. And under this admiration she bloomed. She dared to inch her chair forward until she could see the stage. She clapped her gloved hands when it came time to applaud. Her cheeks were flushed, and her eyes burned bright with pleasure. From her naively excited remarks, even Roger was forced to conclude that this was, indeed, her first visit to the theater. The knowledge made him feel oddly protecting and lordly.

After the performance, he hustled them out before anyone could make his way around to the back of the box seeking an introduction. He had ordered a wine supper at the Clarendon for them, he said.

The name, another Clarendon, gave Carolina an uneasy start, as if the tentacles of Leadville were reaching out to fasten on her. But she soon forgot in her interest in her surroundings: the lights and the white tablecloth and the shiny silver. When Roger handed her an elaborately embossed menu, she was helpless before the array of unintelligible words. She looked up at him imploringly.

"You choose, please. I don't know how. I never ate in a restaurant before."

There was no doubting her. Basking in her evident awe as the French words tripped off his tongue, Roger's chest swelled and he became a bon-vivant, a mellowed man of the world.

He did not even smile incredulously when Floss said, "No, no champagne for her, Roger. She's never touched liquor in her life."

Indulgently he watched Carolina taste the strange dishes, at first timidly and then greedily. A palate accustomed for sixteen years to fried salt pork and creamed dried codfish and potatoes boiled in their jackets was not jaded. His eyes met Floss's over her head in a glance of benign understanding.

Roger shone; he told amusing stories about the great or the merely lucky who dined at tables nearby. About the man with the mustaches who had been all ready to throw down his pick, when somebody dared him to go one foot deeper . . . about the fellow with the napkin draped across his paunch who was down to his pocket piece and finally, in a last-ditch gesture, had bet that against a supposedly worthless claim . . .

Every glance of his blue eyes, between light lashes that squeezed together delightfully when he smiled, was homage to Carolina.

If Floss seemed a little distrait, with her attention wandering to something or somebody across the room behind Roger's back, neither Carolina nor the young man noticed. Nor did they see the slight inclination of Floss's head that meant consent and approval in any language.

So when a small, dapper, beady-eyed man came up to their table, Roger stopped in the middle of a sentence, his face a study in consternation. Carolina stared up at the newcomer vacantly. She had no recollection of ever having seen him before. Floss sat back in her chair enjoying the situation. For the younger man, a fledgling lawyer on a case in which Gilson was one of the clients, had no choice but to introduce him to the ladies. Roger did so grudgingly.

Floss was about to move over to make room for Gilson, when she had another inspiration. She stood up, gathering together her fan and her boa, and announced smoothly that she would be delighted to join Mr. Gilson in a claret cup at his own table. They had several matters to discuss, she said genially.

Carolina expected Roger to be relieved at their thus taking themselves off. But instead he was distracted. He kept glancing over his shoulder at the pair, who had settled themselves for what looked like a long and comfortable conversation. There were no signs of disagreement between them; it seemed only a matter of coming to terms. Henry Gilson's eyes rested approvingly on Carolina. Floss's smile was tolerant but firm. To Roger Jardine, helplessly watching, there was something grossly calculating about that conference, something incredibly calm and carnal about it.

He was at his wits' end. He tried to interpose his slight bulk between Carolina and those two. He fidgeted and wiped his forehead. He gave up all pretense of eating the food that would take half a week's salary to pay for. Desperately he leaned toward Carolina, fixing her with his hot blue eyes.

Once in every life comes a moment when a young person may throw away his life with profligate ease. Usually circumstances: parents, friends, or society, combine to protect him from his brief attack of atavism—his luna madness—his *must*. But there was nobody and nothing to protect Roger Jardine from himself at the moment. He was being driven by something enormously stronger than himself.

"Cara!" he groaned, reaching across and gripping her hand on the tablecloth.

The sudden swift pressure undid her. This girl, who had been brought up on the hem of the red-light district and who had a stark knowledge of the traffic in bodies that went on in a mining camp, had never received a caress in her life, had never experienced the swift, swooning deliciousness of being wooed. She smiled shakenly.

Roger was trapped. His eyes darted from her to the sordid drama taking place at the table across the room.

"Look, Cara, you couldn't care—you wouldn't let yourself care for a horrible old man like that, would you?" He jerked a shoulder backwards in the direction of the tête-à-tête.

She followed his gesture in surprise. She had forgotten all about Floss and the little man named Gilson.

"Him? Mercy, no." She was honestly scornful and completely without coquetry.

"But Floss said she—you——" The sweat broke out in little shining drops again. What had Floss said? How much did this wide-eyed young thing know of Floss's plans? "Oh, Cara, I know so little about you. Tell me what you think about love. Tell me that you believe that a man and woman who care for each other should be—should stay—well, pure, for each other." He was a little incoherent; although naturally he meant that Cara was the one to stay pure, not himself.

Carolina nodded gravely.

"I do, Roger," she said; and it was like a wedding vow.

Roger thought so too. And Floss had told him she would be satisfied with nothing less than a rich protector or a good husband for the girl.

"Say you'll marry me, Cara. I love you, I tell you! I never loved anyone before. I want to marry you. Will you be ready—as soon as I find a preacher?"

Even while he said it, he knew that he was a fool; he knew that he was throwing his life away. And he was glad. When Carolina promised, he felt that all his days had been leading up to this moment.

Floss was coming leisurely toward them. Her smiling exterior hid her anxiety. Had she allowed them long enough? For time was so short. Everything was crowding her—Stelle, the young man, Gilson, even the girl's own lack of ambition. But one look at their faces was all the answer she needed.

II

ON AN AFTERNOON IN APRIL IN THE YEAR 1889, EXACTLY ONE WEEK from the day of her arrival in Aspen, Cara Smith and Roger Walling Jardine III were married in the hotel parlor by a long-haired elderly reprobate who called himself a preacher.

At the close of the makeshift ceremony the old man took a stance on unsteady heels and delivered a little homily ending:

"And so, my dear young friends, as the Good Book enjoins, Husbands, love your wives, and wives, reverence your husbands. That you may truly say to each other, Whither thou goest I will go; and where thou lodgest I will lodge and—er——" He cleared his throat, casting about helplessly with rolling, red-veined eyeballs.

Carolina prompted softly, "Thy people——"

He picked up his cue.

"——thy people shall be my people and thy God my God."

His eye was on a little rim of green peeping out of Roger Jardine's fawn-colored vest pocket . . . Was that a ten? Or might it be two tens nestling cozily there together?

Carolina had only time to think scornfully, A funny kind of preacher. Everyone knew that those words were said by Ruth to her mother-in-law, not by a bride to her husband . . . And then Roger bent down and kissed her hard on the mouth, and she forgot all about a seedy old fellow who fumbled his Bible verses. This was her first kiss, and she was wildly in love.

Floss stealthily wiped her eyes and looked for all the world like the mother of a bride, a little sad and considerably relieved. She was thinking triumphantly, Well, that's one time I bet on a low straight and raked in all the blue chips.

CHAPTER 8

MR. AND MRS. ROGER JARDINE ENTERED THEIR SUITE IN PARLOR A OF the newly finished Jerome Hotel. As Roger closed the door behind them and turned the key, their eyes went homing to each other. Even after four months of married life, there was still something immensely significant about locking the door upon the world at night and turning to each other. It was the very conspiracy of love.

Carolina was conscious of the beating pulse in her throat as she moved away from him across the immense flower-carpeted room before he could touch her. It was delicious to prolong things. And tonight had been truly gay. They had attended a bazaar for the Volunteer Fire Department, held in a lodge hall over a store. There were raffles and fish ponds and fortune-telling booths and little tables for refreshments.

She swept over to the center table and deposited her load of useless loot that had cost Roger so much money tonight. While he waited, she made a self-conscious little ritual of hanging her bonnet in the wardrobe and folding her new dolman with the scrollwork braid trimming. Before they were lost in their lovemaking, she wanted to hear from his lips again that he was proud of her, that he thought her beautiful.

Still keeping an acre of tapestry carpet between them, she began to undress before her marble-topped bureau, lifting her arms to her hair in the timeless, provocative gesture of all women disrobing.

"Oh, Roger, I saw everyone admiring my topazes," she announced happily, unclasping the necklace which had been his most recent gift and laying it on the liver-colored marble slab.

Roger paused in front of the wardrobe, coat in hand, and looked across at her with a flash of pleasure. They smiled at each other briefly: the smile of love.

"It was you, not the topazes."

Quite honestly she thought so, too, but she wanted to hear him say it.

"Well, you were far and away the handsomest man there," she told him with conviction.

He flushed. She could never get over how pleased a nice man like Roger could be with a frank compliment.

He had taken off his collar and his wide stiff cuffs. Now he was leaning back against his own bureau watching her, a little smile playing around the corners of his mouth. He still wore his immaculately white shirt and his black broadcloth trousers, but he had slipped his suspenders off his shoulders and let them dangle rakishly. Carolina, who had seen suspendered men all her life, had to learn that this dishabille, to Roger, meant abandoned intimacy. His reservations, his fastidiousness, entranced her, just as she was entranced by the care with which he polished his pointed shoes, by the earnest way he brushed his bowler hat, and by the studied exactness with which he pierced his cravat with his pearl stickpin. Living with Roger was a series of delicately voluptuous surprises. He was both lordly and beseeching, reserved and impetuous, remote yet close.

"Roger——" she looked over her shoulder at him, "would you care to unhook me?"

He was across the room in an instant, bending carefully over the row of hooks down the back of her rich brown shot silk that was the perfect setting for her topazes (and her milky skin and her ale-gold eyes and her red mouth). She loved looking at him when he was not aware of it. Watching him in the glass, she could see his brow furrowed like a small boy's as he struggled with the hooks, being careful not to tear her dress, wanting to please her.

She slipped the sleeves down off her arms. The dress fell to the floor. Roger bent to kiss the back of her neck, his eyes gleaming.

"Sweet," he said softly against her skin. "Sweet——"

Oh, not yet, she thought, loving him yet wanting to postpone love a little longer.

"Look out, Roger, you're trampling my new dress." She glanced at the floor.

Roger backed away and bent to pick up her dress as she stepped out of it. Sheepishly he shook out the brown frock with its half-train and its fashionable overskirt. He was usually the careful one about hanging up things.

She smiled indulgently. Roger was forever catching her up on some piece of carelessness. This was once she had caught him. He spent much of their time together marveling at her simplicity, at her ignorance, at her appalling lack of worldly knowledge. Like the time he had tried to give her ear bobs to match the topaz necklace and found to his astonishment that her ears had never been pierced. He said he could not imagine any girl growing up in this day and age without having her ears pierced. What must her mother have been thinking of?

Carolina had started to tell him that her mother had probably been thinking of having another baby in the Gospel wagon, or of how to feed seven hungry mouths on nothing at all. Then she shut her lips stubbornly. Even though Roger had kept on looking at her, his eyes bright with unspoken questions, she could not say anything. Her childhood must become a forgotten thing, she told herself; like a bad, bad dream.

"I count time from the day I married you," she had evaded him fondly. "I have no childhood. I was born again on my wedding day——" She was unaware of the Biblical cadences to her speech.

Roger had looked first frustrated and then pleased. And presently he had taken her into his arms, almost as if he did not want to; and everything was all right again.

Now, as she thought again of her mother's meager life, she was overwhelmed by her own undeserved good fortune. She feared that the rich lode of her happiness might fault or pinch out any day now. For Roger was everything a girl could ask for: handsome, gay, good-natured, and tolerant. She did not put it in words that he was everything her father was not.

Four perfect months; well, almost perfect. It had been hard when Roger had proved unexpectedly rocklike about Floss. Why, they owed everything to Floss, and yet he made her stop seeing Floss and even speaking to her on the street. Floss had been big about it. She had tried to explain it to Carolina when they said good-by.

"It shows what a good job I did on you, Carolina. Him thinking you're too good for me now." She paused. "Well, you are. So it's good-by, kid. May all your ore pockets be rich ones!" She had turned and swept off along Hyman Street, her head up, the lace ruffle on her parasol fluttering jauntily.

Carolina had stood there staring after her and wanting to cry.

Roger had had his own unhappiness too. As soon as his family had received word of his marriage, they had shipped his big chest to him with all his belongings in it: his clothes and his college diploma and his mandolin and even his silver porridge spoon and baby's mug. As if to indicate that he was no longer a part of, or indeed had ever been born into, the family at all. True, she was aware that Roger's mother wrote him secret grieving letters. But there was no placating his father.

Carolina had tried to comfort Roger by explaining that families were really not the least bit of use. You could shed them like a snake its skin and feel ever so much freer and happier afterwards. That is, if you did not let yourself dwell on whether Rosalie was outgrowing her tendency to sore throat and what Mat would do this winter with no one to help him with fractions.

Roger had scarcely seemed to hear her. He only looked at her as from a great distance. She had the uneasy presentiment that perhaps he was not one to shed his family so effortlessly.

Of course his father had dismissed him from the family law firm, and that had ended his connection with the lawsuit here. But losing his job had actually proved a blessing, because he had done so much better since, trading in mining shares at the various exchanges along Mill and Hyman Streets.

She thought it was clever of Roger to understand about mining securities and buying on margins and cleaning up profits. He was always shuffling papers called stock certificates, covered with fancy printing, while he talked about how much was "asked" or "bid." He was always poring over pen-and-ink maps showing long narrow coffin-shaped mining claims that overlapped each other in an intricate, lacy design.

To her, a mine was simply a sinister hole in the mountain that swallowed up husbands and brothers and fathers each day (sometimes maiming and killing them) and then disgorged them at the end of their toil, tired and muddy-footed and spotted with candle grease. From her window here in the hotel she could watch the Aspen miners coming off shift after dark, lighting their way down the slopes with candles that made a flickering tinsel festoon along the mountain side.

She was proud that Roger could make money out of the mines and yet stay on top of the ground, wearing a neat business suit and polished, pointed shoes.

"I thought your friend Mr. Canaday, that buys and sells mining stock, was very agreeable tonight," she said demurely, beginning to untie the drawstring of her top petticoat. When she arrived at a more dangerous proximity to her ruffled drawers, she would retire modestly behind the opened door of the wardrobe to complete her disrobing. She was still four petticoats away, however.

Roger scowled. "Too damn—much too agreeable. I don't like the way he stared at you, Cara—bending over you to look at your necklace, and remarking on the scent you were wearing."

Carolina batted her eyes innocently. Actually, she did not think much of this Canaday herself; she had never cared for a waxed mustache and hair slicked sideways over a bald spot. But she enjoyed tormenting Roger. And it was certainly inconsistent of him to object to their having a dish of ice cream with Mr. Canaday, when he did business with him. Roger had said they had a deal on. And not another soul in the whole town spoke to her and Roger. Not that she cared. She could do without any of them, so long as she and Roger had each other. But he needn't act so stiff toward Mr. Canaday, just because he was civil enough to invite them to have some refreshments. She had accepted the invitation quickly, so there was nothing to do but for all three to sit down at one of the small tables together.

She remembered the queer sensation she had as the conversation went on. She had happened to remark that she thought the uniforms tonight lacked some of the dash of those of the Leadville Fire Department. At her words, Canaday had laid down his spoon.

"Are you well acquainted in Leadville, Mrs. Jardine?" he asked in a careful voice.

"Me? Well, in a way," she had answered. "Though not with what you'd call the 'best people,' I guess." She was always one to put her worst foot forward, Letty said.

Then she had stopped abruptly. For Roger was leaning toward her, hardly breathing, waiting for her next words; waiting for her to give something away about her childhood. She had stiffened. Never! She would never tell anyone about her hateful childhood: not Roger, not anyone. She would be open with him about everything else in her life from now on, but not about her past. Not about being Carolina Lawler, instead of Cara Smith. Not about her unspeakable childhood and the singing on street corners and her father praying for her in public—like stripping her naked—and the young

72

folks snickering. She had had to close her eyes tightly for a moment to overcome the loathing she felt for the past.

When she had opened them again she was able to speak casually to Mr. Canaday.

"Oh, I've been in Leadville some—but then I've been in most of the boom towns at one time or another—I can't say I know many folks in any of them."

Mr. Canaday had relaxed; but Roger only looked more compressed about the mouth. As if he realized that he had almost had her for a moment, but she had eluded him again.

Roger, still leaning back on his elbows against the bureau, was struggling to find the right words now.

"Canaday is too—too personal with you, Cara. He makes you conspicuous," he said miserably.

Carolina smiled. She was conspicuous anyhow, she thought complacently. As if a Mr. Canaday could make her more so. She reveled a little in Roger's jealousy. It gave her a sense of power, and she needed it with Roger. For he was always unintentionally making her feel ignorant or inadequate. Only when it came to matters of love did she hold the ascendancy. And she loved him so; oh, how she loved him! She would relent in a minute and go into his arms.

II

How, ROGER WAS WONDERING WRETCHEDLY, DID YOU GO ABOUT telling the girl you were mad about that she is outré? That she is, as his mother would say, "excessive"? That when she laughs—head thrown back and lips parted—or sweeps through a room, or merely picks up a menu in a restaurant, she attracts as much attention as an eagle in a chicken yard? Even Canaday had noticed her overgenerous use of perfume. When a man of his stripe remarks on a thing . . . Yet once when he had tried to chide her, she had whirled on him, eyes blazing, and said—shouted would have been nearer the truth——

"I'll never be able to get too much lovely perfume! You don't understand. Perfume means something to me—something special." A strange girl; a frightening girl.

He could not do without her. She was in his blood like a tropical fever that waned and almost disappeared and then flared up violently again. He wanted to scold her; he wanted to shake her;

he wanted to make her over. But he never stopped wanting her.

The difficulty went deeper than mere manners; it went back to a home life that must have been completely foreign to his, that gave him nothing to appeal to, nothing to catch hold of. She was so beautiful, yet so strange. So—so violent, he thought unhappily, recalling his mother's sleek gentleness that always got its own way through devious, ladylike means. Whereas, with Cara, you felt that if you prodded her too far, she might actually throw things or yell or make scenes. The thought made him squirm.

He simply could not understand Cara. Perhaps if he could find out something about her background—— There was her not minding being a social outcast, for instance. He wondered if she did not know she was one. Or had she grown up in a circle where everyone was a social outcast, so that she was used to it? Surely she must realize that not a single respectable person spoke to them here.

He would not confess even to himself what a blow this fact was, after having been fêted at first as the most eligible young bachelor in town. Now, the only people who addressed them socially were flashy, off-color ones: gamblers, stage people, and promoters like that smart skunk Canaday, who might know a lot about mining properties but who was miles from being a gentleman. Or Floss.

He winced. The thought of Floss was like a constantly aching tooth that he could not keep from harrying: wiggling it, pressing it, unable to leave it alone. How did Cara happen to know Floss Kittredge? The two girls had come straight from Hattie Merkle's that morning; he had seen them get out of the carriage. What was Cara to Hattie Merkle?

It was the same old round of torment that he had been undergoing for the past four months. He knew that bawdy women sometimes had children. What became of them, those poor little accidents of profane love? What kind of a life lay in store for them? If they were girls, probably only the life of a high-class prostitute. He remembered Floss telling him that Hattie had put Cara in her charge. Floss was to look after her interests and school her in the deportment of the courtesan. He remembered, too, that the only people Cara mentioned by name from her past were prostitutes and gamblers. Not once had she spoken of her father or her mother. The only towns she seemed to have lived in were mining camps at the peak of the boom, and everyone knew that fancy women followed the booms. What was she to Hattie?

There was the matter of her education, too. She had read a lot in an unguided way, yet she had the strangest gaps in her learning. She was both innocent and startlingly worldly. Not that she seemed to care a thing about money. There wasn't a mercenary bone in her body, he had to admit. But she was obsessed with the idea of laughter and gaiety. And how she hated church! It was as if she had been indoctrinated to hate church and respectable people and conventions. It was the code of the bordello, of Hattie herself.

And then he looked at her, and his doubts faded. She was so altogether desirable, sitting there before her bureau with her embroidered chemise falling off her shoulders. God knows, he had never doubted her goodness, her chastity—who should know better than he? It was all the other things about her that nagged at him. If he could only find out . . .

His heart melted like tallow as she looked at him in the mirror. What if she did use too much perfume? And was too nice to that cad, Canaday? And was—excessive. She was *his*.

He started toward her in answer to the curving invitation on her lips. And then he halted with an actual effort of will. If he could trap her just once. It was this uncertainty that was driving him crazy.

She had only to say: "My father was a hard-rock miner, Roger," or "—he was a smelter worker," or "—he had a job in a sampling works——" Anything, so long as it was respectable!

Had Carolina but known it, the truth about her parentage would have turned him limp with relief. All that was religiously conventional in him would have responded to the idea of "the cloth" . . . no matter about the Gospel wagon and the street corner ranting and the town's bored contempt.

He began with elaborate strategy, clutching at the first conversational peg he could hang a remark on, the care of one's clothes.

"Mother was always a regular crank about us children putting our clothes neatly away when we took them off. She said that even if we were among the first ones born in Denver City—that's what they called it back in '64—we weren't to live like Navajos. She came from Boston, you know."

"Did she, Roger?" Carolina gazed at him with bright interest. She could see that he loved to talk about home; something maternal in her encouraged him to. Perhaps it would help him.

75

"I remember once, to punish me for some carelessness, she actually kept me home from the big celebration when Colorado was admitted to statehood. In '76—the Centennial State, you know—the summer I was twelve. I was mighty put out, you can bet. Where were you the summer you were twelve, Cara?" he ended with strained sharpness.

Where was she? Carolina put her hairbrush down and stared into the glass at some specter that Roger could not see. A sudden change came over her face as at an old and ugly memory. The pupils of her brown-topaz eyes widened blackly; her nostrils grew pinched.

"I haven't any past, I've told you! There was no Cara until I met you. Why do you keep digging at me?"

"But of course you have a past, dear. Everyone does. Floss was evidently a part of your past. Tell me how you happened to meet Floss."

He was startled at the swiftness with which she leaped to her feet. She whirled, bracing herself with arms outstretched behind her on the marble-topped bureau. She was a young animal caught in a trap, trying to get loose from it, willing to gnaw off a paw to rid herself of the trap.

"Leave me be, I tell you! You don't have to know how I came to meet Floss." She shut her eyes for a moment, the trick she had when a memory was too bad to face. Roger could not know that she shut her eyes now against the memory of her mother, tired out and beaten by life, as she did washings on the sly for the fancy ladies because they paid the best . . . "I don't want ever to think about how I happened to meet Floss. Don't ask me again. That's done with forever. I've left it all behind me, do you understand?"

She was shaking with uncontrollable feeling. When she opened her eyes and looked at him, there were unaccustomed tears on her lashes. Already Roger had discovered that Cara never used tears as a weapon.

"Oh, Roger, isn't it enough that I only want to start remembering from the moment I met you?"

The storm was over. She smiled a little—shyly, surely—holding out her arms to him. It was she who crossed the acre of flower-patterned carpet that separated them; who wooed him shamelessly; her white skin, her white arms, her giving mouth, all wooing him.

He looked down at her torturedly. He tried to wrench his glance

76

away. Then he groaned and caught her to him in an embrace that was fiercer than any thus far; that was hungry and bitter and desperate, like the reaching out of a starving man who knows that the food will probably kill him.

As he carried her toward the vast white bed in the vast and flowery bridal suite of the elegant new Jerome, he was whispering incoherently to her.

"I don't care—nothing else matters—it's enough to know that I can't live without you."

But it is not enough. It is never enough. No man marries a woman and not her past. Perhaps a woman can do that for the man she loves; but a man—never. It may be that a man is too possessive; that far back in his subconscious is the thought that his children's mother must be unsullied. For over and over Roger's unanswered questions were to rise to haunt him. In her arms he could exorcise them; but by the next day they were riding him again, mocking him, plaguing him.

C H A P T E R   9

CAROLINA WAS DRESSING FOR THE THEATER, AND DOING IT RELUCtantly. In the first place, she was hungry; and in the second place, Roger was acting up again.

He seemed to be having a good many of these spells lately where he poked listlessly at his food, or failed to hear her when she spoke; or, if he did hear her, stared at her in an abstracted way that made her want to yell or do something violent to capture his attention.

Was it money? She was used to lack of money. But when she suggested that their quarters here must cost a dreadful lot and that surely there were nice comfortable boarding houses to be found, he had actually looked alarmed.

"For heavens sake, Cara, don't start retrenching now. This is no time. In fact, I want you to wear your new sealskin cape as much as possible."

So it could not be money, she decided innocently as she combed out her front frizzes and arranged the long rope of her hair in a

French twist. Maybe it was more letters from home. She had learned that a letter from home was always followed by one of Roger's moods.

Lately she had begun to notice other handwriting on the envelopes besides his mother's. A demure yet ornate script such as fashionable young ladies affected. His sister Lydia? But Lydia was married and having babies and was much too busy to write. Occasionally Roger referred to a girl in Denver named Sue. But he had also remarked that he had not written to Sue since his arrival in Aspen; and Roger never lied.

She did her best to coax him out of these moony spells. She encouraged him to talk about his family; but as often as not that only made him more depressed. She brought him his shiny beetle of a mandolin and begged him to sing the one about the tavern in the town. Sometimes he would start, and then break off in the middle of a line. Maybe he was thinking of other times that he had sung that song to other girls. Or maybe it was something about the words:

> "Fare thee well, for I must leave thee.
> Do not let this parting grieve thee——"

He was very difficult. One minute he was morose and the next minute he was feverishly gay. Like tonight. He had come rushing jubilantly into their room not five minutes ago.

"Look, honey. I've got tickets for the Opera House. It's 'Little Nell and the Marchioness.' Get into your best bib and tucker. Sorry there isn't time for you to eat, but I picked up a handful of sweets, so nibble them while you dress." He pulled a paper-wrapped package out of his pocket and dropped it on the center table.

She had started to protest. She did not like sweets, but she hated to tell him so. He was so sure that all girls doted on them and only downed enough solid food to "keep from feeling faint." The truth was: she liked things like stew and turnips and cornbread. She wondered who had nursed such delusions in Roger's mind. His mother —his sister—Sue?

It was the same way with her fondness for arithmetic. She could do sums in her head far more quickly than Roger could. Yet he was convinced that all girls were unable to cope with anything stiffer than sickly verses or china painting or "composition," and were completely floored by thirteen times nine. So she had learned to wait until he told her the answers. It was her first and almost only concession to the wifely ideals of her time.

She bit disgustedly into one of the little cakes while she dressed. Her temper was not improved by the realization that Roger had, from the smell on his breath, just visited one of the more lavish saloons, where he could get plenty of stout masculine edibles along with his liquor: crude, delightful things like liver sausage and rye bread and cheese and pickled herrings. Her mouth watered even as she swallowed the loathsome macaroon.

Clasping the topaz necklace around her throat, she thought fleetingly about the handsome saloons here in Aspen: the Brick, because it was the first brick building; the Branch, because it was a branch of a Leadville saloon; the Abbey, because men always seemed to like incongruous names for their saloons. The Abbey was the most high-toned of them all. Roger was always expatiating on its works of art; you'd think that all the men went there for was to look at the paintings.

Roger had returned and was standing in the doorway. She grabbed up her dolman.

"I asked you particularly to wear your sealskin, Cara."

She obediently exchanged the dolman for her sealskin cape. This late summer weather was still pretty warm for a fur cape, but if he wished it——

They were late. They had barely seated themselves in the Opera House before the lights went on for the intermission.

"Might as well go back and promenade a little," Roger said, standing up promptly.

Carolina had hoped they could sit still for a while. She was out of breath, for one thing. And for another, the sweetish cakes were resting uneasily in her empty stomach. But she got to her feet with a yawn. Roger had never been able to convince her that yawning was like scratching; you simply could not do it just because the impulse hit you. You had to restrain yourself. To Carolina, a yawn was still a public act.

The back of the theater was packed with a slowly milling crowd, each member of it intent upon showing off the fruits of his sudden wealth, whether in the form of new sealskins or new jewels or new wives.

But Carolina lacked her usual interest in them tonight. Perhaps it was because she was "out of sorts" over one of Roger's moods, or perhaps it was the little cakes. Whatever the cause, she lifted sulky eyes to Mr. Canaday as he approached. With that sweeping bifurcated mustache and hair slicked crosswise over his bald spot, he looked exactly like a bartender in one of Leadville's cheaper dives, she thought. All he needed was a spotted apron across his paunch.

When he bowed ostentatiously over her hand, holding it too long and too moistly, she pulled the hand away and refused to glance above the level of the middle button of his fawn-checked waistcoat. He was as slick and greasy as a batch of amalgam, she decided with distaste.

"The little lady is looking mighty fine tonight, if I may say so," he began, his heavy-lidded gambler's eyes upon her. "And she has a neat taste in fashions too." He was eying with appreciation the sealskin cape whose rich brownish collar stood up like an Elizabethan ruff behind her shining head.

Carolina glanced down carelessly.

"Oh, the cape. Roger picked it out. He has all the gumption when it comes to choosing clothes; he kind of senses what's right or wrong. But I tell him I know more about people. That's one thing you learn if you've been raised among—well, where I was—you get so you can spot the cheats and crooks at a glance." She lifted hostile eyes.

Canaday was obviously taken aback.

Roger was aghast. He cleared his throat and made desperate little conversational sorties.

"I—er—I hope you're enjoying the play tonight, Mr. Canaday. Quite refreshing, isn't it? I've heard it said that Lotta started the fashion for charming hoydens—as a change from the more stodgy roles. But I suppose you've seen all the great names in the theater —you've traveled so widely. I—we, that is, my wife and I would like nothing better than to hear about your travels. I wonder if you'd give us the pleasure of having a bite with us after the theater?"

Roger waited nervously.

Mr. Canaday waited too—for Mrs. Jardine to second the invitation. Roger looked at her expectantly. Carolina remained stubbornly silent.

"We'll see," Canaday said at last with a certain aloofness. "No doubt the little lady will be too tired——" He drifted away as the orchestra began to twang and rasp.

The crowd closed about them like an irresistible human glacier and carried them back down the aisle. Roger was white with anger as they reached their seats and he helped Carolina off with her fur cape. He might feel reproach or resentment or even fury toward a woman, but he would never neglect to help her off with her cape.

"Did you have to be downright insulting? For all I know, you've queered the whole deal. It would serve us right if he refused to do business with me, after the way you treated him. What possessed you, Cara?"

"You've certainly changed your tune since the last time. You were nagging at me then because I was too friendly with him. You said he was cheap and not a gentleman. Well, I've decided you were right. I've just remembered who it is he reminds me of—Pat McCoyne that ran the lowest dance hall on State Street."

Roger recoiled. That terrible familiarity with the underworld! Would he ever be able to forget it; to make her forget it?

"You don't understand about business; you don't have to *like* the people you have dealings with. I need Canaday in a business way, and I expect my wife to help me, not ruin me. When we leave the Opera House, if we run into him again you will second my invitation to supper. Just be civil, that's all. You're either falling all over a man or else you're looking at him as if he'd offered you a mortal insult."

He stiffened, getting ready for a scene. But Carolina surprised him by looking up at him adoringly. Just when he expected her to raise her voice and make them both conspicuous, she suddenly melted into sweet docility.

"Oh, Roger, I love you when you get all worked up. But are you sure we can afford the supper—with champagne and everything? If we're short, so we can't even buy good hot meals——?" She was thinking of those horrid little cakes, when what she had wanted was a filling meat pasty. "Surely we can't afford to spend the money."

"We can't afford not to," he said firmly, settling his shoulder forgivingly against hers. Her hand went out to meet his under cover of the sealskin cape. His clasp tightened electrically.

They sat there immobile, lost in the clamor of their own senses, inwardly drowning in the swift hot tide of love that beat through their bodies and fused them at their fingertips. The play was forgotten. They were merely two young people whose feeling for each other scared them by its intensity, who were only waiting until they could be alone together again.

But afterwards they were jerked back to the exigencies of the everyday world by the sight of Canaday. Carolina invited him prettily to sup with them.

He kept them in suspense a moment; then he accepted benignly.

Throughout the elegant little supper at the restaurant, during which she tried to hold her ravenous appetite within bounds, she was conscious only of Roger and their waiting love. She had ceased to mind Canaday because he had become non-existent for her. She was in a trance of love; a somnolent young savage waiting to be carried off by her mate.

As the three walked sedately back to the hotel, where Canaday left them with a flourish of his fawn-colored Derby, Roger was thinking approvingly of Cara. He had never seen her so restrained and ladylike. He was gratified. Perhaps she would develop into a perfect hostess after all. Like his mother, he thought. He almost added, like Sue.

The next morning as they were dressing to go out to breakfast—Roger had been assuring her that the frugal Continental breakfast was much better for them than the big hearty meal served here at the hotel—Carolina saw him drape his massive watch chain across his waistcoat and anchor the end of it in his watch pocket with a safety pin.

She almost exclaimed, "Why, Roger, what's become of your watch?" when something stopped her. A certain furtiveness, combined with bravado. Her eyes narrowed sympathetically. She had seen that look all her life. The look of a gambler down to his last dollar, or even without his last dollar, so that he must borrow from the house to start over, who religiously keeps his plug hat gleaming and his boots polished.

She thought tenderly, I won't let on I notice, and I'll try to eat only the cheapest things. She wished she were not so disgustingly hungry these days.

As they started out through the elegant plush-and-marble lobby, she saw the hotel clerk trying to catch their attention by means of hesitant, throat-clearing movements.

"I have to go ahead and see a man," Roger said hastily. "Tell the clerk, if he asks, I'm closing a big deal today and will have the money for the bill by night."

So she had been right in her suspicions. Carolina faced the embarrassed clerk down. There were times like this when it helped to be tall. And her childhood training in stalling off the grocer until Pa could get another job helped too.

Throughout the morning she was thoughtful. Something would have to be done. She could not go on any longer humoring Roger's pride. She would hunt a cheaper place to live.

It was silly to go on pouring out money for this elegant Parlor A. As if she had to live in a hotel with an elevator and bowing waiters; or have a bathroom all to herself, with a marble-topped washbowl, and a tub that you could practically lie down in and didn't need to heat the water for, and a toilet that flushed when you pulled a dangling chain . . . As if she had to have all these luxuries to make her happy.

Roger was nervous at lunch. She suspected that he was about to meet Mr. Canaday. Silently she wished him luck. But luck or no luck, she had made up her mind to look for cheaper living quarters.

As soon as he had disappeared into one of the mining exchanges, she set off on a walk of exploration toward "the Flats," that shabby district down the slope near the tracks and the Roaring Fork river. She proceeded north along Mill Street, crossing the fashionable residence street nicknamed Bullion Row.

She admired the handsome verandaed frame houses, with their wooden lace edgings under the eaves, and the even handsomer brick and stone houses, built to last a hundred years, with their round towers and their turrets that might have been used for gun emplacements.

As the ground dropped away, the character of the houses dropped too. They grew meaner and smaller. Everything about the Flats reminded her of Stringtown. It was a region where laborers lived: section hands, miners, smelter workers. How well she knew such houses. The walls papered with newspapers, the front room that always had a bed in it, the soggy gray bedding, and the pillowcase with a dark center where an unwashed head had rested.

She knew it, and she did not like it. But she would not be unhappy here, so long as she could be with Roger. She would show the Flats that she could keep things clean and pretty. She would show Roger that she could be a helpmeet to him.

She sat down to rest on a fallen cottonwood trunk. She would not admit in so many words that she had found her luxury a bit boring and more than a bit lonely. That she missed her younger brother and sister so poignantly that she had finally risked writing

to Letty begging for news. But Letty had not answered. Carolina
had to console herself with the reminder that Letty was no hand to
write; Letty said so herself.

Of course love was everything. But it *would* be nice to have
somebody to talk to. (There she went, missing Floss again!)

Suddenly she returned to the present with a start. She must be
moving on. She had not found a place yet. This time as she inspected the small shabby houses, they looked different to her. You
had neighbors, she remembered, if you lived in a region like this.
Somebody to talk to while you hung up clothes or emptied wash
water around the shrubs in the yard. And best of all, you had things
to do.

Her healthy, seventeen-year-old body cried out for hard, demanding work. A way to spend herself. Ah, the scrubbing and painting
and whitewashing she would do for Roger. She glowed with good
resolves. She expanded with pent-up energy.

She neared the end of the short side street. Late summer was
kind to the shabbiness here, for narrow-leafed cottonwoods grew
thick near the river. Clematis wrapped their trunks in a thicket of
viny traceries. All winter long, the dried clematis would embroider
the rough trunks with gossamer tufts of white.

She saw few For Rent signs. Aspen was a busy place; and like all
boom towns, it overflowed with failures as well as successes. The
successes lived in Bullion Row; the failures, or the near failures,
sank like sediment down here on to the Flats. "The tailings of the
gulch," Carolina labeled them bluntly.

But for the accident of its inaccessibility, Aspen would have had
its silver boom at the same time as Leadville, in '78 and '79. People
knew that the silver was here, even then. But the fierce ramparts of
the Sawatch range held back development until the railroad came
in '87, bringing the boom with it.

Now Aspen was on the crest. Not that there would ever be a
trough to the wave of its prosperity. Hadn't she heard Roger explain often that the supply of silver here was as limitless as was the
demand? He talked just like the men on Capitol Hill in Leadville.
Aspen was one mining town that would never grow shabby and
full of ghosts, with grass in the streets and the houses and stores
boarded up or in ruins. He was very positive about it.

There was only one more building on this street. It was a typical
run-down rooming house; a tall gray shoebox with the gable end

fronting on the street and the length of it running back toward the railroad siding. Its front door opened, without the amenity of a stoop, directly on the board sidewalk. The upper story seemed to be served by a rickety outside stairway that went up to an open landing on the second-floor level.

She made a little face, thinking of its probable interior: the cracked crockery on the washstands and the wooden bedsteads teeming with vermin. She could not bring herself to go in and inquire. A person would have to be completely down on his luck to stay in a place like this.

The figure that she had been unnoticingly following turned and began to climb that outside stairway. She recognized the profile instantly and halted to avoid being seen. It was Canaday, obviously returning to his bedroom after a day downtown. With the air of old habit, he opened the door at the head of the staircase and went in.

So Canaday lived here! She turned and walked thoughtfully back to the hotel. She forgot all about her original errand, for she was faced with something she must think about first. Why Canaday, the successful trader in mining stocks, should be living down here on the Flats, along with the manual laborers, the failures, "the tailings of the gulch."

She longed for somebody to talk it over with. Somebody like Floss, who had had experience with the Canadays of the world, even though Hattie did not encourage custom from their sort. If she could only talk to Floss.

It never occurred to her to want to talk over a problem with her husband.

CHAPTER 10

CAROLINA WAS UNACCOUNTABLY TIRED BY THE TIME SHE REACHED the door of the hotel. She thought with acrid amusement that at least she would have one more bath in that opulent full-length tub before they were put out.

Maybe if she hurried, she could get past the clerk without his stopping her to ask about money. She glanced uneasily into the lobby before she entered. But she need not have worried. When she finally scuttled past the clerk's wooden-grille lair, he gave her a smile of such respect as can only be purchased with coin of the realm.

Wondering, she let herself into their room. Roger greeted her in high spirits. He was all over his mood. Also he had his watch back. She had never known him to find so many occasions for looking at it.

He had put over the deal with Canaday, he told her promptly. They could eat in the main dining room again (the frugal Continental breakfast had lost its charm); they could have champagne with every meal; they could go to see the Bostonians at the Opera House tonight. Best of all, they could pull out of this accursed place where everyone looked down on them.

Carolina sensed with unusual acuity that Roger had been wretched here, that their ostracism had been a constant raw wound to the thin skin of his pride. So love was not enough. It had been for her—well, almost enough. Poor Roger!

He kissed her with young ardor.

"Won't it be wonderful, Cara love, to shake the prissy dust of this damn town off our feet?" Such language in front of his wife was proof of his pent-up intensity. "We might go to Manitou for the rest of the season and drink the waters." She wondered what on earth he meant by that. "Or maybe try our luck in Central City or Gunnison, or go down to Boulder for the winter."

He was full of enthusiasm. She noted that he avoided suggesting his home town, Denver; just as he avoided any mention of her home town, Leadville.

During the lavish meal in the dining room that night she wore an air of reflective waiting. She realized that having money had stiffened Roger's backbone, and given a gloss to his smile, and quickened his whole spirit. It was like water poured on the roots of his wilted pride. She looked at him with fresh pity. So money was that important to Roger. She, who had seen how fast money could come and go—and mostly go—was maternally sorry to find him so vulnerable.

Back in their room, she begged off from further public proofs of their new affluence.

"I couldn't drag another foot, Roger. I—I took a long walk this

86

afternoon." She did not tell him where she had gone. It seemed a little silly now—her search for cheaper living quarters—in view of his present effulgence.

Roger was instantly solicitous. He took off her high, buttoned shoes with their tottery spool heels. He chafed her tired feet. He tucked a pillow behind her head and brought her a hassock.

She watched him with love in her eyes. It was sweet to be taken care of.

She wished he would talk to her about this deal with Canaday so she could find out more about the latter. Not that she could probably understand a word of it, she admitted humbly. Still, she did know something about people and she had a head for figures.

At first Roger made no move to discuss his affairs with her. After all, women were not made to understand business. But presently his elation overcame his manly reticence, and he took out a thin sheaf of stock certificates and spread them fan-wise before her . . . Such handsome green Spencerian engraving on the heaviest of parchment paper. Such impressive pictures of gods and goddesses and signs of the zodiac and a map of the heavens across the top.

"Oh, aren't they pretty, Roger! What are they?"

"Certificates."

"Certificates?" She had never handled one of these certificates before. The very word had an imposing sound. She had heard of marriage certificates and had often wondered why she did not have one. Shouldn't that queer old preacher have given her something to show she was married? Oh, well, she certainly was; so why worry?

"Stock certificates," explained Roger indulgently, as if he were speaking to a bright, but very young, child. "These represent, all told, five thousand shares of stock in a mine."

Carolina wrinkled her forehead.

"It means I'm part owner," he elaborated, "of the mine these stand for. I traded five hundred shares of Silverbell stock and got these five thousand in return."

Carolina looked respectful. They would get ahead fast, at this rate.

"How wonderful, Roger. But where did you get the Silverbell stock to trade? Wasn't that the name of the company here that was having the lawsuit?"

Roger did not seem to hear. He was doing sums on the back of an envelope.

"I thought that was the name of the company," Carolina persisted, "whose case you were working on before you got fired."

He reddened. She might have said, "Before you severed your connection——" but Cara was never one to soften a phrase to save a fellow's feelings.

"It was part payment for legal services," he admitted.

"To you?" Her expression was troubled.

"Well, the Silverbell certificate was made out to Roger Jardine," he said defiantly.

"But they meant your father, didn't they, Roger? It really belonged to him. Did you sign your name to it?"

Roger scowled; then he nodded.

"But isn't that what you'd call forgery, Roger? Wouldn't your father consider it stealing?"

Roger flinched. She had the crassest way of putting things.

"I don't care what he'd call it!" he said savagely. "I never had a fair deal. And this will set us up for life somewhere else. We can kiss this blamed town good-by. Make a fresh start where people don't know anything about you, darling. Where they'll look up to us, instead of treating us like dirt."

A quick pain shot through her. So it was on her account! Roger had suffered because of his marriage to her. All the while that she was being happy over getting away from her family, Roger was being miserable over being cut off from his. She had not fully comprehended before. She loved him the more fiercely, now that she had discovered the sacrifices he had made for her. She longed to prove her love by impossible feats of courage and self-abnegation. But she could only say admiringly:

"I think it was clever of you to get five thousand shares in place of five hundred. How did you do it?"

Roger looked mollified. Cara had never sounded so wifely.

"Well, Canaday happened to know they were reorganizing this Leadville company—he's got lots of influential friends—so he picked up the stock under the market. That is, if there were a market for it; it hasn't been active lately because the mine has been shut down to install new machinery. But the last time it was quoted it sold for almost two dollars a share. That means ten thousand dollars right here." He patted the certificates.

"You said Leadville. What was the name of the mine, Roger?"

"The Little Saturn. You must have heard of it," he said proudly.

Even Cara, heedless girl that she was, must have heard of the Little Saturn mine.

"Yes, I've heard of it."

"Well, then, I guess you know what a lot of millionaires it's made."

"It was the men who worked in it I heard about it from."

He frowned a little. He was always forgetting that she knew more about the overall-wearing world than the cotillion-dancing one.

"What did they say?"

"That the timbering was rotten in some of the tunnels. And that the company was stingy with the cribbing."

He tried to look patient with such irrelevancies.

"I knew four of the men who were killed in the cave-in last year," she added. "They all left families."

He shrugged. Naturally there were always miners getting killed in mines. Her remark only went to show that women had no head for business. Not a thought for the men who had been made rich overnight by the Little Saturn and enabled to go to Denver and build pink sandstone mansions.

"But suppose, Roger, it isn't worth two dollars a share now? Suppose Canaday was mistaken about it? Or was trying to cheat you?"

"That's impossible. Great fortunes have been made out of the Little Saturn; great fortunes will still be made out of it—that is, unless something has gone awfully wrong. Say, the water has come in—or the ore pinched out—— But the news would be sure to get around."

"It was the ore, Roger. It happened over a year ago. They lost the vein. It faulted, and they couldn't pick it up again. They tried and tried."

He sprang to his feet, his face whitening.

"How could you know? A girl like you."

"I grew up in Stringtown on the edge of Leadville; I heard the men talk. The mine owners made a big to-do about installing new machinery so as to have an excuse to shut down until they could unload on unsuspecting buyers. But the miners in east Leadville know the truth; the smelter workers in Stringtown know it, too, whether or not Harrison Avenue admits it. Except as a long gamble, the Little Saturn isn't worth a thing. I doubt if it ever will be either."

89

Roger sat down. His arms fell heavily across the green certificates. The gloss left his smile; the smile drained from his face.

Carolina longed to cradle his head in her arms. But she dared not. She knew that he did not want that kind of comfort now; he wanted balm for his pride.

"That Canaday! He ought to be horse-whipped. Let's go right out and find the sheriff and have him arrested."

"I can't. I owe Canaday five hundred dollars that I can't pay back now. Besides, I couldn't sick the sheriff on him when I—when I took the Silverbell stock that belonged to my father. Father would consider it stealing. There's nothing I can do."

"Oh, yes, there is! Get your hat, Roger. We're going to make Canaday give back that stock."

She was down on the floor scrambling for her shoes that had been pushed under the sofa; she was on her feet jabbing pins into her hair and straightening her bustle; she was slipping into the voluminous dolman with the inside pocket into which she thrust the glossy and beautiful and worthless shares of Little Saturn stock.

Automatically Roger obeyed. He did not even think to ask her how she knew where to go when they left the hotel and she turned northward toward the Flats.

She had forgotten how tired she was, that her feet hurt, and that her back ached in a funny, nagging way. They walked faster and faster. It must be nearly midnight, she surmised.

"I ought to have warned you harder about Canaday," she reproached herself. "That sleepy, shifty look of his. We'd better not waste any time, because he'll be on the first train out in the morning. That is, unless he smells trouble and sneaks out on a freight tonight."

"But suppose he's already sold the stock?" Roger was no longer a lordly twenty-six to Carolina's seventeen. He was meek and humbled and putty in her hands.

"Wait and see. If he has, we'll study what to do," said Carolina, the pragmatist.

"Now I know why he was so upset that night at the Firemen's bazaar when I happened to mention Leadville," she said ruminatively. "He was afraid I might have heard about the Little Saturn. He must have known away back then that you had the Silverbell certificate and he was planning to unload the Little

Saturn stock on you—baiting you along with that five-hundred-dollar loan. The cheap, fly-by-night crook!"

Roger had to walk faster and faster to keep up with her. His anger mounted along with hers. She had succeeded in infusing him with an iron of the spirit that was not normally his own.

They stumbled along over the uneven sidewalks in the dark. Most of the lights in the houses on the Flats were out now, but occasionally they heard sounds of revelry or voices raised in domestic strife. It was just like Stringtown, she thought absently.

They turned off on to a short side street. There it was, the last house on the right. Beyond lay the railroad siding, and beyond that, the rushing Roaring Fork. She could hear the uneasy stopping and starting of a freight engine somewhere, and underneath all the other noises, the ceaseless tumbling gurgle of the mountain stream.

"We better try the outside staircase." She pointed up to the second floor of the narrow building, where lights still burned.

"How'll we know which room he's in?" he asked.

"We won't go in. You call through the door and say somebody wants to see Canaday outside on business."

They both knew that there was nothing strange about such an anonymous message. Men like Canaday transacted their business in alleys and saloons and in the back rooms of gambling houses. Nor did either of them think it queer that it was Carolina who put the words into Roger's mouth.

"I'll attend to him!" declared Roger as he followed her up the stairs, which swayed flimsily under their tread.

At the top was a railed platform. In the darkness they snubbed their toes against the pile of stove wood stacked just beyond the door for use by the lodgers in their small sheet-iron stoves. They opened the door and looked down a short bare corridor that turned a bend just beyond.

Roger cleared his throat. His voice was a blend of casual, yet clandestine, insistence.

"Canaday here? Somebody to see Canaday on business outside."

There was silence, followed by a scraping of chairs on a bare wooden floor. Steps clumped along the hall, and Canaday rounded the bend in the corridor and came to the door. It was obvious that his eyes could not pierce the darkness outside.

"Back in a minute, boys," he called over his shoulder. "Maybe you better deal me out on the next hand though."

"Only take a few minutes of your time, if you'll just step outside," Roger said easily.

He was doing fine, Carolina thought.

Reassured, Canaday stepped out on to the platform. He was in his shirtsleeves. The chill night air must have struck him sharply.

"Who is it?" he asked quickly. "What can I do for you? Speak up."

"It's me, Jardine. I've just found out how you cheated me. Your Little Saturn stock isn't worth a damn. I won't stand for it!" Roger blustered, trying to maintain the role Carolina had assigned him.

"Your Little Saturn stock," Canaday corrected. "It was a fair and square trade."

"You lie! You knew all the time it was no good."

Carolina could sense the iron going out of Roger; she could feel him wishing he had never been fool enough to start this mad venture.

Canaday remained silent with the contemptuous silence of a man who knows he has the upper hand.

"I want that Silverbell stock back," asserted Roger, his voice rising. "It wasn't mine to begin with. It was my father's; we have the same name. I'll pay back that loan as soon as I can."

He was pleading, not ordering. Carolina longed to shake him, to bolster him up with some of her own strength and hardihood.

"You should have thought of all that sooner, my boy. How was I to know you were trading stock you didn't own? Stealing, some would call it." Canaday sounded pained. "Maybe this will be a lesson to you. But I'm sure your father won't do anything much—you an only son and all——"

It was surprising how well informed he was about Roger's affairs.

"Oh, yes, he will. You don't know my father."

Carolina could stand it no longer. She stepped out of the shadows at the end of the platform where she had been pressed against the pile of stove wood.

"You're a crook, Mr. Canaday. You knew all the while that the Little Saturn had played out."

Canaday concealed his shock at the sight of Carolina. The girl now; she was a different proposition. But he did not lose his unctuous calm. He had been in far tighter spots than this.

"So it's the little lady, eh? Well I'm mighty sorry to have to tell you it's too late. I've already—er, hypothecated the stock with my banker. I needed a little cash. If you want the stock back, you'll have to see him. I'll write his name down on a card for you——"

One hand was feeling for the door handle behind him. The other involuntarily touched his middle in a fleeting, corroborative gesture.

Carolina knew that gesture. She had seen it often. She thought: He lies. He hasn't been near a banker. His sort is its own banker. He's touching his money belt to see if it's safe.

The rage inside her mounted like a crackling forest fire. The sound in her ears was like the roaring of a forest fire. The slight rattle of the doorknob told her that he was outwitting them. In another second he would be inside the hall, with the door bolted behind him. He would be gone, taking with him all hope of her and Roger's ever having a decent future together.

She acted too fast for conscious thought. Her right hand groped behind her, and her fingers closed on a piece of pitch pine. She swung it and brought it down with savage emphasis upon the man's sparsely covered skull. It gave out a thick dull *clunk* against flesh and bone.

She heard a gasp, but the gasp was Roger's. Slowly the figure of Canaday began to buckle. Not all at once, but gradually. First the hand fell away from the knob; then the head wobbled; then the backbone caved; and finally the knees gave way. The whole slack body lurched sidewise and fell in a boneless way down the wooden steps. Only a few feet it slid, and lay there barring their descent down those rickety stairs.

For a moment the world was shockingly silent. Then Carolina began to hear distant, unrelated sounds. The interminable nervous switching of the freight engine below. The interminable senseless gurgling of water over rocks. The rasp of somebody's breathing— her own breathing. The sound of somebody's hoarse swearing— Roger's swearing. But no sounds came from that body lying crosswise on the steps . . . no sounds at all.

Suddenly they heard footsteps in the hall behind them. They shrank back out of sight beside the stacked stove wood.

The door opened, and a rumpled male head was outlined against the lamplight.

"Hey, Canaday, ain't you coming back? I thought I heard a noise. What's keeping you?" The owner of the head peered sightlessly out into the night.

No one answered him. The man grunted uncertainly. Then he pulled his head in and shut the door. Through the warped cracks they could hear him explaining to the others.

"Guess he's gone off. Musta been the ore rattling out of the loading chute—might as well go on with the game."

Roger's hand was icily damp as he clutched at Carolina.

"Let's get out of here—before somebody starts up these steps and finds him."

But Carolina had suddenly become as cold and calculating as Hattie Merkle. Run away now, without getting the stock back? Never.

She felt her way down ahead of Roger and bent over the body. Roger tried feverishly to get past that huddled human heap; he tried to pull her with him. But she stubbornly blocked his way as she undid the man's shirt and reached inside.

Just as she expected, a money belt encompassed his fat middle. She felt a crackling paper—the Silverbell certificate, she was sure. She extracted it with a jerk. From the pocket of her dolman she took the worthless Little Saturn certificates and shoved them back between the man's money belt and his body. As if she had been trained by a mining camp Fagin, she remembered to button his shirt before she stood up.

Roger was almost sobbing as he implored her to hurry. But she was deaf. She knew with stern certainty that they dared not stop yet. For as soon as Canaday came to, he would rush to a Justice, get a warrant, and have Roger thrown into jail. She knew all about it; wasn't somebody always having her father thrown into jail? What matter if Jude Lawler's intentions were good? What matter if Roger had been cheated? At the threat of jail, Roger would give up the Silverbell stock, and that would undo everything. She must have time to get the Silverbell certificate in the mail and on its way to Roger's father. There was only one thing to do now.

"You lift his shoulders—they're the heaviest," she commanded. "I'll take his feet. It's only a few steps to the freight."

"Suppose he's dead?"

94

Carolina did not answer. She had seen men hit a lot harder than this come to in a couple of hours. She picked up Canaday's feet, holding them like carriage thills on either side of her. She waited for Roger to raise the stocky shoulders. Roger grunted as he lifted the heavy weight. The man did not stir. Slowly, step by step, they descended the rickety staircase. She said nothing until they reached the ground.

"There's a loading platform over there in front of that warehouse." She gestured with her head in the darkness.

She led the way, still holding the booted feet. The body sagged in an arc, dragging at times. Roger panted and strained under the greater load. Cinders crunched under their feet, but the sound was blotted out in the larger noise of ore rattling out of a bin and down a chute into a waiting car on the siding.

A brakeman sang out in the darkness, "Only one more to load now, Jim."

The train moved forward a car length.

"The nearest car—by the platform, Roger," she whispered.

Roger rebelled briefly. Generations of law-abiding, civilized ancestors rose up inside him to protest.

"But suppose he isn't dead? Suppose he's hurt and needs a doctor?"

Carolina was oblivious to such distinctions. Her tone was like a shrug.

"He's a thief—and he made you a thief too."

Roger made a last desperate stubborn stand. He halted, and the heavy body sagged on the ground. Carolina tried to move the body alone, but she was balked unless he helped her.

"I can't do it!" he whispered.

"You've got to. If he comes to, he'll have you arrested. It'll be in the papers. Your father——"

At the word, Roger gave in. He was bested. Like a person succumbing to his own private daemon, he obeyed her. They panted slowly up the slight incline toward the wooden loading platform in front of the low black warehouse. Now they were on a level with the loaded cars of ore. Only one more to fill, the brakeman had said. In a minute the whole train would be moving.

With a swing and a labored heave, they hoisted the pursy body over the side of the car. There the body slid a little on the loose ore and finally, with a grisly snuggle, settled itself into the depres-

95

sion between the hump of ore and the side of the freight car. There was little likelihood that the man would be discovered before morning.

The rattle of ore suddenly ceased. They stood stockstill in the silence, flattening themselves against the warehouse.

"That's all," another voice shouted. "Let's roll."

A lantern gave the highball signal; the engine tooted and puffed purposefully; the train slid slowly past the frozen pair and felt its way out on to the main line. The switch was closed; the lantern waved again, and the train was gone.

The enormity of their act now rushed over Roger. He tried to pull Carolina into a run. When she refused to be hurried, he tried to break away from her. But she held on tight to his arm. Now was no time to lose their heads. They must walk, not scurry from this place. With all her strength and will she held him back to an ordinary homeward-bound pace. At last they were on the side-walk heading toward the hotel.

"We'll send the certificate to your father first thing in the morning, Roger," she said evenly, as if that made everything they had done this night defensible and right.

By the time they reached the haven of their own room, Roger was at the end of his endurance. He sat—buckled rather—on a chair and ran a finger around his sweat-soaked collar. His eyes stared wildly. His clothes looked inches too big for him. There was a smudge of dirt across his face, dirt from a loaded ore car.

A sickening revulsion swept over him. He could not bear to look at Carolina and he could not keep his eyes off her. When the distant *whoo* of a whistle sounded as a freight train snaked its way out of the valley, he shuddered. But Carolina only walked calmly over and pulled down the window shade as if to shut the sound out of the room and out of their lives.

Paralyzed, he continued to sit there and stare at her in fascinated horror. Why, she was undressing as if nothing at all had happened. She was smoothing out her dolman and unfastening her brooch and unbuttoning her basque as if they had just returned from an evening at the village singing circle. She was a frightening woman—a formidable woman. He had never felt so alien to her.

CHAPTER 11

ROGER WALLING JARDINE II SAT A LONG TIME BEFORE HIS DESK IN his glossy mahogany law office on Seventeenth Street in Denver, staring down at the contents of the sealing-wax spotted envelope from his son . . . Who would have thought the boy had it in him!

He blew his nose and stared out the window at the impossibly beautiful range of mountains to the west. He had been proved wrong. The lad was sound, after all. Not that he had ever put it into words, either to himself or to young Roger, but he had never entertained too high an opinion of his only son's probity, his stamina, his—well, guts.

His own father, the first Roger Walling Jardine, had been a rabidly upright man, eking out a living on a Vermont hillside. He himself had been a shrewdly lucky man, riding into Denver on the crest of the wave of settlers in the Sixties as attorney for a big mining company. But young Roger had never seemed either strong and honest like his grandfather, or strong and unscrupulous like himself. Roger was, he had feared in his secret solemn bitter moments, merely slimsy—gentlemanly, but slimsy.

He got up and paced the length of Persian rug, his hawk's face soft for a moment. Then he clapped his hand over his middle with a habitual gesture of distress and stopped his nervous pacing long enough to measure himself a dose of baking soda. This dyspepsia was kicking up more trouble every day. Whenever he had a difficult case to try, whenever he was upset by anything, it gave him the very devil. He needed his son here beside him—that's what he needed. And by God, he was going to have him!

For the first time in his life he was unreservedly proud of his son. He wanted him here beside him in the law office, with "Jardine and Jardine" painted on the door. He wanted to ask his son's advice; he wanted to put his arm across the boy's shoulders.

His heart swelled. Sending along that stock certificate when he didn't have to! When he could so easily have argued that he had a right to it, that his father had been grossly unfair to him, that the very least his father owed him was the chance to make a fresh start in some place where his wife's past was not known. (As if a woman of that sort could ever make a fresh start.) He supposed Roger had felt in honor bound to marry the scheming jade— against his will, of course. The poor young idiot probably didn't even know that money would have suited her better.

Well, he'd get rid of her. There were always ways. Marriages in those western counties were often pretty sketchy affairs—not even a license required. He would look into the legal end right away . . .

II

THE MONEY FROM CANADAY DID NOT LAST LONG—ABOUT AS LONG as did the bowing obsequiousness of the hotel clerk. This time Roger showed no proud male reticence about confessing to Carolina the true state of their affairs. Something had gone out of him that night on the Flats. He was beaten, and they both knew it. He guessed dully that he was no stock trader after all. And probably not much of a lawyer. Anyhow, what chance had he to build up a law practice in a town where he had just been fired by his father? He did not go on to say: and where he had married a girl from Stelle Bogart's house. Once more they were headed toward starvation; the sordid kind this time, not the polite kind.

Carolina was alarmed at having the whole responsibility for their affairs suddenly thrown on her shoulders. Earning a living, in her world, was not a pleasant pursuit that could be carried on wearing polished pointed shoes and a cane and a neat sack suit. It was a grim business which required one to crawl out in the dark and carry a lunch bucket and work all day and come home after dark. It was a matter of horny calluses and split, blackened fingernails and candle-grease spots and grime that settled in the tired creases of a man's face.

She raked her memory for "gentlemen's jobs." Except for professional gambling, she did not know any. Then she remembered that the weigh man at the smelter did not have it quite so hard. He was a cut above the common laborers because he had to have a head for figures. Timidly she suggested it to Roger. He applied at the smelter, and that night he told her with a shrug that he had got the job.

"I suppose they also serve who only stand and weigh-it," he said, his pale smile deprecating his bad pun.

Carolina bent her energies in earnest this time to finding a cheap place to live. At first she suggested the south edge of town. But that would bring them close to the Row, where Floss lived, and Roger frowned it down.

There was nothing to be had in the east end. So it left only the Flats. The best she could find was a shack consisting of three poorly furnished rooms less than a block from Canaday's old lodging house and the gurgling river and the nervous, interminable switching of engines.

She was sorry for Roger that he twitched and turned so much in his sleep, after they were settled in the new house. She tried to make it up to him with extra orgies of endeavor: of clothes-washing and scouring and scrubbing.

But even though she had to admit that Roger was less than happy these days, her own happiness welled up within her. She could not down it if she would. For there was so much to do. She was busy all day long and beautifully tired by night. She remembered Leo's saying once, his eyes crinkled up with amusement: "Carolina's fine, so long as she's busy as a moth in a wool sock. But just let that girl be idle——"

Everything had a special zest for her. Hanging out clothes was a delight in the bright sharpness of early fall. The sun had less heat and more brilliance now. The sky was a deeper indigo blue.

"I will lift up mine eyes unto the hills," she thought often with exultation, watching the butter-yellow of the frosted aspens creep down the slopes as the season advanced, watching the first light snow vein the mountain sides, watching the full-bodied gold attack the lower cottonwoods along the river.

She was ready for the cold. Waking up in the mornings now was like waking up in Stringtown, without any of the unpleasantness. The same delicious, drowsy black warmth in bed; the same forbidding black cold when one got up. But it was exhilarating too. For there was the fire to kindle hurriedly, standing in one's bare feet on the cold splintery floor. And as the weeks went by, there was ice to break in the pail that had been filled at the pump the night before. There was coffee to boil and the limp slab of bacon to slice and fry, accompanied by wavy strata of blue smoke above the stove. And then there was Roger's lunch bucket to pack.

It had been such a shiny, undented lunch bucket at first that Carolina had surreptitiously given it some nicks and scuffs. She knew that a man was unconsciously evaluated here, as in String-town, by the hard-serviced look of his lunch pail.

Her neighbor on the south, Mrs. Hubbell, taught her how to make that staple delicacy of the mining camp, a Cornish meat pasty, for Roger's lunch. Carolina found that she had a knack for cooking. Mrs. Slye, on the north, showed her how to piece quilts. She began an intricate design, unsuitably called "Old Man's Troubles," and had gone no farther than the first block before she discovered that she hated to sew. But both neighbors conceded that young Miz Jardine needed no instructions on how to wash clothes; she was a fine hand, they said, with washtub and flatiron.

If only Roger could have been happy here. For now she had neighbors and gossip and a community life to share, as she had not had them back in her luxury days at the hotel.

To her amazement, both the priest and the preacher called on her and invited her to come to church and—respectively—to a raffle and a sociable. This would never have happened at the hotel, she was sure. Both clerics seemed fully aware that she had once lived in Stelle Bogart's house, but apparently they felt it was easier to retrieve a soul that was scouring her front steps with wood ashes than one that was lolling in the best suite at the Jerome. The distance between kneeling to scrub and kneeling to pray seemed much shorter than the distance between Parlor A and a front pew.

But Carolina remained cold to all kinds of religious blandish-ment. She bristled at any recital of the worn old phrases: The Blood of the Lamb—Saved by Grace—Confess Your Sins—— She was reminded too painfully of a weaving circle of bums and Letty's nasal alto and her father's angry thundering.

But when she jeeringly told Roger about the calls, he did not laugh. Instead, he looked pleased. He might casually break half the commandments himself, but he approved of the cloth and he desired the approval of the cloth. He suggested diffidently that they go to church some Sunday. Oh, not to the humble church of either the priest or the minister, but to the fashionable one with the towers and the flying buttresses.

"We might even make a little donation, Cara. There's no quicker way to become accepted in a town," he said reasonably.

Carolina recoiled. She hated religion and everything connected with it. Hadn't she had a bellyful from the day she was born? Yet there was something distasteful about using the church to push oneself ahead.

"But wouldn't that be like blowing trumpets when thou doest alms, Roger? Or like the hypocrites that pray, standing in the synagogues where they may be seen of men?"

Roger stared at her as if she had suddenly begun to talk a foreign language—which indeed she had, as far as he was concerned.

Everything about the mean, neat little house was as pleasantly cheerful as she had hoped it would be—except Roger. He had lost the last shreds of the lordly, debonair personality that had won her. He was a daunted man, hagridden by his own thoughts. She did not know how to comfort him because she could not read those thoughts.

Winter tightened its grip on the flimsy little shack until keeping warm became a serious occupation. Carolina banked dirt up around the foundations, chinked rags in the cracks, repapered the kitchen with old newspapers, and got up each night to replenish the fire. But she liked it; she felt she was pitting her strength and sagacity against her old enemy, winter.

To Roger there was no challenge in the weather. He caught a cold which left him with a deep, raucous cough. The smelter fumes kept it aggravated. He grew thinner and wispier and more withdrawn. Each evening when he came in, with his old-man stoop and his face gray under the smelter smudge, Carolina would think with baffled and irritated concern: But the job isn't that hard, Roger—being weigh man is supposed to be easy work— now if you were swinging a hammer, drilling rock all day——

Nevertheless she would rush to bring him hot water to wash in before she dished up the beans and salt pork and boiled cabbage. Then she would frown because he was finicky and picked at his food. Each day she grew more confused and resentful; and Carolina did not resent in silence.

She knew only two ways to cope with this tired, remote, yet elusive, being. One was with tirades, and the other was with sex. As her frustration mounted, she made the mistake of resorting more often to tirades than to sex.

Roger would shrink from her when she raised her voice, or banged stove lids down with a furious clatter, or ended a quarrel with a peculiarly horrifying gesture of clenched, upraised fist. He would glance over his shoulder toward the neighbors' with a shamed look. He need not have worried. The neighbors considered such sounds the normal accompaniment of married life. But Roger never became accustomed to them.

The gulf between them widened appallingly on the day that he came home unexpectedly to find her calmly reading one of his letters. Or if not calmly, at least rightfully; for she was incensed.

The letter was written in the ornate feminine hand. What was worse, it indicated that it was one of a series.

Dear Roger: Aren't you ever coming back? I can't get a word out of your mother and father about your plans. But as I warned you in my last letter, you'd better or you'll be entirely out of the swim. Denver is becoming quite cosmopolitan, my dear. [The appellation made Carolina's eyes flash.] You should see our new electric trolley cars. Not horse cars or cable cars, but trolley cars! It is considered quite au fait for whole parties to ride out to the end of the line, singing and chaffing each other. Oh, yes, and they're building a lovely pink sandstone hotel on Mr. Brown's plot on Broadway. It will quite put the Windsor in the shade. Remember the ball where you and I eluded the chaperones? Also, they're planning a lot of parties around the cornerstone-laying for the new capitol up on the bluffs.
I have a new frock I'm dying for you to see, Roger, but I won't describe it. I'll wear it for you instead when you come back. You'd better make it soon, Roger, as I caught the bride's bouquet at Polly Isham's wedding the other night.

Carolina could see neither sense nor sequence to that last sentence, yet she was aware that it held some special significance for Roger; just as she was aware of something inimical in it to herself. The letter brought home to her how large a part of Roger's life she had played no part in, and how well another girl, who signed herself "Always yours, Sue," knew the carefree young Roger whom she would never know.

Roger stood in the doorway and stared at her and the letter in her hand. He had every prejudice of his class.

"You're reading my letter!" he accused her. He expected excuses; he was hopeful of excuses.

Carolina brushed the reproof aside. She brandished the letter. Her coppery hair was disheveled; her cheeks were blotchy with anger.

"And who is this 'Always yours, Sue,' I'd like to know? Writing to a married man about a lot of lahdedah parties down in Denver and begging him to come back. I'll bet you've never told her you have a wife up here."

Roger's glance wavered. This was carrying the war into his own camp. For of course he had not told her—that was the reason why he had not written to her at all—and apparently his parents had not told her either. He tried to renew his original attack.

"But you were reading my letter, Cara."

Cara ignored the reproof. In fact, she did not even recognize it as such. There had been no fetishes about privacy or about reading each other's letters in the Lawler household, where there had been neither privacy nor letters.

"She wrote to you—and you're my husband—we're one flesh," she remarked austerely.

He stared. No one had ever used such expressions in his presence before. He had no answer.

Carolina did not like silence for a reply. She began to think of her wrongs, of Sue in Denver who called Roger "my dear," and wrote him romantic, reminding letters. She knew a consuming rage of jealousy which she took to be righteous indignation. She was winding up inside, like a coiled spring, for a fine furious letting-go, full of how-dare-yous and I-won't-stand-for-its, when he looked at her, his nostrils pinching in, and turned on his heel and walked out . . . Before supper too—with a nice mess of boiled turnips and potatoes on the stove—and in the dead of winter . . .

Deflated, sore of heart, she dished up food and defiantly sat down to eat at the bare, scrubbed table. But for once, the food stuck in her throat. She stared at the crackling cookstove with the fire flicking in the cracks and the teakettle that rocked and droned until it burst into a comforting boil. But she could not be comforted.

At last she gave up the dreary pretense and put her head down on her arms and wept. She was seventeen, and she needed someone—a woman—to tell her how to hold her man. Floss could have set her right in a minute, although Carolina did not know that. All she knew was that she was terrified and lonely, and that Roger had forbidden her to see Floss, who had come to mean mother, sister, and confidante to her.

It was long past midnight when Roger came home. The smell of liquor preceded him into the bedroom. But Carolina, who had been tossing for hours, rolled over apathetically and decided she

103

was too tired to quarrel. That, for Carolina, was very tired indeed.

However, she was ready to forgive long before Roger was. He held her off moodily for days. It was humiliating, but she loved him too much to nurse any pride. Finally, youth and propinquity and her rich violent beauty won the argument, and once more they were close together again in the unique and powerful closeness of passion. The ugly little frame house with the cold floors and the rattling windows and the straw-filled mattress was blotted out by the mystery and beauty of their oneness.

Carolina went about her work humming happily after that; nor even knew that the tune she hummed was one of Letty's called "The Cry of Lost Souls."

She did not discontinue reading Roger's mail, which was scanty; but she humored his peculiarities to the extent of not letting him catch her at it. Fortunately Sue did not write soon again.

III

Now the town was bestirring itself, was tensing in preparation for the coming New Year's Day street celebration. Such goings-on, the neighbors promised. Snowshoe races, rock-drilling contests—both single-jack and double-jack—and last of all, a tug of war between the crews of the two largest mines. Bets were already being placed.

Carolina, who had seen snowshoe races and rock-drilling contests all her life, nevertheless was on tiptoe. Her whole being was famished for gaiety; she had been on short rations ever since they had moved into this squalid little house. She brushed her best dress, a rich bottle-green lutestring with matching bonnet, which had been among the last things she had purchased before they left the hotel. She aired the sealskin cape that seemed to mean so much to Roger, if not to her. She mended her tighter-than-skin kid gloves. She was in a holiday mood.

Christmas came and went. She could talk of nothing but the coming celebration. Roger was bored at first; then condescending; and finally grudgingly acquiescent to the idea of going. She shut her ears to his remarks about hoi polloi and bourgeoisie. She did not want to hear; for whenever he used that tone, it meant that he was trying to spoil her fun. This time she would not let him.

New Year's Day was coldly brilliant. As they walked toward the roped-off intersection in the middle of the town, the snow squeaked underfoot and Carolina's cheeks were whipped scarlet. Her blood raced, and her feet skipped lightly to the tunes of Cornish bands, called "Cousin Jack" bands, that played on the street corners. Crowds were gathering; the horses' breaths were like white smoke; there was the rattle of harness, the creak of wheels, and the squeal of cutter runners on the snow.

All around the town, the steep white mountains, etched with their dark evergreen spires, rose like the sides of a cup. Carolina sniffed the cold rapturously and felt a singing in her blood. Why, she actually knew people to speak to, people who nodded and smiled back. What if they were all from the Flats? They were merry, and she was having fun. This was what she had hoped to find when she ran away from home, and when she married handsome, easy-smiling Roger Jardine.

She tried not to glance up at the morose man beside her, but to concentrate her attention on the contests in the open square. First, the single-jack drilling contest, where one man competed against another to see who could bore the fastest into a block of granite. She admired the dexterity with which each man held his own hand drill with one hand while he pounded it with a single-jack hammer held in the other.

She liked the double-jack contest even better; for here two men were pitted against two men. This time one held the twisting drill while his partner hit it with a double-jack hammer. Granite mud splattered. Faster and faster the metal drill ate into the hard rock with a steady boring motion. When she recognized one of the men as her neighbor Mr. Hubbell, she promptly aligned herself with his side and jumped up and down, yelling lustily for him.

Roger caught her by the arm in a shocked way and dragged her back to the present with a sharp injunction to remember herself.

Carolina sighed. That was just the trouble. It had been fun to forget.

During the races she was caught up in the excitement and she shouted again. Then she "remembered herself," and glanced up contritely at Roger, who was looking annoyed. Being a lady was not a particularly entertaining occupation, she decided. She wondered why women worked so hard at it.

At last the tug of war was announced. Most of the men in the two mine crews were brawny Welshmen or Cornishmen, serious, deeply musical, upright—albeit sometimes hard-drinking men—

but men! They felt a fanatical loyalty to their own mines in a contest like this, so that the tug of war became a fiercely primitive struggle. Feeling ran high, as did the bets. The two crews lined up facing each other. There was jockeying for position along the writhing python of rope.

All around the edges of the enclosure craning people moved restlessly. Carriages seesawed back and forth, the horses fractious and wild of eye.

Carolina recognized the leading Madams of the town, out with their girls. A celebration always offered a splendid chance to show off the latter. She saw Lil Jackson and Juliet Herman and Roxy Riordan. Then she saw Stelle Bogart's carriage with four girls in it. Her heart gave a leap of affection as she recognized Floss, looking statuesque and smiling and exceedingly well-dressed. Carolina wanted to wave, but the pressure of Roger's hand on her arm reminded her that she must not.

It was almost time for the starting gun. The men in the tug of war were bowed over the rope, their great muscles flexing, like so many handsome Percherons readying for a haul. The whole crowd held its breath, watching the starter who held his gun high above his head.

Carolina clenched her hands together under her cape. She would not be able to stand it much longer. She would strangle or scream if that gun did not go off.

And then the gun went off—letting loose a wild commotion behind her. Women shrieked. She whirled to see a team of horses reared tall on its hind legs. She heard the snap and splinter of a carriage tongue as the frightened animals twisted and came down. In their frenzy, they bolted for the only opening in sight, a side street. She saw the carriage tip crazily and go over amidst more screams and more shouts.

The animals pulled the scraping, bumping burden of overturned carriage until they were brought to a panting stop, wrapped around one of the new electric light poles. Along the snowy road behind them were strewn several bundles of clothing. The bundles were women, dressed in furbelows and finery, who had been thrown from Stelle Bogart's carriage.

She opened her mouth to scream, but no sounds came. Floss had been in that carriage! She shook off Roger's hand and picked up her long, heavy, interlined skirts and ran—not as a lady runs with gathers held primly in one hand, but like a child who impatiently grabs up its pinafore in both hands. Floss. Oh, don't let anything happen to Floss.

Carolina was a tall girl, strong and well-built. She elbowed people out of her way. With unfeeling haste she stopped to bend over each occupant of the carriage where she had been tumbled out, only to straighten up a moment later and run on to the next as soon as she found that it was only Stelle or Trixie or Doll, sitting up in the snow and swearing as she rubbed her bruises. Where was Floss?

As she reached the overturned carriage, several men were cautiously raising it from the ground. So Floss was under it. She had not been thrown clear, like the others, but had been dragged all that distance. Carolina knew a wave of anguish sharper than anything she had ever experienced.

She knelt beside Floss and chafed her hands.

"Here comes the doc," offered someone respectfully, as Dr. Walgren hurried up, his round fat stomach bobbing in time with his round black leather bag. He dropped to his knees beside Carolina and began to examine the injured girl.

"Keep her flat—ease her over on to a blanket or a coat. Couple of you men carry her across to my office yonder. The other three women aren't hurt to speak of."

There was a moment of vacuity when no one seemed to know quite what to do. Then Carolina stripped off her wide, warm fur cape and thrust it at the doctor.

"Here—use this. I'll come with you."

He glanced across at her quizzically, kneeling down in her bottle-green dress in the snow beside the town's handsomest prostitute, apparently oblivious to both the chilling cold and the gaping multitude. But the tail of his own eye took in that multitude. Not a single soul in it actively wished Floss ill; yet there was something fitting, and at the same time toothsome and stimulating, about an accident happening to a fancy woman.

"Come along then," he said, scrambling to his feet and leading the way to his office.

People made a path for them: the fat little doctor, the two men carefully carrying their burden, and the tawny-haired girl in the green dress with the distraught eyes.

Roger reached her side at last. He had braved even his own

107

hatred of being "conspicuous" long enough to cross that open space and clutch his wife by the arm.

"Cara! You must have lost your mind. A woman from the Row——"

"But it's Floss; she's my friend."

"But you're my wife. And that's the fur cape I gave you. Have you forgotten?" He tried to pierce the terrible fixity of her purpose.

But her eyes were glazed and absent. Once before, he had attempted to cope with this single-mindedness of hers, with this utter inability to see anything but the goal ahead. And once again he failed.

She shook his hand off and hurried to catch up with the procession.

Roger slunk back into the crowd, affronted to his very soul. From the spectators around him he heard murmurs of sympathy or reproach or simple relish. He turned and fled for sanctuary to the saloon appropriately named the Abbey.

In the doctor's office, Carolina sat beside Floss, who lay on the couch, her head pillowed on the fur cape. While the doctor was getting splints and hot water and bandages, Carolina held Floss's hand. But the hand was icily cold, and Floss's face was bluish-white. The only color about her now was the red of the blood that oozed slowly down from a wound under her ash-brown hair and clotted on the soft fur of the cape. Her right leg was twisted queerly under her.

With an aching desire to do something, Carolina gently unpinned the plumed hat. When Floss opened her eyes, the two girls looked at each other, a long look of clarity and understanding. Carolina thought that Floss was dying, and Floss thought so too.

"You mustn't let go, Floss. You're the only friend I've got in the world."

"And you—you cared enough to worry—about what would become of me," Floss whispered. "But what about Roger—he won't like this——" Was that a ghost of a grin? Or a grimace of pain? Injured, nearly unconscious, Floss still understood Roger's reactions as Carolina never would. Floss's eyes fluttered shut.

Carolina was sure that Floss was dead. She dropped to her knees beside the ravaged girl and put her head down and wept. Painfully and tearingly and from deep inside her, she wept for her only friend.

The little doctor waddled back just then, tut-tutting and pooh-poohing.

"She's a long way from dead, my girl," he informed Carolina kindly. "Lost a bit of blood, and that's made her faint. But I'm examiner for the Row, and this one's got the physique of a peasant. Soon as I get that scalp wound sewed up and her leg set, she'll start to mend. Might even be back at work in a month, if the leg knits all right. You better get along home yourself."

She looked up at him dully.

"No need at all for you to stay here," he assured her, helping her to her feet. "My wife can lend a hand. You put on your cloak and run along before it gets dark."

For answer she pointed to the blood-soaked cape beneath Floss's head.

He gave a whistle of understanding. "You did that for her, eh? Well, take my mackintosh off the hook. You'll get your cape back from her later."

She swayed dizzily, putting out a hand to steady herself. Funny; she'd never been one to grow faint at the sight of a little blood. The doctor was beside her, giving her a long, kindly, scrutinizing look. He held out his mackintosh for her. Then he took her by the arm and helped her down the steps outside.

"If I didn't have work to do here, I'd drive you home myself. Now watch out, and don't slip on the ice, and be sure to take some good deep breaths to get over the fainty feeling, and lie down when you get home. And send your husband for me in the morning if you aren't feeling all right." He was insistent.

She nodded, with a puzzled feeling.

It was on the way home that she knew. So that was it! Since the beginning of her womanhood, her body had been fitful and erratic in its rhythms. She had not given it due thought lately—after those first months of watching and hoping. But the doctor knew. Just by looking at her, he knew. She must hurry home to tell Roger. She hoped Roger would be pleased.

But she could not tell him when she reached home, because he was not there. He did not come home that night, nor all the next day, nor the following night.

It was morning of the second day when two neighbors helped him home. He was reeling and coughing, and it took two men to support him. She saw that he was not drunk now; he was merely ill. One whole side of his coat was marbled and crusted with old snow where he had lain in it.

All that the neighbors could tell her was that they had found him lying by the side of the road, half under the high wooden sidewalk where he must have fallen off. They had recognized him and brought him home.

Even then she could not tell him about her wonderful news, because for many days he was too ill to listen. Later, when he was over the worst, she could not tell him because it meant new responsibilities and expenses, and just then he was too depressed over losing his job at the smelter to face any added burdens. He lay there, face to the wall, muttering that he wished he were dead. How would they ever manage now? What was the use of going on?

He grew thinner and gaunter. The stubble shadowing his cheeks was darker than his hair, and it made him look strangely old and wasted.

And so she delayed telling him, until something happened that made it impossible for her to tell him.

C H A P T E R   12

CAROLINA STOOD IN FRONT OF THE JEWELER'S WINDOW AND STARED at the gauds laid out to ravish the pockets of a booming silver camp.

Under her fur cape, her fingers gripped the flat leather jewel case. She was still childishly ignorant of the cost of things, once she left the familiar world of sacks of flour and lengths of calico and bottles of liniment. Fur capes and topaz necklaces were far removed from even her realms of speculation. She had been astounded, for instance, after the driver from Stelle Bogart's house had returned her fur cape, to have Roger mutter something about that being a fine way to treat a cape that had cost more than he earned in three months, nowadays.

She had been appalled. All that, just for a fur cape to keep one warm! But even had she known, she could not have done differently; for Floss had needed it. And the bloody places hardly showed since it had been cleaned; the fur was only a little bit matted here and there. But Roger could not bear the sight of the cape now. It was as if it represented something distasteful to him.

She had no way of knowing that that was exactly what it did represent: his defeat in a battle of wills in which his wife had pitted her strange and violent temper against his strongest wishes and instincts and had come off victor. There was double humiliation for him in the fact that Cara did not even seem to realize that there had been a battle of wills.

She wondered again how much she could get for the topaz necklace. Maybe the jeweler would not buy it at all. She was timid about going inside to ask. Store clerks could always daunt her by their superior knowledge of things.

Even as she was planning to sell the necklace, she was dreading the time when Roger would find it out. He grew edgy over the simplest things, such as lending a fur cape to a friend in need. She did not know how he would take it when he learned about her selling the topazes. Yet if you were hungry, you sold anything you could lay your hands on. It was as simple as that, whether you were in Stringtown or here on the Flats. And they were hungry now. At least she was, and in a day or so, Roger would be too.

She had scraped the bottom of the larder and borrowed all she decently could from her neighbors and held in check her own ravenous appetite in order that Roger might have food. But that was a process which could not go on indefinitely. Now the food was gone, and Roger still lay in bed most of the time with his face to the wall, while Carolina worried.

When she had tremblingly asked Dr. Walgren, outside the front door one day, how Roger really was, the doctor had assured her that Roger did not actually have the consumption yet, but that he was terribly run down and beat out. His heart was tired too. He needed a lower altitude for a while and freedom from worry.

Carolina's brows had drawn together. In her world no one was ever quite free from worry. She wondered how you achieved it.

"Why don't you write his folks in Denver and ask them to help?" he had suggested, as if he were answering her unspoken question.

Carolina had retreated quickly.

"Oh, no. We couldn't do that. We'll work things out for ourselves." She was remembering how harshly Roger's father had cut him off and how stealthily his mother wrote to him.

The doctor had pondered her words for a moment, his eyes on her waistline. She could feel her color rising. Was she beginning to show so plainly? Strange that Roger had never noticed.

"Well, how about your folks then?" the doctor went on kindly but persistently. "You must have some family somewhere. If you don't like to tell them yourself, I will. I'll explain about your husband's health and your own—prospects."

Her hand had tightened convulsively on the icy doorknob behind her.

"No," she said harshly. "I'll never let him know—I mean, I haven't any family."

"You'll have to be doing something," he said drily then. "This don't look like a situation that's going to cure itself."

She stared now at the trinkets in the window. Fifty dollars for the necklace? Sixty? It had to be enough to send Roger down to a lower altitude for a while. She remembered Manitou where you went to "drink the waters." But suppose the jeweler was not interested in a topaz necklace today? A coldness clamped around her stomach. Roger must have that stay in Manitou . . .

"And which pretty gimcrack does she want to buy today?" inquired a sprightly male voice at her elbow.

Startled, she turned to find herself looking down at Henry Gilson. He stared boldly back up at her with the same unabashed, knowing, chipmunk look he had worn in the restaurant almost a year ago when Floss had pretended to dicker with him about Carolina's future.

Carolina had seen him only a few times since, but his eyes had always been admiring, as the eyes of swaggering, ambitious little men often are admiring of big goddess-like women, as if the latter offered an irresistible challenge to their fierce bantam potency.

"I don't want to buy any of them," she said, humoring him. "I want to sell something."

"Can I help you?"

She looked at him consideringly. Maybe he could tell her what the necklace was worth. She drew the jewel case out from under her cape.

"I was wondering how much I could get for this." She pressed

112

the snap, and the cover flew back, revealing the necklace resting on the white plush.

"H'm, very pretty with your coloring——" He tilted his head back, comparing the topazes with her eyes and hair.

"That's what Roger—my husband—said when he gave them to me."

"Why do you want to sell them?"

"I have to. He's had lung fever, you see. He's been dreadfully sick——"

Mr. Gilson looked extremely unperturbed by the state of Roger's health. In fact, he looked as if he were about to saunter on.

Carolina detained him with her pleading eyes.

"Can you give me any notion of what they're worth, Mr. Gilson? Could I get enough to send Roger down to a lower altitude—to, say Manitou—till the weather warms up?"

He seemed to change his mind quite suddenly about going on.

"Excellent plan. I understand there's nothing better after an attack of lung fever than a stay in a more salubrious climate. As to selling your necklace, I've got an idea." He stopped and tugged at the neat bristles of his mustache. "My wife and I will be celebrating an anniversary soon. I'd been wondering what to get her."

Carolina looked relieved. Then she remembered something.

"But I thought she never came back after she left you last year," she said tactlessly.

He cleared his throat. "She, too, needed a lower altitude. She finds it much more beneficial for her to stay in Ohio. I should like to express my gratitude to her—for our years together, of course—and what could be finer than a topaz necklace?" His expression was bland.

She studied him doubtfully, her brows drawn together.

"And so," he continued, "since the time is short and I've not been able to find anything else for her, I'll be glad to give you two hundred for your necklace." He paused, scrutinizing Carolina's face for some expression he did not seem to find there. "In cash too," he added hopefully, as if certain that this would bring the look he desired. "I think you'll find that amount more than fair," he finished guardedly.

Carolina's eyes were downcast to keep him from seeing the elation in them. Two hundred dollars! Surely that ought to keep

Roger at even the most select boarding house for several months and leave enough over for his railroad ticket besides.

And then something magical and breath-taking and altogether unsettling happened to her that quite transformed her face. Color swam up across her cheeks; her eyes grew wide with startled awareness; she looked suddenly dewy and melting.

Gilson ran his tongue over his lips. He had scarcely expected such a warm, such an almost overwhelming response to his offer. She had seemed unattainable until now. He smiled cynically.

What he had no way of knowing was that, as she stood there holding her cape tight about her and looking absently past him, her thoughts on all the things the money would buy for Roger, Carolina had suddenly felt life for the first time—sharp and insistent and vigorous—within her belly. She had been awed and illumined by it. It was proof of the miracle which she had only half-believed in, up until now. She quite forgot the elderly popinjay before her.

He recalled her attention to himself.

"If you'll come up to my office, I'll give you the money now. I have it in my safe."

Of course. The topaz necklace. More than ever she needed the money now. She followed him abstractedly.

Once inside his inner office, he made a great ceremony of unlocking his safe and untying canvas bags and counting out money. He begged her to sit down; but she refused, which vexed him somewhat. Of course he was just as good as any man, he told himself truculently, whether in board rooms or bagnios; but it did put a man at a disadvantage to try to make love to a girl who towered above him. Yet the warm radiance persisted in her eyes. She looked innocent somehow and deliciously pliable.

"How can I thank you?" she breathed as she tucked the money into the reticule fastened to her belt.

"There are ways," he suggested.

But she merely continued to smile dazzlingly beyond him, above him, and around him.

Of course . . . Stupid of him not to realize. Naturally she would have no commerce with him until her husband was decently out of town.

"You'll be back——" he said meaningly. He was standing close to her now. One hand dropped over hers on the edge of his desk.

Her eyes rested on him as if she were seeing him for the first time. He drew his hand away hastily and stepped back. He did not know why he stepped back. For, a moment later, her face was suffused with that dazzling light again.

"You've been very kind, Mr. Gilson," she said shyly.

Kind! He almost groaned. He'd like nothing better than to be kind. He'd like to shower this big tantalizing creature with beautiful things.

"I hope I shall be able to say the same thing of you some day," he said softly.

But either she did not hear or she would not understand. She had kept her cape about her all the while; now she was fastening it at the throat and making sure that the money was safe and drawing on her gloves. Her eyes were downcast; her thick brush of lashes swept her cheeks. He looked at her sweetly curving mouth that could be rebellious and angry and even shrewish, he suspected. A pretty dish, a ravishing dish, he thought greedily. That was two hundred well invested.

She was turning to go. Now she would give some indication that she recognized the day's transaction for what it was.

He waited. But nothing happened. He began to feel aggrieved. It was all right to play this demure and innocent role up to a certain point; then it became provoking. She hadn't given him so much as a side glance or a knowing smile. It was no way for an understudy of Floss's to act. True, he had always understood there was no woman so prissy-good as a former inmate of a house. But this one had taken his money. That was just the trouble. She had taken it as rightfully as if she had just sold him something at a bargain.

"Cara!" he said urgently.

She looked at him in surprise. He had the feeling she was asleep. He'd wake her up! He moved aggressively nearer. She was his kind of a woman. Gold—creamy—carmine. Ripe as a red cherry or a purple plum hanging just out of reach.

Out of reach, be damned. Hadn't he just paid two hundred dollars to bring her within reach? One arm slid around her waist under the soft fur cape. The whole arm-filling solidity of her, yielding yet firm, went to his head like port on an empty stomach.

"Don't, please," she said stiffly, drawing back.

Her stiffness maddened him. She had affected him this way from the very first moment he had seen her and had dickered with Floss about her—before that crazy young blade actually went and married her. Nothing else had satisfied his hunger since, and he had tried all ways of assuaging it. He had to have her. And she was slipping through his fingers again.

"How do I know you'll come back? Maybe you'll cheat me again," he reproached her.

"Cheat you?" She looked amazed.

"You know I've given you four times what your necklace is worth—a topaz is only a semi-precious stone—and don't try to pretend you don't know why, either."

She stared at him in shocked loathing. Yes, she knew. Her years in Stringtown, the comments of the plain-spoken Floss, told her instantly. Hot shame rushed through her. Why, she was a respectable married woman who loved her husband. She gave him a searing look and did the one thing to make him hate her always. This tall Astarte jeered at him.

"You little banty, you. Let go of me. Do you suppose I'd really look at a litter-runt like you? Get out of my way." She pushed him aside so effectually that only the corner of the desk saved him from sprawling.

He winced at the bruise on his flank, regained his balance, and came at her again, belligerently trying to retrieve his lost ground. But she only shook him off again in disgust, as she worked at the catch of her reticule. With a sweeping gesture, she jerked out the contents and flung them down on his desk. Some of the bills fluttered off; some of the silver spilled on to the floor with a rattle and clink, followed by the sound of rolling coins coming to rest in the farthest corners of the room.

Then she picked up her jewel case and sailed out of the room in a swirl of sealskin and gleaming brown silk, her cheeks scarlet and her ale-colored eyes wide and angry.

He stood there for a moment, wrathfully rubbing his hip, his pulse beating with the sick fury of the little man, belittled. If she had only cried for mercy, or begged him to desist from despoiling her, or had acted the least bit terrified of his highly dishonorable intentions. But to fling him aside like a distempered cur . . .

II

SHE WAS STILL PANTING WHEN SHE JOINED THE CROWD BELOW THAT moved along the streets like surging lava.

As always, the high wooden sidewalks were jostling full of miners, off shift, with their shawled wives; of well-dressed ladies from Bullion Row daintily picking their way across the walks from carriage to shop; of an occasional man of substance hurrying about his affairs; and of countless men, without substance, drifting from mining exchange to faro table.

Slowly her agitation waned. She let the crowd carry her along. She supposed she ought to try the jewelry store again, but she searched for excuses not to. Perhaps it would be best to find out first how much Roger's ticket was going to cost . . . That was it, she decided; she would go down to the depot and inquire. Anything to put off the visit to the formidable jewelry store.

She worked her way out of the throngs to the side street that led to the depot. She was glad to draw a clean breath again. She wanted to wash away the recollection of Henry Gilson's licking eyes and importunate hands.

Presently she forgot him completely. Carolina was not oversensitive; she had but a single goal now, and that was to get Roger well again. She pinned all her hopes on his stay down at that watering place. She was glad she had surreptitiously been getting his clothes mended and washed and pressed during the past few days. As soon as she had the money, she would send him away. She trusted to his great tiredness not to combat her.

She decided, with her new, hard-learned fortitude, that she would keep her secret a little longer—until after he returned, well and strong and eager to pick up life. Some deep feminine pride prompted her to wait until he wanted her again before she told him about the fruit of their love. He seemed so far away from her these days and from all earthy need of her warmth and love. As soon as he was better—she told herself hopefully.

She was thankful for her concealing sealskin cape as she walked along toward the depot. Gilson had not suspected. For, without the cape, the doctor had guessed immediately. It seemed strange that Roger could have lived in the same house with her and slept in the same bed with her and not noticed. What unhappy thoughts was he thinking during all those long evenings while he lay in bed with his face to the wall, or sat at the kitchen table staring at his knuckles? It was a dreadful thing to know a man's body so well and to be such a stranger to his mind.

The depot agent told her the price of the ticket. She thanked him and turned away. It was not too much.

Her attention was caught by the gaudily colored posters, advertising various mountain resorts, tacked on the waiting room wall.

"Manitou," she read. "The famous Rocky Mountain Spa. The Saratoga of the West. Elegant Hotels and Select Boarding Houses, $3 to $4 a Day."

She sighed. It was going to cost a dreadful lot. But it would be worth it. For surely, when he came back, Roger would be himself again. Everything between them would be as it once was, back in those sweet, laughing, wonderful days at the hotel, when Roger came rushing into their room to gather her into a quick, hard embrace.

She brushed the back of her hand across her eyes in an oddly childish gesture of grief.

The train was just pulling in as she left the depot. Curiously she stopped to watch it. Trains were still novel and exciting things to her, who had jolted so many weary miles in the Gospel wagon.

The train today seemed to occasion an extra amount of flurry. The agent hustled out to greet the passengers from the last coach. The train crew rallied around. There was a feeling of fanfare and obsequies in the air. No one paid the slightest attention to the ordinary passengers spilling out of the ordinary coaches.

Carolina did not know that she was seeing her first private car and the effect that great wealth has upon hired underlings. She merely knew that the first two to descend from that special coach were disappointing. A colorless middle-aged couple, completely unimportant to her because they were middle-aged. But the third and last passenger called forth a feeling too pure to be envy; it could only have been awe. Never before had she seen "a perfectly turned out" young woman.

The girl, who was a few years older than herself, was the complete perfection of young ladyhood. Her figure was slight to the point of fragility, her complexion was as flawless as the inside of a sea shell, and her mouth was a small perfect rosebud that would never become vulgarly full-blown . . . But, ah, her clothes! The sweep of that overdrape, the chic smallness of that muff, the pert tilt of that bustle, all combined to make a whole that defied analysis.

Carolina turned hastily to go. She felt dowdy and heavy on her feet and uncouthly robust.

As she hurried away, she made herself, with her usual singleness of purpose, dismiss the distracting memory of the girl at the depot as well as the thought that Roger would probably be exposed to others of her kind at the Select Boarding House in Manitou. Unflinchingly she returned to her problem which was still how to get him away.

Suddenly she knew what she must do. She must ask Floss for the money. It was the only way. Of course she would make Floss take the necklace as security for the loan, although Floss would object; but Carolina had her pride.

She drew a long breath. She felt better, now that she had made up her mind. At that moment she saw Dr. Walgren's buggy tied in front of the Cowleys'. Cowley had slipped in one of the stopes deep in the Morning Glory mine and had a bad knee. She watched the doctor come out of the house and go around to unblanket his old white horse.

As she neared him, she heard his usual stream of vituperation directed at the patient mare. Like the rest of the town, she smiled at the epithets addressed to this most docile of beasts by this kindest of men. He broke off sheepishly as Carolina appeared from behind the buggy.

"Hello, Doctor, you aren't riding over toward the Row, are you? I need to see Floss Kittredge in a hurry."

He chuckled. Any other female would have simpered and twisted in a series of ladylike circumlocutions until he invited her to ride along with him. But not young Jardine's wife. She was as direct as a rifle bullet.

"Matter of fact, I'm on my way to Stelle Bogart's right now. Jump in."

He smiled at her in a fatherly way. Spunk—that was it. Too proud to ask either her husband's or her own folks for help . . . He was glad he had been able to be of some use to the young Jardines. They would be finding out pretty soon just how much he *had* smoothed the way for them.

Carolina clambered carefully up into the buggy. All her movements were careful now. She wondered if she dared ask the doctor a few questions about herself. She knew it was not ladylike to mention right out to the doctor anything about a baby before it was

119

born. That was only talk for women. Yet she had no woman, except Floss, and Roger had forbidden her to see Floss. Only this once would she disobey him and it was for his own good.

At the thought of Roger, the quick shining look came back to her face. Roger was going to be all right. Everything would work out. Their lines would fall again in pleasant places.

CHAPTER 13

Dr. WALGREN JOGGED BACK FROM THE ROW TO HIS OFFICE, BEHIND his thick-rumped white horse. He wished he could be like those big-city doctors who simply did their best and then shrugged off untoward results, if there were any. Instead, he got all wrought up over his patients' fortunes. Take Floss Kittredge now. He'd breathe a lot easier when he got that cast off and found that her leg had knitted properly. You never could tell with a compound fracture.

Out on the stoop in front of his office, which was a small cube-like excrescence on the side of his house, his wife Gertrude waited for him. She was a positive-looking woman, whose chin, bosom, and stomach all jutted aggressively. Her iron-gray hair was skewered on top of her head in a knot that looked as unyielding as a coiled metal cable. Her steaming hands were wrapped in her apron as she delivered messages, commands, and reproofs.

He certainly had taken his own time about making his calls at the Row, she said; if he didn't look out, there'd be talk. Old lady Janes had left word for him to stop by so she could complain about her back—it wasn't as though she ever paid for his calls; he better leave her till the last. Mrs. Cornforth asked should she expose the rest of the children to Lloyd's measles and get it over with? No hurry about her either; they hadn't paid for the last two babies yet. And there'd been a call from young Jardine's father, a very polite, distinguished, well-fixed looking gentleman from Denver. He wanted the doctor to drop around at once. He and his wife had come especially to take young Jardine home with them and they needed the doctor to back them up.

"They came in a private car, if you please—belongs to one of the

120

big moguls of the railroad. I asked the depot agent when he went by. I'll bet Jardine Senior is good for a handsome fee if you persuade the young fellow to go home," she finished.

"What do you suppose I wrote that letter to the father for? It's what I been trying to do all along. I don't have to be paid extra for doing my duty." He gave up in despair. Gertrude could always succeed in making him look like a thriftless ninny. He clucked to the horse.

"Remember," she called after him, "the Jardines first—and charge plenty." She reentered the house, her hands still wrapped in her rolled-up muff of kitchen apron.

"Giddap, you old hellion, you!" Dan Walgren slapped the fat white rump vindictively with the lines. "None of your tricks today. And I'm not going to the Jardine place till I'm goddam ready."

The placid, stall-stained old mare flicked one ear and headed toward the Jardines'. Her gait was half walk and half trot, and her rump went up and down so vigorously that one was almost deceived into thinking that she was making splendid horizontal progress.

"Filthy-minded old harpy!" he scolded the horse.

But the horse's feelings were not hurt. Heeding the doctor's twitch on the lines and not his words, the mare kept straight on toward the Flats and the Jardine house.

Dan Walgren was pleased with himself for having written the letter that had brought the young man's parents up here today. After all, when a boy had nearly died of lung fever and a girl was several months pregnant, they couldn't pamper their pride. Youth! Stubborn, cocky, independent, wonderful. He sighed sentimentally . . . Not that he'd suffer through the whole damn business again, if you gave it to him.

He blanketed his horse in front of the little shack and opened the door with a family doctor's lack of ceremony.

He took in the scene in the kitchen in a glance. The father, distinguished, "well-fixed looking," as Gertrude had said, pacing back and forth. The young man, with a blanket around his thin shoulders, sitting beside the scrubbed kitchen table. The acquiline, bloodless woman, whose love for her son had made her both abject and demanding, hovering over him and saying with the harried archness of an adult promising candy to a child if it will take its medicine: "——Mr. Braden's elegant private car to take you back in, Roger dear. And the sweetest surprise——"

121

"I've told you, you'll have to wait till Cara gets back," Roger repeated with tired stubbornness.

"But she hasn't any hold on you," his father blurted testily. "I've been to the courthouse. You don't owe a thing to that little——"

"Your father means," interrupted the mother with smooth haste, "that you've paid enough for your folly, Roger dear."

"Cara is my wife," said Roger with thin dignity.

The doctor was troubled. He wished the girl would get on home. It wasn't good when in-laws used that tone about an absent wife.

After the proper introductions he bent over the young man and laid his ear flat against the bony chest.

"Now breathe." The shallow breath soughed in and out. He listened and nodded with qualified satisfaction.

"No worse. But you do need a change, young man, as I wrote your father. The minute your wife gets back, I want you to let your folks take you two home with them. You better let your mother start gathering up your things now; Cara will be along pretty soon."

"But she'll never be willing——" objected Roger.

The doctor was impatient. Like all benefactors, he could brook no obstacles in the way of his good deeds.

"Sure, she will. She told me only a little while ago that as soon as she saw her friend about a matter, she was hoping to get you off on the train for several months in a lower altitude."

"She told you that?"

"On the way over to the—I mean, to visit the friend with the fractured femur."

"Cara went over there?" He seemed stunned.

"I tried to get her to ride back with me, but she said she had too many stops to make while she did her trading. You know how a woman is, with a pocketful of money."

Roger only stared at the doctor incredulously, as if trying to conjure up such a picture of his wife. His face slowly blanched; the feverish red spots heightened until he looked very ill . . . The sooner they got him down out of here the better, the doctor reflected uneasily.

"Come, come," he prodded Roger with bluff heartiness. "Get a move on, boy. You want to get well, don't you?"

Roger was staring fixedly down at his clenched fists. His knuckles made sharp white cones under the thin skin. The doctor was snapping his bag together and drawing on his gloves. All these his-

122

trionics over a simple matter of a visit home! He appreciated that there were family complications. Still . . .

"I tell you, it's what your wife has been planning all the while. She told me so when she asked for a lift over to see Floss."

Something in his final words seemed to clinch the matter for Roger. He looked up with a brief bitter flash. There was a new edge of resolution in his voice when he spoke.

"You've convinced me, Doctor." And to his mother and father he said, "How soon can we get away from this hole? I don't want to take anything with me. I want to leave it all—everything—behind!"

His father exhaled a long breath. The pinched look left his mother's face.

He guessed his words had done it, thought the doctor complacently.

"If I see your wife, I'll tell her to hurry. She'll want to take a few knick-knacks along, even if you don't." Jovially he took his departure.

The elder Jardine followed the doctor to the door, murmuring something about not being able to thank him sufficiently, but that he would try to do so in a—material way—when he returned to Denver. No doubt about it, he said, the doctor's words had turned the trick and broken down his son's resistance, after he and his wife had failed utterly.

He went on to speak of the doctor's recent letter telling about Roger's illness.

"But for you, I'd never have known how bad things were," he said gravely. "True, I was making plans for him to come back and go into partnership with me. But I might have waited until too late——" He blew his nose.

The sentimental old doctor blew his nose, too, and mumbled something in gratified embarrassment as he went on out to his buggy. He had fixed everything to a T. As soon as Cara got back, the family could all set off together. He'd wager they'd forget about her past. After all, it was her future that counted. And if he was any judge of bosoms and hips, there'd be plenty of young Jardines in her future. That should win over even the most stand-offish of parents-in-law.

Now for old lady Janes and the Cornforths' measles.

A HALF-HOUR LATER CAROLINA TRUDGED WEARILY HOME WITH HER heavy sacks of groceries. On top, well away from the beefsteak and the country butter, rested the package containing Roger's new muffler. She supposed it was silly, for he did not have to have a muffler. But he had lost his that night he had lain out in the snow, and he did like nice things. They seemed to do things for his spirit. She, who would have no money for herself or any prospects for any, once she had supplied Roger with enough for his trip, made tender excuses for buying him a brocaded muffler to send him off in a holiday mood.

She would not let herself think ahead to how it would be after she had put Roger on the train tomorrow. She must not think; she must just keep going. In fact, there was still the problem of persuading Roger to leave at all. It would be terrible, she thought in a rebirth of anxious unselfishness, if he should balk at going.

As she neared the little house she wondered vaguely why there was no smoke coming from the chimney. Then she noted the wheel tracks in the snow. So the doctor had been here to see Roger. She was sorry to miss him; he must have just left. But she knew how important he felt it was to get Roger away.

Floss had been wonderful about the money today. Good old Floss. She had even understood that she must take the topaz necklace until Carolina could pay her back and redeem it.

How tired she was. Her arms ached. Her whole body ached. She was so weary of battling something all the time. The hardest of all lately had been Roger's moods. They frightened her because she could not understand them.

She loved him so. Her whole extravagant, lavish, "excessive" nature yearned to spend herself for him: her last ounce of energy, her last breath, her life itself, in order to give him back his old-time, confident gaiety. She would not, she could not, face the possibility that it was her own lack that had brought Roger to his present state. Or that he had been different ever since that night last fall when she had had to hit Canaday over the head to get back the Silverbell stock. She must lay Roger's condition to some external circumstances: to his distasteful job, to his lung fever, or to his run-down condition. Anything but to the possibility that she had failed him.

She shifted her package to the other hip. Surely Roger would be pleased today . . . She was like an earnest little girl who sorely needs some one to assure her that she had been a very good little girl indeed. Surely when Roger ate the good beefsteak and scalloped potatoes tonight and saw the muffler and knew about the Select Boarding House, he would approve of her. He would smile and light up in the old way. He might even hold her in his arms again before he left on the train, she thought humbly. Then she would tell him her heart-shaking news.

As she went up the walk, she heard the long trailing whistle of a departing train. Usually she paid no attention to trains; they were always switching and puffing and letting off steam close by. But this one made her pause. Then she forced herself to go on. She was being foolish. But she, who had so little of the mystic in her, could not dispel the sense of something portentous and fey about that distant whistle.

As she opened the front door she did not see the slight twitch of the curtains in the Hubbells' side room, or the face that ducked back from the Slyes' kitchen window. She walked into chill silence.

"Roger!" she called with shaky cheerfulness.

No one answered. The kitchen was empty. The front parlor was empty. Unwillingly she approached the bedroom. She looked in upon emptiness. The bed covers had been hastily thrown back. There were signs of a hurried departure.

She went through the house again. It was then that she saw the note, weighted down by the red glass spoon-holder on the kitchen table. It was written in a brisk, cultivated hand, with Greek e's and short forceful tails to the letters.

My son is coming home with me. Surely now you admit that you have been very bad for him. That chapter in his life is closed. I have been to the courthouse. You undoubtedly know that you have no claim on him whatever. Your old friends at the place where he found you will doubtless be glad to take you back.

Roger W. Jardine, Sr.

Pinned to the note was a check made out to Cara Smith.

At first she was too stunned to make sense of either the note or the check. And then she was too horrified. But slowly the words began to pound themselves into her brain. The color rose to her temples; her head went up like an angry filly's; the breath came panting through her nostrils. With a shriek she tore both note and check into little pieces. Then she hurled the groceries to the floor and threw the wrapped muffler into the farthest corner. Sobbing harshly and shouting at the absent Roger and Roger's father, she strode back and forth through the empty house.

With a terrible kind of industry she began to collect Roger's things in a pile: the new muffler, the clothes from the nails behind the bedroom door, even his work-stained overalls from the back porch. He had left everything but the suit he wore, even his fine gloves and his walking stick. There was something ultimately insulting about his leaving everything behind that had been a part of their life together.

She picked them all up and carried them out to the back yard. She poured kerosene on the pile. When she touched a match to it, it flamed upward. There was a snarling crackle as brocaded waistcoats, braid-bound cheviots, and rolled-brimmed hats went up in flames. The leaping evil tongues of fire were repeated in the twin fires in her eyes. Round and round the blazing pyre of their love she paced, pushing in the edge of a law book, the tip of a polished boot, the end of a walking stick.

When it was over, she remembered something else and ran back into the house for it: the brittle, shining mandolin. She banged it down on the ground, shattering it. When it was only a splintered mass, she threw it on the smouldering embers. Not until then did she go back into the house and shut the door with finality. She was seen no more that day.

The curtains fell back into place at the Hubbells' and the Slyes'. It was time to put supper on, and it was getting too dark to see anyhow. Even though they took occasional peeks during the evening, no lights shone from the Jardine house; no smoke came from the chimney; no sounds issued from the small dark cadaver of a house.

The following day the two neighbors met for a surreptitious exchange. Mrs. Hubbell said to Mrs. Slye, "Poor wild young creature. I don't dass go over till the storm's past. Them redheads!"

Mrs. Slye agreed with dismal relish. "But she ain't really a redhead either, come to think of it. I guess that's the trouble. At sun-up when I was fixing breakfast, I saw her creep out and poke around in the ashes for something. It was the remains of that fiddle. She just sat down in the snow with it in her arms and rocked it like it was a baby. Crying she was; you'd have thought it was somebody dead."

Mrs. Hubbell clicked her tongue sympathetically. "I shouldn't be surprised if it was marked—with her carrying on so . . ."

CHAPTER 14

FLOSS LOOKED UNCOMFORTABLE. LIFE HAD NOT TRAINED HER TO mince words, and now she longed to mince them. As she set the jar of beef extract and the wine jelly down on the kitchen table of the small house on the Flats, she avoided Carolina's eyes that were smiling up at her from across the table where she sat placidly featherstitching a small wrapper.

Floss sighed. She could not bear to erase that smile. For all about the neat, ugly little house were evidences that Carolina had begun to hope again: in the sprigged calico curtains awkwardly made by hand, in the blue-and-white checked cloth on the table, and in the tight little bunch of pasqueflowers, softly furred as squirrels' throats, thrust into a tumbler as a child might thrust them. Everywhere was touching proof that Carolina had found excuses for Roger, that she blamed his parents for everything, and that now she was only waiting for him to come back so she could forgive him lavishly.

Floss hooked her cane over the back of a chair and let herself clumsily down into it. Good thing Carolina was too wrapped up in herself to notice how lame she was. She untied her bonnet and laid it on the table and brushed her hair out of her eyes.

"Dr. Walgren wants you to eat well. He says you're a big-boned girl; likely your baby will be big too. You must eat for two, you know."

Carolina flashed her a grateful glance. She did not feel quite so alone, knowing that Floss and the doctor were thinking about her. Floss's concern she could understand, but not the doctor's. It was almost as if he felt responsible for her, as if he blamed himself in some way for her troubles. That was all foolishness, of course. What did he have to do with them?

"I do eat lots, Floss, and I'll relish this food. I'm certainly a lazy piece, lolling around the house, getting big as a locomotive boiler, while I owe you that hundred you loaned me on the necklace."

Maybe it wasn't sensible to have torn up that check from Roger's father. After all, it was Roger's baby she was having. But she was glad she had done it. That high and mighty note! She'd rather starve.

"When I want the money, I'll holler. I'd rather you'd eat now. Women alone never have any sense about eating——" Floss stopped uneasily. That wasn't exactly a tactful remark.

But Carolina was not perturbed.

"If I didn't know you made lots of money, Floss, I would have gone to work long ago to pay you back. I will, too, as soon as the baby is born."

"Well, sure—some day," Floss said vaguely, avoiding Carolina's eyes. "Now do like the doc says and take walks and look out for falls and don't lift things and be careful about getting your feet wet. I knew a woman once, because her husband didn't carry out her wash water quick enough, lifted those heavy wooden tubs and brought on the baby. Born dead, it was. And there was a girl at Hattie's had a sister seven months along and she slipped on the cellar stairs and fell, and she and the baby both died." She recounted these mishaps with gloomy warning.

"I'll be careful. When Roger gets back——"

Floss took a deep breath. She guessed she would have to let her have it. There seemed to be no way to pretty it up either.

"I just came from the courthouse, Carolina." Carolina looked up from her featherstitching in surprise. "I didn't just understand that note Roger's old man left—the part about your having no claim on Roger. So I went to find out. It's so, I'm afraid. You aren't married to him at all."

Carolina's head went up angrily. "I am too! You saw us get married. That old preacher that didn't know his Bible——" Carolina paused uncertainly as the import of her own words struck her.

"That's just it. He was a fake. I figure it's all my fault; I should have made sure. But I haven't had much experience with getting married," she admitted drily. "And so I left it to Roger to hire the preacher. The fellow at the courthouse says there's no record of a Roger Jardine marrying a Cara Smith (or anybody else). I made him look and look. The preacher was supposed to have had your marriage recorded, you see."

Carolina stared lethargically at the tumbler of flowers, her brief burst of anger gone. Floss eyed her uneasily. It was not natural for

128

Carolina to act this way. She had been such a wildcat at first, after Roger left. Then she had calmed down, and now she had begun to hope. This last was the worst of all. It had been better when she screeched and smashed things. It must be her condition that made her act so easy and cow-like.

"I don't care what you say, Floss, Roger thought the preacher was on the square and that we were really and truly married. He *felt* married, I know."

Floss said nothing. She wished she thought so too.

"Tell you what," she said brightly, "you write Roger about the baby. If I know him, that will bring him back from the ends of the earth. Better write today and stop all this nonsense about being proud and waiting for him to come to his senses."

"Or maybe just waiting till he feels stronger, Floss," corrected Carolina, gently but stubbornly. Then she added with her old-time honesty, "But no matter what, I can't do it. I can't use the baby as a—a whip to drive him back to me. Don't you see I can't, Floss?" He must want *her*, Carolina thought, and not be compelled to come back, like some easy little wench's fellow that had got her in the family way. Some day Roger would return to her.

But Floss could not see, at all. A frown contracted her smooth brows. A nice gentlemanly fellow like Roger had to be managed. Hadn't she managed the whole business of getting him married off to Carolina, in the first place? (Well, what had seemed like getting him married off to her.) Roger, back home with his folks, might be different. Maybe he had forgotten Carolina at her best. Maybe he remembered her only in those last gray bitter days. A baby would bring him running, though. Carolina was a fool not to use the only lever she had.

Floss sighed and began to tie the strings of her smart little bonnet under her chin. Awkwardly she got to her feet, holding to the chair until she had a firm grip on her cane. Yes, it was a good thing Carolina was too wrapped up in herself and her hopes to notice how lame she was, or she'd be hell-bound to pay back that hundred dollars. For she would realize instantly that Floss had not been able to "work" since the accident, that she would probably never be able to again.

Well, she mustn't keep Stelle's driver waiting out in front all morning. Stelle had been decent about giving her this job as housekeeper, but it carried no special privileges with it.

129

"Now do like the doc says. And don't fret about the money either. But I wish you'd write Roger."

Carolina was looking dreamily into the distance, seeing the Roger she had conjured up out of her heart's need.

"He ought to be feeling lots better by now, Floss. I'm glad his father and he made up, even if Mr. Jardine was horrid to me. For Roger was simply miserable while they were on the outs. But I don't think he ought to risk coming back until the last of the spring snows has melted," she said with an air of pretty firmness, as if she were being consulted in the matter. "His lungs will probably be weak for a long time. He must take care of himself," she ended generously.

Floss swallowed hard and turned to let herself out of the house. Love made awful damn fools out of women. She was glad she had never been bitten by it.

II

SPRING SLOWLY PRIED LOOSE THE TIGHT-FISTED GRASP OF WINTER. The Roaring Fork was bank-high with muddy run-off water from the melting snows. The almost daily wet snowfalls, which in a lower altitude would have been spring showers, melted by noon.

Carolina walked cumbrously now. Her mind was cumbrous too, moving with a fecund placidity quite foreign to her usual swift vigor. Her neighbors helped her with her sewing, and she stitched her few small garments with awkward care.

Because of the hypnosis of love, or perhaps because of nature's overwhelming desire for a placid environment for its burgeoning young, Carolina's whole nature seemed to have changed. She smiled often to herself, her thoughts all turned inward. Roger might walk in, any minute. Of course he had not written; you could not explain things in letters. But one moment in each other's arms, and everything would be all right again.

Devoutly she swept and scoured and dusted; she was a wife, "readying up" for her husband. Her neighbors whispered together . . . Poor young thing—who did she think she was fooling? And her with her time almost on her, and no sign of the Mister. His folks had certainly put a stop to *that* in a hurry.

Carolina was smiling as she scalloped the edges of a newspaper Mrs. Slye had given her for her shelves. She cut lacy little designs in the folded scallops, reminding her of the paper dolls she had once cut out for Rosalie which, when you unfolded them, became long strings of dancing figures, all holding hands. Rosalie had been enchanted.

She turned the sheet of *The Denver Republican* and stopped, her scissors in air. She laid down the scissors carefully.

Oh, no, she thought, she must be reading it wrong. Her eyes were playing tricks on her. The sentences blurred together in the strangest way, but no matter how she read them, they remained the same. Fashionable Wedding Unites Prominent Denver Families. Miss Susan Cornelia Braden Becomes Bride of Roger Walling Jardine III. Ethereal loveliness of the bride set off by white roses—court train—eight bridesmaids. The groom recently became a partner . . . elegant new home on Sherman Avenue the gift of the bride's father to the happy couple. The paper fell from her fingers. It was as if she had been knocked almost unconscious—almost, but not quite. She picked up the paper again.

Miss Susan Cornelia Braden. She drew in a ragged breath. So this was the "Always yours, Sue," whose letters had told Roger of the parties he was missing and reminded him of romantic past escapades and warned him to hurry back because she had just caught the bride's bouquet.

Ethereal loveliness. Suddenly she knew. The pale and flowerlike beauty at the depot.

She sat very still for a while. Bride . . . bride's bouquet . . . bride's father. The words hammered remorselessly through her brain. But it couldn't be! Nobody else could be Roger's bride because he was already married to her. The preacher had said so. Roger had said so a thousand times, holding her in his arms. "My darling—my wife—my love——" He loved her, and they were having a baby any time now.

Her chaotic mind was beginning to function again, was beginning to wind itself up like a tightening spring. But it was a useless winding up. Coiled springs must have something to let fly at. It was no good if you were all alone in a dark little house that you had scoured for your husband to come back to, sitting before the table where you had cut out clothes for his baby and yours, looking down at the account of his marriage to a girl called Sue.

For the first time she comprehended Floss's warnings about Roger. She began to cry, letting the tears run down without wiping them off. She got to her feet, holding to the edge of the table, and paced back and forth across the small kitchen. Back and forth, back and forth. Why, she was only a—she thought of the short ugly Stringtown word for herself. Her baby was only a—she thought of the longer, ugly Stringtown word for a baby like hers.

She walked faster and faster. Her shell of lethargy was shattered at last. She wanted to hurt somebody. She wanted to lash out, as she had always lashed out when she herself was hurt. But who was there to hurt? Roger was safe, far away in Denver, married to Sue, and living in an elegant new home on Sherman Avenue. Who was there to hurt? And then she knew. She could hurt all that was left to her of Roger—Roger's child. She could hurt herself, whom he had once loved.

She did not wait. She flung herself out the door without pausing for a wrap or even to shut the door after her. She was savagely glad that it was a raw spring day with a mushy snow covering the ground and a sharp edge to the wind. So much the better. She broke into a stumbling run.

She was remembering Floss's anxious commands; she would disobey every one of them. It never occurred to her that there might be a simpler way to accomplish her purpose, even though all her life she had heard of the wretched women of the mining camps who resorted to guns or knives or doses of laudanum in order to quit this too-difficult world.

She hurried across back lots, over the bridge, straight up the hillside that rose just outside the town. She avoided the road and the paths leading up to the mines. She had no idea where she was going; but she chose the steepest way.

Grimly she savored all her disobediences. So she must not overdo, eh? She forced her heavy body pantingly up the mountain side. Sweat poured down her face. So she must not lift? Vengefully she tugged great fallen branches out of her way instead of going around them. On and on she climbed.

Once, she looked back in triumph at the scene below: the narrow black boxes of shaft houses, the skeletal superstructures, the engine houses with their feathers of smoke, the dumps tumbling down the hillside. She looked down upon the town itself, spread out on the floor of the valley like the squares of a game of tick-tack-toe.

She did not slacken her pace. Be careful not to get her feet wet?

Look out for exposure? Her feet squelched in her shoes, and the biting air stung her bare arms.

It was growing dark. Now she had lost the view of the valley as she stumbled down into gullies and climbed up the far sides again and stumbled down into more gullies. She supposed she was somewhere on Smuggler Mountain, but that was all she knew. Be careful about falls? A dozen times she fell. Once she even rolled down a steep declivity until a scrubby juniper stopped her descent. A murdering frenzy lashed her on.

But even rage can consume itself. Her demoniac energy waned. Her steps wavered. She dropped down at last under a pine tree, too tired to move. She leaned her head back against the trunk. If she rested just a moment, perhaps she could drive herself on again. She must have slept briefly, sitting there with her back to the pine tree in the dark wetness, her drenched clothes sticking to her.

She opened her eyes at last. She did not know whether she had slept or been unconscious. She clambered stiffly to her feet, all feeling gone. Well, that had done it, she thought dully. She'd die of pneumonia. No human body could stand such abuse and survive. No unborn baby could, either.

Her sense of triumph had burned out long ago. Even her desire for revenge was gone. Only a vast bruised tiredness filled her. The instinct of a hurt animal to return to its hole was all that motivated her now. She headed back toward home; at least, she thought it was toward home; the way was downhill anyhow.

The early spring twilight was gone. The numbing chill of night enfolded her. There was no need to try to fall now; she slipped and stumbled often in the treacherously slick snow. Her hair hung in wet strings; her hands were skinned and her knees bruised; her skirts slapped wetly about her ankles. An injured animal, she dragged herself along.

She saw the blur of lights. So she was nearing the town again. She met no one, or if she did, she was too near collapse to know it. Her footsteps echoed hollowly; she must be crossing the bridge. Peering out through her dank streamers of hair, she found the path through the back lots.

Only two more houses to pass. She could scarcely pull one dead foot after the other. As she staggered into her own back yard, she saw her door swinging wide. She was beyond fear.

"I will not fear what man shall do unto me." The words said themselves in the dim recesses of her mind. No one could do worse to her than she had already done to herself.

She held on to the door frame and pulled herself inside her own kitchen. She did not stop to light a lamp or start a fire. She slumped down on the edge of her bed, kicked off her squashy shoes, and rolled back underneath the covers. Half-fainting, she lay there, feeling her heart pound until it shook the bed.

Suddenly the child within her kicked out with such force that it brought her sitting bolt upright. So it was starting! Floss had been right. She had brought it on.

She clenched her fists and lay back rigidly. Sweat broke out on her. Let it come. They would both die. She, who had always loved babies, was glad—glad—— She only hoped that Roger would know about it—in that elegant new mansion that was the gift of the bride's father to the happy couple. She waited for the next pain, expectantly, grimly.

The sun woke her, shining brightly in her face. She opened her eyes experimentally. She felt of her bulging body. Nothing seemed to be happening. She glanced out at the ticking clock in the kitchen. It was past noon. She yawned and sat up.

Lord, have mercy, how she ached. But she did not have even a cold in her head. Her wet ribbons of hair had dried on the pillow during the night. She put her feet out on the chilly floor and saw that her bedraggled garments had molded themselves about her body as they dried, like corn-husks about a well-filled ear of corn.

Suddenly she felt ravenous. She had not eaten since yesterday noon. She was skinned and bruised and one ankle was wrenched, but she felt fine.

III

Two weeks later, dr. walgren delivered her of a healthy eight-pound girl. The labor was comparatively easy. It only went to show, he said, that it paid to take care of yourself . . . all those admonitions he had sent her by Floss. Cara must certainly have been in the pink of condition.

Carolina looked out impatiently into the kitchen where Floss and Mrs. Hubbell and Mrs. Slye and the doctor were bending over a bundle, making foolish noises. She was weakly furious. It was her baby, wasn't it? She called out to them.

The doctor chuckled as he brought the baby in and laid it beside her.

At the touch of that small girl child, a dam burst within her. She surrendered to a flood of mother love so fierce, so passionate, so protective, that it washed away her bitterness and even her heart-break. She no longer remembered that once, in a fit of madness, she had tried to do away with this small part of herself that was now no longer part of herself.

Eleven days later Carolina was at the washtub. Not doing the small washing of a tiny baby, but "washing"—overalls and grayish shirts and long grimy union suits for the men who lived in rooming houses on the Flats. She was ridden by the thought of the hundred dollars she owed Floss. For the doctor had let it slip that Floss was no longer the affluent Floss with the preferred room in Stelle Bogart's house. Floss was having to get used to fewer fine feathers, he said; but he figured she liked it better.

"A woman—a man—can do without a lot of things if they feel proud of themselves inside," he said shyly.

There was a quick, stern resolution in the way Carolina worked the pump handle up and down and filled the copper wash boiler and measured out the bluing. Her arms were firm and white and strong; her young body was straight and healthy. And her heart had turned to stone.

C H A P T E R 15

SPRING AGAIN. THE EARLY MORNING AIR WAS FRESH AS ONLY MOUNTAIN air is fresh. Carolina bumped the borrowed and battered baby buggy listlessly along over the uneven wooden sidewalks of the Flats, as she delivered neat little bundles of washing to the boarding houses where the single men lived. She was also giving the baby her airing.

Dorothea, who was eleven months old now, perched among the clean bundles, smiling divinely at each passerby. With each encounter, Carolina brightened a little. Dorothea was undoubtedly the most beautiful child ever to stop traffic in a mining town.

Thank goodness, she was fair and delicate and finely made, instead of weed-strong and ruddy like herself. She did not go on to say, thank goodness, the child looked like Roger, instead of herself; for she took a stiff pride in not mentioning Roger's name, even in her thoughts.

She paused at the corner to glance up and down the street. You got so you did that automatically, if you were young, and had a baby without a father, and lived alone in a tiny shack in the wrong part of town. It would be lovely to be a widow, she reflected wistfully. If you were a widow, there were no questions asked, no sudden stoppage of talk when you approached, no looks exchanged when you had passed. But best of all, you did not always have to be on guard—locking the door the minute you got inside the house—never opening it after dark until you were sure who was outside. She thought of the time or two that she had been careless, and a shudder, almost of nausea, went through her.

But even when she was harried and shamed, she never wanted to be a maid again; for if she were a maid, there would be no Dorothea. And Dorothea was completely rewarding.

Dr. Walgren had named her. Carolina had asked him to. He had answered with a certain diffidence, "How about Dorothea? It means Gift of God. All babies are, in a way; but this one is, more than most."

Carolina had looked at him with a guilty twinge. That terrible night on the mountain! She did not deserve this miracle of a baby. Then in the next moment the twinge was gone. Dorothea—Gift of God. She admired the doctor's perspicacity. Not that she wanted a religious name, she told him quickly. But he reassured her; Dorothea came from the Greek and was not to be found in the Bible. She relaxed. Gift of God her baby certainly was, she decided worshipfully, accepting and rejecting God all in one breath. She would call her Thea.

The buggy bumped down the two steps at the end of the sidewalk to the muddy road, across the deep spring ruts, and up again to the walk at the far side.

Carolina was far afield in her thoughts when suddenly she was jerked back by an awareness of a presence beside her. She turned with a start. Gilson! A futile anger filled her. Would she never be rid of him? He was worse than any of them about sneaking down to her house after dark. Sometimes she was reminded of a wiry, clever, persistent little coyote circling around and around a ewe that it had marked for its kill. But, foo! What could he do to her? So long as she paid her rent and didn't get sick and managed to have plenty of washings to do . . .

He was smiling at her now—cynically and admiringly, as if he had all the time in the world.

But Carolina was no good at playing a waiting game.

"What do you want?" she snapped.

"Why, nothing; nothing at all. I only thought you'd be interested to know that I've recently acquired a small property down on the Flats. A three-room house, I believe. An owner has certain rights, of course. So I'll be down this evening to have you tell me what repairs you need." His voice was that of a model landlord.

She looked at him with loathing. So he had bought her house. She wondered if a landlord did have certain rights. Where could she turn now? The doctor? He was always being called away just when she needed him most. She gave Henry Gilson a harassed glance. He only smiled back in frank anticipation. He had several scores to settle with this savage, contemptuous young beauty.

"I'll thank you to keep away from me and my house!" she told him belligerently. But even to her own ears, her voice sounded hollow. She would have to move at once. But where could she find another place as cheap, in this prosperous, crowded mining town?

She switched past him, trundling the buggy ahead at a furious pace. He did not try to follow her. He did not need to, his manner said. He would be down tonight . . . An owner had certain rights.

She stopped absently at her last place to leave her last bundle and collect the fifty cents that would round out the whole hundred dollars that she owed Floss. It had taken her all these pinching months to gather it together; for Floss, of course, knew nothing about it. If Carolina had not been superbly healthy and able to nurse the baby all this while, it would not have been possible. For first there had been rent and groceries and kerosene and stove wood and soap to pay for. Only after that could she put by anything toward that elusive goal of the hundred dollars she owed Floss.

Her achievement should have brought her satisfaction now. But it did not. She felt a resentful surprise. All the while that she was working she had looked forward to the day when she would be able to pay Floss. And now that she could, she found that the future stretched ahead as just another drab year of putting dirty overalls

137

and sweaty shirts to soak, stoking the stove to keep the sad-irons hot, and wondering when she would make a slip that would imperil herself and her baby.

She slowed her steps. Thea, however, did not care for a contemplative pace; she liked taking the bumps with speed and vigor. She jounced up and down imperiously in her buggy. Obediently, Carolina quickened her gait and took the bumps at a spine-shaking rate. But it was only a quickening of the steps and not of the spirit.

She looked up the street in search of Floss. She wanted to get rid of the hundred dollars. This was the time of day that Floss did her marketing for Stelle Bogart. It was hours before the girls stirred, or began to think of their afternoon drives, so Floss could have the use of the carriage.

Floss found it hard to walk any great distance, but you would never know it from anything she said, thought Carolina admiringly. Floss had steel in her; she kept her head up and asked no favors of the world. And since she had broken with her old way of life, she was different. Maybe she did not laugh quite so easily and loosely as in the old days; maybe she was a little tighter and crisper now. But it was the tightness and crispness of self-respect. Floss *liked* being Floss for the first time in her life. Her gray eyes were straightforward and unabashed.

Her steps quickened as she saw Floss, superintending the stowing of groceries in the bottom of the carriage, as the storekeeper, pencil over ear, bent down with the load of supplies. Storekeepers had suddenly become respectful to Floss, now that she represented the management end of one of their best sources of trade, the parlor houses.

Carolina waved to Floss, signaling her to wait. The storekeeper returned to his shop. Floss hobbled to meet her, leaving Stelle's driver to drowse in the sun. The two girls met with the swift smile of friendship. Floss bent over the buggy to make a face at Thea, which sent the baby off into gurgles of laughter. From the first, Floss and Thea had had a tacit understanding between them.

The two friends moved along the busy sidewalks, both holding to the handle of the baby carriage. For Floss, the buggy was a support to steady her. For Carolina, it was the prow of a boat that she used to push aside the waves of humanity.

Carolina told Floss abruptly about the hundred dollars. She reached for her reticule. Floss looked dismayed.

"I don't want it back. I did it to help you have the baby." Floss smiled down at the silky little duck-tail of hair curling out from under Thea's bonnet. "She's worth it. Besides, I've got the topazes."

"But you don't want them. You just took them to help me out. What would I have done without you and the doc?"

"Fiddlesticks! You hang on to the money."

They walked along through the jostling crowds. All about them was the most intense life; and they felt lifeless. For the first time Carolina sensed that Floss, too, looked upon an arid landscape. Now that she was through with it, Floss hated the bawdy house. Yet she did not know how to break away from it.

They were forced to halt because of the dense crowd in front of one of the mining exchanges. The blackboard set up outside was covered with chalked quotations. A man stood on a chair shouting and waving his arms. He was as impassioned as if he were selling an Indian herb tonic. A buzz of excited comments rose. There was a winy stimulation in the air that elicited a faint stirring of response in them.

"It's gold, gentlemen, gold! This new Mt. Pisgah district is a veritable Golconda. Get in on the ground floor today. Shares in the Bald Eagle are already selling for nineteen cents; last month they were two. The Jim Dandy is eight. The Pegasus, twelve and a half——"

Gold! Although they had grown to womanhood in silver camps, there was something about gold. Fragments of talk boiled up about them—mention of lodes and stopes and drifts and cross-cuts and porphyry.

A voice near them muttered corroboratively, "It's so—what he says. The gold is right at the grass roots—greenhorns stub their toes on it."

Another voice said, "Yeah, a fellow I know says you can mine it with a pitchfork."

"Nestling in a high shallow bowl just west of Pike's Peak lies this treasure chest of nature," continued the stock seller grandiloquently. "But if you delay investing, you may be too late."

The two girls turned on a common impulse and looked at each other. Inured as they were to wild talk and wilder expectations, their nerves yet vibrated to the tension in the air. Gold! Floss's lips pursed thoughtfully. Carolina's eyes, a flecked brown-gold themselves, widened.

"Faint heart ne'er won—a fortune," said the persuasive voice. "Here's your opportunity, gentlemen. Step right up——"

"They say the stage in is so packed it moults a miner at every turn," contributed someone in the crowd.

Men laughed and jostled closer.

"—only opened in January, and already bids fair to become the biggest gold strike since Californy. Who'll take a chance?" tempted the promoter.

Two in his audience would. Perhaps not in the way he had hoped; he was after investors, not recruits. But two were ready to throw their hats over the moon.

Carolina breathed fast, her color coming and going. She clutched Floss by the wrist.

"Why not, Floss? I'm sick and tired of it here—with every woman looking at Thea and me so I know just what she's thinking—and with every man looking at me so I know just what *he's* thinking too."

"Same here," agreed Floss. "Sniffing and saying to themselves, 'There goes one of Stelle Bogart's tarts.' I'd like to be me, with a clean slate. We could use that hundred. Maybe that's what you were saving it for, and didn't know it."

"There's a train in two hours." Carolina's tone was urgent. In only two hours! So that the house would be dark and empty tonight when Henry Gilson dropped by to inspect his property. Oh, they had to be on that train.

Floss drew back in alarm. Carolina always went too fast for her.

"But how could we be ready in time? And what will we do after we get there?"

"I don't know. But we'll make out. Oh, Floss, to shuck off the past—— To have a better future——"

Floss's chin went up. "I'll meet you at the depot," she said. "It's over the mountain for us, my girl."

"Over the mountain!" repeated Carolina raptly.

Suddenly the future looked bright and promising. Carolina glowed with new life. It was like the spring crack-up of the ice crust on a mountain stream that all winter has looked rigid and dead, even though a sensitive ear might have caught a hidden gurgle underneath. It was like the sudden start of sap in the willows along the creek in early spring that turns lifeless twigs to richly massed parades of color. She felt full of eager, straining life.

"I ought to have been weaning her before this," Carolina remarked with a nod at the baby as she parted from Floss. "I may have to start, on this trip."

Thea had no need to jounce demandingly on the trip home. The buggy careened along. Carolina's mind was racing ahead, packing, sorting, closing up the little house.

Her rent was paid for another week; Henry Gilson could have nothing to hold against her. Her eyes shone with a hard brightness. For Henry Gilson would have plenty to hold against her: the fact that she had escaped him, after all his hungry circling . . .

She must not forget to return the baby buggy to the Hubbells'. They would be needing it this fall. She hoped it would last them through one more baby.

There was really nobody to say good-by to. Dr. Walgren was out of town today. She would write to him after they got settled. Dear Dr. Walgren. Where would she be today without him?

For the first time she was thankful for the nearness of the little house to the depot. When she had packed her own and the baby's clothes (unable to resist taking along the last of the flour and sugar and prunes and beans), the telescope weighed heavily.

As she started out, flushed and panting, holding the kicking child on one hip and carrying the bulging gray canvas telescope with her other hand, she could hear the train chuffing and letting off steam. Just as she rounded the corner and staggered up the cinder bank, Floss drove up in Stelle's carriage. They would buy their tickets on the train, Carolina decided warily, so as to leave no tracks behind.

The two girls met, out of breath and laughing, at the steps of the coach. There was something gallant and reckless and young about them as they managed to get themselves and the baby and their luggage and all their hopes up into that hot little railroad coach.

They were still laughing as they fell into their seats. Carolina's green bonnet had been pulled down over one eye by the grabbing baby. Floss dropped her purse, and it required the help of three interested passengers to retrieve it.

Oh, this was fun—fun, thought Carolina hungrily. And she was so wrapped up in the present and the future that she was not even reminded of another journey two years before in this same sleekly varnished railroad coach, with the same crackling stove in the end, the same swinging gilded kerosene lamps, and the same fusty smell of cinders in the plush. That journey, too, had been a voyage into the unknown; but it had been undertaken in a spirit of revenge on her part, and of anxious alarm on Floss's. Today's journey was embarked upon by both of them in gaiety and in hope.

Thea jounced up and down demandingly on the seat opposite them. She wanted action. The two young women smiled, first at her and then at each other. They knew; they felt the same way.

When the train started, they laughed aloud together in a contagion of optimism. Oh, to be off. Over the mountain!

The train picked up speed. The bare branches rushed by, and the little houses, and the muddy cross streets. Neither of them looked back.

C H A P T E R 16

THEA WAS A GOOD TRAVELER. DURING THE TIRESOME TRAIN RIDE AND the stop-overs and the train ride again on the following day, she behaved like one of those babies in a steel engraving who neither squall nor throw up, but merely bounce and coo.

Carolina was tingly with excitement as the eastbound Midland train stopped at Divide to let them off. She tossed her head in its still fashionable green bonnet, picked up her picture-book baby, and followed Floss down the aisle. Outside, she could see the stage coach waiting to take passengers over the eighteen rough miles to the new mining region back of Pike's Peak.

Her very aliveness must have shone in her face, for Floss muttered warningly, "Remember, no laughing or talking to anybody except maybe the stage driver. Everything depends on how we start, in a new place. Straighten your bonnet."

Carolina straightened her bonnet, but she could not wipe the shine of anticipation from her face. Floss watched her with stern anxiety. Floss herself looked sober and refined. She wore her darkest dress and no paint on her face. She would never again use paint. Before she left Stelle's she had given away all her "fast" dresses. Carolina thought she took a quite unnecessary pleasure in her unpowdered face and her drab clothes, but she supposed it was Floss's business. If it made her feel any better——

The men crowded up about the stage coach and the two women. Carolina tried to look remote and ladylike in the midst of the admiring male circle. Apparently she and Floss were to be the only feminine passengers on the stage today.

"You're practically grinning! If you don't look out, they'll take us for fancy women following the boom." Floss's horror was profound. "One good thing—there's nothing so respectable as a baby."

Carolina jiggled her respectable-looking baby while the stage driver, a large friendly young man with very black mustaches against a wind-reddened face, came up to ask the two girls if they would like to sit on the high seat beside him instead of inside the coach. It was a fine spring day, he coaxed; the view was better up there.

They agreed that it was, indeed, a fine day, and that they would be pleased to ride with him—on account of the view.

They felt young and sought after as he helped them up over the wheel, handing the baby up with practiced care. Carolina noted with demure satisfaction that he was careful to put Floss on the outside so that she, Carolina, would sit next to him.

While the luggage was being tied to the "boot" that jutted out at the rear, the men crowded inside the coach, or disposed themselves on the top, or stood on the step. Any way to get to the new bonanza. Carolina listened avidly to the excited hubbub of talk. She would always like men's talk better than women's.

"—tenderfoot's paradise——"

"—couple of farmers, just digging a post hole and they found——"

"—use silver dollars for poker chips——"

Carolina reflected that she would never be anything but a mining camp brat herself. Floss too. It had not occurred to either of them, when they were looking for new pastures, to consider going anywhere but to another boom town. They would have been shy of a plains-country town, where men made their livings from cattle or hay or potatoes. They would have been alarmed by its unfamiliar patterns. Mining was in their blood. They had heard this kind of talk all their lives.

"And which is your grip, ma'am?" inquired the driver.

Carolina pointed.

When he picked up the bulging gray canvas telescope, he pretended to stagger.

"Now look here, ma'am," he said aggrievedly, "you ain't supposed to bring your boulders to Mt. Pisgah—you'll find plenty when you get there."

The men laughed exuberantly.

"That's not boulders!" declared Carolina hotly, and then blushed as they guffawed.

There was no use after that in trying to maintain decorum. Carolina could only throw back her head and laugh with them in her rich happy contralto. She did not even care whether she was "conspicuous."

"If you must know—it's a sack of flour," she confessed, wiping her eyes. "I make good Cornish meat pasties, if I do say so."

This time the laughter turned to a shout of approval. A voice said with jesting awe, "To think she can bake too!"

And with those words, the girls' profession was decided for them.

The driver tightened the last strap around the tarpaulin that covered the luggage. Then he climbed up to his place beside Carolina, picked up his reins, and they were off.

The men yelled—from sheer animal spirits and because they were young and exhilarated by the presence of two pretty women and because each one knew in his heart that by next week he would be rich. Floss's eyes danced in spite of herself. Carolina jumped the baby up and down on her knee and made her crow.

"So it's a home bakery you ladies aim to start," said the driver.

Carolina could feel Floss stiffen; she doubted that Floss could bake a flapjack.

"That's what we thought. That's why we brought along the flour, Mr.—er——"

"Pete. Just Pete. Last name's Ramsay, but nobody including myself ever remembers it."

"Pete, then. And this is my friend, Miss Floss Kittredge." Part of Floss's changed existence now would consist of being "Miss."

"And my name is——" Carolina stopped in complete panic. Why hadn't she thought about it in advance? She was not Mrs. Jardine, and she hated that false name, Cara Smith.

Floss came to her rescue quickly.

"Her husband was taken some time before the baby was born," she explained in a melancholy undertone to Pete. That would explain Carolina's lack of mourning, as anyone could figure out by looking at the baby that the conventional year must be over. The explanation also gave Carolina time to collect herself.

Carolina spoke now with a quiet resolution that might well have been grief. She was tired of lying.

"My name is Lawler—Carolina Lawler."

Pete Ramsay all but uncovered his head in the presence of what he took to be deep womanly emotion.

"You ladies will be a mighty welcome addition to the camp," he said soothingly, like one trying to divert an invalid. "When you see the poor excuse of a hotel—a ragged tent with a stovepipe coming out the side, along with the smell of burnt grease—you'll know why the men would pay gold nuggets for some home cooking. Got any idea of how soon you can get your bake shop started, Mrs. Lawler?"

"As soon as we can find a roof and a cookstove to put under it," responded Carolina promptly. She did not dare look at Floss.

"If you hold out the bait of some decent victuals, your cabin will be up before you can mix a cake. All you got to do is choose a location. I even think I know where I can find a cookstove for you."

Carolina thanked him warmly. He made a great show of cracking his whip over the backs of his horses without touching them and of flicking cones off the branches as they passed. He's just like Mat doing handsprings in front of the little girls, thought Carolina indulgently, liking him for it, and liking even more her sense of power over a handsome male. It had been so long . . .

Pete Ramsay was forced to give his whole attention to his driving here because the road, scarcely more than a trail, skirted along the edge of a gorge. After that, their route lay through forests and over the tops of flat mountains and along narrow shelf roads.

Carolina was observant. It was higher here than in Aspen; almost as high as Leadville, even though it lay not many miles from the open plains. On a smooth stretch Pete pointed with his whip toward the massive bulk of Pike's Peak to their left, pinkish in the afternoon light.

"Looks like a big lion crouching with its head on its paws looking out across the plains toward Kansas, don't it? I always say this new gold camp lays just back of the lion about where you'd expect to find its tail switching."

He laughed at his own flight of fancy, and Carolina laughed, and Thea laughed. Carolina did not know when she had had so much fun. Who would have dreamed that starting a home bakery in a new mining camp could be so stirring? But when she glanced at

145

Floss sitting primly beside her, she wondered if Floss needed to look quite so prissy and disapproving. She hoped Floss was not going to be like Letty, always telling her not to twitch her skirts when she walked and to keep her eyes down.

But she was soon absorbed in watching the maneuvering required to get the stage coach out of the way so that a heavily loaded ore wagon could pass. There was no question here of the right of the road. There were no rights. At wide places, the lighter vehicle must make way for the heavier one, or both go down to destruction.

"You did that to perfection," she sighed admiringly, after a particularly bad stretch. "I believe you could turn this team on the rim of a sombrero."

Pete modestly disclaimed any such dexterity, but his handsome weather-toughened face reddened with pleasure.

"You two ladies got any place staked out to sleep tonight?" he inquired presently. "The accommodations here aren't hardly fit for respectable women, so far."

Floss's felicity over this remark was patent. She relaxed for the first time since they had left Aspen. Carolina admitted that they had made no arrangement.

"I just took Nils Aagard, the assayer, over to catch the train down to Colorado Springs. He left the key to his office with me. He's got a cot in back. It's better than nothing, and you folks can stay there till we get a cabin up for you." There was no hint in his manner that he was giving up his own chance to sleep in a real bed under a roof, although both girls suspected it.

This Pete Ramsay was a wonderful fellow, Carolina thought as she thanked him; and her thoughts were easily legible.

Pete brushed aside their thanks, but his shoulders had a squarer set to them, and his tongue was suddenly loosened as he told them of the wonders of the new camp that lay ahead.

"Nils Aagard—that's the assayer—says this Mt. Pisgah district has always been kind of a riddle. He says they found colors here right from the start, but nobody ever figured there was enough to pay. Then some new gold was panned in the Seventies, and things picked up for a little while. But it wasn't till the Eighties that a real rush started—only to find out it was an April-fool joke. Some crook had salted a mine with gold from a shotgun. They almost lynched a fellow for it. After that, nobody would believe any good of the Mt. Pisgah district."

"Somebody must have believed," remarked Carolina sagely.

"Yeah, you're right—a bullheaded young cowhand named Bob Womack. He gophered so many holes digging for gold, his boss warned him all the cattle would have broken legs. Some cows had already got bogged down and lamed in the piddling stream they call Cripple Creek. But the cowhand kept right on digging till he found ore last January that assayed $250 a ton."

"Did he get rich?" Carolina wanted to know.

"He got drunk." Pete grinned down at her. "Raced off to Colorado City and had a few too many and galloped his horse up and down the streets yelling out his news. Started a regular stampede up here. I got this job driving the stage soon after; there's several loads of men coming in every day . . . and nary a decent flapjack, or cup of coffee, or piece of pie in the whole place," he said with mock mournfulness.

"We'll soon fix that," Carolina assured him. Here was a man! One who obviously relished his victuals, and who would never sulk and have spells and push his food around on his plate . . . When a jolt of the coach threw her lightly against him, against the great sledgehammer muscles of his biceps, a pleasant fire ran through her that she thought had long ago been quenched forever.

At that moment, to Carolina's intense chagrin, her picture-book baby took it into her head to act in a distressingly human way. She fussed and whined and finally yelled. Floss tried jiggling her. Carolina tried jiggling her. Thea only yelled harder and turned her head grimly away from the cold bacon and dry bread which they had brought along.

"She's tired. It's a long trip for a baby," Carolina apologized to the driver. Thea wailed and clawed at the front of Carolina's dress. Carolina lifted her up on her shoulders; she played rockabye with her; she said desperately, see-the-horsies, and Thea-go-bye-bye.

But Thea kept right on yelling. She hurled the dry bread and bacon over the side of the coach. She stiffened and held her breath until her face became the color of a ripe grape. There was a sympathetic lull in the talk behind them, acknowledging the helplessness of the male sex in the face of the nerve-shattering enigma of a bawling baby.

Pete said nothing. He whipped up his horses. At the halfway stop where he changed to a fresh six-horse team, he lifted the two women down over the wheel.

147

"Don't you know, ma'am," he muttered reprovingly to Carolina, "that you can't wean a youngun all in one day? You've got to take it gradual-like. Now you go sit on that rock behind those junipers and nurse the baby. I'll hold up everything till you're ready. The poor little tyke."

Carolina flushed. The very idea—talking right out to her like that! It was mortifying. But she followed his instructions. Twenty minutes later she reappeared with a dry, fed, sleepy baby.

Pete hoisted them up on to the seat again, careful to place Carolina beside him, as before. The baby promptly went to sleep. As they set off, Carolina hoped that Pete's marked preference for her was not based on any lack of respect. After all, he had been a little indelicate, back there.

Her fears were allayed when he confided to her shyly: "I had a wife and baby once. Lost them both of cholera within a week. A man sure gets lonesome for the sight of a little one—and a good woman——"

Carolina's spirits rose. That was more like it. Admiring and respectful both. It accounted for his practiced way of handling Thea. It also accounted for the comfortable way he cupped his hand under her elbow when he helped her up on to the high seat, and for the casual ease with which he snugged her to him when he tucked the laprobe over their knees. It accounted for a lot of things —all of them pleasant.

She straightened her bottle-green bonnet and tried to smooth her bottle-green skirt, a little the worse for all those hours of holding a damp and squirming baby, and smiled radiantly at nothing.

As the horses strained up a long slope, the distant high peaks seemed to rise with them. She asked Pete the name of the rugged white-crested ramparts to the southwest. He told her they were the Sangre de Cristo range.

"That's Mexican for Blood of Christ," he explained.

Blood of Christ. A little chill went through her. From her childhood she had feared and hated the name. Now it brought back her father and his somber preachments. She hoped it was not a bad omen; she had run away once . . .

At the top of the rise, Pete shouted, "Let her go!" and snaked his long whip harmlessly.

The horses broke into a gallop, either because of the crack of the

whip, or the oats waiting in the valley below, or because of something expectant and eager in the air.

The sun had already set behind the bare cone of Mt. Pisgah as
they dropped down into a high mountain valley. It was steeped in
rose and purple twilight, but she could see that it was a shallow,
sparsely timbered soupbowl, surrounded by unimpressive hills. As
they flew down the long incline, the high white peaks—Pike's and
those of the Sangre de Cristos—were hidden from sight by the
nearer hills.

A graceless place, thought Carolina in brief dismay as she stared
at the single street lined with straggling tents and yellow pine
shacks, punctuated here and there by flickering campfires. The
spring ruts were deep. Boxes and barrels were dumped any place.
There was the hollow sound of hammering in the thin air. It was
raw, it was ugly, the view was mediocre—but the indefinable intoxication of quick riches was everywhere.

The horses galloped down the home stretch. The passengers
shouted. Dogs barked frenziedly. The few inhabitants called out
welcoming halloos. They wanted newcomers; there was gold enough
for all.

We follow the booms! thought Carolina with an uprush of anticipation.

CHAPTER 17

THE TWO GIRLS SLEPT THAT NIGHT ON A COT IN A LEAN-TO OF A SLAB
shack that was the assay office, with Thea occupying the top half
of Carolina's gray canvas telescope. They knew they were lucky.
Most of the other new arrivals had slept either under the stars or on
the dirt floor of a tent saloon.

Their teeth chattered as they crawled out of bed the next morning to build a fire in the small rusted stove. Spring nights and
mornings, at an altitude of 9300 feet, are bone-chilling.

They had on their practical second-best clothes when Pete Ramsay arrived to take them to the so-called hotel for breakfast. As they
pushed their way into the crowded, smoky tent, Carolina's nostrils

distended. Pete was right. The settlement cried out for a good bakery. She was actually jubilant over the badness of the coffee and the doughiness of the flapjacks.

"Now if you ladies will give me some idea where you want your cabin, I'll see about getting the land for you," Pete offered, as they finished their breakfast and hurried out for a breath of fresh air. "Building sites aren't in great demand yet. But you wait. By this time next year, they'll be selling at so much a front foot." His was the unquenchable optimism of all boom town inhabitants.

Carolina smiled brilliantly at him. Inwardly she concurred, even as she turned to look at the wavering line of huts and tents that followed the single muddy thoroughfare. A barren, ugly, forbidding place—a boom camp—she thought, and exulted at the prospect. For they were in at the start.

Her gaze traveled down the slope to a handful of shacks and dugouts near the stream. Pete's glance followed hers.

"They call that Poverty Flats down there," he told her.

She averted her eyes. No more Flats for her, she thought grimly. No more poverty either, if she could help it.

The two girls and Pete, with the latter comfortably carrying Thea in the crook of his big arm, wandered thoughtfully along the roadway. Everywhere, Carolina saw battalions of stakes. Already the nearer hillsides were pocked and tunneled, as if by a band of giant moles. She saw men panning gold in the skimpy stream and wondered how they could scoop up enough water to do it. She suspected that a shortage of water would long plague the settlement.

They passed a saloon that was housed in a tent and another that was merely a plank laid across two barrels. The blacksmith shop, she noted, was doing a rushing business already. And beyond that, a large floored tent which said "Lodgings" over the door seemed to be spilling over with men. She peered with interest into the dark interior of an outfitters' log-cabin store, where gold pans and picks and chewing tobacco and miners' candles and bacon and flour were offered for sale; she would come here for certain of her supplies. As they passed the assayer's shack, she realized afresh how fortunate they were to have a roof over their heads, and how much they owed this Pete Ramsay. All three of them smiled when they came to a tattered tent set high on stilts, with an elbow of stovepipe sticking out and steam issuing from the rips, which bore the sign, "Hot and Cold Baths." Beyond that was the inevitable lawyer's office; for the law was almost as prompt in reaching a boom camp as were the fancy women.

As they tried to avoid the deeper mudholes, Carolina noticed that garbage was disposed of by tossing it into the street, where burros foraged at will. No wonder last night's quiet had been punctuated by a bedlam of braying.

At last they stopped on a sloping piece of ground a little higher than the rest. Carolina turned and looked around her. Yes, it had a lovely view of Mt. Pisgah, she decided. There was a fascination about that naked, solitary cone.

She tried to shut her mind to the flood of memories that the name evoked—childhood memories of sonorous Bible words and lugubrious hymn words.

> "—Till from Mt. Pisgah's lofty height,
> I view my home, and take my flight—"

She could hear again Letty's nasal twang lingering happily over the prospects of her imminent demise . . . She shook off the spell.

"Here!" she said gaily, holding out her arms as if to embrace this particular plot of ground. "Could we get this piece, do you think, Pete?"

Pete was sure that they could, and by merely handing over a few dollars, he said. For it belonged to a Jake Hartsell who badly wanted to scrape together enough money to get him down to the plains, since his last spell of mountain fever.

Floss, for all her added five years, was glad to leave decisions to Carolina, who made them with speed and aplomb. Carolina might sometimes be wrong, but she would never repine. There would always be other chances. Why look back?

Word had already got out that the bakery ladies wanted a cabin put up in a hurry. A dozen pairs of strong arms were only too willing to oblige. Whether it was the prospect of good food, or merely the longing of lonely men to be near young and attractive women again, so many amateur carpenters volunteered that they got in each other's way.

By night the sills of a one-room slab shack were laid on granite boulders, and the frame was up. Carolina could not sleep for having to get up and look out the window at the pale bare bones of her house, standing there in the moonlight.

151

She had had them turn the gable end toward the street. Already, in her mind's eye, she saw the high false front that would eventually be put across the gable to make a business house out of it instead of a mere dwelling. She saw the tall black letters, "Reliable Home Bakery." She saw herself and Floss as proprietors—making change —getting on in the world.

Never did a cabin go up so fast or so merrily. Carolina was everywhere at once, encouraging and admiring, while she held a two-by-four or laughed at a daring sally. She loved every minute of it. Thea loved it, too, clutching fistfuls of shavings and waving them over her head, entranced by so much shouting and pounding.

It was Floss who got the kettle from the assayer's shack and scoured it out so that Carolina could make coffee. They had never tasted better coffee, the men assured her gallantly, holding out their cups for more.

Every man among them had promptly fallen in love with Carolina and, with the horseplay characteristic of the American male in his public lovemaking, they "joshed" each other and wrestled like bears and called each other, "you splatter-eared bobcat" and "you old horsethief, you."

The bona fide bachelors were quick to make known their status to her. But all of them eagerly followed her with their eyes. With Floss they were less confident, for she met their amorous pleasantries with smiling indifference. They were forced to conclude that she was a confirmed maiden lady. But Mrs. Lawler now—there was nothing confirmed about her. There was a widow to take the eye of a man! They bragged a good deal to her and showed her promising pieces of float rock which they carried about in their pockets, touching them first with their tongues to make the metal gleam. By tomorrow each of them would be rich and a great catch for—a pretty widow.

Pete Ramsay reluctantly tore himself away to make his stage run to Divide and back. But he more than compensated for his absence when he found a cookstove and had it freighted in to the settlement on the second evening, as well as a precious four-paned window. Floss and Carolina were rapturous.

By the end of the third day, when Nils Aagard returned, they were ready to move into their new cabin. It had a wood floor. Most of the cabins still had pounded dirt floors. It had a window. It had a stove to heat it with and a door to close against the world.

That first night they could not bring themselves to go to bed. They had to walk around and straighten things and drive just one more nail and try the packing-box table first in this corner and then in that. Floss turned out to be surprisingly deft with hammer and nails. Already she had put up a three-cornered shelf for the water bucket.

"By fall I'll have the whole place lined with tar paper," she announced. "All you do is nail it on the studding, and if nobody pushes a chair leg through it, we'll get through next winter nicely."

It was not until the usually unprotesting baby began to fuss that they finally blew out the light and went to bed. The evening of the third day—thought Carolina with weary satisfaction.

They were barely dressed the next morning when a rap on the door announced the arrival of the first of their ubiquitous admirers. It was the quietest of the lot, a shy fellow named Laban Hull. He carried the half of a dressed venison over his shoulder.

"I figured you'd have to have meat to make a pasty," he apologized. "So I shot a deer that first night you ladies got in, and it's been hanging in a tree since. Venison makes a right good pasty," he assured them anxiously, as if to overcome their objections.

Meat! It was their most urgent need. They thanked Laban Hull so effusively that his ears turned scarlet with pleasure and he deposited the carcass on the doorstep and fled.

Carolina set to work at once, cutting up the meat and slicing the potatoes and onions and turnips.

Somehow the news got out. The bakery ladies were making meat pasties! The hum of voices outside the cabin grew.

Carolina tried to control her rising panic. What if the stove did not draw properly? Or the oven baked unevenly? Or she had lost her knack, acquired only last year from her neighbors on the Flats? But she could not fail. Floss was too reassuring and the men too trusting and Pete too proud.

She pushed back her sleeves resolutely and began to mix the pastry. With an empty quart beer bottle (she would never lack for rolling pins in a mining camp) she began to roll out the crust on the flat top of the packing box. Carefully she spread one half of the thin round of dough with the chopped meat and vegetables and then folded the other half over on to it, making a pie shaped like a half moon. A pasty must be exactly right, she thought anxiously; with just enough gravy, for no one liked a dry pasty; but not too

153

much, for no one liked a leaky one. And there was a special trick to "buttoning up" the edges so that the juices did not ooze out in the baking. She tucked two pasties, back to back, in each pie pan. Oh, they had to be good! Everything depended on them.

She piled more pitch pine in the stove. A pasty required an hour in a fairly hot oven, yet it must not be too hot or the crust would be done before the meat and vegetables. She tested the heat with the back of her hand. Now! She shoved in the pans. Then she and Floss stood back, scarcely breathing, to wait.

The men seemed to know by instinct when it was time to take the pasties out. The door inched open; one bushy face appeared, and then another. They crowded in like sheepish schoolboys, licking their lips. Carolina gave them a harried glance as she bent over the oven. Floss had seen to it that coffee was boiling in a big kettle; from somewhere she had acquired a collection of cups. The canned milk was ready.

Scarlet with heat and apprehension, Carolina drew out the first pasty. A long-drawn blissful *ah* went up from her audience. For the steam spurting from the little slits in the crust carried that most delicious aroma known to a hungry man—the smell of cooking meat and flaky pastry.

If only she and Floss could have sampled one first, thought Carolina. But there was no such possibility. She could only count noses —or mouths—and hope. She divided the pale-golden, smoking-hot pasties into equal portions and passed them out. Floss followed after her with the coffee.

Tremblingly Carolina bit into her own piece. She chewed and swallowed critically. Not until then did she dare lift her eyes to meet Floss's . . . It was good. The crust crumbled in her fingers. The venison was tender and savory. There was just enough gravy. It was a miracle of a meat pasty!

The men evidently concurred, for at that moment a shout went up from the bearded, booted crowd.

"It's the best meat pasty in this whole country, ma'am," one of them assured her.

"Or in the old country either," supplemented another, "and I take in all of Cornwall and Wales."

Carolina blushed and dropped her eyes.

"Oh, I've made better in my time. As soon as I get my hand

in——" she deprecated modestly, as good cooks have always done. But in her heart she knew that no one would ever make a better meat pasty.

II

THE NEXT FEW WEEKS WERE LIVED AT A GALLOP. THERE WERE TABLES and counters to build, shelves to put up, a partition to erect that would wall off their sleeping quarters. They were shameless about letting their paying customers help, and the customers insisted.

New strikes were being made every few days. On the Fourth of July the rich Independence mine was staked out by a carpenter named Stratton, who almost missed it because he had once taken a course in geology, and geologists insisted that there could be no gold in such a formation. Two druggists dug where one of them dropped his hat, and the fabulous Pharmacist mine resulted.

Bennett and Myers' cattle ranch, which was to be known as the three-hundred-million dollar cow pasture, was swarming by fall. The two owners finally laid out a townsite which they called Fremont. The chief streets were named Bennett Avenue and Myers Avenue. Lots sold at twenty-five and fifty dollars apiece, a tidy increase over nothing at all.

The Reliable Home Bakery added its false front that fall, and a lean-to containing a bedroom and a storeroom, and an ostentatious glass show window measuring a good three feet by four, carefully carted all the way from Colorado Springs by Pete. The two girls began to collect some savings, which they hid under the plush lining of Carolina's sewing basket.

Thea thrived. She took her first steps, toddling from one admiring miner to another. She said her first words which, to Carolina's faint maternal annoyance, were F'oss and Pete. Floss and Pete were entranced.

Winter set in, but they were all used to high country cold. Except for a spell of croup for Thea, which Floss surprisingly knew how to nurse her through, with a roaring fire and a steaming kettle of mountain sage on the stove, all three stayed well.

Carolina had never worked so hard or been so merry in her life. If Leo Cobb of her childhood had been right when he said she was happiest when she was "busy as a moth in a wool sock," she had every reason for happiness now.

Her new sense of well-being was augmented by Floss's happiness.

155

Laconic and unsentimental as ever, Floss was a different person now. She stopped often to swoop Thea up in her arms to make her crow. She waited on trade and washed dishes and learned to make a meat pasty that was a fair imitation of Carolina's, all the while radiating a crisp serenity.

Undoubtedly Carolina's gaiety had something to do with Pete Ramsay, who never missed a chance to stop in at the end of his stage run. His large and ruddy good looks made her feel small and helpless. In their occasional friendly scuffles in the back of the bakery—oh, always over something he was trying to grab away from her or that she was trying to grab away from him—she found herself overwhelmingly outclassed. He could pick her up off the floor with one arm. He could encircle her and hold her in a vise. She gloried in the feeling. Perhaps she was even guilty of creating such encounters. Or, when she found herself in one, of not extricating herself as quickly as she might.

"Pete!" she would shriek. "How dare you? I'll have you know I'm a prominent business woman."

And Pete would throw back his head and bay with laughter, showing his splendid white teeth.

"You're only a mighty pretty little gal to me, Carolina, that's all you are."

Carolina would laugh with him, caught up in the jolly contagion. All her life she had been wanting such laughter.

There were whole days and even weeks when she never thought of her childhood, or the street preaching, or her father; when she almost completely forgot about Roger Walling Jardine and that last, hunted, bad year in Aspen, with the interminable washings and the whispers of people and the look in Gilson's eyes and those stealthy knocks on the door after dark that she knew she must not answer.

Floss was noncommittal about Pete. But Carolina prodded her until she was forced to answer.

"Sure," Floss admitted tepidly. "He's a lot of fun to have around. Sure, he's a big, comical, good-looking fellow. But that's just the trouble: here he is, thirty years old, and what does he amount to? Has he put anything by? I'll bet he lives up everything he makes from week to week, with a game here and a glass there and a tart on Saturday nights."

Carolina flounced angrily away to hang up her dish towel.

"You sound like you might be Hattie Merkle, totting up a customer's assets!"

Floss shut her lips. Her back was straight as she limped off to bring in an armful of wood.

Most of the time the girls were excellent friends. Floss knew how to handle Carolina. Once, when the latter began to wind up for a dramatic exhibition of temper, with her fist lifted heavenward in a gesture of fury, Floss only looked at her with scornful good humor.

"You're just wasting it, Carolina. I've been laced down by the hardest-tongued Madams west of the Missouri. Save it."

Carolina immediately wilted and went out of her way to save Floss, whose bad leg was bothering her again.

The stream of prospectors thinned to a trickle that winter, but in the spring of '92 it swelled to a torrent again. The name of the town was changed from Fremont to Cripple Creek, and the big rush was on. The same lots that had brought twenty-five dollars in the fall now sold for fifteen hundred.

With each new stage load of prospectors, the girls' business increased and the front door bell tinkled oftener and the cigar box for cash under the counter filled faster.

A hotel went up, and then another, although it was still considered a stroke of luck to sleep in a chair under a roof. A bank, a newspaper, and stores followed. The saloons had mirrors and rails now. There were electric lights for the prosperous, their looped filaments glowing redly inside the bulbs. An epidemic of curbstone trading broke out although there were no curbstones. Prayer meetings were held in a tent on a hill; a church building was under construction.

"Bad women" were numerous; a sure sign of the town's prosperity. Floss and Carolina were careful to look the other way when they passed one of them on the street. They were still too close to these others to fraternize or play Lady Bountiful.

As Floss warned, "We dassent make a single slip, Carolina. Not one. If we do, this wouldn't be called the Reliable Home Bakery. It'd be known as Floss's Place before either of us could say, 'Call the sheriff!'"

Sometimes after work, and over a cup of coffee and a copy of the newspaper, the two friends would compare this self-consciously booming gold camp with Leadville's roaring youth and smile indulgently at Cripple Creek's claims to wildness. This was just cambric-tea wildness to their experienced eyes. Yet Cripple Creek managed to have its murders, and its alley suicides of soiled doves, and its stabbing affrays, along with the best—or the worst—of the mining towns of the Rockies.

"I see where somebody named Freddie May Allen was found dead in an alley today from an overdose of laudanum," said Carolina conversationally over the paper one night.

Floss made no answer. Carolina glanced up in time to see her compress her lips with a shudder. She resumed her perusal hastily. It was hard to connect Floss now with the Freddie May Allens of the world.

"And here's a room advertised for rent 'in a plastered house,' like it was a mansion on high," she rattled on. "And I see where they've got pug dogs for sale. And Pozzoni's Complexion Powder. And gentlemen's silk hats. Foo! Plug hats. When this town hasn't even got water piped in and we have to buy it from barrels."

"Everybody's too busy getting rich to bother," condoned Floss. "A greenhorn came in for dinner today and said he read in the paper back home how the ore here in Cripple Creek is so rich it won't crack, it will only bend—and how the gold is so plentiful they 'prospect with plows, mine with road scrapers, and ship out the scenery.'"

They laughed. That was a boom town for you. And just enough truth lay behind such fantastic assertions to make one give credence to even wilder ones. Hadn't some men, only the other day, been blasting for the foundations of a hotel over in Victor, when they struck gold—so that a shaft house went up instead of a lobby, and now it was called the Gold Coin mine?

As the town grew, it spread out over the vast shallow soupbowl of the valley. Now there were sidewalks, uneven and wooden, and often perched high on stilts. The new hotels, the Portland and the Palace, were crowded. The three brickyards worked day and night, even though most of the houses were still three-room slab shacks boarded both inside and out. Bennett Avenue was lined with mining exchanges and assay offices and clothing emporiums, while Myers Avenue was a solid row of variety theaters and dance halls and brothels.

For baked goods or even a simple meal, people flocked to the Reliable Home Bakery, run by those two nice little women just off Bennett Avenue.

ONE NIGHT IN LATE JULY OF THEIR SECOND SUMMER IN CRIPPLE
Creek, Floss hobbled across the street to borrow some molasses.
Thea was sound asleep in the lean-to, in the trundle bed beside the
larger bed that belonged to Carolina and Floss. Everything was
quiet. The curtains were drawn across the show window in the
front room.

Carolina was finishing up the day's tasks. She snugged the
checked tablecloth over the big pan of bread dough set to rise behind the cookstove. She liked tying up the strings of the day and
putting it neatly away.

She carried the sack of flour into the storeroom. Some day they
hoped to turn the storeroom into a parlor—as soon as they could
afford an organ for it and an ingrain carpet and a center table. She
chuckled at the thought of the organ; for Floss knew only the kind
of songs she had given up forever, and Carolina knew only fire-and-
brimstone hymns that she likewise had forsworn.

She blew out the lamp and went to stand in the open doorway
looking off up toward Mt. Pisgah. The last sunset streak had departed, leaving a greenish afterglow behind the cone. The night
breeze came in sweetly, although there was a nip in it. With the
last rays of the setting sun, there was always this brisk warning slap
in the air. The wind felt good on her flushed face.

She stood there listening to the revelry coming up from Myers
Avenue. There seemed to be a row everywhere. She could hear the
shrill singing in the variety theater two doors down. From the
gambling house next door came only the occasional subdued calling of numbers or the triumphant bark: "Keno!" They were lucky
to be next to a gambling house, which was always the quietest place
in town. What if it had been a dance hall or a church!

Farther away sounded the complaining bray of a foraging burro.
Dogs barked intermittently, rousing each other with staccato out-
bursts that died down with no more excuse than they started. She
could hear the constant thunder of the stamp mills, like heavy
wagons rumbling over cobblestones, and saw in her mind's eye the
interminable stamping of the iron shoes that ground the ore, like
a row of children raising and lowering their feet with a peculiar,
senseless rhythm.

Underneath it all, and above it all, was the breathless asthmatic
sound of pumping that never stopped day or night; and the hollow

tramp, tramp, tramp of feet on wooden sidewalks that likewise never stopped. All these, to Carolina, made up the familiar night sounds of a boom camp.

Everything was going perfectly, she thought. Thea was a beautiful, reserved, patrician little thing past two, with grave, weighing eyes and delicate features—but healthy too. The business had prospered. They were serving two meals a day now. They still kept their savings under the lining of her sewing basket, but soon they would have to open a bank account.

She ought to be satisfied, she told herself, leaning disconsolately against the doorframe. What more could anyone ask than a business of her own, a fine and loyal friend, and a beautiful child? But she did ask more, she thought, looking ahead at the months that stretched into years.

She walked heavily outside to bring in an armful of wood to start tomorrow's fire. The sounds of human revelry were louder out here. Everybody else was happy. She had heard the stage come in hours ago, but there had been no sign of Pete Ramsay since. He was evidently not interested enough to bother.

She sighed and bent down to pick up the wood. But she straightened up at the sound of a heavy tread on the gravel and a tuneless rumbling that was Pete's idea of humming. Her heart set up a hammering. Pete rounded a corner and came toward her swiftly in the dark. The armful of wood dropped. She had not supposed she could be so glad to see anybody.

"Well, if it isn't my girl waiting for me!" He caught hold of her arms above the elbows and lifted her clear off the ground in his exuberance. A great big girl like her, Carolina thought with gratification, her spirits soaring. He smelled of the barbershop—so that was why he was late—and of pipe tobacco and maybe the glass or two he had stopped to take on his way up. And of course, a little of sweat and horses and chewing tobacco. But she was afraid she did not mind any of it; she was hungry for that man smell. Every fiber in her vivid, healthy body leaped in response.

But even as he held her, half-laughing, half-teasing, she sensed the change taking place in him. The boyish exuberance receded, giving way to something far more urgent and demanding. There was a resistless heaviness about his movements—a slow, magnetized quality that was unbearably exciting to Carolina. He set her down, but he did not let her go. Instead, he drew her toward him until she was close enough to feel the warmth and power of him. She was incapable of resistance.

"You're my woman, Carolina," he said thickly. "I started feeling like this the first time I hoisted you up over the wheel of the stage a year ago."

"Did you? I didn't know——" That was a lie. She had always known that Pete was wild for her; but something had stood in the way of her responding wholly to him. At the moment she could not think what it was.

Her mind was a whirling pinwheel of fireworks. Her knees were bread dough. Always before, he had treated her like a playfellow. Now she knew that the scuffling and banter were past. This was urgent. This was what her body cried out for: the answer, she was sure, to all her hungers and her lonelinesses. His hands holding her elbows were shaking. In another instant they would be in each other's arms, in a locked, primitive, savage embrace that would brook neither subterfuge nor delay.

Carolina did not hear the tired limping steps inside the kitchen. When Floss's voice finally penetrated her senses, she had the feeling she had heard it several times. Breathing hard, she pushed Pete away and steadied herself against the pile of wood with her outflung hand.

"I'm outside, Floss. I came out to get some wood. Pete's helping me."

When they had composed themselves, they entered the kitchen, with Pete carrying the armful of wood. He was red of face and uneasy of eye. But Floss was lighting the lamp in its bracket.

"Thanks, Pete," Floss said dismissingly over her shoulder to him. "You can dump it in the woodbox before you go."

Carolina bristled. Before you go! She liked that.

Pete dropped the wood. He fidgeted on one foot and then the other as he dusted off his hands and waited for an invitation to stay. But Floss was obviously closing up for the night. There was nothing for him to do but leave, which he did, reluctantly.

When he had closed the door, Carolina began to take the pins out of her hair. She was "put out" with Floss. Floss need not have been quite so high-handed.

"What's the matter, Floss?" she asked at last sulkily.

"Matter aplenty, I'm afraid," Floss sighed. "I suppose you wondered what was keeping me." Carolina had not wondered at all; she had been much too occupied. "I slipped in to see the new doc that's just hung up his sign. He says I've got to go to Colorado Springs and have an operation or I'll be completely bedfast in six months. He's educated, so he knows. Says I should go right away. It will cost like fury. I haven't got it. And besides, you can't do without me here in the bakery."

Carolina melted instantly. Floss needed her.

"Of course I can get along, and we have too got it—or if we haven't I'll find it. Everything I've got is yours, Floss. You take the stage out with Pete in the morning. I only wish I could go with you."

Floss looked at her, and her face crimped. "You're—nobody ever before——" She turned hastily and hobbled into the bedroom.

Long after she had gone to bed, Carolina lay beside Floss and thought, Good old Floss; I'll never be able to pay her back. Money can't do it. If it hadn't been for Floss——

But her mind, unbidden, kept edging back to that moment under the stars. She could not keep it fastened on Floss and her problems; she could not discipline the errant thrill that coursed through her. Pete was so handsome and so strong. His hands on her arms—his breathing so close to her—— In another minute . . .

She stirred restlessly. At last she crept out of bed and went to look out the back door at the night beauty of the mountains. The air was cooling to her cheeks and her senses. She thought heavily that it was no doubt a good thing that Floss had called to her just when she did. Probably Pete hadn't saved much, and maybe he did have a weakness for a game and a glass. Well, thank goodness, it hadn't gone any further. Once more Floss had stepped in at the critical moment and saved her. She was relieved, and she felt only gratitude toward Floss, she told herself firmly. Certainly, she was grateful.

She began to pace back and forth along the splintered boards of the kitchen floor. Back and forth, back and forth. And it was the restless, frustrated pacing of a woman caged by life.

CHAPTER 18

THEA HAD THE EXASPERATING INDEPENDENCE OF A TWO-YEAR-OLD, insisting upon walking all by herself when her mother was in a hurry to go somewhere; and then, just when the latter was dragging home laden with bundles, suddenly wilting down into a heavy little bundle that had to be carried too.

Carolina hunkered down before her impatient baby in the front part of the bakery and poked Thea's waving arms into a jacket and tied a bonnet on her head. It was August, but in the year 1892 children were not exposed to the dangers of a walk without bonnets and cloaks and ankle-length dresses.

She knew she had no business leaving the bakery so near supper time, with Floss away in Colorado Springs recovering from her operation, and a new helper in the kitchen. But Thea was a persuasive piece. She had only to look up at her mother with her head on one side and her elfin smile (Carolina preferred not to recall that it was Roger's smile), and she melted like butter on a hot flapjack.

Carolina gave a satisfied look around the bakery and lunch room, at the long clean counter with its German-silver casters of condiments and its glass spoon-holders placed at intervals before the row of stools, and into the spotless kitchen beyond from which issued the warm crusty smell of fresh bread. She was proud of her bread.

From the kitchen doorway she spoke to the new helper, whose name was John McGregor. Had she believed in prayer, she would have called him the answer to one. For no sooner had Floss left for Colorado Springs two weeks before than this down-on-his-luck miner had appeared, asking for a job.

The sober Scotch-Canadian in his thirties was sick of golden promises. He was willing to give up being an entrepreneur, willing to exchange a gnawing hunger under his belt and the elusive possibility of making a fortune for regular wages and good hot meals.

"I guess I'm no gambler, Mrs. Lawler," he told her with a half-smile. "I'd rather set my sights for a rabbit, knowing I'll have rabbit stew for sure, than to aim at a bear and miss." The half-smile was at his own expense now. "Especially when the bear turns and takes out after me."

Carolina promptly hired him and found herself liking him in an absent-minded way, although she was too absorbed in her own problems to wonder much about the history of this quiet, lanky, sallow-faced man with the long upper lip and the steady eyes. She was thankful for his thrift and carefulness; it was gratifying to find the potatoes pared thin and the fire banked at night before he left, but it was scarcely romantic. She found it suitable and proper to be respectfully addressed as Mrs. Lawler, ma'am, but it did not make her heart beat any faster. She sensed that his occasional shy twinkle hid a subtler wit than was usually current in a mining camp; but she enjoyed bellowing laughter and a joke that was as plain as a nudge in the ribs. In fact she enjoyed a man like Pete Ramsay, although she would not admit it. For she told herself that Floss had undoubtedly been right about Pete. Floss was likely to be right when she assayed a man. Still it did no harm to pass the time of day with him when he came in from his stage run, she argued to herself.

So John McGregor took on the protective coloration of the bakery and became a part of it. Carolina was always one to undervalue what came easily.

"Do you think you can manage if I go out for a while?" she asked McGregor from the doorway. "I won't be gone long. But that child has been hectoring me to take her for a walk."

"I can manage, Mrs. Lawler," he said simply, and she knew that he could—under almost any circumstances.

She smiled brightly at him, but already he was merging into the background, becoming a tried and useful piece of kitchen furniture.

Carolina reached down for Thea's hand. But Thea jerked her hand away and staggered joyously ahead out the door in a run that threatened to trip her on her long skirts. Carolina followed more sedately.

As she turned on to the wooden sidewalk, she smiled mockingly to herself at the town's pious vaunt that any woman was safe on the streets of Cripple Creek so long as she kept her eyes straight ahead and walked fast. She sniffed. A woman had better not try it alone and after dark, no matter how fast she walked. But if she had a child with her, she was safe at any hour. Her eyes softened as they rested on Thea.

In their year and a half here, she and Floss had not made a single misstep. The town accepted them as a hard-working pair, one a maiden lady of twenty-five, a little on the prim side, and the other a young widow struggling to raise her child.

Carolina savored her respectability. Only those who have hungered and yearned for it can know its lingering sweetness. To think that a child could make such a difference! Until her baby was born, her baby without a name, she had not cared. She had hated respectable people because they reminded her of her father. And then Thea had come into her life, and the most important thing in the world became the safeguarding of her child.

She had almost stopped worrying lately. There was such slight danger of their being found out. Who, among Floss's former customers, would ever recognize this plain, dowdy woman walking with a cane? Who would ever think that Carolina was not the worthy young widow she claimed to be?

She felt secure and successful. She did not admit that part of her complacence consisted of the knowledge that, in spite of motherhood, hard work, and the passing of time (she would be twenty at the end of the month), she was still desirable. Pete Ramsay dogged her shadow. Not that she would ever consider him seriously, she told herself for the hundredth time; but it was nice to be wanted. And there was McGregor in the kitchen always watching her admiringly, besides the swarm of miners out in front offering her jokes and compliments. She did like having men around.

So great was her sense of well-being that she was wholly unprepared for what awaited her. Thea had darted out of sight. Carolina started on a run to catch her. She turned a corner and all but collided with a small crowd. Even then, she did not hear the voice, so intent was she upon retrieving her child from that maze of trousered legs.

And then the sound penetrated her consciousness. For a second she stood quite still, congealed by the harsh, demanding, impassioned voice. Her father! A revulsion so great went through her that she was almost sick, there on the street. Only the fact that mother love is of the body and the instincts, rather than of the mind, kept her from abandoning Thea completely and running wildly in the opposite direction. As it was, she stood rooted to the spot. Then, white-faced—even her lips had a grayish cast—she forced herself to follow her child.

"Did you ever feel a red-hot branding iron pressed against your quivering flesh? Did you ever drink molten slag straight from the furnace? Then you know, sinners, what awaits you unless you repent——"

"Go to it, parson," jeered a tipsy voice from the crowd. "Give 'em hell about hell!" The speaker admired his witticism; he repeated it several times.

There was a squashy impact as a piece of limp garbage struck a man's face. Jude Lawler only brushed it away impatiently and went on.

By now Carolina had caught hold of the tail of Thea's long dress and pulled her back. The child struggled, but Carolina managed to reel her in and pick her up. Thea stiffened backwards in a furious arc and let out a howl of rage.

The sound disconcerted the street preacher far more than had the hurled garbage. He turned toward the commotion. There was a moment of blankness, as his glance rested on the set-faced young mother trying to subdue her child; then his eyes gleamed in startled recognition. But he picked up the thread of his harangue and went on, as Carolina, carrying her protesting child, hurried back the way she had come.

She was panting from more than exertion as she rounded the corner and stopped to lean against the side of the building. She half-expected her father to come after her—preaching or no preaching. Presently she ran on again. She had been so sure she was safe, that she had built a new life for herself. Why had she not remembered that reformers as well as sinners followed the booms? Why had she not expected, now that silver was on the down grade and gold on the up, that her father would come to Cripple Creek?

But he can't touch me, she tried to reassure herself . . . Oh, couldn't he? He had ways, malign and righteous, she remembered.

She slowed to a walk and set the child down. At the sound of running footsteps behind her she turned.

"Carolina!" called out the boy who was racing toward her. His voice broke on a high note.

"Mat!" she exclaimed incredulously. "Oh, Mat." Her tones rounded out rich and soft with wonder and love. For it was her brother, grown lanky and tall, with a few pimples dotting his chin, and a hollow-eyed look that ill became his lengthening frame. Why, he must be fourteen, going on fifteen. He did not look as if he had had a square meal in weeks.

She dropped the baby's hand and caught Mat to her, kissing him unashamedly, the tears blinding her. She saw Mat's bony Adam's apple working. He patted her wordlessly. He was as tall as she already. In another year he would top six feet.

"Oh, Mat, I've wondered and wondered about you all. I've got a bakery a couple of doors down. I just took some fresh bread out of the oven. Wouldn't you like a slice?"

Mat's eyes gleamed like those of a hungry stray dog.

Carolina picked up Thea's hand again and propelled her firmly toward home.

"And there's also some beans and good hot stew. Here we are, Mat." Carolina almost forgot her father in the quick flood of tenderness over being able to "do for" her brother.

It was later than she had realized. The supper crowd was gathering. McGregor was dishing out food and pouring coffee and scurrying back and forth with money to put in the cigar box under the counter.

Carolina shed her hat and grabbed an apron. She placed Mat at the end of the counter nearest the kitchen so she could fill and refill his plate. She was shocked and touched by the amount he consumed.

When the crowd thinned, she brought her own plate and sat down beside him . . . So the whole family had trekked to Creede when the silver boom started there? And Letty had found herself a husband? Not Letty, born to be an old maid!

Mat chuckled with his mouth full. "He's near as old as Pa and has four children and an old mother to care for. He said Letty could bring Rosalie with her. So Letty decided Pa didn't need her as much as Mr. Hinchley did, and that it was her duty to make a home for him."

They grinned briefly at each other, all their old unspoken clan knowledge linking them together. Letty, outwitting her father through her weak, complaining martyrdom.

"But you, Mat—you don't look as if you got enough to eat?"

He flashed her a look. "You know Pa——"

She knew. She recalled those endless blessings before meals because her father preferred praying to eating, while the children fidgeted hungrily.

"I used to worry about how you'd do in fractions after I left," she said.

"Not very good," he admitted. "But I'm all right in other things. I want to be a telegraph operator. If I could only stay in one place long enough to get some more schooling, I could be. I've got a little book. I practice Morse code all the time," he finished importantly.

She sighed. What chance had he, with their father? If she could only help.

The door opened. Chill air rushed in, but no one entered. The talk ceased as men craned to see who stood in that open doorway.

Carolina lifted her eyes with sudden dread, knowing what she would see. Her father stood with hands braced on either side of the doorframe surveying the room from under lowering brows.

Before she had time to reason, or to fight back, or to hate, she was stung into momentary pity by his haggard thinness, by his look of crucified thinness. She saw again in retrospect—far more clearly than she had seen it at the time—the fringe of men about him this afternoon, the limp piece of hurled garbage. Unconsciously she put her hand up to her face.

But the next minute she hated him. For now he was singling out Mat and herself.

"Ah, so there you are! A fine way for children to treat their own father—running off while he preached the Word to gorge on rich foods——"

A half-dozen miners paused with spoons in midair. McGregor in the kitchen stopped rattling stove lids. Even Thea, playing on the floor, was silent. Out of one corner of her eye Carolina saw that Pete had come in through the back door and was gazing at her father. She put her arm across Mat's shoulders; she could feel him tremble.

Carolina thought desperately, I must stand up to Pa now for Mat's sake. Surely he has no power over me.

"Won't you sit down, Pa? Let me give you some stew and a cup of coffee."

He looked as gaunt as one of his own underfed Gospel team. He glanced around the hot little room accusingly.

"This is your place then? I saw the name of Lawler, after I'd hunted through several streets of this modern Gomorrah for Mat."

He seemed to waver; his nostrils dilated ever so slightly at the smell of food. Then he shook off his transient weakness. "Where did you go that night you ran away? Who gave you aid, ungrateful daughter?"

Carolina was silent, fighting the old terrifying spell that, in spite of all her efforts, threatened to overwhelm her again. Her hand shook as she poured the coffee and pushed it toward him along the counter. He made no move to take it. Thea, alarmed by the angry vehemence of the strange man's voice, crowded up close behind her mother.

Jude Lawler stared down at the child with a question in his eyes. "Yours?"

There was no need for her to answer as Thea frowned fiercely up at him from the shelter of her mother's skirts.

Pete was moving forward from the kitchen. When Thea saw him, she turned and ran to him in relief. He picked her up. Jude Lawler looked ominously at Pete.

"Is he the father?"

Carolina tried to answer, but the words stuck in her throat. She could only shake her head.

"So! You have a child, but no husband. Then that is why the name of Lawler is out in front—your name as a maid. You have no husband to give you his name, or your child a name——"

The miners looked down and fidgeted. Manlike, they wished they were anywhere but here, yet none knew how to break away.

Carolina stood there clenching her hands under the edge of her apron. She had only to hold her head high and refuse to answer, she told herself. But so great was the old domination that her words came out against her will.

"I was married—I mean I thought I was——" she whispered.

"You thought you were! Just as you thought you could flout your own father and run away on a winter's night in your lewd finery—and still come to some good end. But God's judgment overtook you, and you fell into the hands of a vile traducer——"

Even as the angry blood pounded in Carolina's temples, she thought that those were strange words indeed to apply to Roger Jardine.

"He was nothing of the sort."

But her father could always best her. "Then where is he?"

Where was he! She shriveled.

"Perhaps it is not yet too late, my daughter. Perhaps your soul can still be saved, even though you may have lived the life of a harlot and eaten the bread of wickedness——"

She began to shake with fury and despair. For she was looking about her at all the crumbling walls of her respectability, of her self-esteem, of her very safety, that she had so carefully built up in the last year and a half. A mad and cruel Samson—he had brought them tumbling down about her. "Like as a father pitieth his children——" Pity! She hated her father. She hated the God that he was like.

She sensed the furtive glances of the men. She understood. No longer would she be "that nice little widow that runs the bakery." From now on she would be "the Lawler woman." They were no worse than most; they were simply women-starved men who would take what they could get. Her sole protection up to now had been their conviction of her "goodness." Floss had known. One little slip, one little proof of a deviation from rectitude, and it meant the end of her guarded security. Never again would she dare walk the streets of the town alone. And Thea? What would become of Thea?

An insane rage possessed her. Her father was wicked. He blasted and killed everything he touched.

"—so let us pray for your soul, my daughter," he said wearily. As always, after a righteous outburst, his own resentment and wrath had spent itself. He was beginning to take a mordant satisfaction in saving his own child.

A crimson mist blinded her. She could kill him; she would kill him. She whirled, reached for the heavy crockery sugar bowl, which could be a lethal weapon in the hand of a violent woman —and hand and sugar bowl were pinioned in brawny fingers. Pete's fingers. For a big man, he had moved fast. She stiffened to rebel; then she wilted.

Pete removed the sugar bowl from her grasp and set it back on the counter again. She could feel the warmth of him at her shoulder, could hear his hard breathing. He reached out and drew her into the shielding circle of his arm. His left arm still held Thea. The three of them faced Jude Lawler.

Then it was that Pete Ramsay committed the finest act of his life. He said with the unshaken calm of a big man who need not bluster or bully, "I guess that's all, Reveren'. Carolina and I are on our way to the Justice's right now. That is, if she'll do me the honor to become my wife. I'll start adoption proceedings for Thea—I'd be mighty proud to call her mine——" He turned and looked at the gaping miners. "A shivaree would be in order, boys, about Saturday night," he said in jovial dismissal.

At his words, a vast and humble gratitude suffused Carolina. For the tension in the room snapped like a too-taut bowstring. The men began to wipe off dripping mustaches and fumble in pockets for change and stand up to go. The whole atmosphere had altered within those few seconds that it took Pete Ramsay to set things right. From the sinister, the situation had become only facetiously commonplace. Men like these were not over-fussy about youthful indiscretions. All they needed to know was that Carolina was removed from the field of prey. And she was—by Pete's words. She had suddenly become a protected wife and mother.

To Carolina Pete Ramsay became a god at that moment.

Jude Lawler did not easily relinquish an unsaved soul. He had known a savage joy in rescuing this lost sheep, in publicly bringing her back into the fold. Now these holy satisfactions were being snatched away from him. For after all, when a straightforward young fellow who tops six feet and weighs two hundred offers to make an honest woman of a soiled dove, there is little "saving" left to be done. He surveyed the situation dourly from under his lion's brows and turned to go.

"Come, Mat," he said and went out.

Mat did not move. He sat staring after his father. There was abject appeal in the glance he turned on Carolina. Her hand tightened on his thin shoulder.

It was then that Pete added the last heroic cubit to his stature, in her eyes.

"Make your home with us if you want to, boy. We'll be glad to have you."

Mat's eyes were doglike in their devotion, and Carolina had to blink hard.

"You can be a witness at the wedding, Mat. Come on, Carolina, get your hat before you change your mind."

Perhaps no bride ever had a stranger jumble of thoughts during her wedding ceremony than those which went through Carolina's mind a half-hour later, before the Justice of the Peace . . . This will show Pa. "Mrs. Peter Ramsay and Miss Dorothea Ramsay."

This time I'll have a regular certificate, even if I don't have any roses or court train. Everything's going to be recorded, right and legal. If only I never have to see Pa again. The bride's attendants were her brother and her small daughter. I'll make it up to you, Pete, I promise I will——

On the walk back to the bakery, with Thea riding on Pete's shoulder, beating him over the head and crying giddap, Mat was suddenly shy, while Carolina was wordless. She was beyond words. Pete was a knight, a savior. He might have worn a nimbus around the crown of his handsome black head.

In delicious perturbation she made up a bed for Mat in the storeroom, succeeded in getting Thea off to sleep, and emptied some hooks for Pete to hang his clothes on. Floss could no longer disapprove of Pete after tonight, she thought in a blur of triumph. For Pete had proved himself. He had stood up to her father like a man. He had saved both her and Thea.

She thought how different Pete was from Roger Jardine. Not weak and disloyal and easily turned aside. Pete was a rock of a man.

She blushed at the uxorious urgency of the arm about her waist and made a laughing pretense of brushing the arm aside so that she could finish putting clean linens on their marriage bed. If she so much as turned toward him . . .

But she did not mind the urgency. She did not mind that Pete would never woo her with the slow persuasiveness of a Roger Jardine, beguiling her and captivating her, until at last she kindled too. Pete was not subtle. But who wanted subtlety, if falsity went with it? Pete was honest and forthright and hungry for his woman. And she was a woman now, and not a skittish girl who had to be wooed with skilful guile.

And then Pete could be put off no longer. The lamp light went out. He had extinguished it with one quick gust and turned to take her.

I'll make it up to you, Pete, she promised silently in a swift, blind rush. I'll be a good wife to you. I'll always do my duty——

It is seldom that inclination and duty coincide so pleasantly.

CHAPTER 19

PETE WAS THE REAL REASON FOR CAROLINA'S STARTING HER FIRST bank account. She had been putting it off with one excuse after another. The truth was that, like all the financially unlettered, she was timid of the whole world of banks and bankers. But the little hoard under the red-plush lining of her sewing basket threatened to burst its hiding place.

The business was prospering. She had enlarged the bakery according to McGregor's advice, pushing the walls back and building on at the rear. Under the sign, "Reliable Home Bakery," a smaller sign now said, "Meals." More and more she had come to depend on John McGregor. She bought a wagon and a staid old horse so that Mat, who was fifteen, could make deliveries after school hours.

Now there were accounts to keep and letters to write. She had a small front corner of the lunch room partitioned off to make an office. But it was never called "Carolina's office," or "Mrs. Ramsay's office." That would have been unwomanly. So, even though Pete was absent all day on his stage trips, the fiction was maintained that he ran the business from the office.

Actually Pete seldom set foot in it. After a vigorous day in the open air, he was much too tired to figure. If he did drop in late at night when his wife was bent over her desk deep in a struggle with bookkeeping, it was only to give her a hug, or to plant a kiss under the coppery curl at the back of her neck, which immediately led to other things—quite unconnected with business.

Carolina was happy. Floss's operation had been successful, although she was still in Colorado Springs. Mat was busy all day in school, and after school he drove the delivery wagon. McGregor —she seldom thought about McGregor, and when she did, it was only to be grateful that he did not need thinking about—continued on his dependable, unflagging way. Pete was the same wonderful Pete, with his vast good nature and his laughing relish for life. Thea adored him and ran to throw her arms around his knees the moment he entered the bakery. Ah, Pete was what she had been longing for and needing, she told herself often. Each day's separation, when he set forth, was a wrench of parting. Each night's reunion, when he came back to her, was a marvel of completion.

And then, as if to add luster to her every other happiness, she found out that she was going to have a baby. Pete was jubilant. He could think of nothing finer, he told her, than to have a small Carolina around. Carolina's eyes filled as she thought of another time.

Everything would have been quite flawless except for the occasional rumors of her father that sifted in from neighboring towns. She had not seen him since the night he had walked out of the bakery; but she would hear of him, preaching in Anaconda, or breaking up a bar in Victor, or being run out of Altman. She longed to erase the memory of him completely, but she could not. She would wake up in the night and see him standing there in the doorway of the bakery, a great lonely crag of a man, looking with brief and haggard longing toward the steaming cup of coffee she pushed toward him, and then spurning it and walking out alone into the darkness, deserted even by Mat. She hated him, she told herself bitterly. But if only he had not gone out the door looking so old and defeated and *hungry*.

But except for these memories, her life was richly content. Everything she touched seemed to flourish. She ventured to hire a helper for McGregor so that, as she explained to him kindly, "You'll be able to peel off that apron once in a while and act like a man."

She could not understand why he flushed and shut the door so hard when he went out.

It was just as well that the business was flourishing, for there were many demands upon it these days. A little vertical wrinkle came and went between Carolina's brows. She had a habit of biting her full red lower lip when she was figuring, and she was always figuring. No matter how much money the bakery made, it was never quite enough.

There were Floss's expenses, for instance. Floss wrote apologetically that now the doctors said she ought to stay on for several months more in Colorado Springs, taking baths and treatments. She didn't know where the money was coming from. But Carolina wrote back promptly that *she* knew; she had almost enough under the lining of the sewing basket. She would send it along in a few days. Pete had approved; he never begrudged a penny she sent to Floss, Carolina discovered.

Besides Floss's expenses, there was Mat to clothe and send to school and feed. Especially to feed. He ate as if, according to Carolina, he "had a hollow the size of the Glory Hole inside him." She loved to watch him eat. And Thea outgrew her clothes and scuffed her small button shoes through almost overnight.

Pete's wages somehow always seemed to go for other things: for the sleek muff he brought her from Colorado Springs; for the doll for Thea and the new checked waistcoat for himself, and—if the truth must be admitted—for an occasional game and glass at the end of the day. After all, she reminded herself tolerantly, you couldn't expect a handsome young racer like Pete to settle down to double harness all at once without an occasional shying off the road.

But no matter how numerous were the demands upon her, she let nothing interfere with gathering together the money for Floss's needs. It was her first debt to life. If it hadn't been for Floss——

She thought she would count the money over just once more before she went to bed. She would be sending it to Floss in the morning. Humming softly, she moved about the dimly lighted bedroom. Thea was asleep in her small bed in the corner. The bakery was closed for the night, with Mat in the storeroom and McGregor gone to his room in the next block. Pete had strolled over to Johnny Nolan's for a game.

She picked up the sewing basket and carried it out to the lighted office. Seating herself at the desk, she ran her hand under the red plush lining. A puzzled expression spread over her face. But of course it was there. It had only slipped farther back. She ran her hand all the way in. In a sudden frenzy she ripped out the whole lining and turned the basket upside down, scattering spools and thimbles and pincushions in all directions. But the money was not there.

When Pete's steps sounded outside the door, a little high and wide and weaving, she was waiting for him in shocked incredulity.

"Pete! The money in my sewing basket is gone."

She hoped he would say that McGregor had taken it. Or that Mat must have yielded to temptation. Or that he had seen Thea playing with the basket . . . Thus love turns women into miscreants when they would find excuses for their men.

She was unprepared for his smiling confession.

"Oh, that. Sure, I 'borrowed' it for a little while, honey. Too bad you took a notion to count it just when you did. Usually I have better luck."

"Usually——?" Her eyes were dismayed.

"Yeah. Usually I get it paid back before you even know it's missing. All I hold out is my winnings." He smiled mischievously down at her. "Just give me a few more days and a change of luck, and the money'll be right back there in that red plush bank of yours, safe and sound."

He slid his arm about her, but she held him off.

"The money wasn't yours, Pete. It wasn't mine either. It belongs to the doctors down in the Springs. I was saving it to send to Floss first thing in the morning."

He was imperturbable. "Shucks, those doctors!" he scoffed. "Won't hurt them to wait a little. You know they all roll in money like doughnuts in powdered sugar. Don't you worry, puss. I'll win back that money in no time."

He tilted her face up toward his smiling confident one. His lips were on hers. She tried to hold back primly; but there was no prim-ness in her when Pete had her in his arms. She melted.

It was not until the next morning that the little vertical wrinkle reappeared as she collected the scattered spools of thread in the office and replaced them soberly in her damaged sewing basket. Her red plush bank, Pete had called it. Very well . . .

An hour later, Mr. Tom Higby, president of the new bank on the corner, looked up from his roll-top desk to see a grave-eyed young woman approaching, her fingers clasped hard on her reticule.

"They said I was to see you, Mr. Higby. I'd like to start a bank account, if you please. You see—that is, I run the Reliable Home Bakery, but I never wrote a check in my life. I wonder if you'd tell me something about banking."

Would he! His narrow chest expanded. He pulled a chair up for her close beside his desk. His eyes were bright behind his glasses as he looked across at her. How few young women really wanted information, he thought, from an older—that is, from a mellower and wiser man.

As he handed her checkbook to her with the final instructions, he remarked, "You should thank your lucky stars you happen to be living in a gold town like Cripple Creek instead of in a silver town

176

right now. Cripple Creek is about the only bright spot left in a nation on the verge of panic."

"Panic?" she repeated. She had been hearing the word everywhere.

"Depression—whatever you want to call it. It's something that happens when money gets tight and prices drop too far. Even the price of silver is down today because of the big output. In addition, crops have been poor for several years due to the drouth, and the farmers are neck-deep in debt. Naturally they want to pay back those debts with easy money. And naturally their creditors—the big money interests—don't want them to."

Carolina listened intently while he explained those cryptic words she had been hearing: "easy money"—"tight money"—"free silver"—"gold standard." It was not so hard, she thought, if you had a head for figures and really listened. In fact, it was exhilarating, like learning to read, to have formerly meaningless symbols suddenly come alive.

This was the first of several discreet little talks between Carolina and her banker. Discreet, for Tom Higby's reputation as a banker was quite as delicate as any woman's. He vastly enjoyed his role of tutor. He was sure that Carolina had a man's mind; but he was mistaken. She had the mind of a mother animal caring for her young. Yet it was a good mind, quick to grasp anything that affected her own, although completely lacking in objectivity. It could be savage and selfish and ruthless, to keep her small world going—in sum, a female mind—which may have been why Tom Higby found it so stimulating.

"The whole trouble is," he remarked impressively one day, "that the country has never recovered from the Crime of 1873."

She wrinkled her brows prettily.

He cleared his throat and settled back in his chair. Dispensing information to a pretty woman was almost as titillating as dispensing gewgaws to one—and a good deal safer.

"Yes, crime," he repeated. "I'm a 'silver man' myself, even if I do make my living in a gold town. It was a black crime when Congress ordered the mint to stop making silver dollars back in '73. Why, do you realize, Mrs. Ramsay, that this country had had bimetallism—and prospered under it—since the days of Washington?"

Carolina had not, indeed, realized. She was still a little vague

177

about this whole bimetallism business anyhow, but she looked impressed.

"Oh, the East tried to offer the West a sop in the form of the silver-purchase acts of 1878 and 1890, but it wasn't enough. It's tight money, I tell you, that's responsible for this present slump. Put the Populists in power, and we'd cure the nation's headache overnight by bringing back the old coinage ratio of sixteen ounces of silver to one of gold."

Carolina decided to become a Populist then and there.

Colorado overwhelmingly voted the Populist ticket that fall, electing a Populist governor from Aspen. But the older moneyed interests of the East were not won over. They were just as sure that the growing sickness of the country was due to a currency already debased, they said, because of the Silver Purchase Act of 1890. They would not rest until it was repealed.

While the doctors argued, the nation grew sicker. All except Cripple Creek resting on its ancient volcanic crater of gold. Throughout the rest of the state, silver mines were closing down. Silver fortunes made in Leadville and Aspen and Creede went crashing. Jewels were sold, and matched bay teams were put up at auction. Pink sandstone mansions were let go for taxes, and occasionally a bullet blasted out the brains of an ex-millionaire. Silver miners from all over the state drifted into the only bright spot on the map, Cripple Creek. Gold was savior. Gold would bring the country through.

Sometimes Carolina tried to talk to Pete about her new-found knowledge and about plans for their investments, whenever they should have any money to invest. But Pete was jocularly unconcerned. He would pull her down on his lap and ruffle her hair and stop her highfalutin words with a kiss. She let him. Perhaps she liked it best when he thus overrode her whims and her dignity. During those first months she showed him only a demure docility. She seemed to have forgotten all about the episode of the sewing basket.

11

ODDLY ENOUGH, IT WAS A QUITE INNOCENT AND PRAISEWORTHY deed of Pete's that ignited her long-sleeping temper. Perhaps it was because she was having her first morning sickness. Or it may have been because, after an interval of peace, she had heard that her father was back in town. Or perhaps it was the sight of Mat's and Thea's quite irrational adoration of Pete that set her off. There is nothing so cankering to a duty-burdened soul as the sight of those nearest and dearest lavishing love on a charmingly irresponsible outer member of the family.

Thea always let out a shriek of joy when Pete came in from his stage run. The first coherent question she put together was: "Who Tunkentell?"

The family was puzzled. Tunkentell?

Thea had elaborated patiently. "Pete loves me better'n Tunkentell."

Pete threw back his head with a shout.

"Sure I do—love you better than 'tongue can tell.'" Whereupon he had christened her favorite doll Tunkentell.

Mat would smile shyly up from his books at the roistering, merry fellow who had first offered him a home. (Her home, Carolina reminded herself caustically.)

Had Floss been there, she could have warned them that Carolina was building up for an explosion.

The final injury occurred late one night when she came into the kitchen to find Pete stealthily setting out with a basket of eatables.

"Where are you taking all that food?"

He shifted his weight. "Oh, just to an old coot that's hungry, it being winter and all."

"A crony of yours, I suppose. Who is he?"

"He looked so frozen up and blue, and nobody stopping to listen to him," he explained sheepishly. "Kind of losing his fire, I guess. I didn't think you'd begrudge him a little food——"

"My father!" she gasped. "You were sneaking food out to the only person on earth I hate."

The very fact that Carolina was haunted by her own memory of that thin, hungry, unyielding countenance added fuel to her anger. And the flame was fanned by her bitter realization that her life had been shaped and even mutilated by her efforts to rebel against her father.

She made a lunge for the basket before Pete realized what she was doing. He stared, open-mouthed, as she opened the back door and hurled the contents down the slope. The food was almost instantly set upon by a snarling pack of homeless dogs that haunted the backs of the eating houses.

He muttered a shocked and feeble protest, but she whirled on him as if daring him to rebuke her. He tried to appease her with his lovemaking, but this time it did not work. She wrenched herself away.

"Everybody against me—father, husband, brother, child——"

"Won't you listen to a fellow?"

She would not listen. She only yelled the more loudly, her bronze hair sliding down over her eyes as she stood there, panting and glaring. She was beautiful and terrible.

He shrugged at last, turned up his coat collar as if against a storm, and ducked out.

She stood a long time where he had left her, until finally her breathing slowed and her heart calmed its violence. Then she began to pin up her disordered hair. Hot, cleansing shame rushed through her. What could have gotten into her?

She opened the cupboard in search of more food. Pete had pretty well cleaned it out. But she found a meat pasty, a wedge of pie, and a few doughnuts. She wrapped them in a clean towel. Then she called Mat, supposedly asleep in the storeroom. He appeared with suspicious promptness.

"Mat," she said humbly, "I'm just a mean old hell-cat. Get your coat on and carry this basket of food down to wherever Pa is, will you?"

Mat was gone only a short time. He returned empty-handed.

"Did he take it?" she asked hoarsely. It had suddenly become tremendously important to her to know that her father had taken the food.

"Not exactly. I set it down beside him, and he pretended not to see it, while he went on preaching. But he didn't kick it over. There wasn't anybody much listening tonight."

They looked at each other, and an unwilling pity fused their glances for a moment. Jude Lawler would far rather be a target for jeers and even missiles, they knew, than to have no one hearing his message. A strange, obsessed, driven man—their father.

"Maybe he's changed a little—in his feelings toward us, Mat."

Mat grinned wryly. "I don't know. Because when he saw I didn't intend to stay and listen, he got pretty mad and turned and began to holler at me about spending all eternity drinking molten slag straight from the slag pots of hell——"

"Oh, no, he didn't, Mat!" exclaimed Carolina helplessly.

At last she went to bed. She left the door unlocked for Pete, but he did not come in. Each time hollow footsteps echoed along the wooden sidewalks outside, she raised herself on her elbow hopefully. But it was not Pete. She could not rid herself of the recollection of another man who had tried to cope with her temper and who had finally, like Pete, turned up his coat collar and walked out into the night.

Pete's drunk had an epic quality. It lasted for days; until his wages were gone and his job was gone. The stage company brought another man up from Canon City and fired Pete without notice. When he finally stumbled home, both he and Carolina were heartily ashamed of themselves and filled with resolves to do better.

He could be a lot of help running the bakery, she assured him brightly. For one thing, he could take over the delivery wagon and free Mat to wait on the trade at meal hours.

The only trouble with this arrangement was that Pete knew nothing about running a bakery (and Carolina did), and the deliveries took only an hour, leaving all the rest of his day to be filled up somehow. Sometimes, close to the screaming point, Carolina would suggest with strained reasonableness that he take Thea for a nice long walk. Eager to oblige, he would reach down for the ecstatic Thea's hand, and the two of them would start off happily.

In the blessed, hard-working calm that always followed, she would roll up her sleeves and tackle a great pan of dough or a batch of pie crust, while McGregor silently scrubbed floors or washed dishes or peeled vegetables. Neither one looked at the other. It would have seemed disloyal.

At night she would hurl herself into Pete's arms in a passion of contrition. It was her fault that he had lost his job. And it was Pete who had saved them, who had done more than honor required of him. They were happy, she told herself firmly; certainly they were happy.

He never fathomed her moods. But he took what she gave without questioning. For, terrible as she was in her rage, she was richly generous in her love.

Christmas came, a gay one in the little household, a grim one throughout the nation. The wretched year of 1893 started its sordid crawl across history. Misery is always worse in winter time, when cold adds inhuman cruelties to human ones.

Maybe Pete would find a job, she told herself. Not, of course, that he wasn't a real help around the bakery. But she thought he might be less restless if he had a regular job.

She knew happy hours planning for the baby. If it was a boy, she would name him Dan after Dr. Walgren. But there were times, as business grew worse, and the panic spread, and hungry miners poured into Cripple Creek hunting for jobs where there were no jobs and begging food at stores and lunch rooms and bakery shops, when the thought of a baby now frightened her. Her responsibilities seemed suddenly heavy, with the whole family leaning on her. What would happen if she took sick? What would become of Floss and Mat and Thea—and even McGregor and Pete?

At such moments her pregnancy seemed a moving box of fate, from which there was no escape, that was carrying her along to a destination she had not chosen. But presently her love of babies would return with a rush, and she would feel warm and placid and maternal again.

III

AND THEN ONE FINE SPRING MORNING AT DAWN HER PAINS STARTED. It was ahead of time, but even so, she was not afraid at first.

"Don't bother that poor doctor yet, Pete," she told him with bright cheerfulness, between pains. "Babies always take a lot longer than you think."

But Pete got up and dressed and hovered anxiously over her. It was funny, she thought indulgently, how a big strong man always quailed at the actual process of becoming a father.

But pretty soon nothing was funny, and Pete ran for the new young Dr. Westerman, who had taken care of Floss and was educated in all the modern ways.

"Better put the coffee pot on for the doctor," she managed to gasp out to Pete as the two came into the bedroom.

But the doctor seemed unconcerned about having his coffee. He did not give her a casual look, as Dr. Walgren had done, and then retire to the kitchen for coffee and conversation while the tedious process went on and on. Instead, he rolled up his sleeves and went to work.

"Is—everything all right?" she inquired faintly.

The doctor did not seem to hear her. He was moving very fast and grunting out orders to the frightened Pete:

"Here, hold this—steady now—that's it——"

Of course, everything was all right, she kept telling herself when she could tell herself anything. Hadn't she done all the proper things this time? Hadn't she eaten a lot and taken nice long walks and got plenty of sleep? No running up and down cruel mountain sides in the snow, trying to harm herself and her baby, she thought with a remembering twinge of guilt.

But all the right things did not seem to make any difference now. The grinding awfulness, and the oblivion, and then the awfulness went on and on—only a thousand times worse than when Thea was born.

And at the end, when she should have been tired and relaxed and empty and blissful, she heard herself ask faintly, "My baby? What about my baby?" and the doctor's grave, answering, judicial voice: "You must be thankful that we saved your life, Mrs. Ramsay. We could not save your little son." He went on saying kind, meaningless things.

Her son! She could not speak. She put her arm in its long cambric sleeve up over her face and let the weak, bitter tears run down.

Pete tried to comfort her, but he seemed a long way off. Yet when he did go away at last and leave her alone, along toward dusk, Carolina felt neglected. It was after dark when he returned. She asked him fretfully where he had been.

"Up to—Mt. Pisgah——"

"Mt. Pisgah! Whatever for?"

"You know—the burying ground."

A knife turned freshly in her vitals. To bury their son. Their red-headed son. The doctor had said he had red hair.

"I was walking along carrying the—the little fellow. I had him all wrapped up pretty in a box McGregor found—and someone fell into step beside me. I didn't look at first—and then I did——"

"Who?" But her throat constricted. She knew.

"Your old man. He carried a shovel. I'd forgot to take one. He never said a word. It was mighty strange for him not to say a word on all that long walk out to the cemetery. When we got there, he dug a hole. And we laid the little thing in—and he spoke words. Something about Moses on Mt. Pisgah and a Better Land Beyond. He filled in the grave and tamped it down and then he stood there bareheaded in the wind and said a prayer. He called it a prayer for a young soul. He said God met young souls and carried them in special——" Pete sniffled and turned his head away.

Carolina's eyeballs burned. Her throat was knotted in anguish. Pa again! Why had he done this? How had he found out?

She tried to harden her heart against him. And then she thought of her baby in its little box, "all wrapped up pretty," and the dirt tamped down over him, and the prayer said, and she was too weak and tired to feed her hate. Her empty arms ached; her empty heart ached too.

C H A P T E R 20

CAROLINA'S EYE RAN DOWN THE COLUMN OF HOUSES FOR SALE. They were few, in a new and booming gold camp. But she had to have a house, and she wanted it in a hurry. Floss's letter had forced her to come to the decision.

"It looks like I'm to be paroled at last," Floss had written blithely. "I can't wait to get home. But I want to say right now, I'm not coming unless you find me a separate place to stay. You got enough families under one roof already. So please get me a room close by, as the doctors say I'll always have trouble walking and will have to use a cane."

That jolted Carolina into action. They would buy a house. Floss could have this bedroom here in the bakery, where there would be neither steps nor icy walks to bother her. Besides, they needed a house, now that Thea was three and would soon be old enough for a room of her own.

"Listen to this, Pete," she said, looking across the top of the newspaper at her husband, who was frankly admiring his handsome cravat in the bedroom mirror.

"For Sale: Fine two-story brick house on Carr. Owner forced to move to lower altitude on account of wife's health. Burt Gallagher."

"The fellow that owns the brickyard," supplied Pete. "House ought to be well built."

"Come, Thea," said her mother to Thea, who was playing with her doll Tunkentell in the corner. "You go out in the kitchen and stay with McGregor while we do an errand. That's a good girl."

Thea looked dubious about the charms of being a good girl.

"Aw, let her go along," said Pete. "If she gets tired, I'll carry her."

Carolina flashed him a look of gratitude. Pete was always like that. She tied Thea's bonnet on with a swift, competent tweak. Then she absently skewered on her own hat, a brown silk pie pan loaded with buckles and plumes.

She gave an automatic downward push to her belt in front. She was wearing the first new dress she had bought since she had come to Cripple Creek. The gored, flaring brown skirt was rounded out in the rear over a fashionable bustle, and the lemon-colored waist was intersected with bands of brown velvet. It was startling and highly unsuitable for a business woman tripping along uneven board sidewalks with their projecting nails, but she loved it. Like the other styles of the Nineties, it became her, with its ballooning sleeves, its deep V-shaped dip to the belt, and its Grecian-bend corseting with protruding bosom in front and protruding bustle in back, which gave all women the naive and shameless strut of courting pigeons.

At not quite twenty-one, Carolina's figure had fulfilled its promise of sixteen, when Letty had wished it were less buxom, although work and worry had kept her trained down like a race horse. Hers was a more poignant beauty now than it had been at sixteen. For she had borne two children and lost one of them. She had loved one man painfully, and lost him, and loved another. And she lived always with the disquieting memory of her father. Just when she thought she could forget him, she would be called to a neighboring town to bail him out of jail for disturbing the peace; for the saloon and gambling gentry never learned to take kindly to having their mirrors smashed and their patrons dispersed by a shouting, rock-heaving Jeremiah.

Yet if her expression was not placidly happy, neither was it frustrated and petulant. For she was the center of her small world, important and needed.

Thea was quite unable to keep up with her mother on that rapid trip up the hill to the Gallagher house. Pete had to carry her.

Carolina gave little more than a glance at the outside of the narrow, two-story house of raw red brick, with its white wooden scrollwork that ran in ornate Spencerian script along the top of the wooden porch and under the eaves and over each arched window.

"It looks fine, don't you think, Pete?" she asked. There was no time to lose; a good house sold fast in a mining town.

They pretended to debate the matter while they followed the

owner through the house; but it was all Carolina could do not to burst into rhapsodies.

"Look, Pete," she said in a whisper, so that Gallagher should not hear and raise the price. "Electric lights and a place for a bathroom."

Suddenly she was house-hungry. She was starved for a place of her own where she could drape the curtains just so, and decide whether the rocker should go *here*, or the lounge *there*.

"We'll take it," she announced breathlessly to Burt Gallagher, turning to add dutifully, "Won't we, Pete?"

Pete nodded and picked up Thea.

As they set off for the bakery, she looked back at the house. How her mother would have loved it. She remembered that her mother had always hated their migratory life and dreamed of just such a neat brick house with its look of settled permanence. True, Hester Lawler would not have liked the grassless plot of pounded dirt that surrounded it; for as yet there was not a lawn in Cripple Creek. But everything else would have seemed a luxury to her: the black-iron sink, the dangling light bulbs, and the porch to rock on.

In the same breathless ferment that she bought the house, Carolina furnished it. She would never crochet dabs of antimacassars, or gild cattails, or paint dustpans to tie on the wall to hold newspapers, or cover nests of tin cans with carpeting for hassocks. But she knew a sharp zest in buying furniture, now that they had a house.

"I'll take this—and that—and two of those——" she said excitedly in the furniture store. "Don't you think so, Pete?"

Pete always thought so.

She picked out a flowered carpet reminiscent of the grandeur of Hattie Merkle's and Stelle Bogart's, and a lamp with a hand-painted globe for a shade, and a parlor organ with the wooden fretwork backed by red cloth. There was talk of these new upright pianos, but an organ still represented luxury to Carolina.

She bought two leather-covered chairs and a tufted couch that reminded her, she told Pete, of the side view of Pike's Peak, with the head rearing up at one end and its supine length tapering down to the foot. The bedrooms she furnished with golden-yellow brass beds and golden-oak bureaus. Then she bought a remarkable patent rocker for Floss that glided back and forth like an ocean wave, the salesman said.

Her high spirits flagged a little when she came to total up their expenditures. She would have to see Tom Higby about a loan. He had told her to come to him whenever she needed money. He said it was good business to borrow money now and then; it kept your credit good. But again she was uncertain and frightened. Maybe they had gone too fast. She was afraid of debt, just as she had once been afraid of banks and bankers.

Then she shrugged off her unease. She could scarcely wait for Floss to see everything. Her new hat, her new house, her new furniture—her new husband. Oh, especially her new husband. She did not admit that deep in her consciousness Floss's unflattering words about Pete rankled like a sliver that has to fester its way out.

II

WHEN SHE MET FLOSS, WHO CAME IN ON THE STAGE FROM DIVIDE, Carolina was airily on the defensive. Even while she was giving Floss an affectionate peck and noting how drab her clothes were but that her limp was better, she was preening herself as wives have always preened themselves in front of their unmarried sisters.

Floss, who loved Carolina, also saw through her. She waited until all of Carolina's fine talk had run down. Then she said kindly, "I take back everything I ever said about Pete. On account of the way you say he saved Thea and you that night your old man rushed in. Pete and I will get along."

Carolina had to be satisfied with that. She hoped it meant that Floss was convinced at last about Pete and that she thought him splendid now. Of course that was what Floss meant, she told herself; for hadn't Floss said she took back everything she had ever said against him?

There is no pleasanter state of mind than the conviction that your best friend envies you a little. Carolina hoped Pete would stay on his good behavior. She wished he had a job. He was not exactly at his best, hanging around the bakery getting into folks' way, or feeling he must play the jovial host in the lunch room and setting everybody up to another cup of coffee.

That same evening, after they had installed Floss in her own room, was scarcely the most auspicious time for Pete to come forth with a confession. He fidgeted outside the door while Carolina called back farewells to Floss.

"We'll go over the accounts together first thing in the morning, Floss. I don't feel we're doing as well as we ought, considering the amount of our business. McGregor thinks so too. Maybe you'll be able to help plug some of the leaks. But get a good night's sleep first."

Pete cleared his throat as they bent their bodies against the steep homeward grade.

"About those accounts—about plugging those leaks——" he began.

"Yes," she said absently.

"Well, before you start in I may as well tell you, I gave a fellow a little grubstake."

"Oh, Pete, not again! What's become of all those other grubstakes? No wonder our supplies seem to melt. How much was it this time?"

"Well, it wasn't all at once. It was sort of spread out." He added defensively, " 'The biggest mine had to start as a ten-foot hole.' "

She had heard that one all her life.

"Sure, Pete, and so did the biggest failure. The Cousin Jacks had another saying too." She gave the words a melancholy Cornish intonation: " 'Silver lays in veins, but gold is where you find it. Where it tis, there it tis—and where it tain't, there am I——' "

"Yes, but this looked good. At the time, that is. He found a piece of float and trenched a couple of hundred feet up over the hill until he located a contact. That took time. Naturally he had to have some grub—and a windlass——"

"You gave him money too?" Her voice sharpened. Money seemed even worse than giving food. He must have helped himself from the cigar box under the counter.

They were entering their new house.

"Well, how could you sink a shaft without a windlass and some black powder and a piece of rope and a bucket? I've been helping him too. A fellow can't be at both ends of the hole at once."

She did not confess that she had not even noticed his absence.

"Who was it you gave it to?"

Pete reached up to switch on the light dangling on its cord from the center of the ceiling.

"Joe Ricketts."

Her color mounted. Not Joe Ricketts! Pete knew only too well what she thought of that worthless old dump rat. Always begging hand-outs—shifty—quoting queer poetry and somebody called Tom Paine.

"You know he's no good!"

"I thought you'd like him because he's down on churches and God," he said in an injured tone.

She batted her eyelashes angrily.

"He's no-account—that's why I don't like him. And I don't like it because you sneaked food out of the kitchen—and money out of the cigar box—to give to him." She still could not bring herself to use a stronger word than "sneaked." Yet her grievances were mounting into an impressive pile. Her voice was rising. "Working against me—undermining me——" Her eyes were wild; her voice would soon become a screech.

But Pete did not give ground. He hauled a dirty piece of paper from his pocket.

"I got him to sign this in return for the grubstake. It gives me a half-interest," he said stubbornly. "If we hit it, we're going to call it the Lucky Friday—that's the day he signed it."

"Half-interest in a hole in the ground!" she yelled. "I'll show you how much your filthy scrap of paper is worth——" She made a grab for it to tear it into shreds.

But Pete leaped, imprisoning her hand, paper and all.

"Behave yourself, Carolina!" he shouted angrily. "I ought to clop you on the ear."

She halted, like a baby surprised out of its purple-faced tantrum. Had Pete only pursued his advantage then, he might have been a match for her. But he weakened and began to justify himself.

"I'm trying to tell you: at the time I gave the grubstake, it looked like a mighty good thing. Of course now—but any day we may hit pay dirt."

She stared at him a moment longer, almost hopefully. Then her shoulders sagged, and the glitter went out of her. She let him extract the paper from her hand. In silence she watched him smooth it out. She turned at last to go.

"Pay dirt!" she jeered feebly, glancing back over her shoulder to see if he were following, half-hoping to arouse him again and to bring back that dominating, lordly Pete, who for one short moment had almost mastered her.

But Pete was clumping across to the desk in the dining room to put the agreement away in the tin box where they kept their papers.

"Pay dirt," she tried a last time. "Lucky hole in the ground!"

But Pete did not rise to her bait; he did not clop her on the ear;

he did not pick her up in his arms and carry her up the stairs.

"Now see here, Carolina——" he began reasonably.

But reason was not what she wanted. She turned dispiritedly and climbed the stairs.

C H A P T E R 21

LOOKING BACK, THERE WERE MANY PREMONITORY SIGNS OF WHAT was to come, like the faint unsettling rumblings high in the hills before a rock slide, or the slow muddy trickle in a dry wash in advance of a roaring flash flood. But neither Carolina nor Floss sensed them at the time. Not when Pete took to leaving earlier and earlier in the morning and staggering home long after dark at night. Not when he brought Thea a new china doll with the bluest of eyes and the blackest of painted china hair; nor when he ceased to drop in at bars in the evening for a game and a glass, but grew lean and sinewy from hard hours in the open.

They did not know, in fact, until he staggered in that Saturday night, arms filled with packages. The last customer had departed, and the lunch room was closed for the day. The family had gathered in the bakery kitchen where so much of their living had been done and their dramas played out.

"Pete!" exclaimed Carolina anxiously, looking at his flushed face and broad grin.

But Pete was not drunk except with exultation. He began to dole out packages all around.

"This for Thea—red button-boots, chick, with tassels on the tops." He tore off the wrappings and let the child hold the alluring little boots. "And for you, Mat, a real man's suit." Mat reddened; how had Pete known that his soul was sick with longing for a suit where the coat matched the pants? "McGregor gets a watch chain; here you are, old man." Pete tossed the small package to the speechless McGregor. "And for Floss a new shawl with a fancy fringe." Floss accepted it self-consciously.

Then he picked up the last package and laid it ceremoniously in Carolina's lap.

"A new dress for my girl. You've hardly bought yourself a thing since you came to Cripple Creek. I want my wife decked out with the best." He stood waiting for Carolina to untie the bulky package. Never had he looked so fond and indulgent.

Carolina was too unnerved to untie the package. Pete had to whip out his jackknife and cut the string himself. She stared down at the brilliant billows of purple and gold, with veinings of black. Like a gold-hearted purple pansy, she thought.

She held it up to her. She would look startling in it, and every head would turn, and she loved each lustrous fold. She was almost afraid to ask how he had come by it.

"It's beautiful, but how did you——?"

"How did I know it would set my girl off?" he teased. "The lady at the store said it would be just the ticket for somebody with penny-colored hair and eyes."

"Oh, Pete," she begged, "you know what I mean."

He relented. He could not contain his secret any longer.

"It's the Lucky Friday! We hit the streak at last." With eyes shining, he began to pace back and forth, his words crowding each other. The shaft was yielding eighty-five dollars a foot as they went down. The ore buyer at the sampling works paid them a hundred dollars a sack. Pete and Ricketts worked in the bottom of the shaft and had two men at the top to handle the windlass. "Next, we're going to put in a steam hoist and build us a head frame," he finished proudly.

Floss was the first to remember her manners.

"I think that's mighty fine, Pete. I congratulate you and I do admire my shawl," she said with honest warmth.

McGregor and Mat thanked him gruffly, as became men of few words, but their pleasure was patent.

"How deep are you, Pete? How wide is she?" asked McGregor respectfully while he draped his watch chain across his concave middle.

"Twelve inches wide, and we're down twenty feet. Getting better every day."

Still Carolina could say nothing. She sat looking down at the glowing billows in her lap. Thea had climbed up on to Pete's knee to have him help her with her new shoes. Carolina was thinking dazedly, I called it a hole in the ground. I quarreled with him over giving Ricketts the grubstake. I made fun of it. She was humbled, not only by Pete's benevolence but by the fact that he seemed to have forgotten all about her spleenishness over the grubstake in the first place.

"Pete, I think it—I think you are wonderful," she said at last painfully. "I'm sorry I acted up so about the mine. I can hardly wait to get my new dress made."

Pete was embarrassed and elated.

"We'll be rich yet, honey. Rich and greasy with money." He kissed her in front of everybody and then did a little buck-and-wing dance in the middle of the floor out of sheer high spirits. "Half of everything that comes in is yours, Carolina. You deserve it," he finished largely.

The atmosphere about him was full of the rich incense of adulation. Pete grew expansive and benign, breathing its unaccustomed fragrance. He scattered fine promises and meant every one of them. His listeners thought how remarkable was Pete and how wondrous was wealth. Now all their problems would be solved, and complete felicity would be theirs forever.

They sat long in the kitchen, talking. It was Floss who reluctantly reminded them that flapjacks must be baked and coffee boiled at the usual hour in the morning. In a state of bemused conjecturing they finally dispersed, Floss to her room, McGregor to his quarters down the street, and the rest of the family to the red brick house on the hill.

Mat carried the sleeping Thea. Carolina and Pete walked behind, openly holding hands. It was just like the night he had "saved" her and Thea, she thought. Pete was prodigious; he was wonderful. She looked up to him. She could scarcely wait to reach their new home —and their new and glittering brass bed—and their new and tender frenzy of love.

In the days that followed, the little group adjusted itself in varying ways to the fact of their modest riches. Floss and McGregor, who were less intimately involved, only worked the harder. Both of them had seen riches seep away as quickly as they had come. Veins could fault or pinch out tomorrow, but people kept right on buying good hot meals and fresh baked goods. And even Pete had to admit that the Lucky Friday was not the Independence or the Portland as yet.

Pete's new prosperity evidenced itself first in his raiment. He decked himself in fancy waistcoats and light-colored derby hats.

And presently he began to go to the mine later and leave earlier. After all, you could hire plenty of miners, he said. He took to frequenting mining exchanges and hotel lobbies, a cigar tilted at an angle under his glossy black mustache, while he studied the quotations and listened to what "the big operators" said.

Carolina was a little awed by both his garments and his manner. And she was as pleased as any vain young wife when he bought her a rustling silk taffeta petticoat and black kid slippers and a beaded card case—although she owned no calling cards.

She was too elated to heed Tom Higby's gloomy headshakings about the state of the nation when she went in to make her next payment on the house loan. It happened to be the day in June that word had arrived that India had stopped coining and buying silver. The price dropped from the already low figure of 83 cents to 62 cents an ounce.

"It's bad, Mrs. Ramsay," he said. "It's a pall over the state—over the whole country."

But he could not reach her that day. It was hard to sense a pall when you were wearing new kid slippers and your first silk taffeta petticoat.

And in July, when she read that the panic had finally struck with its full force and ten Denver banks had closed in three days, she was remotely sorry. But it was like hearing about a famine in China. Pete had just bought Thea a real wicker doll buggy and he was talking about exchanging the once-wonderful organ for a shiny black upright piano.

It was sad, of course, that the silver miners were so desperate and the farmers half-crazy after years of drouth. And that ten thousand destitute unemployed had stormed the state capital, so that Denver had to provide them with tents and bedding and food. She tried to *feel* sad; but it was difficult, with Cripple Creek still fairly prosperous and the Lucky Friday pouring out money. Oh, not in a torrent, but in a good-sized trickle.

Pete kept his promises. Each time that he and Joe Ricketts split what was left from the proceeds of a car of ore, after first putting by the larger part of it for the contemplated machinery and buildings, Pete gave Carolina her promised half without haggling. To that extent, he was fair and generous. But presently she began to be irked because that was the last she ever saw of his portion. He left her to worry about the bakery and provide for the family and pay off Tom Higby, while no one ever knew what became of his share.

She was sure that he ought not to spend so much time hanging around a joint like Nick Bradley's. But she was still respectful of Pete's stubborn shrewdness in giving that grubstake to Joe Ricketts and she admitted in moments of candor that, but for him, the grubstake agreement would have been torn into shreds. But she wished he would stay away from Nick Bradley's. Yet she was not deeply disturbed. After all, no matter how much of his own money he might lose, there was always that magical goose, the Lucky Friday, to lay another golden egg.

In the fall of 1893, when the final blow to a great silver producing state occurred in the repeal of the Sherman Silver Purchase Act, Carolina was triumphantly absorbed in paying off the last of the loan. The house was theirs; nothing could take it away from them now. Always, she had lived in rented shacks, or hotel rooms, or crowded quarters back of the bakery. Now she had a house of her own.

The narrow, supercilious little red brick house on Carr took on a special value in her eyes. She knew a sensual delight when she ran her hand along the banisters, or fiercely polished the glass in the bay window, or swept the tiniest twig off the front steps with high wide flirts of her broom.

Nothing could pierce her happy armor. For the family was safe. Her father had not been heard from for months. Pete and she were having a sweet renascence of love. And they owned their own home!

She closed her eyes and ears to the rising threats of labor unrest in Cripple Creek. She was not unsympathetic toward the miners. In spirit, she still belonged to the Stringtowns of the world. But with her terrible concentration on that which was nearest her heart —her family—she regarded the formation of a union with impatience. It might pinch off even further the trickle of gold from the Lucky Friday. What if some mines in the region did work eight hours a day and others nine and still others ten, and all for the same wage? It was the miners' lookout not to work for the less generous mines. But strike? They had no right. Well, the sheriff would take care of *that*, she reasoned grimly.

II

SHE WAS SOUND ASLEEP THAT NIGHT WHEN PETE CAME STEALTHILY into the house. Suddenly she found herself wide-awake and propped up on one elbow listening. She always slept with her door open because of Thea, across the hall.

She could hear Pete stumbling about downstairs in the dark. His very stealth must have been what had wakened her. For usually he was as noisy as a stallion in a box stall when he came home late. Could he be drunk? But he did not sound drunk. She heard him bump into a chair and swear softly.

She could follow his course across the parlor and out into the dining room, where he stopped to feel around for the dangling light. Then she heard the rasp and screech of a drawer opening in the desk. There was a moment's silence, followed by more tiptoeing footsteps.

She flung back the covers in the dark and jumped out of bed. She had padded to the head of the stairs in her bare feet when she heard the front door close. Heavy footsteps clumped down the front steps and along the walk.

She was nettled. What had got into Pete? Going back downtown at such an hour. Curiosity drove her down the stairs without letting her stop for her wrapper or slippers.

She looked at the clock as she turned on the light. Two in the morning. What had he come home for? Not money, for they kept little money in the house. What then? She was virtually certain that he had been gambling at Nick Bradley's.

She glanced down at the open drawer in the dining room desk and saw the tin box in which they kept their papers. She tried it and found it unlocked. There was only one thing of real value in that box. With a startled leap of the pulse, she lifted the lid. It ought to be right on top—the paper. But it was not.

She dragged out the box and dumped the contents on the desk. Of course it was there—the grubstake agreement with Joe Ricketts. She had seen it only a few days ago.

Her hands shook so that she could scarcely shuffle through the little pile; her marriage certificate, the deed to the house, an insurance policy or two. It had to be there. Why, that grubstake contract was their only wealth. The bakery was only beginning to make a little money again. He wouldn't be such a fool; nobody would be such a fool as to risk their entire future. Besides, he had promised her half the income from it. Right in front of McGregor and Floss, he had promised her half of everything that came in . . . She began to sweat.

195

But the paper was gone. With a face as harshly set as Hattie Merkle's, she turned and ran up the stairs, her long bronze braids swinging. She must hurry, hurry. Some ominous prescience told her that minutes counted now.

She dragged on her clothes with clumsy fingers. She wound her ropes of hair around her head and secured them with a hairpin or two and grabbed up her old sealskin cape.

Then she ran. It never occurred to her to waken her lanky young brother, who might have been some protection to her in the ribald, leering, after-midnight hours of Cripple Creek's red-light district. Carolina had learned to meet her problems alone.

The lights of the district still blazed, as they blazed all night. But Nick's place looked secretive and sullen, with its drawn shades and thick doors. It did not advertise any "lady waiters," or have a corner roped off for dancing, with a band to lure the public in. It was a straight drinking and gambling place, dedicated to the ruthless business of separating a fool from his money.

Breathing hard, she pushed open the door. In spite of all her furtive, skirting knowledge of the night life of a mining town, and in spite of all her hymn-singing on the streets outside such places, she had never set foot in a gambling house before.

The thick fumes struck her like the palm of a dirty hand shoved in her face. Her nostrils quivered. Ever since Stringtown she had observed with a certain scientific detachment that liquids which smelled harmless enough in the bottle, by some strange alchemy, when swallowed, promptly turned into something sour and offensive on a man's breath.

No one noticed her at first, as she stood uncertainly inside the door peering through the layers of blue smoke. The very walls looked smoke-cured.

The room was long and narrow, with a balcony running across the back. On the walls were the pictures common to gambling houses: Custer's Last Stand, a hazy chromo of covered wagons and galloping horsemen, and the usual beer and whiskey advertisements.

To her right stretched the bar with its dented brass foot rail. Two slick-haired bartenders languidly officiated in front of the streaked mirror and the phalanxes of colored bottles. One of them indifferently polished a glass; the other mopped the bar with a gray rag that looked like the body of a dead cat.

To her left were the faro lay-outs. She searched the circle of men crowded up about each table buying chips of the dealer, who stuffed the money into the slot of the "ready box" bolted in front of him. Faro was reputed to be the fairest of gambling games. It would be too slow for Pete.

Her eyes flicked over the group around the roulette table and passed on. Pete must be at the back. She tried to locate him in the smoky obscurity beneath the balcony where the smaller games such as craps and poker and slough were in progress.

Now the lookout at the side of the room had observed her. She tensed, but she pretended not to see him. He was a large, surly-eyed man seated on the lookout's high chair from which he could watch for a pair of dice slipped out of a coattail or an extra ace edged down from a sleeve. She saw him half-rise from his seat, his heels still hooked over the rung under his feet. Nick's place did not welcome women, whether good or bad. They interfered with the systematic fleecing of patrons.

Then she saw Pete seated at a round table in the farthest dim corner under the balcony.

Her heart began to pound. For there was something beaten about his posture, lounging back, hands in pockets, staring at the cards.

She moved swiftly toward Pete until she stood directly behind his chair. Her glance dropped to the cards in front of him. In spite of her father's hatred of "playing cards, the devil's tools," Carolina, like every other child in Stringtown, knew a busted blackjack hand when she saw it. A ten and a six and a seven. Oh, the fool—the utter fool! Didn't he know that in no game is the novice so easily cleaned as in blackjack? That in no house game is the take so sure?

She looked across at the silent dealer staring down at a paper in his hand and then turning it over to inspect the signature before getting ready to fold it and put it in his pocket.

The grubstake agreement! She saw the bottle of ink and the pen on the table in front of Pete. It could not have been more than five minutes since he had assigned all their future hopes to this unsavory gambling house run by the unsavory Nick Bradley.

A wave of such fury pounded through her veins as made all her past furies seem puerile. Perhaps because, for the first time, others besides herself were threatened by Pete's folly. With a scratch of the pen he had thrown away their security. And because her anger was not wholly for herself, it was more controlled and deadly now.

The dealer glanced up from his leisurely perusal of the paper and gave a start at the apparition behind Pete Ramsay's chair. Was she drunk? He did not think so. Doped? Just possibly; there was a queer look in her eyes all right. Fighting mad? No doubt of it.

He scrambled to his feet. Pete turned his head in the direction of the dealer's fascinated gaze and shriveled. All two hundred and more pounds of him seemed to grow wizened and old at sight of his wife.

The lookout had been quietly edging in from behind. He was only a few feet from Carolina now. The rest of the room was still scarcely aware of anything untoward happening.

Carolina spoke to the dealer. Her voice was low as yet.

"I want that agreement back. I'm his wife. He had no right to let go of it."

The dealer looked around helplessly for Nick, the boss. This was no job for a mere dealer like himself, who only worked on a commission; or even for the lookout, who was nothing but a bouncer. It was Nick who had made the deal and set a figure of $2000 on the grubstake agreement when Ramsay insisted he wanted to go on gambling in order to win back what he had already lost. Let Nick handle it. God, how he feared women that came in raising hell about their husbands' losses.

"I'm sorry, ma'am," he said soothingly, looking toward the stairs leading up to Nick's office on the balcony, "but your husband just assigned this contract over to the house; he put it up against $2000 in cash. Nobody asked him to. He insisted that he wanted to, so as to make back his losses."

"What losses?" asked Carolina.

"Twelve hundred dollars that he had on him in cash."

Carolina flinched. The down-payment on the new steam hoist. It did not belong to Pete, but to the partnership; he was supposed to have taken it to the mine supply house this afternoon. And, on top of that, he had gambled away another two thousand, as the betting value of the grubstake agreement. She felt sick inside, but she spoke boldly.

"He had no right to gamble this contract away—half of it belongs to me."

"It don't say so on it. It's made out to Pete Ramsay."

"I tell you he promised me half. Besides," she added, with biting feminine irrelevance, "the game was probably crooked. I want that

198

paper back. I want it back, I say." Her voice was beginning to grow shrill.

"I'm sorry, lady, but it was legal," the dealer protested in the placating tone he used to ugly drunks.

"Legal—hell!" she cried, reverting to Stringtown. "I'll take you to court. Every cent, every bite of food in that grubstake, I provided. You know Pete Ramsay never had so much as a spare shirt to his back till he married me." Pete himself might have been miles away as far as the fiery-eyed woman and the uneasy man were concerned. Or he might have been present as an incompetent child, for all the attention they paid him. "I made every dollar of it. I started the bakery. I added the lunch room. That contract ought to have been made out to me, by rights. But Pete promised me half anyhow. I've got witnesses. I know about verbal contracts——"

The dealer was harassed. He could handle fighting drunks and sobbing ones, but deliver him from a spitting-mad woman.

"I only work here. You'll have to take it up with the boss. I'll go get him," he said hopefully, edging toward the door, still holding on to the grubstake agreement.

But Carolina was not to be outwitted that way. She leaned across the table and with one sweep of her arm sent the nearest covey of bottles to the floor with a crash. The room stilled instantly.

"Don't you sneak out with that paper," she warned.

Suddenly she sensed the lookout closing in on her from the rear. She whirled just in time to avoid his gorilla arms and his silencing palm. She grabbed up another bottle by the neck and sprang to one side. With her back to the wall and the bottle in her upraised hand, she faced them. The crash had brought Nick Bradley scuttling down from above.

Her head was back; her blazing eyes scorched them all.

"Don't anyone lay hands on me!" The lifted bottle was no mean weapon. Suddenly she was Jude Lawler's daughter, tall and terrifying and thirsting for vengeance. "Make a single move, and I'll bust that long mirror with one throw."

She saw Nick wince. She recalled her father's methods and followed up her advantage quickly.

"That isn't all. I'll bring in a dozen fighting-mad women whose husbands have been cleaned out in this crooked hole. They'll smash the rest of your place. Every night they'll smash it up. Think you can buy protection? Well, you can't—not from a bunch of

199

wives and mothers. I'll sick the Purity League on you. We'll close this place up so tight a mouse won't be able to gnaw its way in."

"Who the hell is this?" asked Nick Bradley.

The lookout nodded toward the slumped figure of Pete.

"His wife. She wants his grubstake agreement back. Her old man is that ranting street preacher what hangs around sometimes."

Nick blanched. "Him—God!" he breathed in a pious whisper. He could face the police, the guns of welshing patrons, but not an outraged female—not the church crowd.

"Come up to my office, lady, and we'll talk it over," he pleaded.

"No. We'll settle it here and now." Her arm described a small threatening arc.

Sweating, Nick said to the dealer, "Where's that agreement? I'll assign it back to her. Anything to get her out." He reached for pen and ink. "What's your full name, ma'am? I'm making this over to you."

She told him. He wrote on the back of the grubstake agreement and handed it across to her. She read it carefully.

"Now get out, both of you," he said bitterly, mopping his forehead. "All I ask is never to lay eyes on either of you again."

But Carolina was not through. She was Jude Lawler's daughter in more ways than one.

"But my husband owes you $2000. He lost it to you."

"All I want is that you should get out," repeated Nick doggedly.

"Give me a piece of paper," Carolina commanded.

Nick obeyed.

Bending over one corner of the table, she wrote quickly. Then she held out the paper.

"It's my I.O.U. for $2000. Pete owes it to you. You'll be paid in full."

Nick Bradley stared suspiciously, first at the paper and then at the girl. People didn't pay out $2000 just for the fun of it. He looked questioningly at the lookout.

"Just like her old man. She may raise hell—but she'll pay," he explained.

In twenty years of running crooked gambling games, Nick Bradley had never come across her like. He began to urge Pete up out of his chair. He held the back door open for the two of them. Anything to get them out of here. He didn't know what she might take into her head to do next.

When they had gone, he closed the door and made his way up to the bar where he poured himself a long drink. He drank it neat. Once in a while he dazedly felt of the I.O.U. in his pocket. He had thought there were no surprises left in the gambling business.

Carolina and Pete walked up the hill in the chill darkness, with Carolina in the lead and Pete dragging along shamefacedly in the rear. She was strangely emptied of feeling. She felt neither satisfaction nor resentment. In fact, she felt nothing at all. Everything had been said only too plainly back there at Nick's place. The grubstake had been morally hers in the first place, for she had supplied all the gumption and enterprise and courage. Pete had forfeited every claim.

She clutched the contract so tightly that the pressure numbed her fingertips. They turned on to peaceful Carr Avenue. Not a sound punctuated the before-dawn stillness except their own footsteps. Tap—tap—tap—tap—— There was a measured, lonely sound to them. Two people walking home in the chill small hours, a few feet apart, a whole world apart.

Suddenly she remembered another set of hollow, echoing footsteps, and another silent homeward walk in the dark beside a shamed man, following a crucial effort to retrieve what she had thought was rightfully theirs. And the same empty sadness had climaxed that other effort. She could see a bleak rooming house on the Flats—and a crook named Canaday—and a stock certificate . . . She shook her head in a bewildered way. But this was the Lucky Friday contract she clutched in her fingers. This was her husband Pete Ramsay plodding along behind her like a man in chains. For a minute she hadn't been sure—for a minute she had thought it was Roger.

C H A P T E R 22

IN THE YEAR THAT FOLLOWED, THE WHOLE FAMILY RUED ITS BRIEF spending spree. The new house, the parlor organ, the patent rocker, the glittering brass beds—every bright ornament of their existence they lived to regret. For under the driving lash of necessity—and

Carolina's tongue—they could not forget those debts which Pete had contracted in a moment of folly and which they must now pay for with grueling months of hardship.

There was the twelve hundred dollars belonging to the partnership and intended for the steam hoist, which must be paid off first; for the mine needed the hoist. There was the two thousand dollars on Carolina's I.O.U. to Nick Bradley. Thirty-two hundred dollars in all, merely to regain Pete's original half-interest in the Lucky Friday mine. And the mine, instead of opening up as everyone had expected, was pinching off in the most perverse fashion. Why wasn't it doing better? Carolina wondered.

"Too poor to pay, too rich to quit." How many times had she heard the bitter saying. Sometimes she wondered if she ought not to have let the grubstake agreement go—let the mine go—in order to concentrate solely on the bakery. She knew that both Floss and McGregor would have preferred that. But the gambler in her, the adventurer, could not give up. Surely by next week, or next month, or next year——

Often she insisted on McGregor's accompanying her up to the mine because he had once been a hard-rock miner and because she distrusted Ricketts. When McGregor donned his ancient cap covered with candle grease, he donned a certain authority with it, in her eyes.

Ricketts made no effort to conceal his dislike of them all. He was impatient with his petticoated partner. He scorned suggestions from McGregor, "that baker." And his contempt for Pete, when he found out about the gambling fiasco, was limitless. Ricketts was not distinguished for his sense of gratitude. He quite forgot that he owed everything to that original grubstake which Pete had given him. And Carolina likewise forgot that if it had not been for that same grubstake, there would have been nothing for her to retrieve in the gambling house that night. Easy-going Pete was not one to remind them of their debts.

Oddly enough, it was Floss—who had been set against Pete in the first place—who now came to the rescue of his pride.

"Help me with this barrel of flour, will you, Pete? I never saw such muscle," she would say admiringly. Or, "I wonder if you'd take the wagon and go for that freight shipment? I'd ask Mat, but it takes a real hand with horses to back up a wagon just right."

Pete would brighten and turn to see if Carolina had heard.

Usually she had not. She was burdened and distrait, feeling that she carried the whole responsibility of the family now.

Mat still gave Pete a silent boyish admiration. And Thea still loved him extravagantly. But his wife seemed to grow farther and farther away from him, and he did not know how to bring her back.

Occasionally he would get a job freighting, or acting as night clerk in some cheap hotel, or working in a mine. But he never held a job long. Soon he would drift blithely off to a neighboring town where he had heard that things were picking up.

Pete was not so different from Carolina's father, who was always moving on to a new place when news of a rich strike of wickedness beckoned to him. The last that Carolina had heard of Jude, he was preaching his way from camp to camp in the San Juan country. She always felt lighter and slept more soundly when he was in a distant part of the state.

Usually, a month or two after Pete departed, he would drift home as casually as he had left, and the whole family would know a flicker of delight as he swung back into their lives again, penniless, battered, and insouciant.

Carolina would try to hold him off to show her disapproval. Wasn't he the real reason for their present stringency? And then youth and propinquity and the hunger of the senses would drive her back into his arms again, and once more she would know rapture of a kind. Once more she would think in a rush of contrition, born of their healthy passion, Pete is wonderful; he saved me; I owe everything to him.

But soon the stern regimen of all work and little play would begin to tell on Pete, and he would ease out of the picture again with talk of "other interests" in another town.

For a while after his departure, Carolina would be piqued and angry. She was angry that he refused to worry with her over her responsibilities. She wanted him to feel burdened too. If it was laughter and tolerance and light-heartedness she had once thought she wanted, she had her fill of them now, and she found them weak and rotten props to lean on.

Presently she would forget her resentment in the awful fascination of the problems of making a living. Only the bakery was doing well these days. Something was always hindering the mine. Now it was the strike.

She worried and bit her nails all that wearing, warring spring. She urged Ricketts to give in and grant the men the eight-hour day. For the just side of her remembered what it was like for a man to set off with his lunch bucket before it was light and return again after dark, too tired to do more than wolf down his supper and crawl into bed. Life should be more than that, she decided with grim fairness. But Ricketts refused to listen to her. He turned down the miners' demands, and the men walked out.

She watched the feeling rise as the striking miners of the district banded together and barricaded themselves on a promontory known as Bull Hill. "Deputies," recruited by the mine owners to reinforce the sheriff, began to swarm in from Denver and Leadville and neighboring counties, until some said there were over a thousand of these imported mercenaries in the valley. The whole region was on the verge of a bitter shooting war.

A shaft house was blown up. There were skirmishes here and there. Carolina was afraid to let Thea outside the house. Women dared not go downtown to buy groceries. The miners looted the hardware stores for weapons, and rumors spread that they had installed a cannon on Bull Hill; so the "deputies" laid siege to Bull Hill.

Even the state militia, which was sent in to try to keep peace between the two factions, was all but helpless. When finally Governor Waite, known to favor the cause of labor, came to arbitrate, he was nearly lynched in Colorado Springs by a mob sympathetic to the mine owners. The Governor of a sovereign state! That was too much for the plain citizens of that state. Only then did the owners agree to capitulate. After six months of useless struggle, they gave in on the eight-hour day. The miners had won.

Carolina was spiteful toward Ricketts after this. They had lost six months' work, from January until June. If he had listened to her——

Even though the men were back at work, the mine did not prosper. She blamed Ricketts again. But she knew no way to get rid of him. He was a full partner. She complained to McGregor, but the latter could not assure her that the mine would do better under a different management.

By the end of that summer of '94, Cripple Creek had a population of ten thousand and its first railroad. A network of trolleys connected it with adjacent mining towns. Everything was prospering except the Lucky Friday.

204

It was the bakery and not the mine that finally paid off the twelve hundred dollars to the partnership so they could buy the new steam hoist. And even with the new hoist, it was still the bakery that paid off the two thousand to Nick Bradley, in the following year. He returned the I.O.U. to Carolina with an air of baffled respect.

The family made a little ceremony that night of burning the I.O.U. in the bakery cookstove. Now they could contemplate the future without misgivings. At least Carolina could. McGregor held his peace.

And then, on the very next afternoon as she was nearing the bakery, she saw Floss on the sidewalk deep in conversation with an old crib woman. A block away, Carolina knew the other for what she was. Headed straight for the laudanum route, she thought with the callousness of a mining town. Didn't Floss know better than to talk to one in broad daylight? Floss had always been so careful, even persnickety. Some premonition slowed her steps.

The shabby trull wandered on. Carolina entered the bakery to find Floss working down her bread with nervous thumps.

"Who was that?" Carolina demanded after first making sure that McGregor was not within hearing.

"Mimi. From Stelle Bogart's. She recognized me. I never would have her—she looks as old as sin itself."

"What did she want?" An ague had settled in Carolina's limbs. She held on to the edge of the kitchen table. Mimi. From that past she had been so sure she had buried.

"She doesn't know enough about us yet to try to leech us. But she would if she knew. Stelle let her go when she started on dope. She's down on her luck; business is poor; the competition is terrible here, she says. I urged her to try Leadville. Told her they were having a gold revival over there. She wanted to know how I was doing here. I told her I hadn't 'worked' since my leg went bad, that I'd been forced to take a job in a bakery. I ended by making her sorry for me." Floss laughed shakily.

The two looked at each other from behind that frail blind of laughter. Mimi! If she once found out they had a decent paying little business—a business that was good for a touch now and then——

Carolina stared around her huntedly. She had stopped worrying, with her marriage to Pete, which she had been so sure was a passport to respectability. But now, if this faded old drab should come back into their lives and tell what she knew—about Stelle Bogart's and Floss and the Row . . .

Would she never feel safe again? Or would she always be creeping along on a glacier, hearing a crack in the ice and seeing a fissure open up right beside her, or back of her where she had walked a second ago, or just ahead where she was about to step? Would she never be able to feel secure about Thea?

For a while after this she wondered if people knew. Were they whispering about her as she passed on the street? With a bitter hatred she hated Roger, who was the cause of all her troubles, and her father, who was the cause behind Roger.

Then, as time slipped by and nothing happened, she dared to conclude that Mimi had departed, either from Cripple Creek or from this world.

Oh, they were safe, safe, she told herself once more. She had been foolishly nervous. She was gay again. She resumed her jeering interest in the society columns of the Denver papers which told about the goings-on of the Roger Walling Jardines.

"Listen to this, Floss. 'Mr. and Mrs. Roger Walling Jardine III gave a tallyho party at the Overland Park Country Club last Saturday. It was a most colorful equipage, with the driver of the six horses as well as the footman wearing white breeches and gay coats, and a wicker basket containing golf clubs fastened at the side. The Jardines are said to be mastering the new game. A delicious luncheon of squab and charlotte russe——'" She rattled the paper derisively. "Butler, oh, butler," she called out to her empty kitchen, "see that the squab is done to a turn tonight!"

Floss watched her a little anxiously. Then she relaxed. As long as Carolina could jeer at Roger and his wife, she was all right. It was the silent hurts, too deep to joke about, that warped a person.

Or again, Carolina would say mincingly, running her eye down the columns of *The Denver Republican*, "I see where Mrs. Roger Jardine served an elegant collation to her literary club at her palatial home on Sherman Avenue, and a paper was read entitled, 'Morris, Ruskin, and Carlyle, and the Aesthetic Evils of Commercialism.'" Her ridicule gave way to frank wonder. "Mercy what a lot of ladies' clubs there are! The Fortnightly—the Monday Literary—the Round Table—the Tuesday Music—the Wednesday

206

Morning Music. How can they sit still so long on those hard little chairs?"

"It takes a lot of sitting to improve your mind," Floss suggested.

II

BUT CAROLINA WAS NOT CAREFREE FOR LONG. NO SOONER WAS SHE rid of the worry about Mimi than she took on the worry over the mine. It was definitely not doing well. How much longer could they go on pouring money into it with no return?

One day McGregor quietly insisted upon accompanying her up to the mine. As if to shield her. She glanced sidewise at his thin, worried face. He knew something.

Ricketts came bristling out to meet them. He dragged a piece of ore from his pocket.

"It's played out, I tell you. And I'm played out too." He hurled the piece of rock to the ground.

Carolina turned quickly to McGregor and saw with shocked amazement that he was not surprised.

"The damn' thing's quit on us," went on Ricketts. "A fault cut off the vein. It's no use going on."

I don't believe it, she thought hotly. I won't believe it. She waited for McGregor to contradict him.

"How many rounds have you shot?" McGregor inquired mildly.

"We went down three rounds farther, but it showed only rock. I tried driving off into the hanging wall fifteen feet, but nothing there. I'm through. What's the use pouring good money after bad?"

Oh, tell him he's wrong, she begged silently of McGregor. Tell him all we need to do is hold on and be patient and not give up hope.

But McGregor's voice was alarmingly doubtful.

"Have you thought of going the other way? Through the foot wall?"

She could see Ricketts' lip curl at a suggestion from a man who was more at home in a cook's apron than in overalls. Besides, Ricketts wanted to get away. He was a surly fellow who was happiest with a burro and a pick, eating his lonely meals by a campfire and spouting Tom Paine to an occasional passerby. The onerous routine of a working mine grueled him. He turned to Carolina.

"I got an itch to be moving. I hear there's a stir in gold mining

207

over Leadville way. I'll take a thousand dollars for my share, ma'am. Then you can try McGregor's scheme of driving through the foot wall," he suggested craftily. It was obvious he thought the idea nonsensical.

"I'll—I'll have to think it over," she said weakly. A thousand dollars. Where could she raise a thousand dollars?

As she and McGregor walked down the slope she asked thinly: "What about it? What would you do, McGregor?"

McGregor was a long time answering.

"Well, if I was alone, I think I'd quit. I'd throw my pick in the hole and move on, just like Ricketts. But with you it's different. You're tied here. You'd probably be better off to gamble on it and raise the money and start driving out through the rock, like I said."

The gravel slid and rattled under their feet. If only he were surer of his own judgment, she thought. If only *she* were surer of his judgment. For after all, he had not made any marked success of his own mining ventures. What if he did not know? Yet she could not bear to give up. She had fought so hard.

"How would you go about it?" she asked.

"I'd start back where the slip occurred, take the angle of the fault and start to follow the fault line. Me, I think it let the ore slide off in the direction of the foot wall. I'd go in twenty or thirty feet before I'd give up. I think the ore's still there. But I can't— nor can anybody else—be sure. Ricketts may be right. Many a fault has slipped so far that the vein was never picked up again."

She knew all that. She remembered the Little Saturn and all the secret, costly, desperate measures that were used to try to find the vein again, only to end in failure. She squinted anxiously against the setting sun. Long shadow fingers raked across the flat bowl of the valley, now the site of a populous city. She shivered a little from the fall chill in the air and from the sudden chill that had settled over her spirits.

"I'll see Tom Higby," she said at last.

That night occurred the Great Fire of Cripple Creek. It all started from an overturned stove on Myers Avenue. At first it was just a little fire. And then it was a big fire, leaping ravenously through the business district. The flimsy slab buildings crackled and roared like shavings under a forced draft. There was no saving the bakery; they could only be thankful that it was insured.

Mat drove the delivery wagon up to the back door of the bakery, while McGregor helped Floss out with her suitcase. He shouted to Mat to wait a minute and ran back into the smouldering building, returning presently with Floss's beloved rocker, which he loaded in the back. Mat hurriedly whipped up the old horse, and they escaped under a shower of falling sparks and brands. Afterwards, Floss proudly pointed out the burned spots on the tapestry cover of the chair.

When they reached the brick house on Carr, Floss joined Carolina on the front porch to watch the havoc, while McGregor and Mat took turns climbing to the roof with pails of water to drench the shingles. Pete, who happened to be in town at the time, had promptly hurried to the scene of the fire, where he performed miracles of valor in rescuing trapped citizens. When he staggered home, his face was blistered and his eyebrows were gone and his hair was singed.

Carolina solicitously rubbed ointment on his face and bound up his hands and admired him. For the time, Pete was a hero, home from the wars; and Carolina was his woman.

The fire died down, and then a breeze blew it into sinister activity again. The flames had reached to within a half a block of the red brick house, crackling like a thousand bull whips, before they were brought under control.

Carolina experienced a moment's regret, even though it was to save her own and other people's houses, when the "old" Palace Hotel was dynamited to stop the fire. Buildings, like people, aged fast in boom towns, she thought; where a hotel was ready to be razed after five years, and there was scarcely a citizen over forty. Oh, well, the Hotel National was far handsomer, and that was progress.

There was something symbolic, too, in the fact that her old sewing basket left in Floss's room had been burned. It had not been used as a bank for a long time; her days for hiding money under its plush lining were past.

She was a business woman now, initiated into the ways of banks and banking. But she almost wished that she were not. The old days of the cache in the sewing basket were better; when it was only a matter of taking in enough today to pay for the flour for tomorrow's pasties. Now it was different. Now she had to decide whether to stake everything on a mine that might never pay.

Soberly she and Floss looked out over the smoking ruins the next day and talked about their future.

"The insurance money from the bakery is all yours," Carolina told her. For she knew what it meant to Floss to run a business, to be "Miss Kittredge," standing behind a counter, respected and unassailable. "You can start it up again whenever you like. You've earned it."

Floss looked at her steadily.

"You want to go on with the mine, don't you, Carolina?"

"Yes. I'll put a mortgage on the house." Carolina winced as she said it. The very words, "mortgage on the house," frightened her. But she glanced down at Thea playing fireman in the street with the other children of the block, all screaming, "Fire—fire!" with the happy savagery of children. "I want Thea to have everything nice, Floss. Like—music lessons and polite ways and pretty ribbons——" What she meant was, I want her to feel safe and assured and taken care of.

"Then I'll gamble with you," said Floss, who was no gambler. "It will take everything we can scrape together—insurance money, mortgage money and all—to go ahead with the mine. If you win, I can start up the bakery again anyhow. If you lose—well, time enough to figure out what to do then."

Carolina swallowed. That was like Floss—no fuss, no protests. She knew she ought not to take the money; and she knew that she would.

An hour after she had seen Tom Higby about the mortgage on her house, which he deprecated from her point of view and approved from his own, she was the sole owner of the Lucky Friday mine and had made McGregor her foreman. He let all but one miner go and set about the anxious business of driving out into the foot wall on the slim chance of picking up the lost vein again.

Each day Carolina walked up to the mine to see how things were going, and each day she was met by his set look of negation.

Five feet they went; ten, fifteen, twenty—and still no sign of values . . . Twenty-five, thirty. At thirty-five feet he came to her for further orders.

"It's costing plenty, Mrs. Ramsay; and you've no money coming in from anywhere. We've gone farther already than I figured on. Maybe we'll never pick up the vein again," he said gloomily.

She turned and stared out over the valley. Then her nostrils flared, and her head went up in the old stubborn way.

"I'll put a second mortgage on the house. I've a topaz necklace I can sell. My—my wedding ring can go——"

McGregor bowed as to fate and went back to work.

Each day, McGregor's face—dirty, tired, haggard—told her the answer. The strain was telling on both of them.

Christmas came and went almost unnoticed in the household. Floss managed a new dress for Thea's doll, but that was all. Pete's burns from the fire had been worse than he had let on at first. There were doctors' bills for him, and he had to keep one arm in a sling. And Pete, helpless and imprisoned in a house, was not easy to live with. Carolina spent more and more time at the mine.

Mat, alone of them all, had a job. While he waited to hear from his application for a telegrapher's position in Kansas, he found work with the construction crews that were busy all over town cleaning up debris and erecting new brick buildings to take the place of flimsy wooden ones. Mat's wages kept food on the table and coal in the stove.

On a chill winter afternoon, with her breath coming in feathery white puffs, Carolina neared the mine. This was the first time in her life that she had hated winter. She felt cold and spiritless. Where could she turn next? The last thing had been sold. They did not really own the roof over their heads; only Tom Higby's leniency let them stay on. They could not continue much longer living off Mat's slender wages.

She saw McGregor coming out to meet her. She was afraid to lift her eyes. She noted that his gait was as unhurried as always, but that there was a certain jerkiness in it today. She glanced at him swiftly. His face was as tired and expressionless as usual, but it was different too.

He hauled out a chunk of ore and passed it to her. She remembered Ricketts' hauling out the piece of ore to prove to her that the mine was finished. She thought of all the countless men in her lifetime who had dragged out a chunk of ore to show her. She searched McGregor's face, not the piece of rock.

"It's the continuation, all right. It's the vein that was cut off," he said unevenly.

She began to tremble. There must be a catch in it somewhere.

"You don't mean——?"

"I mean it looks good. The pressure that made the fault in the first place and narrowed the ore down to a thread seems to have been released here below. The vein widens out——" He held his hands apart to show her, trying to keep the excitement out of his voice. He was like a faithful retriever that lays a bird at its owner's feet. "Here it is, Mistress," his gray eyes said. "I've found it for you."

So they had hit the vein at last! Tears stung her eyes. They could eat and keep a roof over their heads. They could get out of debt. Floss could start up her bakery again. They could look the world in the face. And she owed all this to the careful, anxious man standing before her.

"Oh, John—John—— What would I do without you?" She flung her arms impulsively around his neck and kissed him. Her feeling was compounded of joy and thanks and complete trust. It was exactly the way she would have liked to feel toward a kindly father.

But John McGregor entertained no fatherly feelings toward her. He backed hastily out of her embrace. When he spoke, his voice was ragged and his speech hurried.

"It's high-grade, Mrs. Ramsay. It could even be dinner-bucket stuff." He sounded almost incredulous himself.

That night the family talked late. There was a solemn deliberation in their tones, as if they recalled that once before, on the night that Pete announced the original strike, they had let themselves count their good fortune too soon. They would not allow themselves to be hoaxed by fate again. That other time they had tasted riches greedily in terms of bright shawls and tasseled boots and a real man's suit. Now they would tread warily.

But McGregor's half-fearful hopes were fulfilled. The vein was as good as it had been before the fault occurred. Money poured from it once more in a gratifying little stream.

In spite of Carolina's protests that there was no need for her to work again, Floss insisted upon starting up a bakery and lunch room on Bennett Avenue, a new "Reliable Home Bakery—Meals."

"After all," she said, "mines can come and mines can go, but people eat, regardless."

Carolina set herself once more to paying off the mortgage on the house. She had a mystical need to have the house clear. She wanted no lien on the roof over their heads.

She and McGregor were full of sober schemes for developing the mine. Although first they invented a job for Pete where he could do no harm and yet could feel pleasantly important. Then they settled to their planning. They would build a tramway and a sorting house and hire more miners . . .

She began to wear an air of busy importance as she went to and from the mine office every day, stopping in at mining exchanges on the way to read the stock quotations. And why shouldn't she look busy and important, for wasn't she a successful mine operator? Didn't they own their own house, and run a bakery, and have money in the bank? Well, then—why didn't the bliss begin?

Maybe she needed a change of scene or people. She had never yet been outside the mountains, although there was overnight sleeping-car service to and from Denver which, because the sleeper left Denver at eleven at night and arrived in Cripple Creek at seven in the morning, was called by the gambling-minded populace, the "Eleven-Come-Seven." Carolina had never set foot in it. Nor did she know anyone in town except the people she did business with. She knew that Cripple Creek had something called a "bon ton," because the paper was always referring to it. The members of the English Colony ostentatiously played cricket in the shade of Mt. Pisgah every afternoon. But Carolina was a stranger to them all.

"What you need is a bang-up good time," remarked Floss sympathetically, noting Carolina's wan restlessness. "You haven't gone to a party or worn a low-necked dress since——" She stopped lamely; that was not a line of thought that bore further exploring, "—since I don't know when."

Carolina glanced up from the newspaper in her hands. It was the gaily illustrated supplement dedicated to Denver's famous autumn Festival of Mountain and Plain—"the Mardi Gras of the West." Her face wore a look of naked longing.

"Just listen to all these lovely parades, Floss," sighed the same Carolina who had been ecstatic over a rock-drilling contest back in Aspen. "There's a Comic Parade, and a Firemen's Parade, and the Heroes of Santiago, and an Illuminated Night Parade, given by 'those dashing young blades of the town who call themselves the Slaves of the Silver Serpent.' And horse races and Indian races—a whole tribe of Utes are camped out on the edge of the city. And, oh, the balls! There's a ball practically every night. And a King and Queen of the Festival. Look at the Queen, Floss; isn't she pretty?" Carolina held the paper toward Floss wistfully. "See, I'm not so much older than she, am I?"

"No, and you're ten times better looking!" snorted Floss loyally with a glance at the blurred picture of the self-conscious girl who was being crowned Queen of the Festival. Then she bent closer.

"Say—wasn't it her old man struck it rich over in Lake County about ten years ago? He set up the whole town, if I remember."

Carolina studied the picture again.

"Of course. I can see her mother now. Her feet were all splayed out, poor thing, from trudging behind an ox team those weary miles overland when they came West. She said shoes always hurt her after that. It must be a change to sink her feet into deep-piled carpets."

"And carry a fan in place of a bull whip," contributed Floss.

Carolina resumed her reading of the gala edition.

"They give prizes, too, for the best decorated floats. Oh, Floss, I've always wanted to dress up like a goddess or a fairy or something and ride on a float," she confessed.

"You'd be a sight worth looking at, my girl." Floss's tone was maternal. "I wish you could."

Carolina laughed at her own vaporous longings.

"Maybe what I need is a trip to Manitou to 'drink the waters.' Remember how Roger used to think that drinking the waters would cure almost any trouble that rich people had? Although the poor could get well on pump water!" She gave a caustic chuckle. "I see here where the Roger Walling Jardines have taken a box in the first tier of the grandstand at the Festival. You can bet it's the 'best' tier."

All through the years she had followed the newspaper indications of the Jardines' social supremacy. "Mrs. Roger Walling Jardine was hostess at a beautiful sweet-pea tea today——" "Mr. Roger Walling Jardine III has been made vestryman at the church of——" "Mr. and Mrs. Roger Walling Jardine III were among the sponsors of a Subscription Dance given at Kassler Hall——"

There was never any mention of a Roger IV or a small Sue. Carolina extracted a baleful triumph from the fact that Roger who, according to Floss, would have set such store by a child of his own, was evidently childless. A beautiful sweet-pea tea would be a poor substitute, Carolina thought with a misty downward glance at Thea, for a small daughter with soft brown hair and a shy smile.

But even baleful triumph is not very sustaining. Carolina continued to be as restless and jumpy as she was the time before she left Aspen. And now she could not go over the mountain. She had to stay here until the mine was safely established as a producer.

That might take years. A little frown deepened between her eyes.

Carolina herself finally discovered the reason for her discontent. It was at the exact moment that Thea disappeared into the big downtown grade school for the first time. Before that, she had attended only a neighborhood primary class in someone's front parlor. Carolina had taken her to the brick school building this morning, like a score of other bravely smiling but damp-eyed mothers parting with their first-born on the first day of school.

She stood there in the gravelly school yard and watched the little grave-eyed thing in her long skirts and her fresh white pinafore, with her braids down over each shoulder and one hand clutching a new pencil box, as she paused on the steps to wave back at her mother and then turn resolutely to Face Life, all alone.

Carolina turned quickly away so that no one should see her tears. She thought with a clutch at her throat, I haven't any baby. If he had lived, I'd have a red-headed little boy at home now, playing train . . . I'm only twenty-seven. That's what ails me; I want a baby.

As if the decision were all that were necessary, she set off swiftly for home. With her usual unblushing directness, she thought, I wish I'd been nicer to Pete lately.

C H A P T E R 23

CAROLINA PACED BACK AND FORTH, BACK AND FORTH, IN THE narrow confines of the Lucky Friday office, which was merely a boarded-off corner of the hoist house where she worked on her accounts and McGregor kept the time book. As each circuit brought her past the smudged window overlooking the growing crowd around the open shaft across the roadway, her breath came a little faster and she gave an even angrier switch to her skirts.

Somebody ought to throw a stick of dynamite down that open shaft. That would smoke them out—that would teach them a lesson! Oh, not necessarily a lesson that would kill anybody, but just enough to wreck the cage itself, so that the dozen miners barricaded at the bottom would have to climb the whole five hundred feet by ladder when they got over their sulks and decided to come up. They deserved it. Preempting somebody else's property—plotting trouble—encouraging their families to gather around the top of the shaft, knowing you couldn't order women and children away.

Absently she pushed back her tawny pompadour. Carolina Ramsay, at thirty-two, was a handsome woman, with both arrogance and perplexity in her expression. The tiny vertical wrinkle between her brows had deepened recently. Her full ripe mouth that was used to giving commands had grown bitter now.

She was sick and tired of this everlasting strike that no one seemed to want, that yet went on and on. It had started the year before, in 1903, in the reduction mills down in Colorado City, largely over a matter of wages. Only a handful of men were involved. Then, in order to bring the mills to time, the union had ordered out all the miners from the mines that shipped ore to these mills. That meant a walk-out of some thirty-five hundred men in the Cripple Creek district. At first the miners did not want to strike. They had no grievances against the owners. Why should they strike, they grumbled, just to prevent ore from being shipped to the offending mills? Their wages were good, and their hours were short.

But if the men grumbled, the mine owners raged. They paid the highest wages for the shortest hours in the state, and what did it get them? Another strike!

For a while Carolina's mine was not affected, for the Lucky Friday, which was small, did not ship ore to the mills in question. So it was easy for her to be philosophical about the other mines' troubles: the open and stealthy warfare, the damages to machinery, the shots in the darkness, the mysteriously frayed cables that let a cage smash to the bottom of the shaft killing every man in it, and the equally mysterious explosion in a shaft house that buried three officials underground. She complained mechanically about the tiresome, swaggering deputies, about the equally tiresome militia that had been brought in—and withdrawn—and then brought in again. Were the streets never to be free of armed men so she could let fourteen-year-old Thea walk to school alone?

When her own men had finally struck, too, she had grimly hired non-union men and continued operations after a fashion. And then, just three days ago, her original miners had preempted the Lucky Friday, barricading themselves in the bottom of the shaft, and neither threats nor cajoling could bring them up. They warned that they would take drastic steps if she tried to send down deputies after them.

She was afraid they could hold out for a long time. They doubtless had plenty of food. The air was good. They could even drink the seepage water, although it was not palatable and would rise a little every day. For the mine bailed for an hour each morning before work started, although it did not have to pump constantly yet, like the deeper mines. It was all too comfortable for them down there, she decided wrathfully, considering that it was her mine they were in.

She glared at the silent crowd some twenty feet away, standing in the gray patches of late spring snow. What were they waiting for? She noticed that there were a few men scattered among the women and children. What did they all expect to gain from huddling out there? Did they think they could make her give in meekly? . . . "All right, my friends, you've worn me down." . . . Did they think she would be such a milk-and-water fool as to say that? "From now on the union shall be boss, and you can have anything you ask for —from afternoon tea to pink ribbons tied on your lunch buckets." . . . Did they think that by standing out there in the cold they could get her to knuckle under like that?

Never. Nobody was going to bulldoze her. She would join the other mine owners in blacklisting the striking men forever.

At first, when the men had struck, McGregor was conciliatory. But he had changed his tune when they holed-in down in her mine. With his Scotch reverence for another's property, he had become as angry as she.

But what could either of them do? It might go on and on. And if the men became sufficiently incensed, they could wreck the distant mine workings.

She stopped her pacing to stare at the small, cold-looking crowd around the black upright timbers that marked the opening of the mine shaft. The gallows frame. The name had always given her a shivery feeling. Now, as she looked at those shawled women, some with children hugged to their breasts, the baffled look deepened in her brown-gold eyes. Life was so unsettling. One minute it gave with open hands; the next minute it withheld.

Take the Lucky Friday. In spite of all its promise through the years, it still was only "promising." It still was only a modest blade of sylvanite slicing down through the rock, never quite petering out and never opening up into a rich vug—that opulent thickening of the vein which is the dream of every mine owner. Plenty of other mines in this region had hit them. But not the Lucky Friday. McGregor was a good foreman; none better. They had both been so sure she would be rich by now. Not that she cared, for herself——

Life had withheld other things too. Her eyes saddened. She had wanted another baby so. And finally the new young doctor, who was not so new or so young any more, had had to tell her that she would never be able to bear another child. Something had happened that last time . . . She had not been able to believe it. A great healthy thing like her. It had made her channel all her love back upon Thea. Floss had said it could be hard on Thea. That was nonsense, of course; as if anyone could have too much love. Life had played other tricks too. Her marriage to Pete, for instance. Pete was off on another of his "business trips" right now. As always, at thought of him, a helpless, hopeless look came over her face. What could you do with a man who was so pleasant and good-natured and—"do-less"? She knew that the moment he returned, the family, in spite of themselves, would receive him with open arms. Worst of all, she would receive him with open arms. And all the while, each and every one of them would know that he was completely worthless.

But life was generous too. There had been no more ghosts to rise from the past to haunt her. No more Mimis. Even her father seemed to have cleared out for good. The last she had heard of him, he was preaching somewhere over on the western slope. The family had grown used to its little niceties and comforts. Mat had a job in Kansas, where he had recently married. It had been fun to outfit the young couple with linens and silver. Carolina's youngest sister Rosalie had married, too, and she and Floss had been lavish in the trousseau they ordered from Denver for her. Oh, it was pleasant to be able to do for your own, and to have a friend who took as much interest in them as you did yourself. Floss was the same staunch, loyal person, who continued to run the bakery and live in the back of it and feel a prim satisfaction in being "Miss Kittredge."

But the crown and glory and reason for Carolina's existence was Thea. Gift of God. With her slim, patrician look and her pale brown-silk hair and her fleeting Roger-smile, she could turn Carolina into a helpless mass of mother love. It was frightening to love anyone so. For Thea was not tough like herself; Thea was a perfect, crushable thing who would always need to be sheltered and watched over. That was why nothing must happen to the mine or its prospects.

She looked out again at the crowd, beginning to eddy restlessly now. The hot color whipped into her cheeks. Damn them all, she thought, if they aided and abetted those men down below. Or if anything happened, to damage the mine——

She heard McGregor enter the hoist house. He was the only one besides herself who had a key to it in these troubled times. But she did not turn from her resentful inspection, so she failed to note the added disquiet in his face. With the years, McGregor had become merely a little grayer and leaner and more watchful of Carolina's interests. And like the McGregor of the bakery days, he fitted so neatly into her life that she was scarcely aware of his existence.

"What's going on now?" she asked over her shoulder, eying the crowd, which seemed to be moving with a slightly faster tempo, like a river current nearing the falls. She saw a fist shoot up above the heads of the crowd. Still she had no warning.

"Your father's back," McGregor said.

She whirled, her eyes widening. Not her father! Why, he had been over near Ouray the last time she had heard.

"What does he want?"

"I don't exactly know."

"Well, get him out of here. He's a trouble-maker."

"He says he wants to go down in the mine and talk to the men."

"What about?"

"To preach to them—and pray, I suppose. He's offered to take food down, if you'll let him. You're the one has to give orders to operate the hoist." He lifted an eyebrow toward the silent machinery in the hoist room. "The womenfolks are beginning to worry for fear their men may be hungry."

"I hope they starve to death."

"Your old man's got the attention of a crowd for the first time in his life. They're crazy to get food down. It's up to you."

"Well, I say no!"

"The miners could do a lot of damage to your property before they pulled out, if they got mad enough," he said doubtfully.

"But my father—he's just doing this to pester me—to put me in the wrong."

219

"Maybe so. But the women standing out there with baskets of food for their men don't care about that. They only know he's offered to go down. They figure he's a preacher, and so a neutral. They expect you to let him go."

She bit her red underlip. McGregor watched her thoughtfully. Once he started to speak, but he stopped himself. He knew her well enough to let her alone when she had a decision to make.

"My father has never done anything but harm to me, McGregor. You've seen some of it. I don't trust that terrible piousness of his today any more than I ever did. But if you think I'd better——" She left it hanging there.

McGregor turned and went out to the crowd waiting for him around the gibbet-like frame. Then it was that she saw her father, tall and gaunt in his old greenish overcoat, his beard blowing in the wind. She saw him lift his arms in a gesture of assent when McGregor spoke.

Now there was a scurrying to get the baskets piled on the cage. Presently a bell sounded the signal to lower. McGregor started up the machinery.

Thwarted, she stood in the window and watched, her fists doubled into tight balls. All of them were against her: her father —the miners—their families. She was sorry that she had ever given in to the pacific McGregor. Let them starve below. Let the women fuss and fume above. Whose property was it, anyhow? Who had slaved and worried and borrowed and taken risks in order to own it?

She could visualize the cage dropping, dropping, in its deep black slot. One hundred feet, two hundred feet, three hundred . . . It must be down around the fourth level now. Now the fifth. By this time it was at the bottom. She could picture her father talking to the men while they unloaded supplies, exhorting them about their souls. This once they would have to listen to him.

Her lip curled. She remembered that Jude Lawler would do anything to get men to listen to him. Anything.

Suddenly she heard a harsh jangle. The signal to hoist. Something must be wrong. Jude Lawler, of his own will, would never give the hoist signal so soon. Without any preaching; without any praying.

She saw the crowd surge convulsively closer about the mouth of the shaft. She waited for the cage to reach the surface. McGregor set the brake on the hoist and rushed out. The women let him through. She sensed the heavy silence settling over them as they dropped back. She saw hands go up to throats and heads turn, as white blobs of faces looked suddenly toward her office.

What now? she thought. What now?

A path opened up among the thickly clustered watchers. McGregor and several men came through. Slowly they marched across the rutted mine road toward her office, carrying something. Unwillingly she looked and saw the long, limp body of a man. She saw the greenish, frayed overcoat, the flowing beard, and then the blood that dripped. Her father!

They laid him gently on a coat just inside the hoist house door. One of them turned to McGregor.

"I'll go for a doctor now, Mac. Not that it will do any good." The strangers hurried away, as if relieved to get out of the room.

She was suddenly shaking. She held on to the doorframe, her eyes on McGregor, who was kneeling beside her father. He got slowly to his feet.

"No one seems to know what happened," he explained. "Somebody must have tossed a piece of drill steel down the shaft. Maybe one of the crowd at the top. Maybe a miner stationed on a level partway down. Whoever it was likely misunderstood. After all, it was your father. They might have thought he was coming from you—to try to break them down. By now they've found out their mistake—too late."

She could not answer. She could only stare at him with wide blank eyes.

"I'll have to see about getting a wagon or a stretcher. He's going fast." McGregor gave a last look down at her father and then he, too, was gone, leaving her alone with the quiet figure on the floor.

A sickening wave of feeling swept over her. She dropped to her knees beside her father. She must try to make him comfortable. As she wadded the coat up under his head a little, she saw all too plainly the mortal damage done by the piece of drill steel that had fallen from a great height. Like a projectile, it had sliced straight down along the side of his cheek and plunged deep into his chest. The red, red blood from his lungs oozed up through that tight wound at the base of his neck from which the steel javelin still protruded. His face was gray, the dead gray of mold. Her father was dying.

She had not believed he could ever die. She had thought him invulnerable, destined forever to haunt her and castigate her. So this great frowning crag of a man was mortal, after all. She felt a brief surprise, followed by a shocked awareness of the terrible, haphazard, casual ease with which human life snuffs out. Jude Lawler ought to have been harder to kill. He ought not to be going like this, as the result of the tossing of a piece of drill steel down a mine shaft. Surely, so much harsh vigor could not end so easily.

She saw that he was trying to tell her something—groping for words, his eyes fastened on hers. He was not commanding now, or berating, or even judging. He was pleading and uncertain. It frightened her. Her father pleading and uncertain? As soon think of Mt. Massive swaying on its base.

"What is it, father?"

"God—forgive me——" he said faintly but clearly.

"Of course," she soothed.

"Before I die," he said with that feeble persistent clearness.

"You're going to be all right," she lied, with the instinctive hearty impulse of the well to reassure the ailing. "McGregor's gone for the doctor. He'll be here any minute."

"No," said Jude Lawler slowly, the beetling brows a ragged line of pain. "No, I'm done. Shortly I must put off this tabernacle, and I fear——" His face knotted.

She could not believe her senses. Not fears, not doubts, from her father, who had always seemed so sure he knew the inmost will of God. Oh, he could not be wavering in his faith now, here at the very end of his life, right at the last minute of his last hour. She dared not contemplate a world where her father could doubt, on his deathbed. She swallowed, and swallowed again.

"Perhaps I was too harsh with you, my daughter," he went on haltingly. "Perhaps I was wrong. But you were so like me—so devil-ruled. I thought I had to save you. You understand that now, don't you, my girl?"

The burning eyes pierced her. She shrank back from this unfamiliar Jude Lawler, who wanted to make his peace with her. She was frightened by a humble Jude.

"Everything is all right, father," she stammered. She had to end this painful spectacle. She was embarrassed by his humility. "I know what a trial I must have been to you—so headstrong and stubborn." And suddenly she did know what a trial she had been to him, who saw her only as a soul on the brink of damnation who must be pulled back instantly and fiercely.

But everything was not all right. Her words had not eased him nor brought him peace. His bony hand moved restlessly.

"But God—will God——?" he groaned.

So her personal, earthly, daughter's forgiveness was not enough. He wanted that, but he wanted something else. He craved his God's forgiveness even more. She saw now that it was not his faith in God that had wavered, but his faith in himself, in his own worthiness. She saw, too, that God had always been realer to him than wife or children or any human needs for warmth and food and shelter. This gaunt old prophet was agonized now about his Lord. His torment spoke in his eyes . . . Physician, heal thyself, she cried silently to him. You who have sat often beside the dying, father, and eased them into the next world—canst thou not ease thyself?

She was unaware of the ancient cadences into which her thoughts had fallen. She knew only that there was no one to bring him comfort but herself—and she had spent her life trying to forget what he believed, trying to forget the words of the Book. Now only those words could ease him.

Help me to remember, she pled with some outside force. Oh, help me.

Perversely she could think only of the harsh words first. Her father had mouthed them so often. "Woe unto you——" "Upon the wicked shall he rain snares and fire and brimstone——" No, not those! There must be gentler ones that he had offered to the stricken crib woman or to the man dying on a sawdust floor. For such as those he must have held out grudging solace.

Her voice quavered. "The Lord is very pitiful, and of tender mercy——" She hoped that was right. Even dying, he would know if she misquoted.

"Tender mercy!" he gasped between graying lips.

She saw his restless hand still moving. She could not bear to see that unsatisfied groping. With the instinct of all women to soothe, she slid her hand into his. The groping ceased.

"He knoweth our frame; he remembereth that we are dust," she offered hesitantly, wondering if you could bring peace with words you had scoffed at and tried to forget . . . But ah, you could; you could. For the piercing eyes had softened. The hold on her hand relaxed.

"He will not fail thee . . . nor forsake thee." Her voice broke huskily, for she saw that those words were to be her father's shriving. While she watched, he began to cough his life away, lying there with his head on her arm. A harsh, invincible, terrible, humble man, coughing his life away.

But the look in his eyes was no longer tormented. It was tranquil, accepting, finished. The words she had spoken had brought him peace—words she had once learned by rote and learned to hate. . . . Maybe you didn't have to believe, she told herself wonderingly.

She saw a swift hawklike tightening of the features, and then a gradual letting-go. The thing that had lashed him and driven him was quieted at last. He was a spent runner who had finished the race. His hand fell away. The gray marble lips smiled ever so slightly. But was it a smile, or only the strange falling apart of the features that have been knotted by struggle and now are suddenly unraveled by death?

Carolina laid the great hand softly back beside him. She was weeping.

C H A P T E R 24

"Remember to button up your cloak, lovey, when you come out of that hot opera house," said Carolina . . . "And don't forget to thank your hostess for the nice cove-oyster supper afterwards," added Floss . . . "And then be sure to come straight home after *that!*" finished Carolina.

Indulgently Thea submitted to all their last-minute, old-hen fussings.

"Yes, Mama," she said, and "I'll remember, Aunt Floss," and, "Now don't you two worry over me," as she kissed them both with a quaintly mature air and gave them each a loving pat before she turned to the gangly youth who fidgeted in the front hall.

Demurely she tucked her hand under his arm, and the two of them set off to see the high school play called "Who's Who, or All in a Fog." It was her first evening engagement alone with a young man. She was wearing her first white kid gloves and her first "rat" in her silky light-brown hair. Thea was sixteen and a young lady.

Carolina and Floss stood in the front doorway watching and listening. Not until the last faint clack-clack of their receding footsteps was lost among the other night sounds of Cripple Creek did they turn to look at each other sheepishly. They knew they ought to go in out of the winter cold; but they lingered on. It was as if, by standing there, they could hold on to the little-girl Thea that much longer.

How Thea had sparkled, thought Floss wistfully. Well, maybe not exactly sparkled. Perhaps glowed was a better word. Carolina was the one who sparkled, sometimes glittered, occasionally even blazed, when her spirits were high and she was drunk on excitement. Thea gave off a softer light, one that cheered but did not scorch.

They went inside to the parlor and resumed their sewing, Floss her mile-a-minute crocheting and Carolina her lumpy French knots. Floss had to keep her eyes sternly fixed on her own work, for there was something about Carolina in her harsh, unrelieved black, with her unprotected look of recent grief, that tore at Floss's heart. If anything were to happen to Thea now!

Pete's death last winter, only a year after the death of her father, had left Carolina unexpectedly broken. Floss could not understand it. For years, Carolina had had to be the boss and the brains and the will of this whole household. Surely Pete could not have meant much to her. Yet evidently he had meant far more than Floss had realized, for Carolina had not been able to shake off her grief.

Floss had felt only an impersonal pity for Pete himself. He had been taken ill on one of his "business trips" across the state, and had barely managed, like a sick animal, to drag himself home to die. Appendicitis, the doctor called it; Pete might have been saved if he had been operated on in time. A great strong man like Pete. She could not believe it. So jaunty one minute; and a few days later—dead. She would never forget how he had clung to Carolina there at the last; and how Carolina had clung to him too. Maybe she had really loved him; maybe he had really loved her. Not that she, Floss, knew much about love and marriage—having had only a ringside seat at both, as she sometimes said.

Those two deaths had hit Carolina hard. Floss could not get

225

over the way her father's dying had affected her first, leaving her soft and bewildered. The unnatural softness toward the old hellion had extended to her dealings with her miners afterwards. She had refused to take sides against them, even when the rest of the town was up in arms; even after the dreadful explosion that killed thirteen non-union miners in the Independence depot; even when the townspeople rounded up three hundred strike leaders and shipped them out of the state, thereby shattering the union so that now their headquarters were occupied only by packrats. Through it all, Carolina had remained aloof, and afterwards she had meekly re-employed every one of her striking miners. No spirit; no spunk, thought Floss wonderingly. And all because her father had been killed—God knows how—down in her mine. She had made a martyr of him. Yet anyone could see that he had all but ruined her life: twice driving her into the arms of a man merely because he happened to be old Jude's opposite. Floss shook her head.

She looked across at Carolina, whose mouth was crimping as she made futile stabs with her needle at a French knot.

"I thought Thea looked very nice in that shade of blue," Floss offered hastily, to distract Carolina's mind.

"Yes—the dressmaker did a g-good job of draping the shadow-lace bertha—it made her look a little plumper," Carolina agreed shakily. "But, oh, so grown-up, Floss!"

Floss yanked out a botched scallop. Her crocheting went none too well even when she could see clearly.

Neither of them would ever be facile with the more genteel feminine accomplishments. But they had no choice of occupation, since the Lucky Friday had hit the famous vug last year. Even McGregor's eyes had popped. The vug, a great swollen pear-shaped deposit of ore, had been so rich they had shipped the stuff under armed guard each day to the sampling works in Victor.

When it was cleaned out and the vein had resumed its normal size again, Carolina found she had a comfortable little fortune in the bank. And who knew when they might strike another vug? It had been plainly absurd for Floss to go on running a one-horse bakery with Carolina a rich woman—a rich widow, she was now —so Floss had reluctantly sold the bakery and joined Carolina in the house on the hill. Joined her in the rich, idle, tedious routine of running a house that ran itself and concentrating all their love and attention on a sweet-faced, mannerly sixteen-year-old.

"This young Sam Milligan with Thea tonight—I wish we knew something about him," complained Carolina. "I wasn't exactly taken with him, were you?"

"No, I can't say that I was," confessed Floss. "But then, you and I wouldn't be taken with anybody Thea went out with. We're far too persnickety, Carolina. They say no women are so prissy where their daughters are concerned as reformed——" She stopped with a faint chuckle, letting the remark lie there between them. Not that it really applied to Carolina, of course. But they were a pair of old fuss-budgets. Always seeing that someone walked to and from school with Thea, until she rebelled in the eighth grade. Refusing to let her go out with boys and inspecting all the little girls that came to the house and hectoring her about her behavior and never letting her set foot on one of the "bad" streets of the town, until it was a wonder the girl dared sneeze, on her own hook . . . When Floss thought of Carolina at sixteen—bawling furiously in Hattie Merkle's parlor house that she didn't mind if she *did* become a whore—it would serve her old man right——

"But why did it have to be this shifty-looking boy?" asked Carolina. "I know he's been after her and after her, till she finally said yes. But why couldn't it have been a nice boy we know something about? Did you see how he just stood there like a bump and wouldn't look either of us in the eye?"

Floss had noticed. She had not been agreeably impressed either, but she tried to ease Carolina's mind.

"Maybe everything here kind of overwhelmed him," she said, looking around at their recently acquired magnificence—the shiny upright piano, the ponderous mission furniture, the center table with the handsome shaded lamp with its deep fringe of swaying beads.

Carolina was appeased for a moment. Then her worries swarmed back again.

"I can't see why Thea always picks out scrawny strays to like. Remember how she never took to the nice well-scrubbed pets we got her? Instead, she'd come lugging home some flea-bitten dog or chewed-up cat. And now it's this Sam Milligan from Poverty Flats. Poverty Flats!" Her tones were heavy with distaste. "Tailings of the gulch."

Floss knew there was no false pride in Carolina, but the very word *Flats* upset her. It brought back memories.

"They'll play games afterwards at the party. Likely she'll meet some nice boy who'll take a shine to her," Floss offered.

Carolina brightened. They had kept Thea in pretty close. The nice boys of the town had scarcely had a look at her. Tonight they would really see her—so smiling and pretty.

"Now that Thea's a young lady, we ought to be giving a party for her," Floss suggested coaxingly. "Let's see, who should we invite?"

Carolina stared fixedly at a French knot.

"Do you really think we ought to?" she asked with the first tinge of interest.

Floss relaxed. If she could just get Carolina to planning something.

Then Carolina's mouth sagged. "I forgot. You know it's out of the question, with me in mourning and all."

Floss, too, had forgotten. For at times Carolina's black crepe did not look like mourning. It was almost too becoming, she sometimes thought, on a woman with brown-gold eyes and a milky skin and coppery hair; a woman whose passage along the street caused every male glance to follow her like a cloud of dust trailing a freight wagon.

"It need be only a quiet little party," Floss urged. "After all, we owe it to Thea. A girl's sixteen only once."

"If we do give one," said Carolina, weakening, "I suppose I better speak to Tom Higby about having his nephew come up from Colorado Springs for it."

Floss stifled a chuckle. Even the densest mourning could not keep Carolina down long. She had not the least romantic leanings toward that dried up little pod of a man, Tom Higby, yet she had to have him in her train. Just because he was a man (at least he wore pants, Floss conceded cynically), Carolina must consult him on the flimsiest excuse.

He made plenty of chances to be consulted too. Only last week he had dropped in one evening to have her look over some reports —so he said—and she made him sit down and light up a cigar while she settled herself flatteringly to listen to him spout politics.

"It's just like I told you, Mrs. Ramsay," he snorted. "McKinley —and now this young Rough-Rider named Roosevelt—take all the credit for their party pulling the country out of the slump with the gold standard. Gold standard—prairie dogs' tails! It was

228

actually Cripple Creek's flash flood of gold that cured the country. Why, it was almost the same as having free silver, the way it sent prices up again and gave us cheap money in spite of the East."

Carolina hung on his words because anything affecting gold affected her and her family; and because she would always rather hear a man talk than a woman, even if it was only a rattling old husk like Higby.

Not that Higby was so all-fired wrapped up in his bimetallism, sniffed Floss silently. Those big yellow-brown eyes of Carolina's and her parted red lips as she listened may have had something to do with his eagerness to help her understand politics.

She grinned. He probably hadn't slept a wink the whole night after, and then had blamed it on the strong tea he had had for supper . . . Men—men——

But women were just as bad. Here was Carolina, who was only thirty-four and needed a man in her life. Yet as soon as a decent interval had passed after Pete's death, Floss would be willing to bet she would pick out another poor stick to marry, without even a side glance at a good man like McGregor, who was right on the ground. She was too used to him; that was the trouble.

Floss herself understood McGregor and valued him. Slowly she had garnered bits about his past; his bleak Nova Scotia boyhood and his love for a neighbor girl who had promised to wait while he came to the Rockies to seek his fortune. He had sent all his extra money home to help a younger brother through school; and then, when he was just at the point of striking it rich (or so he would always think), he had got the letter saying she had grown tired of waiting and had married the younger brother. He had thrown his pick in the hole with an oath and moved on. He was cold and hungry and at his hope's end when he happened into the hot, savory-smelling bakery that day.

Yet Carolina needed McGregor quite as much as he needed her. He had made her a wealthy woman; he had guarded her with his caution and his wisdom and his honesty. The trouble with her was, she always thought happiness lay just over the hill. McGregor, on the other hand, knew when happiness was right beside him in the kitchen.

It hurt Floss every time she saw his unappeased look. For she knew no way to make Carolina see him. Carolina liked him well enough and leaned on him; but she would have called him an old sobersides. Floss dreaded the time when Carolina should set her cap for another laughing, pleasant, weak fellow like Roger or Pete.

The evening wore on, and the winter wind howled like a pack of lean wolves up and down the streets and around the corners of the house. At length Carolina could stand it no longer. She stood up, rolling her fancywork into a wad.

"I don't care what you say, Floss—" (Floss had not said a word for an hour), "—that child is not dressed warmly enough. I'm going to take a woolen fascinator over to the Ellisons' where the party is. I'll just leave it at the door. I promise not to butt in."

Floss's eyes softened. Poor Carolina. Poor Thea too. She limped out to see Carolina off. How she hated being a hobbling old woman who must always stay at home.

The mile-a-minute belied its name. Floss was still pulling out the same old scallop when Carolina flung herself back into the house a half-hour later.

"She wasn't there!" she said unsteadily. "The party had already begun, but Thea and that boy hadn't come. I waited a while and then—I don't know why, but I thought I better get on home. To be here in case——" Her eyes begged Floss for reassurance.

"You did right," soothed Floss, trying to hide her own uneasiness. What could have become of those two? She wished she knew something about this gangly Sam Milligan who had seemed both shifty and bold in his pursuit of Thea. "They're probably taking the longest way 'round to get home," she suggested with heavy archness. "She'll be all right. What could happen on a four-block walk?"

What could? Floss wished she knew. She must put a good face on things until they found out. She talked about the new birds-eye furniture for Thea's bedroom. How Thea would love it. She talked until she saw Carolina begin to relax. Then she folded up her own sewing.

"It's time we went upstairs. You don't want her to think we're always going to wait up for her, ready to pounce the minute she comes in. Remember, she thinks she's grown up already."

"But she isn't," wailed Carolina. "She's only sixteen!"

Floss smiled with a certain sadness.

"You thought you were plenty old, at sixteen," she reminded. "Old enough to run away from home and get married."

"But that was different," Carolina assured her. "I was old for my age; I knew something about the world. Thea is just a baby," she said, as all mothers have always said of their daughters.

But she turned out the light and followed Floss obediently up to the latter's bedroom. Both of them knew there was no use trying to go to bed until Thea was safely in and had reported on her evening.

The clock had struck midnight when they finally heard a creak on the front porch. Carolina sprang up from her perch on the foot of Floss's bed. Floss sat stockstill, her hands gripping the arms of the patent rocker. It was such a stealthy, tiptoeing creak. There were no young giggles, no whispered good-bys, no retreating boyish footsteps down the walk. Thea was alone.

The front door opened carefully. Someone stood poised uncertainly there. Then they heard the door close and the girl begin her cautious ascent of the stairs. They could even tell when she discovered the streak of light under Floss's door, for she came to an abrupt halt, as if prepared for flight. What on earth——?

Carolina could stand it no longer. She flung open the door, letting the light stream out on the forlorn figure at the head of the stairs.

"Thea!" she cried hoarsely. "What happened?"

For Thea was not a pretty sight. She had a long scratch down one cheek. Her usually dove-neat hair was wildly disheveled. Her coat streamed open, and her new dress was torn. Tears and dirt smudged her face, and she panted like a spent runner. Worst of all was the look in her eyes. She cringed back against the wall under the pitiless light.

"My glove—I must have lost one of my gloves," she mumbled.

"But look at your dress! And your cheek—it's all bloody!" Carolina tried to control her rising hysteria.

Thea put her hand up to her face as if there were no feeling in it.

"I guess he clawed me."

"Clawed you! Tell us quick what happened!"

It was Carolina who was sobbing harshly, not Thea. Suddenly she was afraid to know the answers to her questions, yet she could not stop from asking them.

"Tell us, Thea—tell us!"

"I was at his house. Sam's house. I wouldn't have gone, only he said I thought I was too good to go to a party down on Poverty Flats——"

"So you went," supplemented Floss with desolate irony, "and when you got there, nobody was at home."

Thea looked at her in dull surprise.

"How did you know, Aunt Floss? He said his folks had just stepped out. It was such a dirty house—dirty dishes everywhere— the bedding was dirty too——"

Carolina moaned.

"I must have left my glove there," the girl went on dazedly. "I can't seem to remember——"

"And so pretty soon he said it was too late to go on to the other party and that you might as well make yourself comfortable——" suggested Floss in the same bleak, knowledgeable voice.

Thea nodded bewilderedly.

"And then what?" persisted Carolina, tugging piteously at the girl's arm.

"Well—I was sitting on the couch——"

A wave of sickness swept over Carolina, but she could not tear her eyes away from the wan young face.

It was Floss who, even as she gently guided the girl into Thea's bedroom, got the story out of her, a little at a time. The silent aloneness of the shack—the frightened girl—the lecherous boy— and the lumpy cot with the dirty blankets in one corner of the front room. Thea had managed to break away, but the boy caught up with her, shouting something about her father.

"What was it, Thea?" Floss's voice was grimly level. "What did he say?"

"I told him to let go of me—that my mother wouldn't approve. He just laughed and said, 'Oh, wouldn't she? You ask her about your father some day!' "

"And then what?" prodded Floss. Carolina was beyond speech.

"He said something about my father—in the days before we came to Cripple Creek. How he bet he was nothing but a traveling cheapjack—and then I hit him."

"You what!" gasped both women.

"I hit him good and hard. I said my father was just fine. That I wouldn't listen to a word against him. And then I ran. At first he was following me. And then he wasn't." She gave a little hiccup like an exhausted child. "My father was just fine, wasn't he?" She glanced at Pete's picture on the wall as if for corroboration.

So they had the whole story at last! Carolina leaned weakly

232

against the wall. The hard, dreadful pounding of her heart shook her.

"Yes, lovey, Pete was wonderful!" she gasped in an agony of relief. "Will I ever forget the night he saved us—you and me—the night my father rushed into the bakery and shouted out in front of those men——"

Floss's voice interrupted with the briskness of a slap.

"Carolina, what this child needs is sleep. You too. Come, chick, wash your face and go to bed."

Thea obeyed like a confused child. The two women could not do enough for her. They bumped into each other in a fever of maternal solicitude as they brought her a damp washcloth to wash her face and warm milk to drink and a hot brick for her feet and an extra quilt for her bed. They tucked her in, clucking over her for all the world like two harried mother hens fluffing their feathers over a single chick.

And when Thea said in a weary little voice, "I'm sorry about that glove; I can't remember where I lost it——" Carolina could not answer for a minute, for the sob of thankfulness that rose in her throat.

"Foo! What's a glove!" she managed to say heartily. "We'll buy you a whole bale of new gloves."

The two women tiptoed out unsteadily and shut the door after them.

II

THEA WAS THE ONLY ONE TO GET ANY SLEEP THAT NIGHT. CAROLINA and Floss huddled in Carolina's bedroom, conferring in anxious whispers.

"When she started to tell what he said, I thought for a second —he knew the truth," Carolina said. "And then to have it be only something about Pete——"

Floss looked at her pityingly. Surely, Carolina did not believe that. Yet none knew better than she Carolina's blindness when she did not want to see the truth.

"And what do you think the young whelp was starting to say, when he told her to ask you about her father?" Floss inquired caustically. "Luckily Thea misunderstood, and he never got a chance to finish."

"You mean he knew? About me—about Thea's not having—about Pete not being——? I don't believe it. A mere boy!"

"Mere boys can hear things. Try to think how he could have found out."

Carolina whitened. "It would have to have been that night in the bakery. But it was so long ago. The boy isn't old enough."

"Scandal has a long tail. I've been trying to think. Wasn't there a miner used to come into the lunch room named Milligan?"

Carolina stared, looking back through the years.

"Yes—yes, there was," she admitted thinly. "A Lafe or Jafe Milligan. He was one of the men in the lunch room that night Pa burst in."

"I suspected it. I remember him—a shiftless dump rat. Probably been tramping around from camp to camp ever since and happened to turn up in Cripple Creek, where he heard about you hitting the vug, and it all came back to him. So he passed it along to his kid."

"I'll take a horsewhip—I'll get the sheriff—I'll have them both run out of town!" stormed Carolina, her voice beginning to rise. In a moment it would become a shriek.

Floss gave her a withering look.

"And bring the whole thing out in the open? That would be fine. That would be just dandy for Thea, wouldn't it? With all her young friends knowing and whispering behind their hands and drawing their skirts aside—if they wear skirts—or chasing her after dark—if they wear pants," she said bluntly.

Carolina shriveled, her bluster gone, her wrath suddenly impotent. The only way she knew how to fight was in the open. But you couldn't grasp and throttle a slimy whisper. It slid out of your hand, leaving you defiled and helpless.

"What will we do, Floss?" she asked strickenly. For once, she faced a situation that Floss knew better how to handle than she did. "What will we do?"

"Pull out of here. Before this Lafe Milligan or his boy Sam realize just how much power they have over us. Once we're gone, they'll forget. They're much too do-less ever to follow us up and make trouble. But so long as we're here, either he or the boy will be sure to talk."

"We'll leave on the first train," declared Carolina, white-lipped.

Floss gave a start. Carolina always moved a little too fast for her.

"McGregor can carry on the mine," said Carolina. "Higby can look after my other affairs——"

She brushed the back of her hand across her eyes with her old distraught gesture and set to work. They would take only their personal belongings. Higby could dispose of the rest—all their fine new furniture that only this morning had seemed so grand and that now was merely hampering clutter. They would leave everything behind—everything. It was as if, by leaving it all, she could leave behind the terror that dogged them.

Feverishly she tossed things into trunks and valises and satchels. She had always expected something like this for herself. She had been secretly braced for it, through the years. Perhaps she deserved it, for she had been greedy and headstrong and selfish. But Thea did not deserve it—not that gentle, tender, biddable little thing.

To think that it was her father who had done it. Her softness toward him vanished like a drop of water on a hot stove; her brief sympathy toward him went up in a sizzling puff. She could forgive him what he had done to herself, but she could never forgive him for this wrong to Thea.

She hurled petticoats and chemises and shoes into the open trunk. She dumped in the entire contents of bureau drawers. Glove boxes. Handkerchief cases. Photographs. A daguerreotype of her mother. Old letters. She dared not stop to sort. She must hurry, hurry, before this evil thing caught up with them.

Was she never to know safety from the ghosts out of the past? Never to feel secure for her child? Her heart turned over. All the fierce bravado with which she faced danger to herself wilted cravenly when she thought of danger to Thea.

And it was Jude Lawler's old, harsh words that had done it . . . . Like as a father pitieth his children! Hatred was bitter as salt on her lips, the raw wine of violence burned in her veins.

CHAPTER 25

"WELL, YOU'VE CERTAINLY GOT THE FIGURE FOR IT," SAID FLOSS, tipping her head back to survey Carolina, who was winding a golden fillet around her head before the pier glass in the bedroom of her Denver house.

Carolina's bronze hair was done in an exaggerated psyche knot, the tight golden bands outlining her head in classic beauty. The loose yet clinging golden-colored chiton was girdled in about her hips. Her arms were bare, and the material was caught together on each naked shoulder with an antique clasp.

At last Carolina was "dressing up" to ride on a float. She was to be a Golden Goddess today and ride in her own decorated automobile in a parade at the Interstate Fair, carrying a horn of plenty overflowing with gilded cardboard coins. She was to compete for a prize to be given for the most handsomely decorated vehicle. It was not the famous Festival of Mountain and Plain—discontinued now these many years—but it was the next best thing.

The papers said that one hundred and fifty horseless carriages had been rounded up to enter the competition today, an impressive number for a city of this size. There were to be poultry and grain exhibits at Overland Park, and Ivy Baldwin would walk a wire strung two hundred feet above the street this evening, and after that there would be a masquerade ball for the populace. But this afternoon's parade through the streets and ending up at Overland Park was really society's show window, and Carolina had chosen it as the time and place to exhibit eighteen-year-old Thea.

"You look lovely, too, chick," said Floss hastily, turning to the girl, who was watching her mother with an indulgent smile.

It was so easy to forget Thea when Carolina was around. And Thea seemed quite content to be forgotten, whereas Carolina was always unconsciously bidding for attention. Take these costumes today, thought Floss. "Two Golden Goddesses," was the way their float was listed. And not an eye would see anybody but Carolina. Yet she had honestly intended it as an occasion to call attention to Thea. But with her usual blundering, she had chosen a costume which vastly became herself and totally eclipsed Thea's quieter beauty. Thea, with her silky light-brown hair and her columbine-blue eyes, might have shone as a Silver Queen. But as a Golden Goddess, never.

Carolina was blissfully unaware of all that. This was one of her glittering days. After all, thought Floss compassionately, Carolina was only thirty-six herself, and she had never had any girlhood. Yet the glitter made Floss uneasy. Carolina had been so unnecessarily agitated and voluble about this parade today. Could it have had anything to do with the fact that Roger Jardine was to be one of the judges? Roger was in great demand, now that he had started going out again, after his wife's death last year. Floss had been dreading the day when he and Carolina should meet.

She tried to tell herself that Carolina hated him. Hadn't he all but ruined her life and her child's life as well? Hadn't she cried into her pillow a hundred nights over him, and then finally wrenched him out of her heart forever? No woman could forgive a man for what he had done.

Or could she?

"Oh, Floss, you do think we might win a prize, don't you?" implored Carolina.

"No, I don't," stated Floss. "It's all cut and dried in advance. No outsider stands a chance. Some young society bud will walk off with it—you'll see."

But Carolina would not see. She went on preening in front of the glass and rehearsing her bow for the moment when the silver loving cup should be handed to her.

In spite of the fact that Floss had assumed only the role of companion to Carolina, giving her lameness as an excuse for not going to any social functions, Floss had learned more in their year and a half here about the gradations of Denver society than Carolina would ever know.

"You do the gadding," Floss had said. "You look the part, and I don't. I'll run the house. After all, it can't be so different from running Stelle's place."

It was not so different. Floss was an excellent manager. And she never let herself forget that the mine had hit only the one real pay streak and might never hit another. She humored Carolina by "making a splurge" until they could get Thea launched, but she kept a careful hand on the purse strings. She hired a cook and a second maid, but she did the upstairs work herself. She hired a chauffeur, but she saw to it that he doubled as yard man and butler. William his name was, and he was sitting out in the decorated Peerless automobile now, wearing a gilt top hat for the festivities today. Just as at Stelle's, Floss marketed in the mornings, while William drove her from shop to shop. And as she pressed melons and looked at the color of chicken legs, she picked up gossip about the other fine houses on the Hill. Carolina sometimes

237

suspected that Floss was having a better time in their new life than she was.

"Do I carry this horn of plenty in my left arm?" Carolina asked. Floss consulted the library book in her lap.

"That's the way they've got it in the picture. 'Themis, wife of Zeus,' it says, 'usually represented in art carrying scales in her right hand and a horn of plenty in her left.' You can do without the scales, I guess. 'Considered stately and beautiful,' the book says. You're all of that. You'll be the handsomest woman—the two handsomest women, I mean—in the whole parade."

Carolina laughed aloud, and her excitement kindled darting lights in her brown-gold eyes and whipped the red flames higher in her cheeks.

As if compelled by an irresistible attraction, Thea leaned across and straightened a fold of her mother's robe and tucked up a bronze lock. And her eyes were so fond and so completely admiring that Carolina's own eyes grew soft.

Ah, Thea was worth every effort she had made. Thank God, Thea would never know anything but love and ease and security. Carolina thought of her own childhood—the shack—Stringtown —the washings. She thought of her father, and her mouth set harshly. It was terrible to hate the dead, but she hated him. For a little while after his death she had thought she understood him; she had even faintly sympathized with him. And then all understanding and love had been wiped out by that dreadful night in Cripple Creek when his old, cruel words had risen up to endanger Thea . . . She remembered their frantic flight to Denver, their hunted feeling for months afterwards, and then their slow relaxing. They had escaped in spite of him.

"I'm going to put your mother's old golf cape and a shawl in the bottom of the auto," Floss murmured in an aside to Thea. "She's in a daze today. But it grows chilly when the sun drops. I don't believe those goddesses lived a mile above sea level. So if she gets too absorbed in being Lillian Russell, you put this cape around her shoulders, won't you?"

Thea flashed her a quick smile.

"I'll take care of her, Aunt Floss. She looks magnificent, doesn't she?" she asked, gazing at Carolina, quite as if she were the mother and Carolina the daughter.

"Are you sure, chick, you wouldn't rather be in that other auto with those young girls that asked you to go with them?" inquired Floss in a solicitous undertone.

"No; oh, no!" Thea was softly emphatic. "That would ruin Mother's fun. She knows the parade is mostly for girls, so if I weren't along, she couldn't go at all."

Floss eyed her quizzically. "So you'd rather give up——?"

Thea felt impelled to explain her mother. "If you're cheated out of everything when you're young, you have to try to make up for it later. That's what she's doing now. And I'm trying to help her."

"Well, you are, chick, you are—if that's any satisfaction to you," Floss said gruffly, turning away. "I'll find that cape."

Carolina looked around. What were those two scheming about?

"It's almost time to go, lovey," she said to her daughter.

Thea crossed to her. Carolina slipped an arm around the girl's yielding slimness. Thea was such a lady! She took to the life here like a cottontail to a lettuce patch. She had made friends at once at that nice private school run by the Senator's sister. If only the money would hold out until they got her fully launched. There was enough for one fine, showy year; but that was all. They would have to work fast. Floss had said they must wait until Thea was eighteen. Well, she was eighteen now. Today the world would have a chance to see how lovely she was.

She sighed a little. She wished she fitted into their new life half as well as Thea did. For she was the one who had made the blunders so far. She guessed she just wasn't cut out for living in one of the "best" blocks on Capitol Hill. Although the name never failed to give her an ironic pleasure as she recalled that other Capitol Hill in Leadville where she had once delivered washings. The people in both places were exactly alike—uppity, sure of themselves. About the only difference was that this Capitol Hill had actually snared the capitol buildings for its own.

She had waited for people to call, nostalgically remembering her neighbors in Aspen with their snatches of gossip while they hung out clothes or rolled a baby's buggy out into the sun. This block was made up entirely of forbidding pink sandstone or red brick piles, each with its high iron fence, its haughty turrets, its scowling porches, and its stone carriage blocks or pompous porte cochéres. And in a year and a half, not a soul in the block had spoken to her.

239

She winced, recalling that she had been friendly as a puppy. But they did not care for friendly puppies here. She had tried giving a party for Thea, only to have all but the second-raters send regrets, or worse—simply not answer at all. She had been puzzled and furious; Floss had been merely furious. Carolina had not cared, for herself; it was only to get Thea established.

Well, today would be a start, she thought, snugging the girl to her lightly as they started toward the stairs. Carolina always liked descending the stairs slowly, sinking her feet into carpeting that was as thick and spongy as the deepest layer of pine needles. Halfway down, she liked looking at the lower hall, handsomely gloomy even in the daytime.

That was one of the first things she had to learn when she came to Denver: that the best people shunned the daylight. They kept their houses like rich dark tombs. The well-dressed window in the early 1900's was as heavily swathed as the well-dressed woman.

She had been lucky upon her arrival to find the Gerhart house on fashionable Grant Avenue—or Grant Street, as they called it now—for sale, along with all the furniture. She had added a few pieces herself since.

She flushed, recalling one of the pieces. She had found a prettily carved and padded chair in one of the stores. It had seemed as fine, though not quite so comfortable perhaps, as she had once thought Floss's patent rocker. She had intended at first to take only one. But the clerk was the looking-down-his-nose kind who drove you to putting on airs.

She said grandly, "I'll take half a dozen of these—" she had bent down to look at the tag, "—these Lewis Quince chairs."

The clerk's face had turned a queer red as he said that the chair was a museum piece imported from France.

"Perhaps our importer might be able to find you another of the same period, Madame. But not half a dozen. A genuine Looie Kanz is hard to find."

She was abashed and furious at herself. Looie Kanz indeed! How was anyone to know? She was suddenly transported back to another store and another clerk, who unwound a length of surah from around an iron dress form. She muttered an excuse and hurried out.

She had no way of knowing that, sycophant that he was, the clerk had promptly started the Mrs. Ramsay legend. When he came to tell the story to a few favored customers, she would order "a dozen of those Lewis Quince chairs made to order, and be quick about it!" . . . and he would indulgently explain that he was afraid Looie Kanz was no longer taking orders . . . One can be very witty, in retrospect.

The favored customers would repeat the legend. "—you know, that rich widow—just rolling in gold—a regular Mrs. Malaprop. Did you hear the one——?" When you are only a short generation away from a peddler's pack or a mine bucket or a branding iron, a vast amount of amusement can be extracted from the gaucheries of a later arrival than yourself.

But today Carolina had erased the memory of all her past discomfitures. Together, she and Thea made their way along the lower hall, baronial even to a suit of armor standing on a dais (a terrible thing to dust, Floss grumbled). And as she passed the gleaming metal shell, Carolina disrespectfully reached out and flicked its bulging chest with her fingernails, creating a hollow metal *ping*. It looked so dead, she thought; she felt so alive today.

She glanced swiftly into the vaulted and mullioned-windowed drawing room at the snowy statuary whose marble draperies or marble tresses artfully concealed all disconcerting physiological details. Her eyes rested on the purplish-black mahogany chairs and the spindly gilt chairs and the damask-covered settees, backing up against the wine-dark walls like furniture at bay. Beautiful, she thought. I've come a long way.

Her arm tightened around the girl at her side with a rush of love. Mother and daughter paused for a moment in their glowing golden robes beside Floss in the front doorway. They looked out at the big Peerless, which they had decorated with golden chrysanthemums and golden satin ribbons and golden streamers of crepe paper.

McGregor was standing on the curb with one foot on the running board, talking to William.

"I tried to get him to ride with us today. But he wouldn't," complained Carolina. "I said, as long as he had come to Denver on business——"

"Not McGregor," chuckled Floss. "He'd a lot rather be back scrubbing the bakery floor than mixing with a crowd like today's, all blowing horns and throwing confetti and waving feather ticklers. He says it's too wild for him."

The two women laughed. As if anything could be too wild for one who had lived through a mining camp boom.

McGregor turned and saw them, and his face lighted up. Ceremoniously, as befitted their present glories, he escorted them down the steps and into the automobile.

"Wish us luck," said Carolina, smiling at him. Impulsively she reached out of the open car and gave his arm a squeeze. "I'm all tingly over today. I guess neither of us had much fun growing up, did we, John?"

"No," he said gravely. Then his mouth quirked. "Well, anyhow you're still young enough to catch up."

"So are you, John, so are you."

The car drove off. John McGregor watched it out of sight.

II

CAROLINA'S THOUGHTS WERE ALL ON THE SCENE AHEAD. SHE WAS glad that Floss had no idea of the ferment she had been in ever since she learned that Roger was to be one of the judges today. Of course she hated him. Hadn't she hated him steadily and violently for eighteen years? But she longed to see him, too, so she could flaunt her success in his face, and her happiness, and her beautiful daughter (her lips tightened fiercely). For the whole year and a half that she had been in Denver, she had dreaded and looked forward to a meeting with him. But something had always happened to block it.

Either he and Sue were in Europe "drinking the waters"—which for once had failed to cure a rich person's ailments—or they were in the East, or they were summering at their new mountain cabin in Bear Creek Canyon. When Carolina took a box at the Broadway to see a popular hit, it was to learn that society went only on Monday nights. When she attended a charity ball, the Jardines were "entertaining privately."

They belonged to an exclusive little circle known as the Sacred Thirty-Six, so called because a self-appointed arbiter had decreed that there were only thirty-six socially acceptable families in all of Denver. Even though Denver had a population of 200,000 and boasted of fifty millionaires and had numerous musicians and artists and scholars and inventors among its fifty thousand lesser families, to the cabal at the top, there were only thirty-six families who "belonged." (Floss called them the "Scared Thirty-Six" because she said they all had to take orders from their lady foreman, who happened to be in Europe at the moment but who, according to Floss, had left things in the hands of her equally capable shift boss, a certain Mrs. Warringer.) . . . And then Sue Jardine had died, and Roger circumspectly stayed home for the proper length of time, so Carolina had not seen him yet. Today would be the first time—in eighteen years.

III

ROGER WALLING JARDINE III TILTED BACK IN HIS FATHER'S DESK CHAIR and stared out the window of the Seventeenth Street office building toward the rearing, haughty peaks to the west. He had, as always, the feeling that the chair was a little too large for him, just as his father's office—and his father's shoes—were a little too large for him too. He had kept the office after his father's death of an obscure stomach ailment during the Panic of '93, but he was not used yet, even after all these years, to being the only Jardine left. It gave him a queer feeling to write Finis to his line—a line that went back to Adam, he supposed ruefully. But he and Sue had written it with their empty, sterile, busy lives. He had been almost ashamed of how badly he wanted a child of his own. He had never confessed it to her. He could imagine Sue's look of pained disdain.

Unconsciously he brought his fingertips together in his father's gesture of brooding thought. At forty-five, he was a lean, distinguished-looking man with a clipped mustache and a pleasant salting at the temples, who seemed smilingly deprecatory of his perfect tailoring and his old-world manners. Though, after all, his expression said, someone had to maintain standards in a raw new country, even if it did become a little burdensome at times.

He wished that "standards" were not such expensive things to maintain. Or else that his father had picked a different time to die. For not even a financial wizard could have salvaged much from the Jardine estate during the worst days of the panic.

To the world, it had seemed a pleasant, easy life to be the husband of a rich wife. Or rather, the husband of a rich man's daughter. But the world did not know. It did not know that Sue, so perfect on the outside, was just like her father on the inside. "Darius P. Braden, the great railroad magnate and empire builder." He thought he'd retch if he had to hear those laudatory phrases again.

243

He mustn't forget to drop around after the parade today and pay a duty call on the old hellion, who lay up there on the top floor of the best hotel, attended by a couple of nurses, scheming up fresh humiliations for his son-in-law. Roger suspected that it gave him an interest in life. It took all of Roger's self-control not to let the old man see how galled he was.

He thought back over all those years of doled-out, niggardly sums. Sometimes he had wondered if Sue did not abet her father's penuriousness, so as to keep her husband always insecure, always forced to kowtow to the old despot, always conscious that she held the whiphand in any final disagreement.

He had not been able to put by a cent from his own earnings. It was almost as if Sue had planned to die and leave him penniless . . . They had to belong to the Overland Park Country Club, she said, and then later to the new Country Club on Cherry Creek, where once they had ridden on the slides of old Chutes Park. They had to belong to the Denver Wheel Club. They had to spend every summer week-end, until they built their own cabin to escape the climbers, at an imposing wooden firetrap of a hotel up Platte Canyon, no matter how he hated the "fish train" up Saturday morning and back Sunday night, and no matter how Sue detested rocking on a veranda all day.

When he asked her if she couldn't cut down somewhere, she had turned on him with ladylike spleen and wanted to know why he didn't start on his own Denver Club or his Gentlemen's Driving and Riding Club? After all, she said, the former was just a place to sit in a leather chair and look out the window and the latter cost a tidy sum, what with buying a trotting horse and a sulky and hiring a boy to exercise the horse, all for a few skimming races before one's friends around the oval track in City Park . . . It showed how unreasonable she was.

He gave a harassed sigh. His law practice was fair. But it was not enough to keep up Sue's big house and his clubs and the new mountain cabin. Yet he dared not give up any of them, as that would be an admission of his ignominious circumstances. His only hope was to wait for the death of old Braden—who might live forever.

He supposed he could marry again. He was in constant demand for dinner parties. But he was much too worldly to be deceived into thinking that this meant that he was considered a good match for a young and personable heiress. Every mother in town knew that he would not have a cent until Braden died, and only then if the old man chose to "remember" him. Not that Braden had any closer heirs; and he had promised Roger often enough. Yet Roger knew that if he displeased the old man in the most minute way, the latter would joyfully cut him off without a cent and leave everything to an orphanage or something equally preposterous.

Yes, his only hope of escape from his father-in-law was to marry again. It would have to be to some rich, plain, elderly widow, he reasoned cynically; for he was definitely not a good catch. He recoiled fastidiously from the idea. He was a man of too fine sensibilities, he told himself, with too keen a love of beauty . . . besides, it would be just his luck to have his plain, elderly, rich widow turn out to be parsimonious too.

As always, when he remembered the chill, grudging women he had known, his mind turned back to Cara. Yet what could be so fruitless as thinking about her? She was gone forever. But he could not put her out of his mind—her generosity, her rages, her rich and riotous beauty. She represented the one mad, uncalculating, glorious period in his life. And he had lost her through his own scoundrelly acts. He tried to justify himself. He tried to remind himself that she had been outré—excessive—gauche—violent. But all he could remember about her now was that she had been divine to love and divinely generous in her loving.

He flinched at the memory of his own conduct. Once more he marshaled all the old arguments, the old excuses, and they looked shabbier than ever before his eyes.

Well, what was done was done, he reflected bleakly. You could not go back. He ought to try to give some thought to the rich, plain, elderly widow. But he couldn't do it; he hadn't the stomach for that sort of thing. It meant that he had better keep his fences up, with his father-in-law, and not do anything to upset the old man right now. He blanched at the thought of Braden's ever getting wind of the Aspen chapter in his life. Stelle Bogart's—Floss—and a beautiful young thing from the Row . . .

Just thinking about it gave him the cold shakes. If it ever came out! But it couldn't come out now; he had covered his tracks too well. In the early days there had been the chance. But not now—not after eighteen years.

Young Burton, who worked on briefs for him in the outer office, stuck his head in the door remindingly.

"It's almost time for the parade, sir. You're to be a judge and sit in the reviewing stand, you remember."

Roger came forward in his chair with a swoop. He looked at his watch. He had barely time to make it. He grabbed up his hat and made a dash for the street, elbowing his way through the throngs toward his automobile. As he got the great shiny ark of a Pierce Arrow into motion he thought that the limousine was just one more expensive piece of show that he did not have the money to keep up, nor the courage to let go of. So he kept it, hoping that something would happen soon.

As he left the car beyond the clubhouse at Overland Park and took his place among the judges in the stand overlooking the oval track, he thought that the whole parade today was a piece of nonsense. But the young belles gloried in it, and the mamas used it as a chance to show them off, and he had promised to give his vote to a Hooten granddaughter. He had had a good deal of Hooten business in his time. It wouldn't hurt to be obliging.

There were the usual bands and anxious mounted policemen. The usual lavishly or skimpily decorated floats. He recognized the black electric driven by Mrs. Pickens to show off her two sandy-haired daughters. She might have saved herself the trouble, he thought cruelly; they looked like nothing so much as goldfish in a square glass tank, with their round little carp mouths and receding chins.

Presently he saw the Hooten girl. With her, in the back seat of the lumbering Pope Hartford, rode another innocuous young thing, also in a big garden hat. The decorations were a hodgepodge of paper poppies and dusty goldenrod and yellowing aspen leaves. Not bad. Not especially good, either. With a firm pencil he gave "Number 14, Miss Cynthia Hooten, 'Indian Summer,'" first place.

And then he heard a low whistle from old Judge Klinkenberg at his side. He saw the other lean forward, licking his lips.

"Gad!" exclaimed the old man, stroking his fluttering goat whiskers, "Some women were just made to ride on floats! Wouldn't mind seeing that one as Lady Godiva either." He prodded Roger with a bony elbow.

Roger drew away, but his eyes were on the approaching open car too. It was a rather nice sight at that—the flowery golden chariot.

The sun touched the gilt top hat of the driver and gleamed on the bronze head of the Juno who was standing up in the tonneau with her back to the driver, holding a great golden cornucopia. At that moment one bare shapely arm flung a handful of gilded coins out into the roadway.

Bravo! he thought, as urchins darted in after the cardboard coins. There was something lavish and theatrical and charming about that gesture.

He glanced down at the score card. "Number 28, Two Golden Goddesses, Mrs. Peter Ramsay and daughter Dorothea," he read, and looked again at the float and noticed the demure young girl in the back seat gazing adoringly up at the older woman.

A ripple of mild interest animated him. So this was the Mrs. Peter Ramsay everyone was talking about. The Golden Widow. Bizarre—vulgar—beautiful—and rich. He bent forward in his chair.

By now the automobile was almost abreast of him. He waited for the woman to turn and smile at the judges as the other contestants had done. But she kept her face toward the rear, still tossing out her golden coins.

And then at last she turned, as if to lift her gaze, and his grip tightened convulsively on the splintery arms of his chair. He must be crazy! It was an illusion—the result of his fevered thoughts back there in his office. Yet it couldn't be anyone else. He'd know her anywhere. That regal pose. Those deep-lashed eyes. Even the curve of her arm.

The knowledge burst on him like the fiery shower from a Roman candle. God help him, but she was beautiful! He ran his hand inside his collar; the damn' thing was choking him. His world had suddenly gone mad; it was whirling end over end like a falling leaf. After eighteen years—Cara!

He wanted to attract her attention and he was afraid to. He hadn't expected ever again to encounter her in this life. What if, when she recognized him, she denounced him publicly as he so richly deserved? He must think—he must decide what to do next.

An instinct that was swifter than reason made him drop his program and stoop to retrieve it. When he raised his head, the automobile had already swept by and was diminishing in the distance.

Cara. Returned to him out of the past that he had thought was dead. And that now had come alive again—breathlessly, beautifully alive. He wiped his forehead.

Gradually he began to piece together what he had heard about her. Chiefly that she was a widow and rich. The thought haunted him. "A rich, young, beautiful widow," not a "plain, elderly" one. And once she had loved him—oh, how she had loved him. And here she was, free; and he was free. What could be better than that they two——? God, it offered a glorious escape!

He made no further marks on his score card that afternoon.

IV

AS WILLIAM TURNED THE AUTOMOBILE ON TO THE OVAL TRACK AT Overland Park for the judging, Carolina saw the bunting-draped judges' stand in front of the clubhouse, and a little drum began to beat in her brain. It beat in her veins; she could feel it beating in her heart. After all these years—Roger!

Unable to bear her immobility any longer, she leaped to her feet and began to fling her cardboard coins out into the crowd. She had to do something.

She was facing the back of the automobile as if it were indeed a golden chariot. She could tell that they were nearing the judges' stand. She would make herself wait, she vowed, until they were exactly alongside it; then she would turn and smile dazzlingly up at the judges—and at Roger.

But the smile never materialized. For when she raised her eyes, there was no one in that row of middle-aged men hanging over the rail who looked even remotely like Roger. Disappointment stiffened her lips. He wasn't there. The row of faces became a receding blur.

She sat down limply in the back seat beside Thea. The latter reached out and covered her mother's hand with her own. The Peerless circled the track and returned just as the winners were being announced. They strained their ears, but the voice from the megaphone made no mention of Number 28. Girls in flowery hats were already climbing the steps of the judges' stand to the accompaniment of staccato bursts of hand clapping. So they hadn't won a prize.

"Let's get out of here," Carolina said curtly to William.

"Don't you mind, Mother. Aunt Floss said the prizes were all cut and dried in advance. You were far and away the most beautiful person in the whole parade," comforted Thea.

Carolina felt suddenly sheepish. Her daughter comforting her! A fine way for a grown woman to act—making such a fuss about dressing up in a yellow nightgown and tying flowers on the family automobile just to win a gimcrack prize. Would she never learn? Just because she had always longed to dress up and ride in a parade . . .

She wondered if all the delayed pleasures of life—when you finally got them—did not come too late. You could not go back. You could never reread an earlier chapter; you could only turn the page and read ahead. She sighed and put a hand over her eyes.

"I believe I've got a little headache from the sun"—and the disappointment and the disillusionment—"I'll lie down when we get home."

Thea looked relieved. If it was only a headache——

CHAPTER 26

THE AIR WAS FULL OF THE HAZE OF FALL AND THE HAZE OF BURNING cottonwood leaves. Pyramids of leaves were ranged along the sides of the streets like smoking Indian teepees. Little boys dug holes in old dry irrigation ditches and roasted potatoes in the smouldering leaves. Every iron fence blazed with frost-crimsoned woodbine, and the sky was the fierce October blue of Colorado.

Once in a while, Carolina was homesick for autumn in the high country; for the thin hot brightness of the noontime and the chest-piercing cold of the nights; for the ruddy masses of fireweed and scrub oak; and for the incandescent gold of aspens creeping slowly down the slopes with the frost, leaving lacy gray networks of branches behind.

But on the whole, Carolina was concerned only with the present. She had an impatient feeling that they ought to be doing something about Thea. The parade when she had exhibited Thea had been two weeks ago. Why weren't they planning a party for her? But Floss stubbornly held her back.

"We don't know the right people. Oh, yes, Thea has made friends at school; but they haven't invited her to any of their parties yet. And who do you know to invite? A couple of salesmen that hope to sell you something. Your lawyer—your insurance agent—

the mechanic that's teaching you to drive your new auto. A fine guest list that would make!"

Floss had learned fast. Already she had a cynical knowledge of the folkways of the strange little tribe called society. She knew which corners of visiting cards were turned down to signify various occult things. She knew which wines to chill and whether wild duck should be served well done or "pink around the bone." She had even picked up the elegant nomenclature of bridge whist, with its stilted, "May I lead?" and "Pray do."

But Carolina only shrugged when Floss tried to school her in such esoteric matters. It was Thea they had come to launch, not herself, she insisted. Yet she had a sense of time flying, as swift as cloud shadows scudding across a valley, and along with it their money. And what had they accomplished so far? Nothing—exactly nothing. Oh, Thea was happy enough doing something called "social service" down at the new Neighborhood House on Galapago Street. Carolina thought it involved working with raffia and dirty-faced children. But where did it get her? Thea was certainly the oddest girl.

In the meantime, the social year was starting for everybody but Thea. Society was tuning up its fiddles. Covers came off furniture, and light thin summer curtains were replaced by morose heavy winter ones. Young men set off to eastern colleges, properly ac-coutered with felt pennants and peg-top trousers and bulldog pipes and high white collars. Young ladies registered at Wolcott or went east to be "finished," each with her allotment of chafing dishes and burnt-leather pillows and combing jackets and Maxfield Parrish prints. Matrons got out their card cases and inspected their white kid gloves and decided which newcomers to snub. One could not loll any longer; one had responsibilities.

Carolina and Floss sat at the breakfast table on a fine fall morning discussing the situation. Thea had not come down yet. It was best to talk of such things when she was not around, for she showed an appalling lack of interest in being launched. In fact, she acted downright contrary about the whole business. They supposed that, in a way, it was a tribute to their success in making her feel secure, in never letting a hint reach her of what really lay behind that last dreadful night in Cripple Creek. They knew that one had to feel terrified and hounded and exposed, really to value safety and social preferment.

Thoughtfully Floss spooned out a section of the sourish new fruit called grapefruit that all the best people were puckering their mouths over. She still wore her hair in a prim sexless knob, and she might have been the head of a strict girls' school, except for an occasional lapse into the blunt idioms of her youth or an occasional twinkle of her eye, that was neither prim nor sexless.

Carolina was going through her mail disgustedly, flipping aside requests for donations, invitations to serve on charity committees, and last opportunities to invest in the chance of a lifetime. Suddenly she stopped, staring at a thick vellum envelope. She slit the flap.

"Well! Mrs. Joshua Cooper Warringer requests the honor of Mrs. Peter Ramsay's presence at dinner . . . Floss—— The shift boss of the Sacred Thirty-Six!" Her tone was first astonished and then jeering.

"Let's see." Floss held out her hand suspiciously. A member of the Sacred Thirty-Six could not possibly be inviting Mrs. Peter Ramsay to dinner yet (oh, perhaps to a big reception, provided Mrs. Ramsay made a large enough donation to a favorite charity), but not to dinner—not without calling first—not without letting Mrs. Ramsay climb the bottom rungs by herself. There was something wrong here. Floss turned the invitation over and over, as if to find a clue. But it looked genuine enough.

"Well, why don't you go?" she asked at length.

"Not on your life. It's a rigged game. I can feel it," declared Carolina with unexpected acumen.

Floss inwardly agreed; but she continued to study the invitation.

"Still, it's addressed to you. If you were to write an acceptance, like the book on manners shows how, you'd find out soon enough if it was a mistake or not. Why don't you risk it?"

"I'm not going to. If it was Thea they were inviting—but what do I want with high society?"

"Nothing, for yourself. But a lot, for Thea. This might be the quickest way to meet people, even if there is something queer about it. Then perhaps we could get up Thea's coming-out party by Christmas."

"Well——" Carolina temporized.

Floss did not elaborate on the fact that they must work even faster than they had once thought. McGregor's trip to Denver two

251

weeks before had been expressly to warn Carolina that the Lucky Friday was petering out and that she would do well to salvage anything she could from her fortune.

To Floss, he had gone even further. He had admitted, under pressure, that he had driven several new drifts out with his own money—east on the third level, west on the fourth. But it was no good. The ore was not there. He begged her to put a curb on Carolina's wild spending.

Floss had to tell him that there was no curbing Carolina just now. Until they got Thea launched, they must go right on throwing money around like drunken miners on Saturday night. If they wore sacking and ate crusts when they were old, they must cut a swathe for Thea now.

McGregor accepted the edict with his kind, worried air and went back to the mine—probably to drive another drift with his own money, Floss thought. It would cost him forty dollars a day. When a Scotchman spent his own money like that . . . Yet she knew how useless it would be to try to plead his case with Carolina.

Carolina was still turning the invitation over.

"What could I wear—if I went?" she asked at last timidly.

Floss knew that the battle was won.

"How about your cloth of gold?" And why not? If, as she suspected, Carolina was being invited because she was the latest gossip sensation, let her startle them. Let her look like a flashing gold nugget. She would be beautiful too.

Carolina brightened. Her cloth of gold! She had been longing for a chance to wear it, with its opulent train, its narrow waist, and its daring décolletage from which her shoulders rose, milk-white and sumptuous.

"And my bronze coq-feather boa?"

Floss pretended to ponder.

"Sure. Unless it turns cold, and you wear your new wrap with the ermine collar."

That completed the rout of Carolina's last scruple.

11

ON THE NIGHT OF THE DINNER PARTY CAROLINA PACED NERVOUSLY back and forth in front of her pier glass. Why had she ever gotten herself into such a fix? She had a good mind to send word she could not go . . . She was indisposed. There had been a death in the

252

family. She had sprained her ankle . . . She was far more alarmed by the Sacred Thirty-Six than she had ever been by swindlers or gamblers or striking miners.

She picked up her gold-mesh bag and her long gloves and gave a palsied dab to her pompadour. She wondered if her legs would support her out to her automobile.

There was a dank chill in the air as she stepped outside. She drew her ermine collar higher. A surly autumn wind carried the threat of snow, along with dust from the plains so recently ripped up by hordes of dry farmers who had come west to plant wheat. On any other night she would have sniffed the icy promise with anticipation. There was only dread in her tonight.

As William drew up under the Warringer porte cochère, she had a last urgent impulse to turn back. But the door was already being opened by the Warringer butler. She would have to go through with it now.

She took as long as she dared to divest herself of her wraps. She was the last to arrive. Drawing a deep breath, she started down the hall. She heard every voice still as the butler announced her. She found herself standing in the doorway of the rose-and-gold drawing room, a tall rose-and-gold woman, staring back at them defiantly.

She could not know that their silence was caused partly by curiosity, partly by homage, and partly by guilt. For they had all been chattering like a flock of blackbirds when the butler announced her. Chattering about her too. They had no sooner arrived, a few minutes earlier, than Margareta Warringer had motioned them to come close. She had a surprise, she told them mysteriously. A special guest. Someone they were all simply dying to meet.

Who? they clamored to know.

The Golden Widow, she announced theatrically.

There had been a moment's stunned silence. None of the rest would have dared. The insolence of Margareta. As if to prove that her position was so impregnable that she could invite anyone, even the impossible Mrs. Ramsay, exactly as she would have invited a trained bear to perform for them. The women envied and hated their hostess. The men straightened their shoulders and drew in their stomachs and ran the tips of their tongues over their lips. If half the tales they had heard about the Golden Widow were true . . .

"I'll see that you all get a chance to meet her first, during the cocktails," Mrs. Warringer promised. "I've arranged to have dinner served a little later than usual."

She was mockingly pleased with herself. By this time she was convinced that the whole thing was her own idea. She had quite forgotten that a couple of weeks before, Roger Jardine had murmured in her ear that all the parties lately had been terribly stodgy, didn't dear Margareta think so? Dear Margareta did. If only someone, Roger complained, had the imagination and courage to jolt a dinner party out of the usual rut by injecting something daring into it—something amusing and even startling—like, say, inviting the fabulous Mrs. Ramsay. But it would take a leader——

Mrs. Warringer prided herself on her imagination and her daring. How else had she got where she was?

Tonight Roger Jardine waited perspiringly, fingering his neat mustache. If anything went wrong now, he was ruined, he thought as Cara's name was announced and Mrs. Warringer sailed forth to greet her guest. He retreated to the shadows of the music room where he could see without being seen. Cara must not catch sight of him until the last minute.

"So nice of you to come, Mrs. Ramsay," he heard Margareta Warringer say in her fruity finishing-school drawl. "I know you'll forgive my not calling first. An old woman like me can scarcely keep up with all you charming newcomers."

Roger saw Cara regard her hostess appraisingly. Didn't she know she was supposed to protest laughingly, "An old woman —you? How delicious, Mrs. Warringer!" But instead Cara gravely took in each detail of the bulky velvet-gowned woman before her, with the bosom like pendant squashes and the beaded band around the wattled throat and the cold blue eyes and the rigid gray pompadour. Suddenly Margareta Warringer looked old and flabby and past her prime.

He grinned involuntarily. For years, Mrs. Warringer's satellites had assured her that she was devastating, in a mature and witty Continental way, of course . . . Nothing so establishes a woman's reputation for wit and charm, he reflected, as a fortune the size of the one left by Joshua Cooper Warringer.

So far, everything was going perfectly, he decided, as he watched the tray of cocktails go around. He frowned slightly at the cocktails. They blunted the sense of taste, he maintained; a sound, conservative wine with the dinner was better. But Margareta was always one for flashy innovations. He saw Carolina gingerly pick up a thin-stemmed glass.

Yes, so far it had been a perfect *coup de théâtre*. Mrs. Warringer, half-deriding, half-sponsoring Cara. Cara herself, not exactly sure why she had been invited, but winning the first round by her sheer beauty. He saw the men crowding up casually to be introduced, trying to conceal their eagerness; he saw the women holding back, trying to conceal their hostility.

He had made and discarded a hundred plans that first sleepless night after he had seen Cara in the parade and knew that he wanted her again. He dared not go directly to call upon her. He remembered her temper; she would probably have him thrown out. There was only one commodity he had to offer her, now that he was poor and she was rich, and that was social advancement. All women craved it, he reasoned from experience. He had seen them sacrifice love, honor, and respect to get it. He would use it as a bribe, as a gag for her sharp tongue. For surely, seated next to him at one of Mrs. Warringer's famous dinner parties, she would not dare denounce him. It would give him a chance to plead his cause.

Yet suppose he were wrong? Suppose she was not awed into silence? What if she turned on him stridently? The thought was too appalling to contemplate. But it was too late to turn back now.

III

AT FIRST CAROLINA'S MIND WAS A JUMBLE OF IMPRESSIVE NAMES and somewhat less impressive faces. As her hostess towed her from group to group, she was conscious of the morbidly expectant silence that greeted her.

But Floss had warned her the last thing: "Remember, Carolina, they can't make a fool of you if you avoid both talk and liquor. You haven't got the head for either, you know."

So she kept her mouth shut and merely turned the glass in her fingers. Presently the conversation around her was reluctantly resumed again. She listened carefully.

As always, she found the men easy enough to understand. Men were much alike, whether they wore jeans or dangling black coat-tails. She had only to smile . . . An ex-Senator shook her hand and forgot to release it. A mining machinery manufacturer tried to induce her to inspect the new Corot in the picture gallery. A cattle king began to enlighten her about the mistakes of Congress.

It was the women who baffled Carolina. They talked a language to which she possessed no Rosetta stone. She listened, a blankly staring outlander. She noted that all of them were either ornamental or rich; none was both poor and plain. Women had to pay their way in one coin or another, she reasoned astutely. You didn't get into this circle for nothing.

As the talk became more general, she was impressed by its chief characteristic—in contrast to her own and Floss's bluntness—an unctuous, cooing, worshipful note when one of the group spoke to, or of, any other member of it . . . You flatter me, and I'll flatter you. After all, we few must stand together. What if we are bored? At least, we're exclusive.

Carolina stared at them curiously and a little resentfully. Floss had coached her well before she came. Oh, she was willing to admit that some of them represented more than mere gambler's luck; there was occasional "family" behind a few of them and undeniable ability or civic vision behind others . . . Two of the women had been genuine southern belles whose impoverished but aristocratic families had sent them west on visits, much as they sent their sons out to prospect. The two beauties had promptly struck it rich, matrimonially speaking, and had settled down for life to work their claims. The ex-Senator had endowed a college, even if he had bought outright the legislative body that elected him. The banker, once the headstrong son of a great English house, had introduced improved Welsh mining processes for treating refractory ores that added greatly to the wealth of the region. McGregor spoke of him with respect.

But most of the rest of the assemblage owed their presence here in this overheated, satiny, gilt room to blind luck, whether of themselves or their fathers or their husbands.

As the talk went on, centering now on one member of their tight little lodge, now on another, the honeyed adulation in their tones made Carolina's gorge rise and her fingers itch like those of a small boy holding a snowball while a silk hat passes by.

But at that moment her hostess, accompanied by a gentleman, approached.

"May I present Mr. Jardine, Mrs. Ramsay? He's been dying to meet you. He'll take you in to dinner. And now I'll leave you two——" Mrs. Warringer rustled away.

"Indeed, I have been hoping to meet Mrs. Ramsay, ever since

she came to Denver," Roger said formally, bowing over her hand.

Carolina was too surprised to note that Roger did not seem in the least surprised. She tried to pull her hand away, but he tucked it firmly in the crook of his arm as he began to steer her toward the dining room in the procession of other guests.

"Roger—I never thought——" she began agitatedly. The very touch of his broadcloth sleeve upset her. But she could not free her hand without making a scene. All the furious and reproachful speeches that she had made up during the past eighteen years deserted her.

"I saw you in the parade a couple of weeks ago, Mrs. Ramsay," he said in the same careful tone for all to hear. "I was one of the judges."

They were entering the great dining room now. The table gleamed, like a blinding white island, under the shaded candles. She saw the rich sheen of gold plate and smelled the sheafs of heavy-headed roses. The upper part of the room was in dense gloom.

Roger seated her in ceremonious silence before he took his place beside her. She watched him pick up his oyster fork; she picked up her oyster fork. Floss had said to copy what her partner did. She had not told her what to do in case the partner was Roger. He had all the advantage of a surprise attack. She could not get her wits together.

He bent toward her. For the first time he spoke for her ears alone.

"I never dreamed this Mrs. Ramsay I'd been hearing about was you, Cara," he said cautiously. "I was—quite bowled over. You seem to have done well for yourself," he finished almost jealously.

"Yes—yes, I did——" she managed to say.

"You didn't wait long to marry either," he muttered accusingly, "judging by the pretty daughter I saw with you the day of the parade."

An electric shock went through her at his mention of Thea.

"Did you expect me to wait?" she inquired, with a flash of her old asperity. Let him know that losing him had been like tearing out a vital organ? That she had mourned him and missed him and ached for him until the day she found his wedding notice in the paper—and then had tried to kill both his child and herself? Let him know even that it *was* his child? Never!

Roger gave a furtive look about the table to see if anyone was listening. Then he bent even closer.

"Knowing that you married well lifts a load off my mind, Cara," he said earnestly. "You can't imagine how I used to wonder and worry about you. For fear you would go back to Floss—back to the old life——"

The old life! A little whitish triangle appeared around her mouth.

"I didn't go back to Floss. She came to me. She's my companion here in Denver in my Grant Street house."

Roger started. But before he could frame an answer, the woman beyond him claimed his attention. And at the same time Carolina sensed that her neighbor on her other side was murmuring into her ear. She turned and saw by his card that it was somebody named Judge Klinkenberg. He was remarking gallantly that the gold plate must be in her special honor tonight.

She looked at him inquiringly.

"Your hair, you know—and your eyes, Mrs. Ramsay—and your costume tonight as well as two weeks ago in the parade. No wonder you are known to your admirers as the Golden Widow," he said daringly.

So that was what the town called her. Floss would like that, when their gold was melting so very fast. The elderly beau's eyes were fastened on her appreciatively, and his little goat whiskers went up and down. He muttered something about rare pleasure—lovely woman—Titian beauty—all the while edging nearer until she could feel a questing bony knee underneath the tablecloth.

The old fool, she thought wearily and moved farther away. She supposed it was partly her own fault. Maybe Floss had been right when she said her clothes were too flashy—and her automobile too red—and her laugh too loud.

I guess to a lot of old toms I just look like so much catnip, she thought ruefully. She answered the old man tolerantly enough.

After a time the table conversation shifted again, and the Judge transferred his attentions reluctantly back to his former partner.

"Please, Cara, don't think I liked doing what I did," pleaded Roger under his breath as if they had not been interrupted. "But I was ill. And my father and mother were so insistent."

She forgot her pride. Suddenly she had to know. She gave a harried glance to right and left.

"But, Roger, there at first, you did feel married to me? Tell me you did!"

"Why, of course." He looked surprised.

258

Her façade threatened to crack. She poked fiercely at her quail.

"Then how could you have done what you did? How could you have gone off and left me, just because you found out our marriage wasn't legal? That we weren't married at all——"

"What's that?" he asked sharply before he remembered where he was.

"Oh, I know all about it," she muttered brokenly. "Floss went to the courthouse to look. There was no record. The old preacher was a fake. But, oh, Roger, we were one flesh. In the eyes of God, we were man and wife. Say we were!"

"Why, yes—certainly——" Roger looked stupefied.

Her eyes, fixed on him in limpid anguish, begged him to go on.

"I felt like a dog about what I did, Cara," he explained huntedly, indecision written all over him. The look of a man who says, Shall I go on and clear my conscience—or keep still and save my skin? He opened his lips to speak, and the woman beyond turned to him with an arch question.

"Oh, Roger, I hear you're another who's having his stable converted into one of these new garages. Is it true?"

Roger answered her with thinly disguised relief.

The elderly satyr on Carolina's other side looked at her hopefully.

"I trust you have a kind heart, Mrs. Ramsay, and will take pity on me while my wife is away and let me call some evening——"

"Any time, Judge, any time. My companion, Miss Kittredge, and I are always pleased to have folks drop in."

She almost laughed at the look on his face. But he quickly collected himself and began to talk about his golf game and the latest chit-chat of the group. Carolina knew nothing about either, and she told him so.

The old dandy was nonplussed by such candor. In his world, women pretended; their whole lives were a fabric of pretense. He did not know how to carry on a conversation with a woman who refused to dissemble.

At last the table turned back the other way.

"That final day, Cara, the doctor said he took you over to the Row. To see Floss," Roger accused, as if to free himself of eighteen years of self-reproaches.

"Yes, to sell her the necklace. So you could have a trip to Manitou to drink the waters. I bought you a new muffler too. The trip was to be a surprise. But when I found you were gone, I was so mad I took your mandolin and threw it on the fire. I'm sorry, Roger."

He flinched. She was apologizing to him!

"I wish I'd known, Cara—about why you went to the Row. But I was ill. And my father and mother were so determined. And Sue was waiting for me on the train. I realized she thought we had had an understanding. After all, we'd been brought up together in the same sort of background—with the same—er, standards——" He broke off lamely, knowing that each word was only making it worse.

"So it didn't make any difference what happened to a girl without your background—without your standards——?"

Her voice began to rise. Blindly she crushed her fork down through some sweet tissue of hot meringue and cold ice cream and ate it without tasting it. He was just like all the rest of them here tonight—setting such store by his precious "standards" and his sacred "position."

"Cara!" he warned softly. "Pull yourself together!" Then, in a louder voice, "I understand the new play at the Tabor is very good, Mrs. Ramsay."

Cara was unable to answer.

Their hostess was trying to attract Roger's attention.

"Do tell us, Roger, what you think should be done with the Hooten bequest," she begged deferentially. After all, Roger had made rather a reputation for handling estates; his manner with elderly widows was unsurpassed.

Carolina had a chance to collect herself. Gradually she became aware of the conversation eddying about her. On and on it went, and now it was all about the late famous Jacob Hooten. At the time of his death, the papers had lingered thirstily over the details of his silken bedsheets and his orchid conservatory and his jeweled dog collars (for canine, not feminine throats). And his young second wife and his tentacular fortune which had started in mining and had finally reached into cement and sugar and railroads and stockyards. He had left the bulk of his money to his plain daughters by his first wife and to this childless, ornamental second wife. But he had made a special bequest to the city of fifty thousand dollars for a civic memorial to himself. The entire table seemed overwhelmed by an act of such prodigal generosity.

My, weren't they buttery-talking about that fifty thousand? thought Carolina. Fifty thousand dollars given back to a region that had yielded him millions. If he had dug a stone's throw away in either direction on that rocky slope near timber line, he would have died a ward of the county. But, by the fantastic luck of mining, he had turned up the right boulder with his pick, and hence had been enabled thirty years later to die a rich man's death of cirrhosis of the liver.

"Tell us, do you think they ought to change the name of one of the parks to Hooten Park?" persisted their hostess to Roger. "Or name the new boulevard after him? Or put up a statue?"

While Roger hedged in the best legal tradition until he found out what she wanted him to say, Margareta Warringer's eyes strayed to the woman beside him. They flashed coldly as she recalled that her trained bear had done no tricks as yet to earn her supper.

"What do you think about it, Mrs. Ramsay?" she inquired suavely, needling Carolina. "But then, I suppose you never had the privilege of knowing dear Mr. Hooten, you're such a newcomer here." *Upstart* was what she meant.

Carolina's nostrils flared.

"Well, I never knew him in Denver," she admitted.

"You knew him somewhere else then?" prodded Mrs. Warringer. The conversation around the table stilled hopefully.

"I had the privilege, if you can call it that, of knowing him when I was a little girl. But we mostly called him Deadbeat Hooten then. Or Dirty-Shirt Hooten."

A "distant" Hooten relative halfway down the table stiffened.

Carolina was dimly aware of the sensation she had created, but she was unaware that her own voice had the clear carrying quality of one who has sung in the open air.

She went on, "He worked for wages in the early days—when his wife could get him to work at all—until he happened to strike it rich. Then the family moved out of the gulch and up to the hill. Capitol Hill, they called it too."

Margareta Warringer reddened. This was not the way a trained bear was supposed to act. The distant relative was explosively angry.

"I don't believe you ever knew him!" the latter snorted. "How could you?"

"My mother used to take food to them when they were poor. And when they were rich, she washed for them. I remember what a time his wife used to have—his first wife, that is—even after they moved up on the hill, to get him to change his underwear in cold weather. He claimed it was weakening. And you know how long the winters are up near the divide!" Carolina's laugh had an edge to it. The attention was breathless. It went to her head like liquor. "But even after the money was rolling in, he hated to let go of it. He'd squeeze a penny till he flattened it clear out. Many a time, my sister and I would go back two—three times—to collect for the washings."

Carolina lowered her blazing eyes to her crunchy dessert. Her cheeks were scarlet. There! That would hold them. Syrup-tongued. Bootlickers.

The quiet finally forced her to look up. Not a fork moved. Why, they looked like Lot's wife, all turned to statues, she thought in mounting panic . . . What have I done? I've ruined everything for Thea. I've blasphemed their deity—ten million dollars. She looked wildly at Roger beside her, but he was patting his lips with his napkin. She looked at her hostess, but the latter's face was a peculiar purplish shade.

Oh, Thea, forgive me! I couldn't resist it. It was like getting off a tight corset. But I've spoiled your chances of coming out now. I shouldn't have done it.

For the first time in her life Carolina regretted her ungoverned temper. Perhaps her father ought to have beaten it out of her after all.

She heard a movement beside her; the silence was broken by a queer cracked sound. She turned in astonishment. For it was a laugh, a high nervous laugh. She saw that Roger was not looking at her at all, but at his hostess.

"What did I tell you, Margareta?" he exclaimed. "You've done it again!"

Mrs. Warringer looked a little doubtful, as if undecided whether to be affronted or complacent.

Roger was gathering momentum now.

"Mrs. Ramsay is quite right," he declared with unnecessary vehemence. "Will I ever forget, in spite of his show-off charities, how I had to file suit to get my fee for defending him in that damage case? Deadbeat Hooten! And all of us excusing it by calling it the carefulness of the rich." He threw back his head and laughed again, and the laugh sounded almost real this time.

By now Margareta Warringer had made up her mind. Roger Jardine had told her that she had done it again.

"And will I ever forget the grease spots—" she snatched up the hilarious theme, "—and dear knows what else—on his brocaded waistcoats. And all of us laying it to the amusing eccentricities of the rich. Dirty-Shirt Hooten indeed!" She collapsed delightedly.

There was a shocked rustle around the table. After all, this was their God they were laughing at, for it was ten million dollars. Yet it was Margareta Warringer and Roger Jardine who were committing the sacrilege. And not one of them, even the distant relative, but had either suffered under Jacob Hooten's bearlike humor, or been disappointed by the terms of his will. For he had strewn sly promises right and left, only to cheat them all in the end by leaving everything to his immediate family except that fifty thousand dollars that was to buy him a specious urban immortality.

It was as if they had all been waiting for someone to destroy the conjure of the Hooten name. The rustle turned into a ripple. The ripple swelled to a shout. Deadbeat Hooten! Dirty-Shirt Hooten! They laughed as none of them had laughed in years. And with their laughter, they wiped away their fawning and their reverence. First the acquaintances; then the friends; and last, the distant relative. Carolina had freed them of a tribal fetish.

At that moment she became one of them. Yesterday her remarks would have made her the butt of their derision. But tomorrow she would be quoted as an outrageous wit. Eccentric, yes; but established . . . "Did you hear her say she'd had almost as much fun as on the night the smallpox scare closed all the joints on State Street?"

There was plenty of precedent for her success. Granted beauty and boldness and wealth (oh, always wealth), a woman could even make capital of her humble beginnings, until not only Denver accepted her, but the whole fashionable world as well. There was the gold-logged merchant's pretty wife who boasted in European circles that she had never worn a pair of shoes nor seen a tablecloth until after she was grown. There was the blithe Irish lass whose mate had struck it rich, and who, after she became the rage of Newport, loved to tell how she had burned up her husband's first hundred thousand in the cookstove by mistake.

Carolina became "the inimitable Mrs. Ramsay." She had not changed an inch; she would never change. Society had to accept her as she was or not at all. Society had accepted her.

Back in the drawing room, people clustered about her delightedly. Even the women were disarmed now. They drew her out about the owners of great fortunes who had got their start in mining camps, as well as about her own meager background. She recounted rib-nudging anecdotes concerning the origins of several supposedly impeccable Denver fortunes. But she was equally candid about the shack in Stringtown and the washings. She told about starting the bakery and then striking it rich at last. She was a welcome leaven to a group grown soggy with pretense.

Only Floss could have sensed the gaps in her account—about her own father and her child's father, about her harried flight from Aspen and then her harried flight from Cripple Creek.

It was Roger who brought up one of the sponsors of the next Subscription Dance, to be held at the Woman's Club. She understood from Mr. Jardine, she said, that Mrs. Ramsay had a very charming young daughter. Could they have the pleasure of putting her name on the lists?

Could they! Carolina looked meltingly at Roger, and her last defense against him went down. He had fixed up everything for Thea after all. He had undone the damage she had wrought tonight. He had saved them both—he was wonderful.

She forgot that this was not the first time in her life that a man had saved her and had seemed wonderful.

CHAPTER 27

The first guest to leave the Warringer dinner party returned to announce disgustedly that it had been snowing hard all evening. The ground was thickly covered.

The few who owned automobiles bemoaned the fact. Why had they ever given up their horses? Those who had carriages offered lifts to the owners of motor cars.

Roger said quietly to Carolina, "Your man will never be able to come for you, and my Pierce is hopelessly stalled. I'll call a hack and drop you off at your house."

Carolina nodded dreamily.

The ride home in the closed carriage was all too short. She had barely started her little speech when they drew up in front of her house.

"Oh, Roger—I wanted to thank you——"

He made no answer. With a startled leap of the senses, Carolina saw him pay off the driver and dismiss him. He was coming in! She watched him stolidly stamp out a path ahead of her up to the house. She followed and unlocked the door.

She ought to object, to suggest that he come back another time. This was no hour for a lover of long ago to be entering her silent house with her. Thea was spending the night with one of her school friends. The servants were housed on the third floor. Floss slept in her own suite in the back wing, far from street noises. She said it was still a luxury to get most of her sleep before midnight.

But Carolina was incapable of protest. Roger followed her across the great drawing room and into the snug library beyond. She was without will and without plans. As he slid the folding doors shut, one part of her mind was gratified because Floss was such a splendid manager that the well-oiled doors gave not a creak; the other part was all vibrant awareness of Roger as he laid his coat on a chair and placed his hat and gloves upon it. No matter how highly charged the moment, Roger Jardine would always stop to fold his coat and lay his hat and gloves upon it.

He lighted the fire laid in the grate and drew the curtains. Setting the scene delicately. She was almost frightened when he finished and came toward her, his glance resolute and hot and bright. He helped her off with her ermine-collared wrap and gathered her cold hands in his. She grew weak under his touch. For he was the old Roger who had mastered her so long ago and had never really let her go. She began to tremble. She leaned against the table behind her to steady herself. He was so close—so close.

"I was never able to get you out of my thoughts, Cara," he confessed gravely, continuing to hold her hands, while he looked deep into her eyes. "For all these years you've haunted me. You've reproached me. You even got in the way of my married life."

Her heart gave a thick hard bound. He had been miserable too!

The years faded away like mist. It was as if Pete had never been. She could not tear her eyes from him. All the old intoxication, the agitation, the self-warnings that were so delicious to disregard, were back.

"Then why did you do it, Roger?"

"Because I was a fool! I didn't find out till too late that I'd thrown away the loveliest thing in my life. If they'd only let me alone. But my mother harped so on your lack of 'background'—for my children's sake, she said. And my father kept insinuating things —how I'd never be able to trust my own wife—and my wife would never dare mention her own mother—and probably she didn't even know who her father was——"

"My mother was dead, and I hated my father," she said simply.

He looked taken aback.

"Then how did you—er, happen——?" he stammered. "You and Floss came straight to the train that morning from Hattie Merkle's."

"I had just run away from my father. Floss gave me shelter."

"Was your father—cruel to you?" he asked. He had all the aversion of his class for the sordid details of the quarrels of the poor.

"He shamed me in front of people. I couldn't forgive him. I never wanted to hear his name again."

"How did he shame you, Cara?" he asked reluctantly.

"He prayed over me."

"He what?" It was probably the last thing in the world he had expected her to say. "He did what?"

"He was a street preacher and he prayed for my sins in front of everybody. So I ran away—to Floss, who was always good to me."

He stared at her dazedly. He shook his head as if trying to clear away the misapprehensions of twenty years.

"So Floss was telling the truth all the time. You were as green as grass." He laughed shortly, and it was not a merry sound. "God, what a fool I was! To let them wean me away—because of my children. And then I never had any children. If they'd left us alone —my parents and Sue—you and I might have made a go of it. Perhaps even have had a family——"

She had a still, shining look about her.

"You had children, Cara. You had a daughter——" he said enviously.

266

"Yes, I had a daughter. Pete and I lost our only son. Did you—want children so terribly, Roger?"

"Yes, terribly. Sue never seemed to mind—but it was a great grief to me——"

"Was it, Roger?" Something trembled on her lips. There was a fluttery beating at the base of her throat. She would tell him. He had smoothed the path for Thea and given the child a future tonight. She would make him the gift of his daughter, now.

"Oh, Roger, you were wonderful tonight, after I'd ruined everything. You rescued Thea and me. I was so ashamed the minute I let go with my tongue."

"I was proud of your spunk. Proud of your beauty too."

She thought wonderingly that it was probably the first time Roger had ever been proud of her.

"Roger, I want to talk to you now—about Thea," she began diffidently. It was not so easy after all to say, "Here is the daughter you have always longed for."

"Yes, yes," he said with loverlike impatience, completely misunderstanding her. "We'll see that she gets a fine coming-out party, don't you worry. Margareta will pour; you're her protégée now. That guarantees you. You need have no more fears about your daughter's success."

He was staring down at her, at her lips parted and soft and giving. He drew her to him eagerly, cradling her chin in his palm, feeling the softness of her, feeling the velvet and cream of her. Then his lips were on hers, hard and competent and hungry.

"Roger!" she whimpered, and it was both a plea and a surrender. She was conscious only of the hard beating of his heart and the hard beating of her own. Her knees were a limp weakness, and her will had dissolved. Her only strength was in her arms as she pulled him to her.

She sensed that he was the one who was holding back now, with the beset restraint of a man honorably in love.

"When can we be married, Cara? Don't put me off. We'll arrange everything about your daughter. Only set the date, beloved."

His kiss said, Hush—Hush . . . Stop thinking about anything but us. I want you for my wife this time—openly, honorably, with pictures in all the papers, and "The Voice That Breathed O'er Eden," and a whole platoon of ushers . . .

"About Thea's coming-out party," she persisted. "It will probably have to be at your house, Roger. I may not even have a house by then. But thank goodness, you can't lose yours to the bank before we get her launched."

She felt a startled rigidity.

"What's that?"

"I don't know how much longer I can hold on, Roger. It's all a big joke about my being the Golden Widow." She laughed mockingly. "I never was, because the mine hit only that one rich pay streak. Floss and I came to Denver just so as to get Thea launched in life. When that's over, we'll be cleaned out. We've no time to waste. That's why I was so grateful to you tonight for getting her started right." A little smile wreathed her lips. Now she could tell him. Now she could say, "And the lovely part is, she's yours, Roger —she's yours."

"You mean to say—" his voice was barbed, "—that you're only hanging on by your fingernails too?"

"Too?"

"That's all I'm doing. I've never had any money. Sue's father is rich and has promised to 'remember' me. But that's the only prospect I have. And there's many a slip twixt a promise and a codicil!" he said savagely.

"Oh, I'm sorry, Roger. Now I wish I were really and truly rich. But what do we care, once we get Thea settled in life? We'll have each other and all the beautiful years that are left. As you said yourself, if only your folks had let us alone, we could have worked things out."

"Yes, I said that," he agreed. But he knew that love alone was not enough for him, even though he would never care for any other woman again. He looked at her, and her beauty smote him. He could not let her go now. God, how he wanted her! Achingly and fiercely. For eighteen years he had wanted her.

"But our love needn't wait, Cara darling," he assured her in a rush of feeling. "I never got over you. You were like a fever in my blood."

He caught her close to him. They were back in the flowery magnificence of Parlor A again, back with their first love and all its sweet unthinking madness. He was carrying her across to the great white bed . . . no, to the tufted leather couch on the other side of the library. His eyes were fixed on hers with intense, unmoving brightness. She struggled to keep her will from falling away into oblivion . . . But they would be married right away, she told herself dreamily.

The tick of the thick snow on the glass bound them in. The privacy of the silent house and the complete cessation of traffic outside bound them in too. He was the mad one now, the hurrying one. His ways were the old skilled ways of love, insistent, inciting. She was blinded by his kisses, by her own hair; bruised by his embraces, deafened by the pounding of her own blood.

She made a last effort to hold him off. Only one impulse in her was stronger than passion at the moment, and that was her love for her child.

"Please, Roger, hadn't we better wait—for Thea's sake? It's such a little while till we can be married. I could be ready next week. Or tomorrow."

"But I couldn't be," he said bleakly. "I can't marry till old Braden dies."

She stared up at him in bewilderment.

"But I thought you said he might live forever."

"I did. And he probably will—to spite me! And so long as he does, I'm only a monkey on a string, dancing to whatever tune he grinds out. If you had only held on to your money, it would have made it possible for us to marry now, instead of having to wait." How that fact rankled. A rich, young, beautiful widow—she had seemed an answer to prayer. And the worst of it was, she had spoiled him for any other woman now.

"You mean, he would mind if you married again?"

"Would he! He was always jealous and touchy about his daughter's position. If I were to marry now—or if he were even to find out about our past, yours and mine—I'd be saying good-by to a million dollars just like that." He snapped his fingers bitterly. "I've waited too long and put up with too much, to be cheated out of it now."

She could still scarcely believe what she heard.

"Oh, Roger, money isn't so much. It's only walking on Aubusson carpets instead of hit-or-miss. It's only 'drinking the waters' instead of wearing a mustard plaster. Love is still the same," she assured him with innocent earnestness.

He looked at her flushed and disheveled loveliness. The blood began to pound in his ears again.

"That's what I'm trying to tell you, darling," he assured her. And he was wooing her again—with his body and his hands and his voice. But she sensed the difference in his lovemaking this time. Gone were all his recent restraints, his gentlemanly compunctions. "There's no need for us to wait, Cara. What if we must put off being married for a little while? We can still have each other—and our love——"

Now she knew exactly what he was offering her. Furtive love, backstairs love, while they waited for an old man to die. She would eagerly be poor with a man she loved; she would work for him, go hungry with him—but she would not lie and skulk for him.

With sorrowful clarity she perceived that he was, indeed, the same old Roger. The years had not changed him at all. She remembered the Roger at Stelle Bogart's who had wanted her any way that he could get her. Without a marriage ceremony if he could; with the ceremony if he must. And when he found out that the ceremony was a fraud, he had even slid out of that.

She pushed him away from her gently and finally. She was crying.

"Oh, Roger, you haven't changed a bit. I thought—I guess I hoped——"

Roger was not easily dissuaded. He was used to getting what he wanted, and he wanted Cara with all the mature passion of his being. After all, it wasn't as if he didn't intend to marry her the minute old Braden died . . .

But he could do nothing with this cold shell of a woman. All the ardor and eagerness had left her. Mechanically she sat up and began to wind up her hair and to smooth her dress and her face—her bright, scarlet, kissed face.

At last he took a grudging departure . . . No, he wouldn't attempt to call a hack in this weather; none could get through. It was only a few blocks' walk to his house.

They maintained a polite crust of good manners while she told him to be sure to change into dry things the minute he reached home and to drink something hot; and while he thanked her and bade her a strained good night. But his voice had a sulky intonation. It was the voice of the young Roger of nineteen years before, when Floss had told him that Cara Smith was not for him, not without marriage anyhow.

Carolina watched him set forth into the unbroken whiteness that slid off into blackness beyond the range of the porch light. And when she shut the door after him, she knew that she was shutting him out of her heart forever. There would be no opening of either the door or her heart to Roger Jardine again.

She waited there for a moment leaning heavily against the door. Then she straightened up and marched along the great gloomy hall.

Nearing the suit of armor on its dais, her gait quickened; and as she passed it, she reached out and gave it her usual impertinent flick with her fingernails.

We'll have either James Buford or Belle Conti cater for Thea's coming-out reception, she thought. And ropes of smilax and barrels of carnations. And the shutters closed and lots of candles. And chicken salad and ice cream in molds. And a harp . . .

Suddenly she began to run up the long flight of stairs.

C H A P T E R 28

CAROLINA LEANED ACROSS THE HIGH SHOWCASE OF THE MOST FASH-ionable jeweler's shop and looked at watches suitable for a young girl. The place was as good as a club, Floss always said. You were sure of meeting only the upper crust in it, for the lower crust bought their lockets and bangles and plain wedding bands at lesser shops on side streets. Here, the same clerks had grown old in their neat black suits and wing collars. Here, the same families, some of them dating clear back to '59 or '60, had bought their gold-lined baby porringers and their massive flat silver and their diamond earrings for two whole generations. Denver was becoming simply hoary with traditions, everyone agreed.

Carolina was constantly interrupted to exchange bows and smiles with some member of the inner circle. For now that she was "in," people vied for her favors. The current saying was that Mrs. Ramsay was just like the gold dome on the state capitol—"A trifle flashy perhaps, but genuine."

Carolina smiled mockingly back at old Mrs. Palfrey, at the same time holding up for the other's inspection a dainty bauble of a watch suspended from an enameled fleur de lis pin.

"When I was my daughter's age," chuckled Carolina, "I was glad enough to tell time by the clocks in the saloon windows. But Thea says all the girls have watches now to pin on their shoulders."

Old Mrs. Palfrey let out a pleased snort. That would do to tell. Almost anything Carolina Ramsay said did to tell. She beamed kindly upon this handsome young woman whose mink stole was a little glossier and whose willow plumes drooped a little lower than any other woman's in town. A few more examples of such candor, and she herself might admit that the Palfrey Wholesale Hardware had started as a peddler's pack on her late husband's back while he made the rounds of the mining camps in the Sixties.

Carolina returned to her study of the watches. She knew she had no business spending money on such foolishness when they were almost down to their last thousand. But a girl was young only once. She longed to shower things on Thea while she still could. Her eyes were suffused with tenderness. For it was not true, as she had implied to Mrs. Palfrey, that Thea had asked for a watch. Thea never asked for anything; she was provokingly satisfied with what she had. She had merely admitted, when Carolina and Floss had questioned her, that yes, some of the girls were wearing these smart little shoulder watches pinned to their shirtwaists.

So at the breakfast table that morning, before Thea was up, the two women had argued earnestly with each other about why they really *ought* to buy a shoulder watch for Thea now. Floss said the child had a birthday coming soon anyhow, and it was better to buy her something that would last . . . and Carolina had said that besides, if they got her a watch, she would have no further excuses for being late every afternoon coming home from that dratted Neighborhood House.

Such a girl! You could not count on her to make the slightest effort to get herself established in life. In fact, they had to push her along in spite of herself. Her coming-out party just before Christmas had been the talk of Capitol Hill. Mrs. Warringer poured. All the right people came and drank the punch and ate the ice-cream roses and doves and listened to the harp and admired Thea in the candlelight.

Carolina hated to admit how much of the success of Thea's début she owed to Roger. In fact she preferred not to think about him at all. For on that snowy night, she had indeed shut him out of her heart forever. So that when old Braden had finally died last month and had handsomely "remembered" him with a life interest in his estate (even though it all reverted to an orphanage at Roger's death), she had been faintly astonished, but not moved, by Roger's instant proposal of marriage . . . Too late, she thought sadly, and told him so. He, who hated scenes, had made rather a scene; and it was Carolina who had looked on, remote and indifferent this time. Roger was outraged and incredulous. When he finally departed, he was still unconvinced.

She had only one concern now, and that was Thea. The girl had drifted through her coming-out party like a spun-glass Christmas angel, all glisten and far-away joy. She had been besieged with invitations . . . Wouldn't she like to join the Wednesday Music Party? the girls wanted to know. They understood that she sang charmingly . . . And how about the dance at the Country Club, the young men clamored—or the play next Monday night at the Broadway?

At Christmas she had received any number of copies of Omar Khayyam and pairs of French kid gloves and sheafs of American Beauties with four-foot stems sticking out the ends of the boxes.

But did she settle down and go steady with any one of her several suitors? She did not. She just floated about with that air of wearing a circlet of stars and scattering rose petals wherever she went. Such a look as fairly clutched at your throat—and nobody to focus it on. It wasn't natural. Frittering away her afternoons down at that Neighborhood House as if she had years and years . . .

Yet Carolina and Floss had not dared to goad her by telling her how short their time was here and how low were their funds. For they knew what would happen. Thea would instantly insist that they stop spending money on her and let her get a job. She could teach—she could take one of those new business courses—she could work for pay at the Neighborhood House. She had already suggested the latter several times—as if being launched in society was a matter of complete indifference to her. What could you do with a girl who was so plaguey unselfish and unworldly? All they knew to do was to continue to parade the young eligibles of the town before her and hope that soon she would feel a stirring of romance toward one of them.

Surely the ball that she would give for Thea this spring in the white-and-gold ballroom on the third floor of her Grant Street mansion would turn the trick. There was something about a ball. Carolina, who all her life had been cheated out of balls, invested them with a magic efficacy. With waltz music and palms and flowers and dashing young men—and a balcony that opened off the ballroom right out into the treetops and the moonlight—what girl would be able to resist romance then?

"Please wrap this one, and I'll take it with me," she said absently to the clerk, holding out the desired watch.

II

SHE WAS SO ABSORBED IN HER OWN THOUGHTS THAT SHE ALMOST missed seeing the pair stepping off the streetcar a block from home. William had to slow down to let them walk across in front of the Peerless. Carolina strained forward in her seat incredulously.

Thea! With a strange young man, pausing now under the elm on the corner to say good-by as if they had paused there for a hundred other such good-bys.

Carolina shrank back so as not to be seen. She need not have worried. The sun was in their eyes. But it was more than the sun that blinded them—it was a hurting kind of glory as they looked at each other.

She turned around to stare back at them. Long and hard, she looked.

"Stop, William," she began. Then she said, "No, never mind. Go on."

She carried with her an indelible picture of the tall young fellow with the athlete's shoulders and the high, fine forehead, who was bending over Thea. And of Thea giving him back his look, like an exchange of vows.

Where could Thea have picked up such a shabby young man? How well Carolina knew the signs. The crest of black hair worn a little too long; for hair-cuts cost money. The overcoat rubbed napless along the edges. The broken shoes; he probably got splinters in his feet when he hurried along board sidewalks . . . The very kind of poverty she had schemed and slaved and fought to save Thea from.

With a futile rage at life, she thought of everything she had done for Thea, and now the girl would chuck it all. She remembered Thea's passion for strays, for the mangy cat and the limping cur. She had never shown any interest in the glossy, well-scrubbed pets her mother and Floss had brought her. But this was different; this was too important a matter for Thea to be allowed to let her sym-

274

pathy rule her in. They must interfere. Carolina must put her foot down.

She was seething as she ran up the stairs, calling out to Floss. But already the old, dogged, obtuse side of her that refused to face what she could not bear to face was saying desperately to her other self: The beautiful ball will knock all this nonsense out of her head about mooning around with a range-lean young maverick. It will show her the advantages of an attractive and eligible young man— the "Scion of a Prominent Denver Family"—somebody with "standards"—and "background."

The ball, she was almost sobbing as she ran to tell Floss. The ball!

C H A P T E R 29

THEA RAMSAY OPENED THE DOOR OF THE MEXICAN CHILI PARLOR, which was run by a Greek and patronized by everyone but Mexicans. She stood there for a moment adjusting her eyes to the hot steamy gloom after the raw spring sunshine outside.

In spite of a braid-trimmed navy-blue suit appropriate for a woman of fifty, and a high net collar whose stiffness left red marks in the tender flesh under her ears each night, and a sailor hat designed for a militant suffragist, she looked uncommonly pretty. In fact, she looked nineteen and very much in love.

She threaded her way past the candy counter filled with violent pink, or morose brown, candies and through the maze of round tables, each with its litter of ice-cream-parlor chairs. Perhaps to more critical eyes than hers the shabby little chili parlor in this shabby part of town, with its faded fly-specked crepe-paper festoons and its Cremo cigar ads on the walls and its uncomfortable chairs whose hard yet yielding metal spirals gouged into her back, left something to be desired as a setting for love. But not to Thea. Because here she and Jim Blake had met often after he had finished coaching his boys at the Neighborhood House.

Oh, they had met in all kinds of places. In the cemetery back of Congress Park (unaware that the dead have always thus offered a trysting place to lovers so that life may go on). On Manhattan Beach at Sloan's Lake where they could snatch a dizzy ride around the lake in the little boat. At Elitch's Gardens, which had rustic summerhouses just designed for people in love and a bear pit where two could lean over the railing with shoulders touching and an Old Mill from whose darkened tunnel they always emerged, with Jim looking very stern and Thea's hat on crooked and her lips much too red.

She looked down impatiently at the beautiful new watch that her mother and Aunt Floss had given her last month. He ought to be here.

And then he was here. The bell on the door gave an explosive tinkle. She felt an electric shiver course through her as an abrupt, black-browed young man shouldered his way in and headed straight back to her without a glance to right or left. With the same lack of ceremony he hoisted a leg over the seat of one of the spiral-backed chairs and let himself down into it, all without taking his eyes from her.

Absently he dropped a florist's twisted cone of white paper on the table between them and leaned toward her, drinking her up with his eyes. And Thea leaned toward him, a sunflower following his sun. As he reached over to cover her hand with his, a swooping, delicious, sickening feeling went through her.

"I don't know whether you're pretty or not," he said huskily. "But I do know you're beautiful."

She tried hard to look judicial.

"Prejudice! Just overweening pride of ownership."

A look, quick and flashing as lightning, passed between them. The hand on hers tightened.

"I wish I did—own you completely. Oh, Thea—in a couple of weeks now!"

They were lost in unabashed rapture for a moment. They scarcely saw the steaming bowls of villainous chili con carne deposited in front of them. Presently Thea spoke wistfully.

"You wouldn't change your mind about the ball tonight, would you, Jim? You've no idea how romantic it would suddenly become for me if you were going to be there. As it is, it's all such a waste. The lovely music and the flowers and the lights dimmed for the waltzes and everything. Just a waste. With me wondering what you're doing and wishing I were with you."

"Darling!" he said, which seemed a quite satisfactory answer. Then he laughed.

"Me at a ball? Shucks! I don't know how to dance, for one thing. And for another, I haven't any dress suit. You're seeing my best—and only—suit at the moment, Madame. My wedding suit, as a matter of fact."

The words brought them to a full stop. They sat in trancelike stillness. Their wedding. Thea felt her whole heart and body hollow out with yearning. Her face was luminous.

But when she finally answered, her tone was resigned.

"I guess maybe it wouldn't do for you to come, after all. We'd have too many explanations to make. If you come over next week the way we've planned, then we can both break it to her together. Poor Mother! I've hated all this deception. But I had to do it for her sake—in order to give her this one blissful year. You see that, don't you, Jim?"

"You're sweet," he said gravely.

"She's waited all her life for this—the pretty clothes and gaiety and dance music. It's making up to her for the awfullest kind of girlhood. I didn't have the heart to tell her when we fell in love. I had to let her have this one gay, frivolous year."

"Well, thank God, the year's up!"

"And it isn't as if she could have more than this one year, either. They don't think I know that the money is almost gone and that they're just hanging on till they can give the ball."

"I'm afraid I'm going to be a pretty bad blow to your mother—with her heart set on society for you," he said with a little grimace.

"It's funny about the society part. She isn't the least bit grasping or ambitious for herself—only for me. I can't imagine why, when she scorns it so. It's an obsession with her—my being secure."

"Which means making a good marriage," he said roughly.

"Oh, I am, Jim. I am!"

His eyes caught fire. He leaned swiftly across the table and bent his head over her quivering lips.

The proprietor in the back room stuck his head in and as quickly withdrew it. This was no time to ask a couple whether they wanted more oyster crackers.

When they finally stood up to go, Jim Blake said devoutly, "Thank the Lord, too, that this is the last time I'll have to take you home on the streetcar and say good-by to you around the corner. I want everybody to know. I want to stop total strangers on the street and tell them I love you. That we're going to be married as soon as my school is out——"

"And live happy ever after," she said with complete certainty.

It was then that he remembered the white-paper cone. He picked it up awkwardly.

"I—I got you some flowers to wear tonight." She knew that they were the first flowers he had ever given a girl. "So you wouldn't forget me."

"Oh, Jim—as if I needed flowers to remember you by!" she said with the artlessly banal and startlingly original fervor of love.

II

CAROLINA STOOD IN THE MIDDLE OF HER BALLROOM AND LOOKED about at the gay debris of the party—at the overturned chairs, the wilting flowers, and the nearly empty punch bowl surrounded by its litter of glass cups containing only pink dregs—and thought that it had been a total failure. She had thrown her hopes and her money away.

Oh, not that her guests had not enjoyed themselves. They had. She had thought they would never go home. And everyone—simply everyone—was there. The tide had turned that night last fall at Mrs. Warringer's dinner party when Roger had turned it. And it wasn't that Thea had not been a success tonight; she had been. In her summer cloud of a frock, with her cheeks flushed and her spun silk hair half falling down from dancing so much, she was almost a belle. A dozen men begged for dances, for her favors, for future engagements. And through it all, Thea kept her head and smiled and acted like a perfect lady.

Carolina wanted to sit down in the middle of the smudged dance programs and the wilting petals and cry. For that was just the trouble. Thea was just too damn' ladylike! Carolina had overheard young Dick Saunders ask her if he might take her to the next Subscription Dance, and Thea's only reply had been that she would let him know, but she really expected to be out of town by then . . . As if there were the faintest likelihood! And when Arnold Palfrey —grandson of the Palfrey Hardware—had begged her to go out on to the balcony with him to look at the moon (hadn't she and Floss agreed beforehand that the balcony was worth half the price of the

278

house?) didn't Thea merely smile demurely and say, "Remember, I'm the hostess, Arnold, and I mustn't neglect my guests."

Carolina brushed away an angry tear. Not an ounce of indiscretion in the whole one hundred and twelve pounds of her! It was maddening. Here she had counted on the ball to make Thea forget the threadbare young man. To cinch a good husband for her. To wind up the year. And she might as well have flung her money into Cherry Creek during a flood.

It was enough to make any mother wild. Thea sailing through the evening as serene and impersonal as a summer breeze. Coming up to say solicitously at intervals, "Mother, are you having a good time?" "Mother, it's the best party of the year." "Mother, you look simply marvelous tonight." As if it made any difference how she looked or what kind of a time she had. And all the while, cheerfully ruining her own chances by refusing even to go out on the balcony to look at the moon with the most eligible young man in Denver.

Carolina longed to shake her, to wake her up, to startle her into some kind of activity. Didn't she realize that her mother had staked her last chip on this affair tonight? . . . But of course Thea did not. Floss and she had been only too careful to see to that. It was their fault that Thea was so sublimely unworried.

Wearily she righted a chair and picked up a punch glass from the edge of a window sill. She began to turn out the lights. There was no use planning another affair. There wasn't enough money for one anyhow. She had shot off her last round and uncovered no ore.

She started dispiritedly down the stairs to her own room on the second floor. Thea's door was open. She looked in and saw the girl standing before her bureau smiling divinely as she unpinned a wilted bunch of violets from her shoulder and put them in a glass of water. Suddenly all of Carolina's frustration over the party and her rage at life centered on that bedraggled nosegay.

Thea looked up and saw her mother standing silent in the doorway.

"Oh, wasn't everything perfect, Mother? I thought it was a complete success."

"Did you?" Carolina asked with acrid gloom.

"Of course. Didn't you?"

"No. I thought it was a fizzle."

Thea stared at her mother, and Carolina stared back. As her

glance returned to the offending bunch of violets, Carolina began to shake all over.

"Will you have the goodness to tell me"—she pointed to the violets—"where you got hold of that ratty little bouquet, and why you scorned the roses Arnold Palfrey sent you? You might as well have tossed them in the garbage pail, the way you treated them. Chucking them off in a vase in one corner. Don't you know, violets aren't even worn at parties? The least you could have done was to carry the roses for a while. But no, you had to wear that moth-eaten bunch the whole evening through. Why, Arnold Palfrey is the best catch in Denver. Not a girl there tonight wouldn't walk a tightrope over Sixteenth Street to get him. But you—you couldn't even carry his roses—or step out on the balcony with him——"

Thea had backed away. Defensively she put herself between her mother and the faded violets.

"What got into you? Why wouldn't you carry Arnold Palfrey's roses?" Carolina's voice was rising.

Thea looked at her mother in amazement. She scarcely knew this strident-voiced woman whose hair was beginning to loosen and her face to flush. Not for years, not since Pete's death, had she seen her mother like this.

"But the roses were so kind of big and overblown, Mother. They didn't suit my dress—or my tastes." There was a thin, high-bred, adamant look about the girl that baffled and maddened her mother. "Can't you see? They were too—well, conspicuous?"

Carolina stopped her lithe pacing.

"Conspicuous!" she repeated the word. It seemed to have a goading effect on her. "I spend money like water—I give the nicest party of the year for you, so you'll know eligible young men and have a chance to marry the very best. And one of them sends you a sheaf of lovely roses, and what do you do? Wear a miserable little wad of violets instead. It was a slap in the face, that's what it was. And then you say the roses were conspicuous. You're as bad as your father." . . . Thea was just like Roger, she raged to herself. She shut you up, and shut you out, just the way Roger used to, without fighting back. They both escaped you, like quicksilver held in the hand. You tried to hold on to them, and suddenly you opened your hand and there was nothing there.

It all came back over her again with a rush—her rancor over old grievances. Just when she thought she had forgotten, something would bring it all back to her with stabbing freshness. She took up her pacing again. Now she was lifting her fist heavenward in the old angry exhorting gesture.

"So they were conspicuous?" she repeated, as if she could not let the wounding word alone. "You're exactly like your father, I tell you. You look like him—you talk like him. Too good for ordinary folks, he was. Too prissy-nice. All manners and education and breeding. Always talking about 'standards' and 'background.' Always saying, 'Not so loud, Cara.' Or, 'Must you use so much perfume?' Or, 'Don't you think that color is a trifle conspicuous?' . . . Conspicuous!" The word was a corroding and humiliating echo out of the past.

She was a clock that must run down before it can stop striking. She lost all control of her words. They poured forth with the rush of a cloudburst, of a flash flood in a mountain canyon. She was screaming now. When at last she paused for breath, she was like a drunken man who can not recall what he has said in his cups.

"I'm sorry, Mother," Thea said dully. "Truly I am. I wanted you to be pleased tonight." Her voice sounded crushed and forlorn. But it sounded strained, too, as if she were holding back a great welling-up inside her.

Suddenly Carolina was ashamed . . . Because she had railed at her daughter for being a lady and for not committing any indiscretions and for keeping out of entanglements. It was only Thea's future she was thinking about, she tried to tell herself. But deep within her was an awareness of the differences between herself and her child. A sense that perhaps Thea was made of finer stuff than she. There was the sadness, too, of knowing that she could no longer make decisions for her child; that Thea would make them for herself now. For the first time she sensed the steel and flint and thin, tensile strength of her daughter's character. They were two separate people from now on.

Tears scalded her. She brushed them away with the back of her hand. She felt suddenly very tired. For like old Jude, when her wrath had spent itself, she was spent too.

"Forgive me, dear," she said brokenly, unaware of the damage she had done. She would have died for Thea, but at the moment she was unable to give her understanding. She was sorry for Thea and sorry for herself. She bowed her head and went out.

Long after she had gone, Thea stood before her bureau looking at the photograph of Pete Ramsay. She stared at the bold black eyes, at the swaggering shoulders, at the devil-take-me smile. She turned the picture over and looked at the inscription on the back. It was written in the illiterate hand of a man who is more at home with a pick than a pen. "To my littel girl Thea," he had scrawled there long ago, "from Pete."

She studied the inscription curiously and fearfully.

"To my littel girl," it said, but not "to my daughter." And "from Pete," it said, not "from your father."

She lifted her eyes to the mirror and studied her own reflection carefully. Then she looked down at the picture again. Comparingly, thoughtfully, she studied the man in the photograph and the girl in the mirror.

At last she set the picture back with great care and backed away from it—as if it had suddenly acquired a new and ominous identity of its own.

C H A P T E R 30

THE NIGHT BREEZE BLEW THE LIBRARY CURTAINS IN AND OUT, IN AND out, with soothing regularity. There was a languor in the air. For even a skittish and cantankerous Rocky Mountain spring, which comes late and leaves grudgingly, must finally capitulate to summer.

The green study lamp made a round puddle of light on the desk, brought out the ivory flesh tones of Carolina's forearm, and cast a reflected upward light on her glinting, high-piled hair. She nibbled the end of her pen and wished she had not quite so good a head for figures. For she was going over the bills from last week's ball, and they were alarming. She sat back and looked at them—caterer, florist, orchestra, gown shop . . . And a lot of good it had all done. She might as well have saved her money.

The money was really worse than wasted, for Thea had been in a state ever since. She refused to answer the telephone; she turned down every invitation; she brooded in her room. In a less ladylike girl, it would have been called a tantrum. What on earth ailed her? Where was all that radiance that had shone around her this past winter? She had suddenly turned into a moping, woebegone creature, who looked as if she had lost her last friend—or her first love.

Now and then Carolina squirmed uneasily, wondering exactly what she had said that night in her fit of temper. But surely, she told herself, Thea would not have the sulks just because her mother had flown off the handle. Thea never held grudges. What then?

A bell sounded in the far regions of the house. Carolina heard Floss's limping footsteps nearing the front door. There was no second maid now. She and Floss divided her duties between them. William was gone too.

Carolina laid down her pen at the sound of a man's voice. Curiosity finally drove her out into the darkened drawing room where she could look into the hall without being seen.

Floss was standing with her back to Carolina, talking to a hatless young man. In a flash of dour recollection, Carolina recognized the threadbare fellow who had got off the streetcar with Thea the day she had bought the watch, and who had stood under the elm tree on the corner with her saying a lingering good-by. She bristled instinctively, and the conversation that reached her ears did nothing to abate her resentment.

Floss was saying guardedly, "I don't know about your seeing Thea tonight, Jim. She's certainly in the dumps. Have you two quarreled? She mopes around with her eyes looking like a couple of smoke-blackened powder holes."

Carolina's breathing roughened. So his name was Jim, and he and Floss knew each other. She liked that! She'd settle his hash in a hurry. She moved forward.

"It's not Thea I came to see," she heard him say. "It's her mother. Is she at home?"

"Yes." Floss hesitated. "But I don't think it's a very good time to talk to her. She's going over her bills." Her voice held a hint of acid amusement.

But Jim Blake did not look amused. He merely looked as if he had not slept for a week.

"I am Mrs. Ramsay," Carolina announced in her best uppercrust voice. "Is there something I can do for you?"

Floss turned toward her anxiously. "This is Jim Blake, Carolina."

"I'd like to see you for a few minutes," the young man said.

"Very well. Come into the library." Carolina wheeled and switched on the lights in the drawing room.

He followed her unseeingly through the smothering grandeur of the great room and into the smaller one beyond. She sat down at her desk and motioned him to be seated too. But he remained standing, staring frowningly at the handsome woman with the imperious brown-gold eyes that held a hint of temper in them. She stared back quite as appraisingly at the big-boned, angular young man, whose black eyes held more than a hint of temper at the moment, and whose hair stood up in a rumpled black crest.

"Well?" she asked shortly. For she was not going to let herself be won over by this Jim Blake just because he was tall and hungry-looking and reminded her of her brother Mat. Or because his hair was the kind that probably made a fool girl itch to run her fingers through it; or because his fine dark eyes were hollow with suffering.

"What have you done to her?" he shot out.

Her eyebrows went up. "Thea, I suppose you mean. I was about to ask you what you had done to her."

"She won't see me. She won't answer the phone. She won't meet me—where we always meet. All I get is a note saying everything is off. She can't explain. But she won't be able to see me any more. I thought maybe something had happened the night of the dance."

Her lips twisted. "No," she said with slow bitterness. "I can assure you that nothing happened the night of the dance—nothing whatever."

He ran his hand through his already wild-looking hair.

"Then what's wrong? Tonight's the night we were to come and tell you."

"Have you known my daughter long?"

"A whole year. We met down at the Neighborhood House where I coach in my spare time. I loved her from the start." He turned and looked at her fiercely. "She loved me too—or anyway she said she did. I wanted to tell you right off. But she said no. That you had been cheated out of your fun when you were young, so you must have this one gay party-year first." The fierceness left him. "She's—she's a very sweet girl," he said with anguished restraint.

The restraint touched her against her will. She thought of those two, planning what was best for her happiness, and she had to choke back hysterical laughter. A whole winter wasted because Thea wanted her mother to make up for her lost youth, while her mother wanted Thea to ensure herself a comfortable old age. And in the meantime Thea had given her heart to a shabby young man with romantic dark eyes and shoes that needed patching.

"And so," she prompted thinly, "you were both coming to 'tell' me tonight——?"

"That we want to be married right away. And then I get this note from her saying the whole deal is off because of something she's found out that will hurt my career. I must just forget her and go on as if nothing had happened." His tone was savage with his own hurt. "Forget her! As if you could cut off your right arm and forget it. As if you could plan your whole life and work around a girl, and then, all of a sudden——" He stopped because he could not go on.

"And what, may I ask, is this work you're talking about?"

He looked at her in surprise. "Why, preaching, of course. I'm finishing up at the seminary out on the edge of town."

If he had said he was apprenticed to a bank robber, Carolina could not have looked more shocked. Her horror showed in her face.

"Not preaching! How *could* you want to be a preacher? You don't know what you're getting into: the hardships—the loneliness. Always spied upon—set apart—poor——"

"I know. I'm a preacher's kid myself. My dad had a little cowtown parish out east of here."

"But Thea's not made for the life. She's soft. She's never so much as darned a stocking or put a tub of clothes to soak. She couldn't stand up under it. Maybe—she found out in time."

His eyes flashed. "I don't believe it. And she is not soft. She might look it—but she isn't. She's steel underneath—and spunk —and spirit. I talked my head off at first, trying to discourage her. I told her all the bad things—and God knows, I know them. I felt I had to—even when I was crazy about her. But she said she didn't mind. She wanted to go with me—anywhere. We talked and talked."

She listened incredulously. Thea was like that? But of course, she was nothing of the sort. How could he know? Why, Thea laid sachets amongst her underwear and had to have the ribbon in her corset covers match the ribbon in the beading of her petticoats. She couldn't bear the sight of blood—and she was the worst old sleepyhead mornings. Thea a preacher's wife? Never. There must be some mistake somewhere. But as she watched the young man's fiery certainty, her own certainty wavered.

"But have you got to be a preacher?" she almost wailed.

"Yes, I've got to," he said simply, and she knew that he had. He sat down in the chair by her desk and leaned toward her earnestly. "It's like this . . ." he began.

He wasn't much good at talking. He would never be a glib and unctuous man, impressed with his own priestly function. But he tried to tell her now, albeit stumblingly and awkwardly, why he felt the way he did. He was certain, he said, that mankind had been given a pattern, if it would only use it, for living decently in this sick, imperfect world and for getting ready for another one. But it was not an easy pattern to follow, he told her; it was a challenge to every drop of fighting blood in you. The very best you had to offer was still not good enough, he said with desperate sincerity.

She listened numbly. He never mentioned a jealous God that rained snares and fire and brimstone and tempests and watched unwary feet take hold on hell. His God seemed concerned with the living—like the father that pitied his children.

Suddenly she had a compelling need to talk to him about her own father. She began to tell him, as if Jim Blake were the elder and she a troubled girl. He would never know how strange it seemed to be talking freely about Jude Lawler, after all these years of held-in hate. For in her whole lifetime she had known only that one brief period of sympathy toward her father, following upon his death, before his own harsh words of long before had risen to imperil Thea and to destroy her own fragile feeling for him.

"He made God seem awful when I was young," she confessed. "He shamed me in public, praying for me on a street corner. Calling me names out of the Bible. So I ran away . . . Then, a few years later, he found me and denounced me again—only then it was worse on account of my baby——"

"I'm sorry," he said. And she could feel his sorrow. "Some of us ministers go at things all wrong. We feel scourged and driven, thinking how short life is and how long eternity stretches. We think we've got to wake everybody up before it's too late—like yelling at a sleeping man when his house is on fire. I guess it's this awful sense of urgency that makes us harsh and impatient at times——"

She nodded unwillingly. "That was Pa. At the end, he said he was sorry. He asked my forgiveness. He said I was so much like him he had to try to save me, he had to try to beat it out of me."

"That's what I meant. He was mistaken in the way he went about it. But his message wasn't at fault—only himself, the instrument that delivered the message. That's true of all of us; what we have to say is bigger than we are."

Her eyes looked afar off. "At the end he wanted reassurance when he was about to die. Oh, not about his faith—that never wavered—but that God could forgive him. I remembered some verses. You know how they get sort of ingrained into you? I didn't even believe them myself, but I spoke them out loud anyhow. And they comforted him. About his God. I guess the words were bigger than I was," she admitted.

"Yes, and bigger than he was, bigger than any of us are," he said gently.

She looked at him with strange respect. This young man, who had never set eyes on Jude Lawler, had made him understandable to her. Through the mists of her hatred and her resentment and her fear, she saw her father clearly at last. A driven, haunted, violent, aspiring, God-hungry man. Erring often. Cruel even. But never losing sight of the message he felt he must impart.

She supposed she had been slowly moving toward this understanding for a long time. But it had taken a stranger, a fledgling parson who loved her daughter, to bring it about.

She felt a swift contrition for her self-absorption. He had let her pour out her troubles to him; he had even put his mind and heart on them when he was miserable himself.

"And so you want to marry my daughter Thea," she mused with a bitter twist of the lips.

His answer was an eager tensing of body and spirit.

"I did so want her to make a good marriage, Jim. So she would have an easier life than I had. I didn't want her hands all wrinkled from soapsuds and her hair smelling of steam . . . Wait till you have children of your own! You'll want to spare them things. Even if in doing so, you cheat them out of love. But if you two really care for each other——" She got to her feet slowly and started for the hall.

But in the far doorway of the drawing room she paused. For there, coming down the stairs was Floss leading a white and tear-stained girl by the arm. Carolina bit her lip. Didn't Floss beat all?

287

She must have been listening to every word and had gone up after Thea. Floss, who pretended to have no use for love.

When Thea came into sight, Jim started toward her.

"Thea!" he blurted almost angrily. "Why didn't you answer the phone? I've wanted to tell you—I've been the Reverend Jim Blake since this morning. And I've got the charge we wanted—the mission field in the Southwest—I leave in a week."

Thea's only answer was a brief involuntary lifting of her lashes. How she loves him! Why, it's the life she wants more than anything else on this earth, thought Carolina chokingly, picturing that life . . . the 'dobe huts and Indian brats and open sores . . . the flies and sun-baked dust and loneliness. And love.

Her throat felt cramped from holding back tears. And helpless laughter too. To think it had to be a preacher! By what a winding path had Thea returned to all that her mother had run away from. Returned to her Grandmother Hester. So Hester must have looked at her headstrong young parson when she followed him out of Ohio. Maybe Hester's mother, too, had wrung her hands and tried to stop her . . . Only Jim was different. He was not another Jude; he only shared the same relentless urge that will always drive a small and set-apart portion of mankind toward its salvation—or its doom.

"You shouldn't have come, Jim. I told you not to!" Thea rebuked him with sudden spirit.

"But can't you see, he had to?" Carolina explained, not even stopping to smile at the idea of her aiding Jim Blake. "He loves you, baby. Real love is much too scarce in this world to turn your back on it."

"But I'm not," came the anguished denial. "It's only that I—can't let him ruin his life for me."

"What?" Carolina and Jim spoke at once.

Thea was silent.

"What do you mean?" cried Carolina.

"You're crazy, Thea!" said Jim almost roughly, trying to catch hold of her hand. But the girl only shrank away from him and closer to Floss.

"Please just let the matter drop, Jim. Don't—don't ask me." She would not look at either her mother or Jim.

The paperweight fell from Carolina's fingers to the desk with a small thump of finality.

"Look at me, Thea. Is it me you mean?"

Thea kept her eyes down. Her face was drawn with misery.

Carolina turned in tortured comprehension to Jim Blake.

"I guess—she must have stumbled on something I've tried to keep from her. Thea, lovey, how did you find out?"

"From you." Thea's voice could barely be heard. "That night, after the ball. You said something about my being like my father —so educated and prissy and all. But what I remembered of Pete —didn't fit. So I started in to find out for myself," she admitted shamefacedly but doggedly. "I went through your keepsakes, until at last I found something—in the right hand drawer of your desk there——"

Carolina covered her face with her hands. The wedding certificate of her marriage to Pete. The precious paper that she had acquired at so great a cost, that made her a legal wife, that protected Thea. The irony of it tore at her. She pulled open the drawer and rummaged till she found the tight little scroll tied with faded ribbon.

"And I thought it fixed everything up for you, child—so you'd be safe."

"It was the date on it," whispered Thea. "I was over two years old. Your name is—your maiden name."

Carolina lifted her head and stared off into space, and her face looked tired and naked. So it was all out in the open at last. Her shame. Her subterfuges. Her desperate efforts to protect her child.

"But, your mother——" stammered Jim.

The girl moved swiftly to her mother's side and put her arm around her and faced Jim defiantly.

"Don't you dare say a word against her, Jim Blake! You don't know the truth at all. I don't know half of it myself. All I know is, she was terribly hurt and brave. She ran a bakery and took in washings, to take care of me. She'd have fought tigers for me if need be!" She stood there shielding her mother from the censure of the world. "She—she bought me a little gold bracelet with a bangle on it once, when—she didn't have enough to eat. I've still got it——" Her voice broke.

"That's what I'm trying to say, Thea," Jim explained patiently and bewilderedly. "That your mother was brave and good, no matter what happened to her. And it's over and forgotten long ago.

289

Nothing makes any difference now, except that you and I will have each other."

Thea's head drooped. Her arms fell to her sides. She looked suddenly bereft and alone.

"But it does make a difference. I can't marry you. If it ever came out——" There was the same steely quality that Carolina had encountered before. "—that your wife was a——"

Carolina stared strickenly at these two and wondered how to keep them from ruining their lives.

"But I thought I was married to Thea's father," she assured them piteously. "Until I found out I wasn't. That's why I married Pete Ramsay; to give you a name, Thea. He adopted you legally. You aren't—what you say you are, in the eyes of the law——"

Thea shrugged, dismissing "the eyes of the law," with forlorn contempt.

"Then the stumbling-block is that your real parents aren't married, is that it?" persisted Carolina. "That's what keeps you from marrying your preacher?"

Thea made no answer. It was all so useless, her look said. What was the good of torturing themselves?

Jim tried to reach her again; but she drew away from him as if she dared not let him touch her. Floss kept patting her soothingly.

"Look here, folks," she said sensibly. "None of us is in any shape to plan now. I'm going to put this girl to bed with a sleeping powder. Jim, you come back tomorrow night after we've had a chance to talk things over here. You're all so strung up trying to do the noble thing for each other, you're liable to make a mess of the whole business. Run along now, Jim. And Thea, you come up to bed with me." She led Thea, unresisting, toward the stairs.

Jim started after them; then he stopped himself with an effort. Carolina watched him—his bitter young face, his painfully working throat. When the girl was out of sight, he turned back to her wretchedly.

"She told me she'd be happy! Even when I tried to tell her what a tough time preachers' wives had, she insisted she'd love it. She said she'd gladly teach anybody from Hottentots to Eskimos, if she could be a help to me—if we could be together. But maybe it was too much to ask."

"No, not after the way she looked at you tonight, son. She's hell-bent on going to heaven your way. It's only this awful conscience of hers we've got to reckon with." How terribly Thea must love him, Carolina thought, to be willing to give him up for his own sake. "I've an idea. You let me see what I can work out."

After they had said goodnight, she stood in the open door and watched his hasty gait with the little nervous hitch in it that expressed his anxiety better than words. When he had disappeared beyond the arc light, she turned back to her problems. She put her hands up to her temples. There was something crazy and fantastic about having to scheme to marry off her soft, pampered, lovely child to an impecunious, rock-jawed young parson. If anyone had told her an hour ago . . .

CHAPTER 31

CAROLINA STOOD FOR A MOMENT UNCERTAINLY AT THE FOOT OF THE stairs. She ached to go up to Thea, but she knew that Floss was right. What Thea needed most now was a good night's sleep. As she hesitated, with her hand on the great carved newel post, her face was unguarded and soft. Oh, to make everything right for her child. She had blundered too often before. There must be no more mistakes.

She turned with weary resolution toward the library again. Her shoulders were square now; her head was high. For she had made up her mind what she must do. And she must do it serenely and cheerfully, so that no one would even know that it was a sacrifice. Not Floss. Not Thea—oh, especially not Thea . . . She did not let herself face the thought that even this might not be enough. For it was all she knew to do.

She began to go through the papers in her desk, sorting, tying into bundles, discarding, like one preparing to go on a long journey. There would be just enough money left to pay the bills. She would leave instructions so that Floss could attend to everything after she was gone. The house and the furniture could be put up for sale at once. After the mortgage was satisfied there might even be something left over.

The doorbell gave a soft cautious whir. She started. It was almost midnight. Who—at this hour?

She got to her feet stiffly and moved out into the darkened hall, where she stood staring at the grotesque shadow on the etched-glass door of a person outside. She opened the door a crack.

John McGregor! In all the world she could think of no face she would rather see just then than his sober, comforting, worried one.

He looked a little dazed at the welcome he received. She caught hold of his arm and drew him inside, laughing shakily.

"Oh, John, how wonderful! You'll never know how good you look to me. I'll bet you're hungry. Let me fix you something—a sandwich, a cup of coffee. I'm starved myself. We'll see what there is in the icebox. A fine to-do, isn't it, when a woman doesn't even know what's in her own icebox?" she jeered at herself. "But this is the cook's last week. A perfect old tyrant she is too."

He had never seen her like this, so feverish, so excited. He tried to calm her with his sober talk.

"My train was late. I thought I'd come by the house and see if anybody was up. There was a light in the library——"

"Yes, I was going over bills. Such lots and lots of them. My, those merchants don't know what a chance they took!"

"That's what I came to see you about."

But she would not listen. She dragged him toward the kitchen.

"Here, we'll sit out here. It's more fun," she cried, drawing two chairs up to the kitchen table in the large spotless gloomy kitchen, with its brown wainscoting and its mustard walls and its dun-colored floors.

He leaned back against a cupboard and watched her rush about, while he listened to her scurrying tongue. She gave a blithe snap to the red-checked cloth as she unfolded it and spread it on the table. She set down the cups and plates with a nervous rattle. She measured coffee and sliced bread.

"It's almost like the old days, isn't it, John?" she asked. "Being together in a kitchen again, with a stove and cupboards and lots of shiny pans." Only she knew that this time it was different. McGregor's eyes followed her openly now. Or maybe she was seeing the look in his eyes for the first time. She mustn't notice; she mustn't even think about it.

The sharp, good fragrance of coffee filled the air as they sat down at the small table opposite each other. Maybe she ought not to have brought him out here after all. There was something about a table set for two—at midnight—in a quiet kitchen. Maybe it would have been better if they had sat formally in the library. For he was watching her with a certain male intensity. A treacherous tide of feeling rose within her.

At last he made her stop to hear what he had come all the way to Denver to tell her.

"I shut down the Lucky Friday for good today. I'm sorry, Carolina." He was unaware that it was the first time he had ever called her anything but Mrs. Ramsay. "I did everything I could to prevent it. I—er—drove several drifts in different directions—till my own money gave out too. I figured it was a good gamble," he said sheepishly.

"Oh, John, you shouldn't have!" She was shocked. She had thought that, no matter what happened, careful McGregor would have plenty salted away out of his salary. "You ought to have held on to what you had. What will you do now?"

"Oh, there's a promising new mining field opening up down in the San Juan country. I hear it looks pretty good. I can always find something."

"But I don't deserve all you've done for me." Impulsively she reached out and touched his arm. She felt his muscle tighten and drew her hand away hastily.

"Pshaw." He made a deprecating gesture and began to speak hurriedly of the last days of the Lucky Friday.

"It was like shooting a good horse," he admitted. "Letting the fires go out and the pumps stop, boarding up the windows of the hoist house, nailing a Keep Out sign on the door . . . I'll see a fellow here tomorrow that's interested in buying the machinery. I hope to salvage a little for you that way."

She tried again to thank him.

"I don't have the words, John—but all through the years——"

John McGregor was not an easy man to thank.

"There was nothing I'd rather have done with myself—through the years," he said quietly. "Only trouble was, you never seemed to want help from anybody. You always seemed to manage, by yourself."

She was looking at him fixedly through the bright iridescence of her tears, her mouth trembling into a smile. She had got up to get the coffee pot; now she set it down quite suddenly and turned to him . . . Not need anyone? Self-sufficient? Her heart overflowed toward this man who had been a part of her life for so many years. Why, she had always needed him, she thought, and only now had found it out.

As he stared back at her, at the shimmering brightness of her smile, at the softness of her mouth, at the *need* in her eyes, he stood up quickly, pushing his chair back with a harsh scrape. He had seen something in her face at last. He came toward her hastily.

"Carolina! I guess you know how I've always felt——" He was a man afraid to believe. Slow to hope. But now he dared to hope.

But even as he watched her, he saw her face grow pinched and white. She moved back from him suddenly, as if she dared not look at him or even be close to him. She must keep the length of the kitchen between them, the whole world between them.

With her look of hunted retreat, he stopped instantly. He would never press an advantage.

Her voice held a strained lightness when at last she spoke.

"I don't know how to tell you, John," she said, with her too bright smile. "But I'm going to be married. I've decided to accept a proposal of marriage from—from a Mr. Roger Jardine. We're old friends. It's very suitable——" There was no use telling him her haunting doubts—that even marrying Roger might not be enough to make things right for Thea—but that she had to do it because it was all she knew to do. "I'm going up first thing in the morning to tell him. He's staying at his mountain cabin right now. But I wanted you to be the first to know——" she mouthed the worn old phrase despairingly. "Wish me luck, John. Wish me luck."

She tried to laugh. But the laugh was not a success. It ended in a little rasping sound.

McGregor simply stood there with his hands holding on tight to the back of a chair. She could not lift her eyes to his face. All she saw were those corded hands that had worked so hard for her, holding on tight to the back of a chair. Suddenly she remembered Roger's well-tended hands—gracefully unfolding a damask napkin—twirling a wine glass by a crystal stem. And she had a great longing to reach out now and touch these hard, lean, tense hands on the chair back, with their work-blunted nails and their calluses —she wanted to lay her cheek down softly on them.

CHAPTER 32

As always, Floss. was making things easy for her. she stowed a package of sandwiches in the front seat of the Peerless and checked over the necessities of a motor trip—the can of gasoline and the pail for refilling the radiator and the rope and shovel—quite as if it were an everyday occurrence for a woman to drive alone up a steep and winding mountain road in the year 1909.

"I'll tell Thea you took a notion to go up and see Mr. Jardine on a legal matter and you didn't want to wait for the train and then have to hire a rig at Morrison. She probably won't wake till noon anyhow, poor child. Then this evening when Jim comes, you might telephone to them—what you've decided."

That was like Floss. No exclamations. No sympathy. But a look of profound pity and understanding. She had not argued when Carolina told her what she planned to do.

She had only said, "Thea's happiness is the important thing, Carolina. You and I don't count any more. And this Jim—I've been watching him for quite a while. He's the one, all right . . . Funny thing about preachers. They're like prospectors—always got their eye on future riches, so they don't ever make what you could call first-class husbands. Their wives always come second. But think you can tell women that? Never. They crowd after both kinds—and stick to 'em afterwards all the way to heaven or hell. It's like that with Thea. She's got to have Jim or nobody. She'll be happy too. Not your kind of happiness, nor mine. But happy."

That had helped Carolina. It made it easier to talk and smile and keep her shoulders back. It didn't seem so hard—what she planned to do—while they were fussing around over the car in the bright summer sunshine on the circular driveway in front of the stable.

But she had a moment of pain when she leaned out of the automobile to kiss Floss good-by. Why, this was farewell. Once she was married to Roger, she would not be seeing Floss Kittredge again. Oh, she would see that Floss did not want. But she remembered only too well Roger's violent prejudices on the subject of Floss and his look of shocked disapproval when she had told him that Floss was making her home with her. She knew that Floss realized, too, that they were bidding each other good-by forever. What a bumpy, twisting road they two had traveled together—and now they had reached the end of it.

"G-good luck!" was all that Floss could manage. She ducked her head and began to fuss with one of the brass lamps frowningly.

"I'll be all right," Carolina assured her, as if Floss were referring to the trip. "I learned how, back in Leadville, to chain a log to the rear axle on a down grade; and if she balks going uphill, I'll just back down and make another run for it."

"And McGregor—what shall I say to McGregor?"

"I told John last night," Carolina said heavily. Then her head went up and she managed to smile. "Tell him to turn everything into money that he can. If you have trouble selling this big ark of a house, it ought to be fine for keeping boarders."

She laughed shakily, and Floss joined her. Boarders on Grant Street! It was a palpable absurdity. Everyone knew that Grant Street would always be Grant Street, as sacred to wealth and power as—as the House of Hohenzollern, say.

Floss stood on the stone carriage block and watched the automobile until it turned the corner. Carolina did not look back.

It was a hard trip. The narrow winding road up Bear Creek Canyon, built almost on a level with the innocently turbulent creek, had been laid out for swaying Concord coaches and plodding ore wagons and strings of burros, not for erratic horseless vehicles with frail tires and mysterious insides. Carolina had to stop several times to refill the radiator from the creek. Once she inquired the way to the Jardine cabin.

She had no fear of physical dangers. Her nagging worry was about Roger himself. What if—in spite of his having asked her as soon as old Braden died last month—he had changed his mind since about wanting to marry her? But he'd have to! She'd make him see that there was no other way to fix things up for Thea. A month ago he had been eager and impatient and even petulant with desire for her. But you never could tell about a man. Some only wanted what was hard to get. Others you could count on to the end of time . . . Her mouth trembled. She mustn't let herself think.

She turned in at the stone gateposts surmounted by elk horns bearing the Jardine name and stopped before a large, sprawling, verandaed house that was a far remove from the "cabins" Carolina had spent her childhood in.

When the automobile came to a bucking halt, she sat there in the sudden hush. It was so quiet. Only a bluejay squawked overhead and a horse nickered somewhere. The rest was the familiar stillness of swishing branches, the familiar fragrance of pine needles steeping in the sun. Where was everybody? She wondered if she ought to have warned Roger she was coming, as Floss had wanted her to do. Perhaps he was away for the day. Perhaps he had guests.

She saw a curtain flick at a kitchen window. Roger had said he kept a married couple on the place as caretakers. Then she saw Roger and a workman coming through the pines beyond the stable.

Carolina knew a sudden panic. She tried to tuck her wind-tossed hair up under her floppy hat; she rubbed a lace-trimmed chamois skin over her face, suddenly remembering Floss's axiom that a smart woman always looks her best when she asks a favor of a man.

Roger halted in stupefaction when he saw her . . . Cara, alone in her automobile! It was unthinkable; it was delightful. His eyes grew bright, but he covered his eagerness. With conventional politeness he came toward her.

"Mrs. Ramsay! What a brave woman—to drive alone all the way from Denver. To what do I owe my good fortune—business or just wanderlust?" He was remembering the people who worked for him, and his own position as an eligible widower and her position as an attractive widow.

She tried to frame words as he helped her down from the automobile and escorted her toward the cabin and up the steps of the porch. Dully she noted the holiday air of the place, the Indian rugs and knobby hickory furniture and gay cushions. Sue knew how to do things. She must tell Floss—and then she remembered with a stab that she would not be telling Floss anything again.

Inside the house he helped her off with her linen duster and her gauntlet gloves and the long veil which she unwound from the wagon-wheel hat. All the while, his eyes held that warm expectant shine. She had not known that his eagerness would seem almost worse than his reluctance. You had only to give a woman plenty of time, his expression said—that is, if you were rich and she was poor . . .

"Roger, I've come to tell you I'll marry you," she announced quite unnecessarily.

Roger was too much of a gentleman to gloat.

"We've cared for each other for a very long time, Cara," he said with quiet satisfaction. "We'll be married in the fall. I always think that for mature people—not that you're so very mature, darling, at thirty-seven—there's something suitable, symbolic even, about a fall wedding." He tried to turn her face toward his, but she resisted him.

"Please, Roger—can't we be married at once? I'd thought maybe —this afternoon——?"

He looked first startled and then pleased. Such precipitateness was flattering. He smiled at her even while he shook his head. Wasn't that just like the old impetuous Cara? his look said. Yet she sensed a certain condescension in him too. For now she was a penniless widow, no matter how handsome, who had driven all the way up a perilous mountain road (there weren't a dozen women in all of Denver who ventured to drive beyond the city limits) to beg a man to marry her.

"The same Cara," he chided indulgently. "But we can't go quite that fast, my love. It takes time, you know, for the engravers and the caterers and the notices for the papers. In a month, I'd say, at the earliest."

There was no doubt this time that she was to be Mrs. Roger Walling Jardine III, with all the fixings. Carolina considered the prospect without emotion.

"It has to be now, Roger!" she blurted. "Because of our child." It was out. Starkly—without suavity or finesse.

Roger suddenly ceased his routine gallantry. He stared at her. He caught hold of her wrist.

"What's that? Who—whose child?"

"Ours. Yours and mine."

A cord tightened in his jaw. A blue vein thickened on his temple. His breathing grew harsh and irregular.

"My God, Cara, what are you talking about?"

"About Thea—our daughter. She was born soon after you left me."

He looked suddenly haggard; the very outlines of his skull seemed to show through his face.

"But you said her name was Thea Ramsay."

"I never said Pete Ramsay was her father. She was two years old when I married him. I should think you could have told she was yours, Roger, just by looking at her."

Sweat shone in little drops on his forehead. He began to pace back and forth.

"Why didn't you tell me there in Aspen, Cara?" he turned on her; then he had the grace to look ashamed. "Or anyway, why didn't you write me afterwards? I'd have come back from the ends of the earth . . . my daughter!"

"That's what Floss said. But I couldn't—use her as a whip to drive you back to me."

"Dorothea Jardine," he mused agitatedly. "I wonder why I didn't sense she was mine. She does look like me. We'll have to see that she makes a good marriage."

"That's what I came up here about. That's why we must be married at once. She's in love with a young minister." She ignored his frown of distaste. "But she won't marry him because she's just found out she's—illegitimate."

He stopped his pacing abruptly. He grew breathlessly still.

"She—er, thinks that?" he asked, like one sparring for time.

"She's only just discovered it. She doesn't know yet who her father is. My one hope is that if we're properly married now, we'll be making amends to her. We'll give her a *right* feeling, so she'll go on and marry her Jim. But, oh, Roger, I can't be sure. Maybe nothing we can do now will save her happiness for her!"

Roger was not paying attention to her words. He was lost in his own speculations.

"Do you suppose she'll hate me, when she finds out?" he asked gloomily, all his thoughts turned inward upon himself.

"You wouldn't expect her to be proud of you, would you?" she lashed out at him. "You aren't proud of yourself, are you?"

He flushed. The blow had hit home. She could see him weighing something in his mind. Then he spoke defensively.

"Perhaps she won't hate me quite so much when she finds out that I may be guilty of plenty of other crimes, but not of that. That she's perfectly legitimate."

Carolina frowned. "I don't understand."

The uneasiness in his face gave way to acute discomfort.

"You and I were legally married . . . Don't look at me like that! No names you can call me will be as bad as the ones I've called myself. But you must believe me, Cara, when I tell you I never dreamed during all those years before you came to Denver that you didn't know our marriage was legal. And our divorce too."

She sat down suddenly in a rustic settee, clutching at its arms. She was not a fainting woman, but her face took on a greenish cast. The room upended crazily—stuffed animal heads, bead portieres, brass jardinieres, Indian throws and all.

"When I found out from you the night of the dinner," he went on apologetically, "that you had been under the misapprehension all these years that we weren't really married, I was—well, stunned. I knew I ought to tell you the truth then. But I was afraid you might fly out at me. And I *had* to keep you quiet. My father-in-law would have cut me off quicker than he could call up his lawyer, if he'd known about that secret early marriage. He always really hoped to find out something, I think. My only chance of inheriting was to keep you from talking. I figured that as long as you went on thinking we'd been 'living in sin' you'd never mention it."

She listened in a stubborn daze. One does not easily revise the convictions of twenty years.

"But we couldn't have been married. Floss went to the courthouse to look."

"That's what my father thought, too, for there wasn't any record in Aspen. But like a careful lawyer, he checked and found it recorded in the next county, at Glenwood Springs. Probably the seedy old preacher, who wasn't a fake but only a renegade, had to drink up his fee before he remembered he was supposed to record all marriages. But by then he was miles away, so he just went to the nearest courthouse and recorded it there as if it had taken place in that county. It's very simple, really."

"But I never heard of any divorce."

He looked hang-dog.

"That's where I was a bit unethical—I mean damn' dishonorable! Father argued that if you knew, you'd contest the divorce. He didn't know how proud you were. So we—I—pretended I had no idea where to find you. A lie, of course. We published the summons the necessary number of times in the Glenwood Springs paper, hoping you wouldn't learn of it in time to fight the divorce. The records are all there. I supposed that of course, in a matter of weeks, you'd find out about it."

Still she said nothing. She could only stare at him unbelievingly.

He wet his lips. "Please, Cara, try to understand. People are more lax now about divorce than they were twenty years ago. Then it made you a pariah. Look at the Tabors—never accepted in spite of all that money. Father convinced me that Sue wouldn't marry me if she knew I was a divorced man. So we never mentioned either the marriage or the divorce. And nothing ever came out. I married Sue; and then there was her father to look out for, because he was rabidly jealous where she was concerned. And so, when I found out you didn't know, I figured it was better to wait till after his death to tell you. After all," he finished with a lame attempt at self-justification, "I wanted to marry you then, you remember."

He grew afraid of her long silence and her judging eyes. He had expected her to rage. Now he wished she would. A stormy Cara he could understand; this frozen one was a stranger.

"I—oh, Cara, you make me feel like a dog. Don't look at me like that!"

But Carolina's expression did not change.

"So, to keep me from letting the cat out of the bag—from endangering your possible inheritance, you allowed me to go on through this whole past year, still thinking I was—that Thea was——" She looked at him incredulously. You weakling! her eyes said. And once I thought I loved you . . .

"I did start to tell you a time or two. But can't you see how it was? I had a position to keep up. God knows, I'd earned old Braden's money. And you were so unpredictable when you were angry. There was the danger you might spoil everything."

She looked at him as from a great distance and from a great height. Twenty years—and all for nothing. She thought of him and Sue, so busily maintaining their "position," while she was taking in washings and bending over a hot oven and hoarding dimes in a sewing basket. She pictured all those elegant "responsibilities" of his life with Sue, while she was desperately trying to care for Thea and fend off the Gilsons and the Mimis and the Sam Milligans of the world. Well, anyhow, I *lived*, she thought grimly. While those two were going through the figures of a minuet—bowing, cavorting, grimacing.

Suddenly she was in a hurry. She could not get away fast enough.

"It's a long drive—I must go, Roger."

Consternation clouded his face.

"But you can't go now! I give in about the date, darling. We'll be married this afternoon. There's a minister over in the valley. Don't forget, it's for Thea's sake too," he pleaded with her.

But Carolina was already gathering up her duster and her gauntlet gloves. She did not wait to wind her long veil about her hat.

"We won't be married today, Roger—or ever."

Still he refused to accept her verdict.

"But Thea—you said Thea needed for us to be married." He was openly begging now. Until then he had not known how much he wanted her.

"Not any more. She needs only to know that her parents' marriage—and their divorce—are properly recorded somewhere. You have just presented her with the only wedding gift of any importance to her, if that's any satisfaction to you, Roger. I'm sure she won't hate you nearly as much now—when I tell her."

There was no rancor in her voice, only a breathless, shining haste. If she had ever wanted revenge, she had it now, when she no longer cared about it.

CHAPTER 33

PARTINGS ARE SELDOM ACCOMPLISHED IN THIS LIFE WITH NEATNESS and finish. Carolina could not start the Peerless. It took all of the caretaker's cranking and Roger's experimental tinkering to get the engine to come to life, with explosive, shuddering jerks. By then it was late afternoon, and a storm was hanging low and rumbling up and down the canyon, and the high peaks to the west were already veiled with advancing sheets of rain.

Roger, chivalrous Roger, who was more inept even than Carolina about an automobile, insisted that he would drive her back to Denver. That winding mountain road, with the creek rising and dark coming on, was no place for a woman alone, he declared.

Carolina tried to dissuade him.

"But I don't mind, Roger. I'm not a bit afraid." She looked at him levelly; she could even smile ironically at him. "Long ago I had to learn to travel a dangerous road—alone."

He reddened, but he climbed into the driver's seat.

They drove in strained silence, too absorbed by their thoughts to give much attention to the rapidly rising creek, flowing with roily sinister swiftness. Once or twice Roger tried to reopen the conversation. She had made allowances before, he pleaded; surely she would make them again. But she remained bafflingly remote.

Actually Carolina's mind was cauterized of feeling. She knew only a racing need to get back home. She did not stop to analyze all that awaited her there.

They were halfway down the twisting Bear Creek Canyon road when the storm overtook them. Gray, sluicing sheets of water descended upon them, pounded on the flimsy top of the open "touring model," lashed in through the sides. There was no time to stop to put on flapping curtains. They could only crouch together on the front seat trying to peer through the scouring rain.

The creek beside them was already over its banks. The deep ruts in the road were sloshing full. As they plowed along, the wheels sent a thin brown sheet of water fanning out on either side of them. The foaming yellow tongues of wavelets lapped at the edges of the road. Floating objects bumped past—fence posts, uprooted trees, a drowned calf.

They shouldn't build roads down on a level with mountain streams, she thought dully. A canyon such as this only served as a giant funnel to collect all the water rushing in from the side draws until it carried a tumultuous flood. She peered up through the rain at the rocky walls towering above them. The walls were so high. The canyon was so narrow. She knew how cattle felt in a chute: penned in, helpless.

She gripped the upright bars that supported the top. Her linen duster was plastered to her. Her hair whipped in wild wet strings under the drenched wagon-wheel hat. The lightning made her wince; the thunder deafened her. It was growing dark.

On rickety bridges they crossed and recrossed the creek, that had turned into a churning tumult. If only the road held. If only the bridges held. They had no choice now but to race down the canyon, trying to get out of the narrow, rocky chute before either the road or the bridges went out, or before a wall of water overtook them destroying them in a flash flood.

Ahead of them was another bridge. She saw the turgid waters boil across the floor of the bridge, and the debris jam up behind it, butting at it with the force of a battering ram. They had to get across that bridge. Behind them lay death. Only ahead was there any hope of safety. Now she was suddenly cruelly alive; every nerve in her strained forward to push the car across that bridge.

At that instant she felt an involuntary tightening of Roger's muscles beside her as he shoved on the brakes and slowed the car. To her horror, it came to a slithering stop, while he peered ahead at the swaying bridge.

"Don't stop now, Roger!" she screamed. "We're trapped if you do. You've got to make a try——"

There was another fatal moment of hesitation on Roger's part. Careful Roger, indecisive Roger, who had won so many of the privileged things of life by default. Now, when every second counted, he delayed. She had to scream at him again and shake him by the arm before he reluctantly sent the car jerking ahead. It picked up speed as it ground through the sheet of water that swirled across the floor of the bridge.

She could feel the bridge sway queasily; then it began to buckle and disintegrate like a pile of jackstraws under them. Open water yawned ahead.

"Jump!" she screamed.

A fleeting glance at him showed her a staring Roger, still gripping the wheel as if he could not believe that he, Roger Walling Jardine III, could be asked to leave the safety of the car for that roaring, murderous water below.

She landed on a section of the rapidly collapsing bridge to which a piece of railing was still attached. She clung to its doubtful security as long as she could, feeling the tilting floor switch and sway like a live thing shaken by a monster.

While she gripped the railing, the heavy car glided past her, swept along by the powerful current as effortlessly as if it were a child's doll buggy. Briefly she saw Roger, frozen to the wheel, staring lividly. And then the car turned majestically over and came to rest upside down, wedged against a pile of boulders that parted the current here. With Roger under it.

"Get out, Roger!" she shrieked vainly, as the bridge section to which she clung tore loose and she was flung headlong into the fuming current. "Get out, Roger!" she was still shrieking as she went under, swallowing great gulps of dirty flood water. She fought the watery madness until she had battled her way to the top again.

She tried to flounder toward the overturned car, but she was help-less.

Then the current perversely lifted her and smacked her against the very side of the car. She held on to it sobbing; she beat against it; she threw her whole puny strength against it, trying to dislodge it. A human being was under there. Roger was under there. But she was impotent. The car would lie like an overturned beetle with its curled feet in the air until the next caprice of the flood pried it loose and sent it lumbering down the stream again.

Another wave swept her on. Her shoes had been sucked off. Her hat and veil were gone. She managed to rid herself of her hamper-ing duster. The waters were not so deep as they were mad and ungovernable. Frequently she touched bottom, but only for a second, and then she was hurled along again. She was wholly at the mercy of the current.

Floating objects hit her from all sides. Giant hands picked her up and flung her at the boulders that reared up in the stream bed.

A person could endure only so much, she thought dimly.

A great blue spruce, its fan of interlaced roots upended like a flat disc, bobbed along. She grabbed at one of its limber outer branches. Gradually she pulled herself closer, worked her way in among the bushy branches and hung there panting, finding a brief surcease from the battering of water and debris.

She had become only a creature of instinct, following the same blind impulses that prompt all wild things in time of forest fire and flood. She clung to the spruce branches like a newborn animal clutching its mother's fur.

She knew that she was being slowly beaten into insensibility and that she must reach safety soon. But the flood now covered the entire floor of the canyon from one sheer wall to the other. There was no sign of roads or bridges.

I don't think—I can stand—much more, she gasped. Then a fresh impact of water hit the tree, turning it over and over and tearing her loose from even that meager anchorage. She was back in the flood again . . . Why do I try? Thea is all right now.

But instinct lies deeper than reason. She was incapable of reason-ing, yet she knew with a tenuous certainty that she was still needed. She had to live. There was something more she must do for her child.

God—help me to keep going, she prayed with sudden fierceness.

She fought now to stay alive with all the fury of her mother love. For some deep prescience had warned her that if she drowned now, all knowledge of Thea's true history drowned with her. The only other person who had known was Roger, and Roger was dead. If she did not come out alive, Thea, with the blind stubbornness of the very good, would insist on ruining her own life and Jim Blake's life as well.

Carolina was no longer a beaten, exhausted, expiring thing. She drew on new resources. She fought the insensate flood that would have destroyed her. She clutched at bits of floating wood that betrayed her and let her down. But each time she came up struggling. It was as if all of old Jude's rage at sin and her own fury at whatever balked her had combined within her to battle the elements. And she was fighting for something more important than her own life.

When a heavy timber lurched along just out of reach, she made a lunge for it, missed it, and went under again. As she came up, one end of the beam bumped into her, scooping her up limply. Everything went dark for her. But some reflex of despair made her grab it and hang on, and kept her plastered tight against it. The timber bobbed and turned in an ungainly fashion. Then it swung about in a slow curve and landed her on a gravelly bank, less sheer than the rest. It dropped her like a piece of flotsam.

At first, when she could think at all, when she felt the solid bank beneath her—she was too spent to do more than lie there, half in and half out of the water, breathing harshly. Her lungs were bursting, and her heart was laboring. She could feel the water sucking and pulling at her feet and legs; she could even feel the bank beneath her beginning to crumble and dissolve. But she could not move.

When at last she was able to stir, she gathered all her forces together and dragged herself up to higher ground. Inch by inch, she hunched herself up the bank. Her left ankle was useless, but that seemed a small matter.

After an eon she was free of the current that pulled at her. She could feel the sharp prickle of brush under her cut and bruised hands. It was good to be hurt by land instead of water. Good gravel. Blessed underbrush. Wonderful thorns.

For a long time she lay there in the steady washing downpour. But she realized that it was lessening. The flashes of lightning were feebler now; the thunder growled more distantly. The night was black and starless and thick as a blanket around her. Fortunately there was no wind. Her clothes were like a cold wet skin on her.

At length she began to feel again, if numbly; to think again, if hazily. But she was still not quite of this world; she was suspended somewhere between life and death.

She was not grateful yet for survival for her own sake, but only for Thea's. The thought of Thea was a slow warmth in her veins, bringing her back to life. She pictured Thea's years ahead with her young preacher. Not soft years or easy years. Maybe years filled with hardships and disappointments. But they were Thea's path of happiness.

For the first time she saw the girl as she was. Why, she only looks like Roger on the outside, Carolina realized in surprise. Inside, she's part me. And part her Grandmother Hester, who followed her hot-head to the ends of the earth. And part her Grandfather Jude, who destroyed himself obeying his conscience . . . But I have saved her, she thought with tired content. And in her new wisdom she saw that it was good that Thea and Jim were going a long way off to live. The best thing she could do for them was to let them work out their own lives from now on. She even managed a weak chuckle at the thought that what she had spent her whole life running away from, Thea had gravitated to, irresistibly.

Her own past grew suddenly plain before her in the clear light that a brush with death sometimes sheds. She knew a brief ironical compassion for those two men—Roger and Pete—whom she had turned to in her effort to escape her father and what he stood for. Their weaknesses had only hardened her and tempered her, until she grew to be more like her father every day. She had never really escaped him for an instant . . . Maybe you never escape, she thought.

But she did not hate her father any longer. Probably she would never *like* him, she thought regretfully. But at least she understood what lashed him on, what made him the way he was.

It was a relief to understand. To be free of the compulsion to jeer at all words with a religious significance. To stop hating. For now that she had stopped hating her father's words and her father's God, she could pick up beliefs again. Hatred offered such weak support when trouble hit you, like floods or illness or grief. You were so little and frightened then . . . but ah, how cocky you were so long as the weather was fair and you were feeling fine and the ore was running rich!

"I believe . . . help thou mine unbelief," she said aloud, quite simply, to her father's God.

Then, like a comforted child, she slept. Waking and sleeping and waking again—she managed to get through the long night hours. When at last she roused herself, she found that the storm was spent. The high waters were already receding. By daylight the torrent would be only a creek again. Flash floods were like that.

She was weak from loss of blood from her cuts, and chilled to the center of her being. She wondered if she would ever feel warm again. But her strength was coming slowly back, and with it an awareness of the world she was returning to.

Her money was gone. She ought to feel dreadful, after the way she had slaved and worried to get it. But she didn't. Being rich simply hadn't been much fun. She wasn't cut out for it. Being alive was all that counted now. She was alive—alive. They would be sending out searching parties as soon as it was light.

For the first time she began to think about herself. Why, she was free at last to follow her own heart. Her mind, which had been skirting around the edges of her happiness, began to contemplate it wonderingly. She felt herself trembling with a deep inner trembling that was not from cold.

Already a gray wash was taking the place of the black blanket overhead. As the world took shape, she looked curiously about her. She was lying on a steep talus slope at the foot of a towering rock wall. Charred, snaggled stumps rose from the brush. When the first faint color swam back into the landscape she saw that the brush was fireweed, coarse and ruddy and blooming.

She smiled, recalling Leo's words of long ago. That she was like the fireweed. For the fireweed was the first thing to push dauntlessly in after a forest fire, to be followed later by the blithe aspens and last by the sober pines. And she was the fireweed, with the pioneer's urge to be first into the raw, wild places of the earth.

What was that talk about the new mining camp opening up in the San Juan country? They would be needing a bakery and a lunch counter first thing. She thought of great rubbery mounds of dough set to rise behind the cookstove in a warm kitchen. Ah, to be warm again! She thought of the sweet crusty smell of the loaves as they came from the oven. She wondered if she had kept her knack with meat pasties. Miners never tired of them. Let's see, one would need tables and counters and a stove and lamps—and flour and sugar and beef and lard——

Suddenly she felt wide-awake and eager again. Already life was plucking at her sleeve. She sat up—a little warily, however, for her body was bruised and her ankle ached. Then, with the immemorial gesture of a woman attacking a new day, she lifted her arms and began to coil up her hair.

She could scarcely wait. She and Floss needed honing by life; they had grown rusty as unused picks. Their days in that great useless house had been only an endless ordeal of making bunchy French knots. It had been a long time since either of them had found zest in living. McGregor too . . . Suddenly she stopped skirting her happiness and opened her arms to it. "John!" she cried to the morning, "I'm so slow to learn. I've been such a long time getting ready."

They would be among the first ones in . . . The Reliable Home Bakery. With the three of them gathered in the kitchen after a hard day's work. There was something about the crackle of pitch pine in a cookstove and the yellow light of a reflector lamp.

She could scarcely wait for the sun, for rescue, for the new life to begin. Oh, hurry, hurry, she cried. They had wasted so many years. She and John and Floss—the three of them. Her blood quickened; her heart quickened. It would be over the mountain again . . . over the mountain!

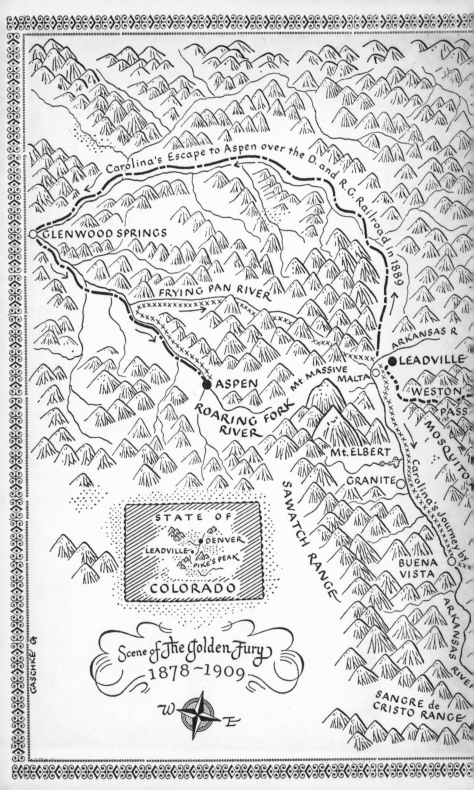